PRETTY LITTLE SINS

KINGS OF BOLTEN

K.G. REUSS

BOOK TWO

Copyright © 2022 by K.G. Reuss

All rights reserved.

No part of this book may be reproduced in any form or by any electronic or mechanical means, including information storage and retrieval systems, without written permission from the author, except for the use of brief quotations in a book review.

Editing: N-D-Scribable Services

Cover Design: Moonstruck Cover Design & Photography, moonstruckcoverdesign.com

Formatting: Books from Beyond

*For all those times when a lover said no but the book boyfriends said,
"Yes, baby. YES. You're such a good fucking girl."*

FOREWORD

Dear Reader

First off, thanks for waiting for what seemed like forever for this book. It went through the underworld and back to get here. But it's here. YAY!

Next, Deadly Little Promises, book three in Kings of Bolten, is up for pre-order. As always, ignore the Amazon date. It's just a placeholder and will release later this fall.

This is a crossover series. You will meet other characters. It may give you anxiety and change everything you think you know. Take notes. Pay attention. Everything happens for a reason and will lead to intense moments of screaming and panic.

I'm creating an entire universe where my characters all live and suffer together. As things progress, you'll find other characters in different books. Make sure you're paying attention to names. Everyone in my universe has a story ;)

Hang tight. It's going to be the most amazing and roughest ride ever. I promise. I'm not the torture queen for nothing.

This is a WORK OF FICTION. Please don't get all twisted about believability. If I wanted realism, I'd not write fiction books. Suspend disbelief and just try to have a good time. It'll be loads of fun.

For all information on content, check out my website www.kgreuss.com Click the appropriate book link for a list of scenarios.

Everything you need to know is there. Know your limits. I have none, so keep that in mind when reading this book and any of my other books. Things can escalate to a place you won't be able to come back from quickly.

You've been warned.

Happy reading.

-K.G.

ONE
BIANCA

My body screamed at me as I tried to roll over in the soft bed in a room I didn't recognize. I made to sit up, my head still fuzzy, only to realize my arms and legs were tied to the wooden bedframe.

"What the fuck?" I groaned, wincing.

The back of my head felt like it had been hit by a sledgehammer. The ache extended into my shoulders. I licked my cracked lips, taking note of my surroundings as much as my restraints would allow. White walls. The smell of cedar. Modern but definitely a cabin.

I blinked in confusion after looking out the window where all I could see were trees.

Was this hell? I was supposed to be dead. Levin had pointed a gun at my head. *Was hell a cabin in the middle of a forest I couldn't escape? Where I had to live with my sins?*

Fallon.

My mind rapidly replayed the last things I remembered. Levin had shot him. Fallon had planned to betray me. Levin and the kings had tried to kill me.

My guts churned, and bile rose in my throat. I needed a bathroom or at least something to throw up into.

"H-help," I called out hoarsely. "S-someone. Please."

A tear streaked down my cheek followed by another. I tugged against my bindings, whimpering in frustration. Just when I thought I'd totally lose it, the door to the room creaked open, and Vincent sauntered in.

With his dark eyes trained on me, he approached quickly. His hair was a mess, but he was dressed to perfection like always—designer jeans, tight, black Henley, a bracelet on one wrist, and rings adorning his fingers.

"Hey, baby B," he said softly, moving to my restraints.

"I-I need the bathroom."

He didn't question me. He simply made fast work of untying me. The moment I was free, I scrambled out of bed toward the door he pointed to on the other side of the room. I rushed forward and shoved open the heavy wooden door with my hand over my mouth and made a beeline to the toilet where I heaved my guts into the porcelain. Sobs wracked my body. I vomited as I clung to the white bowl, the pain of knowing Fallon was gone repeating in my head. The pain of his betrayal burned hot in my chest.

"Baby B?" Vincent called out, coming into the bathroom.

"G-get away from me," I choked out before heaving into the toilet again. I didn't know what hurt more—losing Fallon or knowing he was going to hand me over to a world of hell or the kings' betrayal.

Vincent didn't listen. He approached quickly and twisted my dirty blonde hair away from my face. A twig fell to the tiled floor. I vomited again.

Vincent placed a warm hand on my back and rubbed gently, cooing softly, "It's OK. I'm here. You're OK, B."

I shoved him away after another painful dry heave, causing him to fall back on his ass since he'd been crouched beside me.

"Don't fucking touch me," I snarled at him, wiping my mouth with the back of my hand.

He held his hands up in surrender, his dark eyes filled with worry. "Easy, B. I'm here to help—"

"Fuck you and your help. You've done enough." I wrapped my

arms around my knees in an effort to make myself smaller as I sank to my ass, my back against the wall.

"Listen, I need you to relax. We have to talk. Things are happening—"

"I want to leave. Now. I need to go to the police."

"And what would you tell them, sweetheart?" He dropped his hands and cocked his head at me.

My body shook. "I'd tell them I need to report a murder."

Vincent nodded thoughtfully and clucked his tongue after a moment, seemingly unconcerned with my threat. "Well, that would be a good idea, even a great one, but you're forgetting one important thing."

"What?"

My bottom lip trembled as I tried to keep the tears at bay. He shuffled on his knees to the sink, ran water into a small cup, and handed it to me. I snatched it from him, quickly gulping it down.

"There's no body. No body, *no crime*."

I saw red.

Chucking the cup aside, I lunged at him, knocking him onto his back. I punched and hit wherever I could. He didn't fight back until I clawed at him. Then he grabbed my wrists and flipped me onto my back like I weighed nothing. He loomed over me, the blood from the scratches I'd made on his cheek dripping. They matched the healing wound I'd given him from the night Fallon died.

"Don't be mad at me. I didn't make the rules, B," he said with a snarl, pinning my arms over my head. "And stop attacking me. I'm on your side."

"Fuck you, Vincent. You're on *your* side. You were fine with Dominic and Levin killing me—"

He slammed my arms back to the floor when I made to get up. I winced at the pain coursing through me and let out a hiss.

"Let's get one thing straight. I was *never* OK with harm coming to you. I'd have taken your place on your knees in those fucking woods if I thought it would've made things better. But I can't do shit to help

Levin if I'm dead. He's a brother to me. *My best friend.* Same with Dom. We protect our own."

I let out a bitter laugh. "I guess that tells me where I stand, since I'm the one who had a gun pointed at my head."

Vincent let out a growl of frustration. "That's not what I meant."

"It's what you said," I snapped back. "Now get off me, and let me go. Not only are you an accessory to murder, but you're also a kidnapper."

"I'm not, and you know it."

I had enough of this. My arms might've been pinned, but my head wasn't. I reared back before surging forward and smashing my forehead against Vincent's pretty face. He let out a curse and released me as blood gushed from his nose, splattering my face and the white t-shirt I was in. Figured the assholes had gotten me naked after I'd been knocked out. Being clocked in the back of my head instead of shot was the only explanation I had for why I was still alive and being held captive, not to mention the searing ache in the back of my skull.

I brought my knee up and nailed him in the groin. He let out a cry as he toppled away from me, falling to his side. I wasted no time getting to my feet and rushing from the adjoining bathroom to the bedroom door. Not bothering to look around, I raced down the hall, my bare feet slapping against the polished wooden floors. Clad in nothing but a long, white t-shirt and panties, I took the stairs two at a time. I'd run naked if I had to. I shoved through the front door only to crash straight into Dominic coming in from outside.

The force of the impact sent me tumbling to my ass with a cry. My elbow smacked off the floor, sending a shockwave through my arm.

Dominic's heavy boots thudded as he approached. He stopped and stood over me.

"Going somewhere?" He raised his dark brows at me, his green eyes glinting.

"I want to leave," I said in a shaky voice.

"You will, but not until we're finished." He kneeled beside me and offered me his hand.

I stared at it for a moment, knowing my chances of survival greatly depended on appeasing him, so I placed my palm in his and let him help me to my feet.

"Would it be presumptuous of me to assume Vincent is wounded somewhere in the house?" His gaze skirted over my face and shirt dotted with Vincent's blood.

"You wouldn't be presumptuous," I said, lifting my chin to glare at him while tugging my hand free.

A small smile cut his lips up, his eyes sparkling. It was a disarming look. He looked... happy.

"You killed Fallon," I accused.

"Did I? I don't recall it being me who pulled the trigger."

"Don't split hairs, Dominic. I want to leave. I'm not staying in a place with the men who killed my—"

Dominic's hand shot out, and he squeezed my face. "Don't finish that sentence, wasp." He'd gone from seemingly happy to downright terrifying within the span of a heartbeat.

I swallowed and glared up at him. "I *want* to go."

"And I said you will, but first we have something we need to do."

"What's that?" I demanded sourly as he loosened his hold on my face.

Tenderly, he ran his knuckles along my jaw, a tiny smile on his face that didn't quite reach his eyes. "You'll see."

And with those cryptic words, he took me by the arm and hauled me back to the room I'd just escaped from and placed me on the bed. His eyes lingered on me as he backed out.

"I won't restrain you this time. I'll be back. Don't try to run. There's no way out. You're wasting energy you're going to need later. I promise you that."

He closed the door behind him, leaving me alone to wallow in the pain my heart was in. The click of the lock blended with my sobs.

TWO
DOMINIC

"You look like shit," I muttered, glancing at Vincent, who pulled the ice pack from his face as I sauntered into my bedroom in one of my many safe houses.

This one was my favorite—a modern log home nestled deep within hundreds of acres of woods in the middle of nowhere. I could've had a shack with the bare necessities, but I wasn't that sort of guy.

He shot me a sour look and gave me the finger.

"I guess our little wasp has a sting, huh?" I unbuttoned my shirt and tossed it onto the bed, not feeling an ounce of humor.

I was so exhausted my head hurt. I'd spent the night before not only worrying about Bianca knocked out in the room next to mine, but I'd also had to deal with my father when the order came in to kill her. I'd told him I was dealing with it and had struck a deal to keep Natalia Vasiliev alive, citing my desperate need to torture her, proving my power to the Bratva. I had my hands in a million pots, stirring all of them in the hopes I could cook up something in the small window of time I had left.

"She's got a damn sting all right. Let's say I wasn't expecting her to kick my ass," he grunted, pressing the cold pack back to his face. "I grabbed the ice pack out of your tiny ass freezer." He nodded to the small fridge and freezer combo in the room. "Where is she? I was going to go after her but decided I needed ice more than I needed another kick to my balls. Since I knew you were here, I figured you'd keep track of her."

"Her room. I had to lock her in. Thankfully, she can't get out through the window. I didn't want to tie her down again."

"Wouldn't put it past her to put her lamp through the window anyway," he said with a sigh as he adjusted the pack.

"She can try. It's shatterproof." I grabbed a pressed dress shirt from its hanger and put it on.

"I can't believe you're doing this."

"Well, you know what'll happen if I don't. She'll be dead before sunset." I swallowed and grabbed the black, silk tie from its spot on the dresser and hastily knotted it as I stared at myself in the long mirror. This wasn't how I envisioned my wedding day. I always assumed I'd marry some bitch arranged by my father or one after my money. Not this. *Never* this.

But at least I gave a shit about Bianca. Maybe I wasn't the best at showing her, but I was new to the entire relationship thing. Or whatever the fuck it was we had.

Vincent frowned, remaining silent. He didn't need to say anything. I knew how he felt. He was broken because she was going to be *my* wife with my last name. If there was one thing about my best friend, it was that he was a romantic. Sure, he went through women like toilet paper, but he wasn't like Levin and me. Where Levin and I just fucked to feel good, Vincent was searching for a connection. If he didn't feel it, he moved to the next option. He'd found that connection with Bianca, and I was the bastard taking it away.

"Father only offered me a small window of time to get my shit sorted with a plan for her. I need to deliver my plan to him sooner rather than later. I'm not sure how long I can push him off." I paused, carefully straightening the cuffs of my shirt.

"I meant what I said," I called out, slipping into my suit jacket. "She's still yours as much as mine. She gets my name on paper, but she belongs to all of us."

Vincent grunted, refusing to look at me.

Sighing, I moved and sank down beside him on my bed. I reached out and tugged him to me, embracing one of my best friends.

"She's still ours," I whispered as I hugged him. "I swear it to you."

"You really think your jealous, possessive streak is going to let that happen once her name is beside yours on that marriage license?" He swallowed and stared at me.

I rested my forehead against his, my hands on either side of his face. "I'm a prick. I don't deny it, but if you feel even *half* of what I feel for her, then I'd be the biggest asshole to take that from you when I promised it to begin with. I'll learn to control myself. When it's you and Levin, it's not so bad. I want this. I accept this. I promise, Vin."

Vincent nodded and breathed out. "You never break a promise."

"Usually," I murmured, thinking about how things didn't quite go the way I'd thought they would in the woods.

I hadn't *really* broken my promise. Levin had failed to perform, something I'd prayed for. For fuck's sake, I had a priest locked up in an upstairs bedroom. Shit had escalated rather quickly.

Either God or the devil listened to those silent pleas. Whichever one, I'd thank him when we met someday.

I pressed my lips to Vincent's forehead and pulled away.

"I believe you," he said, his dark eyes on me as I got to my feet.

"Good." I grabbed my dress pants from the hanger, unzipped my dark khakis, and let them fall to the floor before tugging on my pressed pants. I caught Vincent's gaze lingering on me, seemingly lost in thought, so I cleared my throat.

He snapped his stare back to my face.

"You OK?"

He nodded. "Yeah. It's just a lot, man. She's going to hate us. I don't want that."

"She'll understand. She's a good girl." I zipped my pants and put my belt on, studying my reflection in the mirror.

Vincent's phone buzzed, drawing his attention. "Levin will be here in ten. He's got Stella."

Perfect. My plan was already rolling out without a hitch. I huffed out a breath. In a few short hours, I'd be a married man. Bianca D'Angelou would be my wife. And then, I'd put my baby inside her, an heir to the De Santis throne. We'd rule it our way. Together. As a family. A real one, none of the shit I grew up with.

Sometimes saving a life required making a new one. I was willing to do whatever it took to keep her alive, even make her hate me.

Maybe I was getting a hang of this love shit.

THREE
LEVIN

"I think you should've gone with the white chiffon," Stella complained as I drove us back to the safe house Dominic was holed up in with Vincent and Bianca.

"I think I should've run your ass over and left you twitching in the street," I shot back, irritated I'd spent the entire fucking morning with her whiny ass.

"It's her wedding day, you dick. The least you could've done was get her something fancier and the right color, even if she is being forced into it." She crossed her arms over her chest and glared out the windshield.

"Her wedding day is bullshit. You think she's going to be excited to see your ass there?"

"You think she'll be excited to see yours?" She glowered at me, a sneer on her lips.

"I know what she likes. She wouldn't want to be stuffed into some cupcake-looking curtain shit." I tightened my hands on the steering wheel. "She'll like this." At least, I hoped she would. I'd never picked out a wedding dress before.

Dominic had sent me on the errand to get me away from torturing Fallon in the basement. He'd passed the fuck out around four AM after

I'd nearly drown him in a bucket of water when he refused to tell me anything unless I'd let him see Bianca. I'd gotten pissed and told him she was rotting in a hole somewhere already, which made him weep. It made me sick, and not in a pissed off sort of way. In the heart sort of way. I felt his pain as he sobbed her name softly. I hated to admit it, but the dickface obviously cared about her. And *that* did piss me off. He was a fucking lord. I'd come at him with a hunting knife before Dom intervened, suggesting I get some sleep and try again after the wedding so Fallon had some time to heal and come to his senses.

So, there I was, acting like a wedding planner on a twelve-hour crunch with a bitch I couldn't stand sitting in the seat beside me. Since Stella had come crying for help and Dom had agreed, it looked like she'd be spending a lot of time with us. It meant she was the only chick we could use for the next step. Vincent had suggested Bianca's friend Aubrey. But given how close Aubrey seemed to be to Bianca, we didn't think she'd allow Bianca be held captive and forced to marry without a fight. And for fuck's sake, we needed a break from all the damn fighting for a minute. The last few days had been a fucking nightmare.

Bianca had been out for nearly two days. Fallon only came to when I kicked him in the ribs as he lay on the floor in a secret, soundproofed room in the basement. I was sure all of fucking Ivanov's and D'Angelou's men were looking for Bianca if Hail had gone to them. If Stella was telling us the truth, Hail was remaining quiet about everything, but he was silently cursing us all into an early grave as he searched for Fallon.

"So will I be marrying one of you too since I'm also under your protection?" Stella asked.

I snapped my gaze toward her in disgust. "Fuck no."

She frowned. "Why not? She can only marry one of you. I mean, yeah, she gets Dominic, and he's a hell of a catch, but you and Vincent aren't bad."

The frown slipped off her face as she reached over and rested her hand high on my thigh.

"Remember that time during the prom last year when you let me suck your dick behind the auditorium? Then we almost fucked—"

I shoved her hand away from my groin. "Fuck off. I was high off my ass. I'd have fucked a roll of toilet paper if I thought it would scream for me. Plus, Ivanov pissed me off that night more than usual."

She pouted at me. "So, you're just not going to pull over and fuck me then?"

"I sure the fuck *am not*," I said with a grunt, accelerating. I needed to get the hell back to the safe house so I could be free of her ass.

"But I'm horny," she whined, sliding her skirt up.

I ground my teeth and said nothing.

She let out a breathy moan as she slid her fingers beneath her panties. I kept driving as she fingered herself.

"Stella, I will kick your ass out. Stop."

"Why?" she moaned softly. "Is it because that big cock of yours is weeping to be in my pussy?"

The sound of her fingers in her wetness echoed through the interior of the car.

"My big cock is going back to the house to fuck Bianca. Not you. *Never* you. You can stop this shit because it's not happening."

She giggled and rubbed herself faster, her head falling back against the headrest. "I bet she'd let me between her legs."

I smashed on the brakes, the tires squealing as we slid to a stop. A final groan left her lips as she came on her fingers. I slammed the car into park, got out, and went to her side. She stared up at me with rounded eyes as I wrenched her door open and tugged her out.

I wrapped my fingers around her throat and slammed her against the side of the car.

"You are nothing. Do you understand? I don't fucking want you. Vincent doesn't want you. Dom doesn't want you. Bianca sure as fuck doesn't want you. Stop playing your fucking games. *Bianca is our girl.*"

She stared up at me. "You think she's going to want *you* after she marries one of the biggest future mob bosses in the country? Aside from that De Luca asshole everyone has been talking about, Dominic is it. Why would she want a henchman when she can have the boss?"

I scowled down at her, my chest heaving. "Fuck up again, and I'll put a bullet in your head. I don't care what arrangement you made with Dom. I'll kill you and piss on your corpse. Do what you're fucking told. Got it?" I released her.

"Yes," she mumbled, sniffling.

I rolled my eyes. Leave it to Stella Monroe to play the victim.

"Get in the fucking car. Not another word until we get to Dom."

She slid back onto her seat and put her seatbelt on, her arms crossing over her chest.

Fuck. I can't wait to get away from her.

But I'd be stepping out of one mess into another because Vincent said Bianca was awake and pissed off.

She was probably going to kill me because I'd nearly killed her.

And in a few hours, she'd be my best friend's wife. *I'd never have her like Dom would. She'd never have my name. She'd never fully be mine…*

I exhaled as I got back into the car and pulled onto the road, stuffing my ugly thoughts away.

I hated the pain in my chest. If this was love, it sucked.

FOUR
VINCENT

Stella stomped into the house, looking sullen and pissed off. *Great. Two women with nasty attitudes. Just what I needed.* I hadn't expected my baby B to full-on kick my ass the way she had, but I wasn't mad about it. I probably deserved it after the shit that went down in the woods two days ago.

But damn.

Pretty sure she broke my nose and bruised my dick.

"What's your problem?" I asked wearily.

"Levin." Stella glared at him as he strode past with garment bags in his arms.

"Seems he has that effect on women," I said.

He ignored my comment. "Where am I taking the dress?"

I shrugged. "I don't know. Dom said he was going to tell B." I checked my watch. "We're cutting it short on time. The romance king wants to marry at dusk in the clearing. I made her a bouquet from some wildflowers I found." I gestured to the assortment of flowers on the kitchen table I'd tied together with some twine I found in a drawer. "The priest is restrained in a room upstairs, praying."

"Those aren't too bad," Stella said, peering over at the flowers and ignoring everything else I'd said like it didn't faze her a bit. "A little thin, but the bouquet could be worse."

I was surprised by her compliment. Or half-compliment.

"Thanks. There wasn't an abundance of flowers to work with considering how late in the season it is. I did what I could." I licked my lips nervously, suddenly self-conscious about what B would think of them. *What if she hated them?*

"Don't sweat it," Levin called out. "I had to buy the dress. I didn't know what I was doing either."

"Am I doing her makeup or what?" Stella's hand landed on her hip as she glanced between us. She wrinkled her nose. "What the hell is wrong with your face?"

"B smashed her head into it," I grumbled.

Stella paled. "I'm not going in there to do her makeup if she's going to be violent. I didn't sign up for that shit."

"We're a violent lot," Levin muttered. "Best get used to it."

"I'm not going in there alone. No way. She's a freak anyway—"

"Shut the fuck up," I snapped the same time Levin did.

Good to see he and I were on the same wavelength.

"What's going on?" Dom's deep voice boomed out as he came down the stairs, looking dapper as fuck in his wedding attire.

His pitch-black hair was slicked back, and his green eyes glinted in the overhead light. Without knowing him, anyone would recognize he was all power and domination. Knowing him only made those things a certainty.

Stella's eyes widened.

"I-I was just telling these two"—she pointed her manicured finger at us—"that I'm not going into Bianca's room if she's hurting people."

"Scared?" Dom lifted his eyebrow at her as he stepped off the last step and adjusted his cuff links.

She scoffed. "Hardly. I just don't want to be torn up by some rabid trailer trash."

Dom moved quickly, stopping in front of her. She stumbled back, her eyes wide and filled with fright.

"Who am I?" Dom demanded.

Her gaze darted around, confusion on her face. "Dominic?"

"Dominic *who*?"

She licked her lips. "*De Santis*?"

"And who the fuck are you?"

"Stella?"

He inched closer. "Wrong fucking answer. *You're a nobody.* A nothing. Consider this your one warning from me. Insult my bride again, and I'll fucking hang your bloody corpse from a tree so the wild animals can eat you. Got me?"

"Y-yes," she stammered, visibly swallowing.

"Good. Now get your shit so you can help my girl get ready. Today is a special day for her. If you ruin it, you're dead. It's that simple."

"Right," Stella murmured, her sass put on the back burner.

I peered at Levin who'd watched the scene unfold without an ounce of emotion on his face, but when he glanced at me, there was something in the blue depths of his eyes. It flashed through them quickly before he got a handle on it and schooled his expression.

"Dom? The dress?" Levin called out, holding the bag up.

Dom swallowed. "Give me a moment. I, uh, need to talk to her. Make sure Stella has everything she needs to get Bianca ready."

He smoothed down his suit with a trembling hand.

"Dom." I stepped forward.

He looked at me, and, for the first time, I saw fear in his eyes. "Yeah?"

"Don't."

Surprise crossed his face. "What?"

I shook my head. "Don't talk to her. I'll help Stella get her ready. Just meet us down there. Have a drink with Levin or something to relax."

Dom blew out a breath and nodded. "Yeah. Yeah, that sounds good."

I grabbed the garment bag from Levin and then snagged Stella by the arm, hauling her toward the stairs, her bag still in her hand.

Dom was nervous. Terrified. I guessed I would be too if I was set to marry someone who'd probably smash her head into my face the moment she met me at the end of the aisle. Despite the certainty of violence, Dom was a lucky man. B was one hell of a catch.

This was fucked up though. She'd escaped one arranged marriage only to fall right into another one. I hoped she understood this was Dom's way of saving her even if he would be breaking her spirit and probably her heart.

He was willing to force her into this, willing to risk his own life, willing to make a baby with her all in the hopes of saving her life because Matteo wouldn't kill his own grandchild. I knew Dom needed a male heir to keep his father happy. Bianca's pregnancy would keep her safe until we figured something else out. And who knew? Maybe Matteo would welcome her with open arms. I doubted it, but weirder shit had happened.

"He's not going to tell her she's getting married? He's not going to propose?" Stella asked as I led her upstairs.

"No."

"You know, I don't really like Bianca all that much, but even I have to admit this is fucked. You do realize you're doing the same thing to her that Hail was going to do, right?"

"Yep."

"Then why do it?" She jerked out of my hold and glared at me.

"Why the fuck are you so pissed? It's not like you're being forced into marrying him."

She rolled her eyes. "Like I'd complain. He's Dominic De Santis."

It was my turn to roll my eyes. "Yes, all hail King Dom."

"You're an idiot," she grumbled. "I don't know how you're missing the point, but since you are, I'll spell it out for you. *This is her wedding day.* It's the most important day in a girl's life. They plan this for years. They dream of their dress. The venue. The perfect man. The romantic proposal. So yeah, he's messing this up before he starts. She's going to hate this."

"B loves Dom. She told him."

"That was before Levin knocked her ass out after holding a gun to her head under Dom's command."

"Levin needs to keep his mouth shut," I grumbled.

"It was a long car ride, and he got pissed because I tried to get him to fuck me."

I snorted. "Levin isn't going to fuck you, Stella. Ever."

"Why?" she asked with a pout.

"Because he fucking hates the lords, and you've been letting Hail and the guys take you to pound town since freshman year. It's never going to happen." I paused. "Plus, he's in love with B."

"Has he told her? Has he even fucked her?"

"Not any of your business."

She let out a laugh. "That's what I thought. I still have a chance."

"Try it. You'll get your ass kicked. Levin doesn't fuck around. His temper is always simmering just below the surface like Dom's is. The only difference is Dom usually explodes right off the bat. Levin lets it stew and brew if you catch my meaning. That's probably worse."

She shrugged. "What about you?"

"Not interested."

"We've had sex before—"

"I was hard up."

"Mm, I remember how hard." She reached for me, and I shoved her hand away.

"Not happening either. Chill the fuck out, you nympho bitch. Just do your job. Stay in your lane. Dom isn't the only one who'll string your dead body up."

She flinched away from me and straightened her back. "Whatever. You won't be able to handle seeing Dom with her. You'll come around." She fixed a beauty pageant smile on her face.

I shook my head at her. Bitch was crazy. I had to admire her optimism though.

"Let's just get B ready. Don't say shit about the wedding." I moved to Bianca's door and pulled the key out of my pocket.

"So you're just going to shove her down the aisle?" Stella let out a laugh, shaking her head in disbelief. "You're all idiots. I'm glad I'm here to see this."

"Shut the fuck up," I grumbled pushing open the door only to get smacked in the head with a lamp.

My vision darkened as I stumbled back. Stella let out a shriek and dove aside as B took a swing at her too.

This was the third time she'd attacked me in a day. There wouldn't be a fucking fourth.

FIVE
BIANCA

"Eeek!" Vincent lunged at me, swaying from the blow to his head. I hefted the lamp up again, swinging, desperate to get the hell out of there. When I caught sight of Stella lurking behind him, my fury rose.

The lamp came down again, this time catching him in the arm. He let out a snarl and tackled me, knocking me to the ground. His hand cradled my head as we went down, preventing it from slamming on the hard floor. The lamp tumbled away, out of reach as Vincent held me down.

"Stop, B. Don't."

I attempted to smash him in the face again with my head, but apparently, he was a fast learner and rested his forearm at my throat to stop me.

"Stop," he panted out again. "What are you doing?"

"It's not obvious?" I ground out. "I'm trying to get away from a house filled with murderers and bitches."

He let out a sigh, his breath feathering across my face.

"Baby B, no one is here to hurt you."

"Tell that to Fallon."

"What happened to Fallon?" Stella peeked around the doorway. "Hail's looking for him. He's been missing for a couple of days."

"Because he's fucking dead," I snarled, my heart breaking all over again for so many different reasons. "They killed him."

Stella's eyes widened. I hated the bitch, but in that moment, I'd love nothing more for her to rush back to Hail and inform him the kings killed one of his men. If they wanted their precious war, they'd certainly get it with Fallon's death. He was an enforcer's son. He was a lord. I was sure Mikhail Ivanov wouldn't let his death go unpunished.

"You-you killed Fallon? Levin said—"

"Shut the fuck up, Stella. *I* didn't kill anyone," Vincent said, staring down at me.

"Then where is he?" I demanded, my voice cracking. "I saw Levin shoot him. Twice!"

Vincent closed his eyes for a moment before opening them. "B, Fallon was going to sell you out. Let it go."

"*You* let it go. I'm going to sing like a fucking canary once I'm out of here. You're going to have to kill me to keep me quiet. You'll have to whack me!" Hysteria washed over me as I screamed as loudly as I could beneath him.

"Stop! Fucking stop!" Vincent clamped his hand over my mouth, his dark eyes flashing. "What the fuck? Chill."

My chest heaved as I tried to breathe through my nose, the tears prickling my eyes. Vincent's bruised face morphed into an expression of sadness.

"Don't cry," he whispered. "I swear to you everything is going to be OK. Please, B." He leaned down, resting his forehead against mine, but I jerked my head to the side, and he ended up nuzzling my neck.

"Fuck, I hate you this way. I know you're hurting. It won't last forever, OK? Come on. Please. I meant what I said in the woods."

My body shook as I remembered his words. *I love you.* He'd held onto me so tightly, his tears mingling with mine before he pulled himself together to leave me.

To fucking leave me.

"I hate you," I choked out, my heart hurting. "I hate you so much."

He stiffened against me, silent, and then he nodded.

"I know, and I accept that. But I'm going to fight for you, B. You're mine. *Ours.* That's never going to change no matter how much you scream you hate me or them. I *know* you. I fucking know your heart. Buried beneath your hatred is pain. I feel it too." His voice trembled. "Together. We'll get through it together."

I clenched my teeth, hating the anguish he spoke of. I wanted him so much it hurt, but I wanted to punch his face in too because Fallon was gone.

Fallon. Just thinking his name made the wounds in my heart bleed again.

"Come on, baby. Don't do this. I need you to be happy today. Please, don't cry. I promise we'll leave here. We're going back to Bolten. Things are going to get better. Just give us a chance to explain things. OK? Can you do that for me? Give us the benefit of the doubt?"

I shook my head. I wasn't giving anyone shit.

"B…"

But I'd never get away if I kept fighting. I needed them to let their guards down. Once they did, I was running to the end of the world and hiding.

"You promise?"

He nodded. "Yeah. Just get up and be a good girl. Stella is going to help fix you up for tonight."

"I hate Stella."

He smiled, the action not reaching his eyes. "Me too."

"I'm right here, you jerks," Stella called out, sneering down at us as she stepped into the room.

"Wish you weren't," Vincent said with a sigh.

I had no idea why she was there. It was probably more of their secret bullshit. God knew Dom and Vincent sure spent enough time meeting with her before all this shit went down. Levin was probably telling the truth about Dom and Vincent taking turns on her in the men's bathroom at homecoming.

Remembering that only made my anger boil.

Keep it together, Bianca. Be cool. Calm. Let them relax.

"I want to get up."

Vincent studied me for a moment before shifting his weight off me and standing. He held his hand out for me, and I took it, allowing him to pull me up into his arms. My heart stumbled as I stared into his dark eyes. His forehead was bleeding again along his hairline where I'd clocked him with the lamp. Had it been any other time, I would've kissed his hurts and tended to them for him. Now, I restrained myself, hating the war waging within me. He was part of the reason why Fallon was gone. Hell, he'd even shot at us.

"Let's get you a shower." He clasped my hand and led me to the bathroom. Turning back to Stella, he said, "Set everything up. We'll be right back."

I could practically hear her eyeroll as she let out an exaggerated sigh. Vincent ignored her and closed the bathroom door. The room suddenly felt too small as I stared up at him.

Wordlessly, he reached out and skimmed his fingers beneath my shirt as he made to pull it up.

"I thought I'd lost you," he murmured. "It broke me."

I swallowed. I let him take my shirt off. Immediately, I wrapped my arms protectively around myself, covering my breasts so he couldn't look at me. He seemed hurt by the motion, his eyebrows drawing together on his forehead.

"I cried"—he whispered, stooping to push my panties off—"when I thought I'd lost you."

"Please," I pleaded softly, stopping him.

"What is it?"

"Can you turn around? I don't want you to see me."

He studied me for a moment, looking crestfallen. Finally, he nodded. Spinning, he put his back to me and turned the water on before facing the window.

Hurriedly, I shoved my panties down, stepped into the shower, and closed the shower door, letting the frosted glass hide me from his eyes.

"You know, I can see you naked whenever I want, right?"

I ignored him and began washing my hair with the shampoo inside the stall. My favorite shampoo. It wasn't a coincidence.

"All I have to do is close my eyes. See? You're naked right now in my head. You're on your knees. You're moaning for me, taking my cock—"

"Stop," I snapped at him.

He let out a deep sigh and went silent.

I quickly washed my hair and body. Then I stood there, letting the water pelt me, mixing with my falling tears. A soft sob escaped as I covered my face, angry and broken because everything was so screwed up now. I should've run away the first night I was with Fallon. We both could've escaped.

Or not.

He might have delivered me to Dominic's dad instead. Or worse.

But I liked to think Fallon wasn't that guy. I had to cling to that hope or forever be broken. Fallon was good. He was so good. He just wanted to save his sister. I would've done anything to save someone I loved too, even died for the chance. I needed only good memories of him, so I focused on those, while pushing the thought of his betrayal away. It just kept coming back though. Eating at me. Tearing at me. Devouring everything I was.

Maybe this was hell.

I'd been so lost in my thoughts I hadn't heard the shower door open, but I felt a warm, naked body behind mine. Strong arms wound around me as I cried.

"I don't know what to do," Vincent whispered. "What can I do to make everything better?"

"Finish your job," I managed to choke out. "Kill me so I'll stop hurting. So I'll stop thinking."

"You really loved Fallon, huh?" The sadness in Vincent's voice made more tears fall.

"Like I loved the kings."

Vincent turned me in his arms and peered down at me beneath the shower's spray.

"Not loved. *Love.* You *still* love us. You're just hurting right now. I promise the pain will eventually go away. Fallon was going to turn you over to an unimaginable nightmare, B. He wasn't a good guy—"

"He was!" I slammed my hands onto Vincent's hard, wet chest. "You didn't know him! You never knew him!"

"You didn't either," Vincent said softly, letting me slap and punch him. He didn't even flinch. He simply stood there taking it.

He was right. I didn't know Fallon as well as I'd have liked, but I loved what I did know, and that fucking mattered.

I sagged against Vincent, breathless with tears still running down my cheeks. He eased us to the tiled floor and held me as I sobbed, his fingers raking through my hair as I let out my tears.

He remained silent. When the water finally ran cold, he released me and rose to his feet, snagging a towel to wrap around his waist. He grabbed one for me too and had me covered and tucked against him in a matter of moments, his lips placing soft kisses on my face and shoulders every now and then.

"I'll get you something to wear," he murmured in my ear before leaving me in the bathroom to stare into the foggy mirror.

I wiped away the condensation and took in my sad face. My blue eyes held no sparkle and were bloodshot and puffy from crying. My lips were stiff, like they'd lost the will to smile. This wasn't the girl I was. Or at least it hadn't been.

I feared I'd never find her again amid the ruins of what the kings had destroyed.

SIX
BIANCA

"I don't want her touching me." I glared at Stella as she stood holding a hair dryer in my bedroom. I'd already put the silk slip and stockings on while she'd waited outside the door.

"B, she needs to get you ready—"

"For what?" I snapped. "I don't need to be ready if I'm escaping."

Vincent let out a soft chuckle. "You're never escaping us. It's silly to even think like that. We'd find you. I'm exceptionally good at locating what I want. And Dom is fan-fucking-tastic at it. And Levin—"

"I get it," I griped. "You're the gods of hide and seek. I still don't want *her* touching me."

"Please, like I even want to," Stella said with a roll of her eyes. "I'd rather be doing anything else."

"Like Hail, you fucking turncoat. I can't believe Dominic even trusts you."

"Dom and I go way back," she shot back. "We have history—"

"Just dry her hair, Stella. We're going to be late, and Dom hates that shit." He turned to me. "B, let her do what she needs to do. If you do, you'll be that much closer to getting the answers you want and maybe a bit of freedom."

I studied him in the mirror's reflection before grunting, "OK."

Stella set to work, drying and styling. I was certain she was pulling too hard with her brush on purpose. When she burned me with the curling iron on the last curl, I launched myself from the chair and swiveled to her. She stepped back, her eyes wide.

"Total accident. If you come any closer, I'll burn you again." She held the curling iron out like a hot sword.

"I'll have it stuffed down your throat before you make it to me," I volleyed back, eager to try because she pissed me off that much.

She didn't even need to say anything. Her presence alone was enough to set me off.

"Calm down. Both of you." Vincent got between us. "B, let her do your makeup—"

"I can do my own." I flopped back in my seat, grabbed the luxury makeup, and began rubbing moisturizer on my face before doling on primer.

Vincent watched from behind me for a moment, his dark eyes taking in every movement I made.

"Stella, leave," he finally said as I set my foundation.

I had no idea what we were doing, but I'd dress like a clown if it meant I could get the hell out of there sooner.

Stella didn't need telling twice. She rushed out of the room, calling Levin's name.

Bitch.

I finished my eye makeup with a black-winged liner, Vincent never taking his eyes off me. Butterflies flapped wildly in my guts, but I didn't dare let them soar. I couldn't. It felt like a betrayal to all my damn confusion. I'd pluck their damn wings off if I had to. I needed time to think, and I needed to get the hell out of there and run like Fallon had told me to.

"Here," Vincent said softly, unzipping the garment bag lying across the bed and pulling out a beautiful, black lace and beaded dress.

"What's that?" I asked, my voice shaking as I got to my feet. I'd expected something red. Definitely not something that looked like I was about to marry Dracula. The dress was beautiful though. The accompanying veil was black and beaded.

"Your dress. Put it on."

I backed away. "No. Tell me what's going on."

"Please get dressed. You put it on, and I'll tell you whatever you want to know."

I shook my head. "It looks like a wedding dress, just in black."

"B, please. Be a good girl for me, and do what you're told, OK? I really don't want to have to call help in here to get you dressed."

"Where's Dominic? Levin?"

"Downstairs, waiting."

"Which one am I-I doing this with?"

"Does it matter?" he asked softly, confirming my suspicions without admitting it.

"Yes. Levin killed Fallon. Dominic is holding me here. You…"

"It's not me, B. I wasn't lucky enough," he whispered as a sad smile tilted his lips upward. "I promise you can walk down the aisle and punch the lucky bastard in the face if you want. Might make this whole thing easier on a few of us at least."

"I'm *not* getting married," I hissed, my back against the wall as I shook my head. "No way. I came to the kings to escape an arranged marriage. I-I can't—"

"Bianca," Vincent said sternly, stopping my near panic attack with his use of my given name. "You're doing this. There is no out. No negotiation. *This* is us keeping you safe like we promised."

"Levin held a gun to my head! Dominic ordered him to kill me! Then Levin knocked me out. The back of my head still aches like a son of a bitch, and you think I'm going to happily accept this bullshit?" My panic was gone only to be replaced by pure fury. "No. No way. I'm not doing it. Kiss my ass."

I stormed forward to leave the room, but Vincent caught my arm and stopped me. I tried to break away from him, but he tightened his hold and backed me against the closed door, his body pressed against mine.

"I don't like it either, but this is what it takes to keep you alive. You want to find your dad? You'll have a greater chance with the last name De Santis than as a D'Angelou, trust me on that. You want revenge on every fucker who's ever hurt you? As a De Santis you can get it. Trust me, B, this is the way to have everything you've ever wanted."

"What about love? What about you?" The words slipped out before I could stop them.

His expression softened, and he loosened his hold. "You'll still have me. You'll *always* have me."

"Not if I'm married to Dominic."

He swallowed, his dark eyes raking over my face. "Yes. Even if you're married to Dom, you still belong to me, to Levin. A piece of paper won't change that. I won't let it."

"What if I don't want this?" I whispered. "M-my dad isn't here to walk me down the aisle."

He rested his forehead against mine and breathed out. "I'm sorry, baby. We all make sacrifices for the ones we love. This will just be one of yours."

I gulped, hating everything about this. I should be planning which college I'd be attending and thinking about my major and parties, not worrying about becoming a mob prince's wife and staying alive while mourning the loss of someone I loved. Someone who'd planned to betray me.

To save his sister. He would've come back for me. Right?

This was bullshit.

"Please, can you be a good girl for the night and do this?" Vincent murmured, cradling my face. "I don't want anything to happen to you. It broke my fucking heart the first time I thought…" his voice trailed off. "I can't do that again. So, please, if you ever gave a half a shit about me, do this. Stay alive for me."

I exhaled. "OK."

To win, to survive, to become queen of the bullshit, I'd submit.

But just for one night.

And then, I'd let all hell loose.

SEVEN
DOMINIC

I rocked back and forth on my heels in the clearing, dressed in an all-black Bespoke suit, my heartbeat thundering in my ears. Levin stood beside me in his suit as the priest trembled on my other side. I needed the old fuck to make it through this wedding without him having a heart attack. The way he was shaking and gasping, I wouldn't be surprised if he dropped dead at my feet, and not because I shot his ass.

I'd given Stella the task of creating an aisle with candles and rose petals for Bianca to walk down, my sad attempt at making this special for her. I trusted Levin bought her a stunning dress because I knew she'd be upset if she had to wear my white t-shirt on her wedding day instead of something she felt beautiful in.

She was going to hate me after this. I knew that much. Hell, she probably hated me now, but I promised myself I'd try to fix this shit and make it up to her. I didn't know how, but I was good at making shit up on the fly. Hopefully, this time would be no different.

Stella moved to sit on a tree stump, her arms crossed.

"Go make sure Bianca doesn't need anything," I said to her.

"She threatened to choke me with a hot curling iron. I'm not going back in there."

I suppressed a smile. *Of course, she did. That's how my queen should be.* "Go. If she tells you no, then you stay inside and wait for our return. I don't want you out here agitating her."

Stella rose and gave me a sour look but left the clearing.

"Where is she?" I asked softly, staring at the path that cut from the safe house to the clearing.

"Probably gutting Vincent," Levin said with a grunt.

Probably. I'd seen how fucked up his face was from her forehead smashing into it. My wasp had a wicked sting. It only made me want her more. I supposed that said something about how fucked-up and twisted I was.

We waited in silence for a few more moments before movement on the path caught my eye. I watched, my guts twisted and my heart banging hard, as Vincent emerged in his suit with Bianca on his arm, a vision in all black.

A black veil covered her face, so I couldn't see her features, but her dress hugged her body in all the right places before cascading into a trail of midnight behind her.

"Beautiful," I breathed out, not realizing I'd spoken until Levin grunted behind me. I'd have to thank him later for picking out such a perfect dress for my wasp.

It felt like forever before they finally reached us. I locked eyes with Vincent for a moment and noted the pain hiding within the dark pools. I'd meant what I'd said about not taking her from them. I wouldn't. At least not completely. She did belong to me until I deemed otherwise and set her free to them.

I inclined my head at him as he placed her palm in mine and backed away, pulling his phone out to take photos for us.

Her fingers in mine weren't gripping as tightly as I'd hoped, so I gave it a gentle squeeze and turned us to face the priest.

He gave me a shaky smile before clearing his throat. "D-dearly beloved," he started.

Bianca's hand trembled in mine, her chest heaving. I'd never wanted to hold someone so much in my life as I did in that moment.

She had to hate me, but there was a tiny part of me which prayed she loved me and would still want me.

I tuned out the sound of the priest's prayers as I gripped her hand tightly, my mind on the possibilities of what it meant to be married. The responsibilities I'd have to my wife.

I hadn't started the year at Bolten imagining I'd be married before Christmas, but there I was, forcing my enemy's daughter to marry me in the middle of nowhere. And actually wanting her to be my wife.

"Repeat after me," the priest said, his voice still quaking. "I, Bianca Elizabeth D'Angelou, take thee, Dominic Matteo De Santis, as my lawfully wedded husband…"

I stared down at the sheet of black tulle in front of me, my breath held.

She remained silent.

The priest fidgeted.

I clutched her tighter. "Wasp," I urged in a low, dangerous voice.

Whether she said the words or not, *this* was happening. But damn, I really wanted her to say the words.

There was a beat of silence before she spoke, her voice soft, "I, Bianca Elizabeth *Walker*, take thee, Dominic Matteo De Santis as my lawfully wedded husband…"

I exhaled, both her hands in mine, as she continued to speak her vows softly into the evening air, her voice quivering slightly with each syllable.

Levin handed her my silver wedding band. She pushed it onto my ring finger wordlessly and perhaps a bit too roughly, but it was done.

The priest gave us a wobbly smile of encouragement before he instructed me to repeat my vows.

I did, my voice low and even. When I got to the end, I decided to add something. "I vowed to keep you safe, Bianca. I told you I *never* break a promise. Nothing has changed in that respect. If anything, my commitment to you has grown. I'm sorry if this isn't how you wanted things to go, but this isn't a game to me. I don't take these vows lightly. I belong to you as much as you belong to me." I slid the diamond I'd picked up earlier that day onto her slender finger. "Always."

Levin cleared his throat and stared at his feet as Vincent snapped more photos with his phone. I couldn't see Bianca's face through the veil, so I waited, hoping once it was lifted, she'd say she gave a modicum of shit for me and my efforts.

"I now pronounce you husband and wife. D-Dominic, you may kiss your bride."

Gently, I reached out and lifted the veil from her face, staring down at her beauty. Her blonde waves whipped around her in the gentle breeze, her red, plump lips parted. Her blue eyes glimmered beneath the setting sun. She was the most breathtaking thing I'd ever seen.

And she was mine.

I leaned in and pressed my lips to hers, urging her to let me taste her as I gathered her closer to me. Just when I didn't think she'd kiss me back, her lips moved slightly beneath mine, making me melt against her in a way I'd never done with anyone else before.

Suddenly, she broke the kiss. Her hand came up and smacked me across my cheek so hard it made my ears ring. I stared back at her, shocked, as everything around us went silent.

"You son of a bitch," she snarled at me before raising her fist to clock me.

I caught it before it hit its mark as she lifted her other hand to smack me on the top of the head repeatedly with the bouquet of wildflowers Vincent made. Petals flew with the ferociousness of her attack.

She tried to kick me, but thankfully, her dress was too snug to lift her leg higher than a small fraction. A snarl left her lips as she fought against me. We were both panting by the time Levin restrained her against his front, her back to him.

She glared at me, her hair now a wild mess. Levin had her arms pinned behind her back.

I stepped close enough to thumb her bottom lip. "You couldn't behave, could you, *wife*?"

"Guess your brand of lesson teaching doesn't work on me," she seethed, her chest heaving.

I trailed my fingers down her face before running them across the tops of her creamy breasts.

"Good. I like you like this, wasp." I glanced to Levin. "Let her go."

He released her immediately.

I leaned in, deciding it might be fun to play a little game with her. "I'm going to turn around and count to ten. I want you to run as far and as fast as you can. I want you to try to escape me. I want you to cry for help. I want you to get dirty as you scramble through the night. Don't let me catch you because if I do, you'll never leave again." I brushed my lips against the shell of her ear, enjoying the way her body trembled for me.

I whispered a final word into her ear, "Run."

EIGHT
BIANCA

My chest burned as I sprinted as fast as I could while wearing the black wedding dress through the thick forest, my hair a wild, tangled mess around me. I kept casting quick looks over my shoulder to see if Dominic and the guys were chasing me.

As far as wedding traditions went, I wasn't a fan of this one. A chance to escape my killer husband seemed like a trick, but I'd give it my best.

I tripped over a fallen log and fell to my knees, gasping for breath. It took me a moment of struggling to get up in the heavy dress, but I was on my feet, moving again within seconds, the hem hefted high so I could run. I'd kicked my heels off the second Dominic had turned his back on me.

Vincent and Levin had both given me varying looks of concern when I'd hesitated to flee, but fuck it. I was a fighter, so if Dominic wanted to fight, I'd give him a hell of a round.

A twig smacked me in the face, creating a burn across my cheek. Dominic had given me that head start, but I wasn't so sure I could outrun him, considering I didn't even know where we were. I'd been lucky so far and had to be a good ten minutes into my journey through the darkness.

My chest ached from the exertion, so I stopped, gulping in air as I leaned against a large tree trunk.

Something in the undergrowth snapped, making my heart pound harder. *Could a bear get me out here? A wolf? Christ, what if fucking Sasquatch got me?*

I pressed myself harder against the tree trunk, my breathing loud. I quickly covered my mouth to muffle myself and peeked around the trunk, trying to see. Another twig snapped. I swallowed a whimper and dropped my hand, urging myself to peer out farther. I pushed off the tree enough to get a good look around while leaning, listening as the leaves rustled in the breeze.

I started to ease back into my hiding spot but didn't make it that far. A warm hand covered my mouth, silencing my scream before it could start as I kicked and bucked against the hard body.

Dominic turned me and pressed me against the tree trunk, his jacket and tie gone

"You're fast, wasp, but not nearly fast enough," he said in his low, accented growl.

I stared at him, my chest heaving.

He cocked his head at me, a tiny, wicked smile tilting his lips upward. "You're so beautiful."

It wasn't what I expected him to say. His hand dropped from my mouth.

I tensed as he leaned in and pressed a tender kiss against the corner of my mouth before he trailed his lips down my jawline to my neck.

With his other hand in my hair, he gave it a gentle tug to angle my neck for him. I panted as he nipped at the sensitive skin, his fingers moving the strap of my dress aside so he could kiss my collarbone.

"Dominic—"

"Shh," he said softly, brushing his lips along my neck again.

"Please," I whispered. "Stop."

"You're my wife, and it's our wedding night." He kissed the corner of my lips again as he gave my breast a soft squeeze.

"I'm not your wife. I'm your captive."

"You're not, *mia regina*," he murmured, placing a kiss on my lips and making butterflies flutter in my guts at his term of endearment. "You're more than that."

"You tried to have me killed."

"I'm sorry."

I let out a bitter laugh. "*You're sorry?* Dominic—"

"Shh."

"No."

I pushed against him, and he backed off, his green eyes drinking me in. His hair was a windswept mess. My heart skipped as I stared at him, but I was pissed, and good looks aside, he was a monster.

"You killed Fallon."

"I didn't," he said softly.

"You ordered it," I retorted, knowing he was going to argue that Levin was the one who pulled the trigger.

"I was upset."

I scoffed. "So your response is to kill people? People I love—"

The moment the words were out of my mouth he shoved me back against the tree, his eyes darkening.

"You didn't love him," he snarled.

"I did," I choked out as I peered up at him. "Just like I loved you."

His lip twitched and trembled. "You still love me, and you know it, wasp. Good girls don't tell lies. As for Fallon, he was a lord."

"He was a good person."

"He was going to give you up to hell."

"He would've come back for me. And he trusted if he failed, you'd come for me." At least that was the argument I kept having in my head.

"No." Dominic shook his head at me. "He was a piece of shit who was sent to kill you."

"*You* were going to kill me," I shot back. "How does that make you any better than him? He was at least going to give me a fighting chance."

Dominic's hand shot out and wrapped around my throat. I clawed against his hold as he restricted my airflow.

"I fucked up, wasp. What do you want from me, huh? A fucking written apology? I'm sorry I was going to go through with killing you. And I'm so grateful Levin knew my fucking heart and didn't carry out my order. I'd be devastated."

A tear slid down my cheek at his words. He loosened his grip.

"But I'm not going to apologize for anything else. I'm not sorry you're mine. I'm not sorry I bargained for your pussy. And I'm not sorry my last name is yours. I'll never be fucking sorry for wanting what I want." He released me completely, and I sagged to my bottom, gulping in air.

"Fuck," he growled, tugging at his hair before looking to the night sky through the treetops. "*Fuck.*"

He swooped down and lifted me into his arms, cradling me against his hard body. I didn't fight him. I was tired. So tired of a lot of things. I let him carry me because I knew there was no escape. If he could find me in the middle of nowhere, he could find me anywhere.

"I lose it sometimes," he said softly as he marched with me in his arms like I weighed nothing at all. His breathing was still deep and even. "I don't fucking mean it. I'm still learning how to treat a woman I care about. I'm not used to having one around me so much."

I swallowed, not saying a word.

"The last thing I want in this world is for you to be hurt. I don't like the way it makes me feel. I don't like how *any* of this makes me feel. I'm always worried about you. I can't stop thinking about you. You've invaded every fucking thought I've had since I met you. I-I feel out of control and on the edge, but I can't let you go. I don't want to let you go. I've never felt so many emotions at once in my life. I-I don't know what they are."

He grew silent for a moment before he spoke softly, "Is this what love feels like?"

"Yes," I whispered, sniffling.

"Then I love you so fucking much it feels like it's choking me." He pressed a fierce kiss to my head before falling silent.

I kept quiet even though my emotions stirred, and my heart ached for him.

Anger was sometimes stronger than love.

So instead of whispering back to him, I closed my eyes and tried to ignore the thrum of his heart.

NINE
LEVIN

"Here," Vincent grunted, handing me a glass of whiskey.

I took it and swallowed the contents in one gulp. He scoffed and gave me the entire bottle. Then he grabbed another for himself off the shelf before flopping down beside me on the couch in my room.

"Think he caught her?" he asked.

"He's probably fucking her as we speak," I muttered, lifting the whiskey to my lips. I took a deep drink, relishing the burn of liquor as it snaked its way into me. I hated feeling the way I did. Seeing bumblebee walk down that makeshift aisle in her dress made my heart ache in ways it never had before. When I'd made the decision to save her, I knew what it would mean. But damn, it sucked.

Not that I didn't trust Dom to keep his word, but I also knew him. She was his *wife*. It would be stupid to think he'd just toss her back to us right away. Or ever. I guessed there was a part of me that figured maybe he'd want to keep her to himself after getting her. Lord knew how fucking perfect she was, even if I'd never admitted it out loud.

I'd done some fucked up shit to Bianca. I'd lied to her at the dance. I'd made her run. I'd chased her. I'd held a gun to her head. She believed I killed Fallon.

Hell, I'd knocked her ass out and stuffed her in my trunk next to Fallon. I was a big offender. Deep down, I knew she had to hate me, but shit, it sucked. There was still a tiny part of me that hoped she didn't.

"You should've buried yourself in her when you had the chance," Vincent continued. "It was paradise."

I grunted, remembering how hot her mouth was on my cock the two times we'd done that. Yeah, shit had been good.

"Seriously, what are we going to do if Dom can't let go of her? You know he struggled to share before. And that was before she was his wife."

I shrugged and took another swallow of my whiskey before lighting a joint and taking a hit. I blew out the smoke and settled back against the soft leather and looked over at Vincent. He took the joint and inhaled deeply, coughing out the smoke after a moment.

"Fuck you, I guess," I said.

Vincent chuckled and took another hit before passing it back to me and taking a drink. "Might have to."

The sweet fuzziness of the high covered me, relaxing my muscles. Half my bottle of whiskey was gone. I would feel it tomorrow. I peeked at Vincent's bottle. He looked like he'd be joining me in the struggle.

"It wasn't so bad, you know?" he said softly after a brief moment of silence.

"What wasn't?" I gazed up at my ceiling, reveling in the spins it brought me. Fuck, I needed the release from the day.

"That night with B. Kissing." He cleared his throat before going silent.

We hadn't discussed our kissing or him rubbing my cock until I'd nearly exploded. I'd have done anything for her in that moment.

I took another hit and blew out the smoke. It hung over my head like a storm cloud.

"Yeah."

"I've never looked at another guy before."

"Me either," I said, shifting in my seat to better position my head against the top of the cushions.

"It's not like I want to be with a guy or anything. I want B." He paused and cleared his throat again. "But I can't help but wonder what it would be like, you know?"

I did know and didn't know what the fuck to think about it. It had felt good. Great even. But maybe that was because I'd been rock-hard and weeping precum from my cock because Bianca's tits were pressed against me.

"Yeah," I grunted.

"Think she'll want it again?"

"Maybe."

"What will we do if she asks?" He fixed me with his dark stare.

I took a hit from the joint and exhaled. It joined the cloud lingering above me. "I don't know. Go with whatever feels good."

He nodded. "Good. I didn't want to do something to piss you off. I only want to make her happy."

"Same, I guess."

"You *guess*?" He let out a soft chuckle. "She's got you wrapped around her little finger. You did, after all, basically tell Dom to fuck off when you went against his orders."

"The second worst moment of my life was holding a gun to her head while she cried. There was no way I could do it. Not to her. Never her," I said softly, my throat tight with the ugly memory. "Maybe if I'd never known her. Even then I'm sure I would've hesitated. Killing a fucking angel seems sacrilege."

Vincent took the joint from me and inhaled a hit. "Fuck." He coughed. "Well, she's married to our best friend now. If there was ever a doubt that Dom gave a shit, it's gone now. He's taking the ultimate steps to keep her alive."

"He is," I murmured. "I just hope he remembers we give a shit too."

"He won't forget. He promised."

We both fell quiet as we drank and smoked. I tensed as heavy footsteps thudded on the stairs. A moment later, Dom passed by my cracked doorway with Bianca sleeping in his arms as he carried her in her black dress.

"You did good with the dress," Vincent commented, turning back to me as Dom disappeared.

"Probably not good enough for her to forgive me anytime soon."

Vincent huffed out a laugh. "She kicked my ass several times today. I'm sure she'll be coming for you too." He got up and grabbed another bottle of whiskey before flopping down beside me again and taking a deep swig.

"I deserve nothing less," I said softly, my chest aching with worry.

What if she never stopped hating me?

The thought brought me little comfort, so I tipped my bottle back before I sparked up another joint.

Fuck it. I'd cry about it tomorrow. For now, I wanted to make sure I could drown out the sounds of Dom fucking her if he got the chance.

TEN
DOMINIC

I lay Bianca in my bed and gazed down at her. She'd fallen asleep during the walk back to the house. Her diamond ring glinted in the soft glow from the lamp on the bedside table. Her breasts were nearly popping out of her dress.

Levin had done a damn good job picking it out.

I sank down onto the edge of the mattress and raked my fingers gently through her hair. *I will do everything in my power to be a better man for you, mia regina.*

I had to get my shit in check. I couldn't snap at her the way I tended to with everyone else.

Tonight was my wedding night. I should be making love to my wife, but my wife hated my guts. I sighed and stood. Gently, I covered her with a blanket. I needed to put a baby inside her. She wasn't going to let me between her legs anytime soon though.

She'd missed a few days of her birth control pills. I didn't know shit about how they worked, but I figured missed doses were a good start. I'd just have to be a prick and keep them away from her from now on. Or get some placebos and hope she never found out. I'd always been a villain. Nothing had changed, except now I was a villain in love with a queen and willing to do anything to keep her breathing and mine.

I scrubbed my hand over my face, hating I had to do it like this. It wasn't like I didn't think I'd ever have kids. I just figured I'd do it later in life. *And to have kids with Bianca?* Fuck, I'd be so lucky.

I glanced over at her. She was still on her back, her lips parted as she slept. Sighing, I shifted back to her side and placed a kiss on her forehead.

"I'll be back," I murmured before easing away and turning out the light. I left the room, locking the door behind me so she couldn't leave. Then I went downstairs to the basement.

When I got there, I unlocked the secret room hidden behind the bookcase. Purposefully, I strode down the steps, leading to another level of the basement, an area even deeper. Fallon sat inside the large cage with his back to the cement wall. He looked up at me as I entered, his face swollen and bruised.

"Come to put me out of my misery?" he asked with a grunt, his voice a soft rasp.

"Maybe." I dragged over a chair and sat facing him.

He scoffed and looked away. His hands were handcuffed behind his back and his ankles were tied. He wasn't getting away.

"Then fucking do it already. You already killed Bianca. Let me join her."

"Don't be so dramatic," I said with a roll of my eyes.

He swallowed and watched me carefully, his brows crinkling. "What are you waiting for?"

"Levin, mostly. And you. Can't kill you just yet if you have information about Stefan."

"My father is going to come looking for me. They'll get the call I'm missing. Hail won't fuck around when he can't find me. He'll go straight to his father."

"I don't care much about that," I said with a shrug. "It's not like they have proof I have you."

"You're missing too, asshole."

"Am I?" I leaned forward and rested my elbows on my knees as I surveyed him. "I'm known for disappearing from campus for days at a time. No one bats a lash. So are my guys. Plus, it's only Monday. Classes just started back up. We took a long weekend. That's all. No one will question us. And if they do, it'll be their funeral."

"You're a fucking prick." He shook his head at me. "What did you do with Bianca's body? Huh? I fucking hope you had the decency to give her a proper burial and not just shove her in a bag and dump her somewhere." His voice cracked, and a tear trickled down his swollen cheek.

"She's been taken care of properly," I said softly.

He let out a soft sob. I let him cry for a moment, something tearing at my chest.

Finally, I asked the question I didn't know if I even wanted the answer to. "Did you love her? Really *love* her? Not just to fuck around with."

He peered up at me. "I planned on dying with her if it came down to it. I intended to fight as hard as I could to save her. So yeah, I loved her. I'd have given up anything for her."

It was the answer I'd dreaded. My chest burned with the knowledge.

"But it doesn't matter now. She's dead." He sniffled. "You know, she just wanted to find her dad. She missed him. I didn't have much information to help her. It's one of my biggest regrets that I never found him for her. I feel like I failed her in so many ways. The agony of it won't stop. I just want you to kill me."

"Love is torture," I said, getting to my feet and walking away. "Let it destroy you. It's what you deserve for what you'd planned to do to her."

"I didn't *want* that, De Santis," he called out to me. "I didn't want any of that, and you know it! *You fucking know it!* You never loved her. Not the way I did. She was a mere pawn to you. Something to use and destroy. You ruin everything you touch. You're just like your father!"

I froze at the doorway but didn't turn back to him as he wept softly.

"I fucking loved her," he choked out. "You don't get to take that from me. Or her. It doesn't matter what you say or do. It will always be a fucking truth you'll have to live with. She chose me. *She fucking chose me.*"

"There is no choosing," I said. "Not for her. Not anymore."

"Piece of shit! Fucking asshole! You'd better hope I never get out of here alive because I will kill you for hurting her! I'll gut you for taking her from me. I swear it. I fucking swear it," he wailed.

I closed and locked the door behind me. Hurting, I leaned against the wall in the stairwell.

As much as I wanted to be a good man, I knew I wasn't.

I'm a monster, the villain.

And in my story, the villain always wins.

Fallon Vasiliev wouldn't change that.

ELEVEN
VINCENT

"Where's your blushing bride?" I asked, coming into the kitchen the following morning to find Dom fixing a breakfast tray with food he'd prepared.

Eggs, bacon, pancakes, waffles, fruit, orange juice.

"In bed," he muttered.

"How'd last night go?" I swallowed and watched him.

He was frowning, his green eyes downcast and his shoulders heavy.

He shook his head. "It didn't. I caught her and brought her back. She fell asleep halfway here and stayed that way all night."

"So your union is unconsummated? Nice." I grabbed a pancake off the platter he'd made and poured maple syrup over it. "I can fix that for you if you'd like."

"Hell no," he growled. "I got it."

"She hates us."

"Tell me something I don't know, Valentino."

He shot me a sour look as he adjusted the glass of orange juice on the tray before looking back at me.

"Your face looks like shit."

"She hit me with a lamp when I went in to get her ready for last night."

He raised his brows at me. "She did?"

I nodded. "Nearly knocked my ass out. She's wild, man."

A tiny smile touched his lips. He'd smiled more in the last few weeks than in the entire time I'd known him. It made me happy to know one of my best friends was in love with the girl of his dreams. She was the girl of my dreams too though. Levin's as well.

"I know you just married her and all, but do you think I could see her—"

"No. Both you and Levin need to make an appearance at school today. We need to decide what we're going to do with Fallon when you get back. I'm not his fucking maid, so me nannying his ass isn't going to happen."

"How about I stay behind and take care of things here, and you make the appearance—"

He shook his head. "I know you want to see Bianca, but I need to get her to talk to me without trying to take a swing. *I need this. Please.* Just give me a couple days."

"Fine," I grumbled, hating it but accepting it.

"Besides, it should be me who fucks my wife first." Dom picked the tray up and glared pointedly at me.

"I get it." I gave him a tight smile and watched as he left the room.

Levin appeared a moment later.

"Dom said there was food." He stalked past me and grabbed a pancake, stuffing it into his mouth.

"I don't know if that son of a bitch is going to let B off her chain long enough for us to have her again," I said glumly.

I'd always trusted Dom. He'd never steered us wrong before. I still found it worrisome though because with B he was different. And that difference was fucking terrifying.

"He will. If he doesn't, I'll just take her." Levin shrugged and grabbed another pancake like it wasn't a big deal.

I sighed, knowing it wouldn't be that simple. "Dom wants us to make an appearance today at school. We'll go there, smile like fucking assholes, then come back."

"What would be the difference?" Stella sauntered into the room, dressed in her uniform, her dark hair in a high ponytail. "You're always assholes."

I gave her the finger while Levin ignored her.

"Dom made breakfast. Eat then we're leaving," I said, nodding to the small stack of pancakes.

She wrinkled her nose. "No thanks. I don't do carbs this early in the morning."

"You're a fucking party animal," Levin muttered, grabbing another pancake and stuffing it into his mouth.

She sneered at him and picked up her backpack. "When do I get my phone back?"

"Never. You know what Dom said. You have the burner we gave you. It'll have to do." I snatched my bag up from the floor as Levin moved forward.

"This is stupid. I'm not dumb enough to betray the kings—"

"We're not willing to find out. We can track what you do this way. If you fuck up and talk…" I made a neck-slitting motion which made the blood drain from her face.

Levin shuffled past me and snagged a black bag off the table, slipping it over Stella's head without a word before he went outside.

She sighed as I gripped her hand and led her out. She may have an arrangement with us, but she still didn't need to know how to get to our safe house.

We followed Levin out to his car, and I slid onto the passenger seat after stuffing Stella into the back. I'd dumped the priest back at his house last night, vowing to filet him like a fish if he ran his mouth about what went down.

"Dom wants us to figure out what to do with Fallon," I said as Levin backed out of the garage and onto the two-track dirt road through the forest.

"He's not talking. I've tried. Without bumblebee, he's dead inside and doesn't give a shit. He has nothing to live for," he said gruffly.

"Do you blame him?"

He shook his head. "No. I'd be the same way, I guess."

"Me too. So what do you think? Should we just kill him and bury his ass?"

"You can't kill Fallon," Stella cut in, her voice muffled through the bag. "Hail will lose it if Fallon is murdered. Like, Fallon is very important to the lords. Hail always talks about his skills."

Levin snorted but said nothing.

I sighed. "Anyway, peanut gallery input aside, we will have to kill him if he doesn't cooperate. We can't let him run around. If Hail finds out Fallon was going to betray him, he'll be dead anyway."

Stella made a noise to protest, but I glared at her over my shoulder even though I knew she couldn't see me. "You know it's true."

She mumbled, crossed her arms over her chest, and sank back in her seat.

I expected Levin to jump on the idea of killing him, but he was quiet. When he finally spoke again, his voice shook, "If we kill him, she'll never forgive us. You know she won't. If we're scared of losing her, that would be the wedge to make it happen. We have a chance to bring her back to us. I think we need to keep him alive."

"Do you think she'll jet on us and run away with him?"

"I really fucking hope she still gives a damn about us after everything we did. But if she did run, I wouldn't blame her. She deserves better than a couple murdering assholes."

I nodded, silent as my guts churned.

"She loves him," Levin said, his voice taking on a frustrated tone. "We can't change it. I-I don't know how we're going to get out of this. Either he dies or he lives, but if he lives, they're going to come after us if he talks. The entire Bratva."

I shrugged. "We wanted a war."

"We did," he murmured. "But it could mean she's still not safe, so is it worth it? Matteo might not harm her, but Ivanov sure as fuck would. We didn't think this through enough. Now with Dom married to her, she has a bigger target on her back."

I ground my teeth, thinking about all the shit that could go wrong. Levin was right. We didn't think it through.

"So now what?"

"Let's see how today goes. Keep in touch with Dom. If anyone asks about them, we'll say they decided to take a long weekend together. As for Fallon, we don't know shit. Got it?"

"Yeah," I said, sighing. "I can't wait for this day to be over so we can get back to the safe house."

"If Dom lets us come back. He might make us stay on campus to keep up appearances."

Motherfucker would do something like that.

He'd be honeymooning with baby B while we were stuck trying to clean up the mess. But I'd do it. For B, I'd do anything.

AT LUNCHTIME, I sat on a table in the courtyard, watching students mill around. I didn't have much of an appetite and was waiting for Levin to show up. Not much was happening at Bolten. No one was talking about shit. Dom and B's absence didn't seem to be a big deal, but it probably would be if it lasted for more than a couple of days.

Ivanov and the lords were at their table near one of the old oak trees, their disciples by their sides. I hadn't heard any murmurings about Fallon being gone, but it was just day two. I knew the lords had to be looking for him. I hoped with Dom being absent as well, the lords wouldn't think Fallon had run off with B. Of course, maybe they thought she had, and Dom was looking for her.

Ivanov peered across the courtyard at me for a moment before taking a step toward me. Then another. And another. I got to my feet and braced myself, knowing we were going to meet head-on in just a few moments.

"Where's Bianca?" he asked the moment he reached me.

Nice to see he didn't split hairs.

"Away with Dom."

"Yeah? Where?"

"I'm sorry. At what point did it become your business knowing where the fuck our girl is?"

"*Your* girl?" Ivanov scoffed. "Please. De Santis has his dick branded on her tits. She's his, and you know it."

"You're wrong. I would know because I fucked her over the weekend."

His face reddened as he spoke, "I don't give a fuck what you do with your whore."

I raised my brows at him. "Really? Then why did you ask?"

"Fuck you, Valentino."

"Right. Well, now that we've established that, off you fuck," I said, giving him a scamper off motion with my fingers.

"Honestly, I'm just wondering if you've seen Vasiliev. Figured you might know where I could find him. You know, coordinates to the lake you dropped him in or the hole he's buried in. Glad he seemed to put up a good fight because you look like you got your ass kicked." He rubbed his nose, indicting my blackened eyes from B's headbutt.

"Yeah, seems like a solid theory," I said, nodding and pulling out a joint. I lit it and took a deep hit. "But I don't know where your bitch is. I haven't seen him."

"If I find out you killed a lord, *a fucking enforcer's son*, you're dead. If you think shit's bad now, just wait."

"Like I said, I don't know where your boy ran off to. Maybe he got sick of your shit and left. You know, like Bianca did."

He shoved me hard in the chest, barely rocking me back. I followed up by landing a solid punch to his jaw. The crack was a sickening, satisfying vibration through my fist and arm. Before he could retaliate, his guys hauled him back.

He wiped at the blood on his lip as Levin joined my side.

"I want Vasiliev back. You have seventy-two hours to bring him to me alive. If you don't, I'm going straight to D'Angelou to tell him everything. Your precious whore won't be safe anymore. You fucking know it's true."

He backed away, glaring at me, before turning and striding back the way he came with his guys.

"We need to talk to Dom," Levin said, watching as Ivanov returned to his spot. He'd arrived just in time.

"We gotta endure the rest of the day. If we leave now, it'll look suspicious."

Levin clapped me on the shoulder. "Fine, but leave the moment classes are out. Meet me in the back lot."

"Right."

We may be in more trouble than we'd thought because the way Ivanov was scowling made unease crawl through me.

But the real question was how to deliver a dead man to this asshole without risking B's safety because I knew Dom wouldn't just give in.

Just another fucking day in paradise.

TWELVE
BIANCA

"Why is Stella still here?" I asked as I stared down at the tray of food in front of me.

It was lunchtime now. I hadn't touched a bite of the breakfast Dom had brought me despite how good it had smelled. He'd gotten angry and dumped it into the trash before storming from the room and locking me inside.

"She's not here now. She left for Bolten with Vincent and Levin. But to answer your question, we have a deal with her. She needs protection too. You know that." He sank onto the window seat and stared outside.

"Does that protection include fucking her whenever you feel like?"

He snapped his attention back to me and locked his green eyes on mine. "No."

I figured he'd yell at me for the jab.

"You're my wife, wasp. I won't be fucking anyone else but you for the foreseeable future."

I scoffed. "You won't even be doing that, sweet husband."

A muscle popped along his jaw before he turned back to the window.

"Where did you bury Fallon?"

He scoffed and shook his head.

"I want to know."

"It's not really any of your business," he said, not bothering to look at me. "He's gone. That's all that matters."

Anger surged within me, and I heaved the bowl of soup at him. It hit him in the arm, splashing the remnants over his pressed, black pants and onto his dark Henley.

The bowl crashed to the floor and shattered, sending glass shards skittering across the hardwood. He stared down at it for a moment, his Adam's apple bobbing before he rose to his feet and approached me slowly.

My heart jumped into my throat, but I refused to back down.

When he reached the bed, I glared up at him, noting the anger clouding his handsome features.

"Why can't you behave?"

"Why can't you let me go?"

"Because you're mine." He visibly swallowed, his body corded with tension.

"This wasn't part of our arrangement. You know that. *You* forced me to marry you. *You* killed Fallon. *You* tried to kill me. Excuse me for saying this, but fuck *you*, Dominic."

He slammed me onto my back, his large body looming over me as he pinned my arms.

"Behave," he hissed.

"Fuck. You."

"You will, sweetheart." He breathed out. "If I wanted it, I could take it. Don't think you're holding back on me. You're not. You're only prolonging the inevitable."

"I swear I'll take your ass down if you lay one finger on me."

He chuckled softly, his breath feathering over my face. "Don't threaten me, wasp. We both know you're not cut out for war."

"Tell me where Fallon is buried."

His green eyes swept over my face. "What good would it do? He was going to betray you."

I hated hearing the words, but it didn't change a damn thing. "I need to know."

He shook his head. "You never will."

"Tell me where he is," I said louder this time.

He shook his head again.

"Tell me. Tell me. TELL ME!" I screamed it. "Tell me where he is. I want him. Tell me. Tell me. I need to know. *Fucking tell me!*"

Hysteria washed over me as I screamed, tears pouring down my cheeks. I had to know. It was like facing my fears. Having confirmation that he was gone would be brutal, but I needed it like my next breath. "Tell me! Tell me! Tell me!" I repeated the words over and over through my sobs as I dragged in gasping breaths.

Dom's brows crinkled as he shook me. "Stop. Stop it, Bianca. Stop!"

"Tell me. Please, Dominic. Tell me where he's buried. Tell me where you put him. Please. Please, tell me," my words came out choked and garbled as the pain of losing Fallon flared bright hot in my chest.

It overtook the rage. In my mind, I saw Levin knock him to the ground again. I relived the sound of the gunshots firing into the night, my screams on repeat in my ears as I called for him.

"Tell me," I whispered again.

Dom released me and got to his feet, letting out a frustrated snarl as he ran his fingers through his black hair.

"Fuck!" He punched the wall, putting a hole through the plaster before backing away and opening the door. He didn't look back at me. He simply slammed the door closed behind him and locked it, leaving me to weep on the bed, alone.

I FELL asleep after Dominic left me only to open my eyes later to see the sun setting through the trees. Slowly, I got to my feet. I was still clad in the white t-shirt of Dom's I'd changed into that morning. I moved to the broken bowl still on the floor. I picked up a shard of glass and went back to the mattress where I tucked the sliver safely beneath it.

Emptiness was the only thing I felt within me. Nothing mattered. I imagined I would've felt the same way if something would've happened to Dominic, Vincent, or Levin. This situation cut just a bit deeper though, given what they'd done.

I shuffled to the adjoining bathroom and turned on the shower. Not bothering to take off the t-shirt or panties, I got in.

The hollowness morphed as I bawled softly beneath the warm spray. This was the worst. If I had just stuck it out with Hail, maybe Fallon would still be alive. Maybe he and I would've been able to run away together. Maybe Fallon would've delivered me to Matteo, and I'd have been rescued by him once he got the chance to free his sister. Maybe everything would've been different if I had just stayed away from the kings. Maybe I would be different.

I didn't want people to die because they got tangled up with me. Fallon may have made arrangements to have me delivered to hell, but he'd admitted it in the end and sworn he was going to save me. The kings had done none of those things, opting to simply put me on my knees and make me believe I was going to die. *Why didn't they just kill me?* It was a question lurking in the back of my head, but because I knew they were prone to being assholes, I could only assume it was to torture me some more.

I should've run when I had the chance.

But I didn't. I'd gotten weak and gone to the kings. Now, I had the same thing I'd been trying to run from—a cage, a marriage I didn't choose. Maybe I wasn't getting burned with a cigarette, but I was definitely on fire inside.

I wasn't sure how long I stayed in the shower, but eventually the water ran cold as I closed my eyes, dreaming of a solution.

The answer probably rested in the shard of glass beneath my mattress if I could get the courage to use it. I wanted to go out on my own terms. Not on my fucking knees before men who'd claimed they loved me. *Why should I suffer more?* But living while knowing Fallon was gone was a pain I wasn't sure I could bear. Knowing I'd never get the chance to hear him really explain things to me. Knowing my death could happen at any moment was suffering.

I hated these emotions. They were choking me.

Warm arms encircled me, and I shivered as I was eased out from the cold.

"You're freezing," Levin murmured, wrapping me in a warm, heavy towel.

I hadn't even heard him come into the room.

"Come on, bumblebee. Open your eyes and tell me how much you hate me."

I cracked my lids open to find apprehension on his face. We hadn't spoken since shit went down. He pushed the wet strands of blonde hair away from my face. My heart broke all over again as I stared at him. He'd been planning to kill me. He'd pressed a gun to my head. He'd killed Fallon.

"Let's get you warmed up."

The strength left me as I shut down. I had no fight left. It didn't matter. Not much did now. My fate was signed, sealed, and waiting for delivery.

Levin sat me on the bathroom counter, concern on his face. "I'll be right back, OK?"

I said nothing. He left quickly only to return moments later with another t-shirt and pair of sweatpants. Wordlessly, he peeled the wet shirt from me, doing all the work of moving my arms for me like I was a broken doll.

His eyes swept over my naked torso for a second before he quickly toweled me off and slid the fresh shirt over my head. Once that was done, he worked on removing my panties and hauling the too-big sweatpants up my legs to my hips.

He remained quiet as he lifted me and brought me back to the bedroom where he placed me on the bed.

"Be right back," he said, moving back to the bathroom. He returned a moment later with a brush. He crawled behind me on the mattress and brushed through my long tangles before weaving my hair into a thick braid down my back and tying it off with a rubber band.

He lay down and eased me down onto the mattress next to him, his arms wrapping around me. "I'm worried about you, bumblebee. I'm sorry I wasn't here when you woke up, and I'm so fucking sorry I hurt you. I want you to know it gutted me to do it."

I remained silent as he paused.

"I couldn't pull the trigger," he whispered. "I thought I'd be able to when it was time, but I just couldn't do it. A world without you in it would be fucking worthless. I would've followed you to the grave. I know I would have. And I know you hate me right now. Hell, I know you hate us all, but please, don't do this. Don't shut down." He placed a kiss on the top of my head and hugged me to him tightly.

I closed my eyes as a tear trickled out.

"I'm sorry about Fallon. I am. I know you fucking despise me. Fuck, it's killing me so much to know it. I feel like my heart's being torn from my chest and stomped on. You're still here, but I feel like I'm losing you. I-I don't want to lose you. I only just found you."

He grew quiet after that, holding me against his body in Dom's bed, before his breathing turned deep and even.

Deciding sleep was for the best, I closed my eyes again, wanting the nightmare to end.

THIRTEEN
LEVIN

Two hours later, I'd untangled myself from Bianca's sleeping body and had forced myself to leave her side. I'd poured my heart out to her as much as I knew how, yet she'd stayed silent the whole time. There wasn't anything else I could tell her. Laying my heart at her feet made me feel weak and worthless. And she hadn't even given a shit.

The fear that she was already gone made my heart ache. I wasn't the sort of guy who laid it all out for people to see. Burying my emotions was what I did, and it had worked just fine until Bianca had arrived. Now, I was skinned raw and sick to my stomach because the girl my best friend had married didn't want me and didn't give a fuck. This was what emotions got a guy. Fucked up.

"How is she?" Dom asked as I came downstairs.

"Sleeping," I muttered, sitting down on the couch. "Where's Stella?"

"In her room, bitching about not having her phone." He rubbed his eyes.

Vincent came into the room and flopped down in the chair across from me.

"Ivanov was pissed today, threatening to go to D'Angelou if we don't produce Fallon. We need to figure out what we're going to do."

"I know," Dom said, staring off into the distance, twirling the wedding band on his finger.

Lucky bastard. It wasn't like I'd ever considered getting married. Hell, I never thought I'd find a girl I could stand to be around past getting off. But now that I knew Bianca, everything had shifted gears practically overnight. I wasn't sure how to navigate this new territory. Clearly, I was great at fucking it up.

"Seventy-two hours. We either kill Vasiliev and get rid of his body or we set him free," Vincent continued.

"If we set him free, he'll run and talk," Dom said.

"If we kill him, we'll break Bianca further," I added, sighing.

I'd like to kill the cocksucker. He'd been wooing our girl, and she'd fallen for it. Add to it that he'd planned on giving her over to Matteo made me want to keep punching the fucker in the throat until he choked on regret. But then he'd said he knew who'd killed Stefan. Son of a bitch knew how to save his ass, that was for sure.

Dom snapped his focus on me. "If he lives, he'll take her from us. You know he will."

"I hope not. She loves us. It has to mean something," Vincent said, his voice quiet. "You know she does."

A muscle thrummed along Dom's jaw as he spun the ring faster on his finger.

"I hate everything to do with the lords, but that girl upstairs..." Vincent said, his voice thick with emotion. "I really hate to say this, but maybe we need to bargain with Vasiliev—"

"Never happening," Dom snarled, glowering at Vincent as he leaned forward.

"Maybe Vin is right," I said, hating the words as they came out of my mouth.

Dom fixed his glare on me.

"Just listen, man," Vincent rushed on. "She loves him too. You know she does. She'll hate us forever if we don't let him live. Maybe she'll love us again, or at least give us a chance, *if* we let him go. Don't you want your wife to be your *wife*?"

Dom's hands balled into fists for a moment as he breathed in and out deeply, like he was trying to suppress his rage. I hated the idea of letting Vasiliev go too, but the alternative seemed to be losing bumblebee if we finished Vasiliev off. Plus, if he were dead, I'd never get answers about Stefan, and the bastard said he knew something.

"I'm not letting him go. We'll kill him."

"Bad choice," I said. "You know it. I know you hate him, I fucking do too, but I was just upstairs with Bianca. She was sitting in the shower with cold water raining down on her. She was like ice. She's checking out, Dom. She's leaving us, whether we want her to or not. I hate to say it, but Vasiliev has to live. Or maybe he lives long enough to die. The lords could find out and kill him themselves. It'll save us a hell of a lot of trouble and not really be our fault if that happens."

It was a slimy as fuck thing to say, but fuck Vasiliev. I didn't give two shits about him. What I did care about cared about him, so I'd have to deal. For now.

Vincent nodded quickly. "Levin's right. Maybe we can get him on our side. Maybe he'll spill everything he knows for B—"

"No," Dom shouted, getting to his feet. "Not happening. Don't fucking bring it up again or you'll join him in the basement."

"Don't threaten me for trying to bring our girl back." Vincent rose and faced off with Dom. "I know you fucking hate the lords. We all do. But you're punishing B with your hatred. He might love her enough to join us—"

Dom let out a snarl and stormed away from us. His footsteps pounded up the stairs a moment later.

"Damnit," Vincent groaned, falling onto the sofa and sighing. "Fuck, man. What are we going to do?"

I shook my head. "I don't know, but whatever it is needs to be done soon."

"We need Vasiliev to talk, and we need to make B happy again. We've just gotta get Dom on board with the Russian asshole."

"Maybe he'll realize it when he goes upstairs and sees what an empty shell Bianca is becoming. Let's just let him think it over. In the meantime, maybe you should go talk to Vasiliev," I said.

"Me?" Vincent snorted. "Why not you?"

"Because…" I said softly. "I still might kill him for touching our girl and for not giving me the information he has on Stefan."

Vincent sighed and got up. "Fine. But if I kill him, you can't get pissed."

"I won't. It'll be nice to not have a hand in his death this time."

Vincent scowled and flipped me off before leaving to go see our *friend* in the basement.

I hoped he'd weave some magic because if he didn't, we were fucked.

FOURTEEN
VINCENT

I stepped into the basement's dungeon, a term which made Dom roll his eyes, and focused on the asshole in the room.

"We need to talk."

"Go fuck yourself," Fallon said, not bothering to look at me as he rested his head against the cement wall behind him.

"Sure, after we're done. But seriously, do you want to live or not?"

"Not," Fallon said easily like we were discussing the weather.

"Fuck, man, come on. I'm trying to help you."

"Then just kill me and get it over with."

"How about a truce. Or a negotiation."

"Not interested. Kill me. My sister is probably already dead."

"She's not. What if Dom can save her? What if we can?"

Fallon's eyes opened, and he focused on me. "What?"

I licked my lips, trying to gather my thoughts. "Dom is set to take over the palace his father has for him. Your sister is there, or at least will be going there. Dom can free her. He's ready to make arrangements. In fact, he's already started."

"Why would he do that?" Fallon narrowed his eyes at me.

"Because you told us what you know about Stefan Seeley," I said, hoping he caught my meaning.

"And you'll tell me where Bianca's body is so I can say goodbye? So she can have a proper fucking burial?"

"Sure, man."

He sneered at me. "How do I know you're not fucking with me just to get information out of me?"

"You don't, but if you want to make sure your sister is going to be OK, then you should probably start cooperating."

He glared at me. "You know what I don't get about you pricks?"

"Enlighten me." I sighed and pulled up the stool.

"How you could kill Bianca like she didn't mean something. How you could harm her the way you did."

"Right." I nodded. "It's business, man. It's all business."

"Fuck you and your business. I'd rather die knowing I left you pricks hanging than give up what I know. Natalia is probably already dead anyway. You're trying to play me. Just kill me. I'm ready to die."

I ground my teeth together. *Great, not only had Bianca checked out, but it looked like this asshole had too.*

"I don't think you know what you're giving up," I said.

He scoffed. "You know, a few weeks ago, I might have begged for my life. She gave me a reason. If she's gone, what's the point? In the little bit of time I was fortunate enough to love her, I realized that once you find your person, life makes sense. I've spent a lot of my life struggling to find my reason. Then I did. Now it's gone. I'm done. If you don't kill me, then I'll kill myself. Either way, I'm out." He closed his eyes, going silent.

Fuck.

I didn't have shit else I could say to him. Reason was beyond him now without Bianca. And B…shit. She needed him too, or we'd lose her.

I headed back upstairs, knowing I needed to talk some sense into Dom. I'd probably have a better chance of convincing a vampire he didn't need blood than convincing the mob prince to tell Fallon that B was alive… convincing him that B needed Fallon just like she needed us.

Or like I hoped she still needed us.

Letting her know Fallon was still alive meant we might lose her, but I'd rather lose her to her own happiness than see her destroyed by her sadness.

Love was a real bitch like that.

I LAY in bed that night in the safe house and stared up at the ceiling, thinking about my baby B and what the hell I could possibly do to make her give a shit again.

A gift? Maybe some flowers and a date night? I could cover Stella in honey and leave her out for the bears...

A soft knock on my door had me tumbling out of the idea of buying her a pet iguana she could dress up.

"Come in."

My door cracked open, and Dom popped his head in. Immediately, I sat up.

"What's wrong?" I demanded, swiveling so my feet hit the floor.

"Bianca." He stepped into the room, his hands in his pockets and his head down. He looked like someone had canceled Christmas.

"She OK?"

He sighed. "I don't think so. She won't talk to me. When I went in tonight, she was just sitting in a chair staring at the fucking wall. I'm worried." He sank onto the edge of my bed. "I tried to talk to her. I told her I care about her and wanted her to come back to me. I kissed her, but she didn't move an inch. I touched her. Nothing. She's my fucking wife, and I can't even have her the way I want." He yanked at his dark hair, his chest heaving.

"Calm down," I instructed, worried he'd put his fist through another wall at any moment. "She's upset."

His legs bounced as he stared at the floor.

"I talked to Fallon," I started.

"Fuck him."

"Dom, man, listen. I know you don't want to hear this—"

"Then don't fucking say it," he snapped, jumping up to pace.

I steadied my breathing and plunged on, acutely aware his fist might meet my face after the words left my mouth, "She loves him. He loves her. Just like we do. Keeping him a secret is only going to kick us in the ass. If she finds out he's alive and we really did end up killing him later on, it'll be over. We'll lose her for good. You know this, man."

He shook his head and went quiet, a muscle feathering along his jaw in the dim lamplight.

"If we want our girl, we have to keep him alive. And like Levin said earlier, maybe the lords will take his ass out once they realize he's on our side… if we can get him there. The trash takes itself out. It's not ideal, but it is a solution."

"Fuck," he grunted. "Damn it."

"I have an idea."

He let his head fall back for a minute, his eyes closed. Finally, he looked at me.

I cleared my throat. "We let him know she's alive. Let them see each other…"

Dom's balled his hands into fists, so I rushed on.

"Once he knows she's alive, he might be more willing to talk. Then we cut a deal with him. Besides, if B is as pissed at him as she is at us, we might not have anything to worry about concerning her running off with him."

"I'm not sharing *my wife* with that piece of fucking trash." He glared at me.

"If he's one of us—"

"He will *never* be one of us. He's a lord. They're no good."

"We aren't either, man," I said softly. "We're just as fucked up, only we have a girl we're trying to keep. Just think about it, OK? For B."

He blew out a breath and closed his eyes again before he finally nodded. "I'll consider it."

I stared stupidly at him, shocked he'd come around so quickly. I figured I'd be working on it for weeks.

"For Bianca," he said thickly.

I nodded. "For Bianca. We have less than seventy-two hours. No rush."

He ran his fingers through his hair before bidding me good night.

Dom hadn't said yes, but he also hadn't punched me in the face for the suggestion.

It was progress.

FIFTEEN
BIANCA

I'd been Dominic's wife for two days. He'd tried to kiss me and touch me, but I'd refused to react to him. I was empty inside. *How could I trust him after everything that had happened?*

I stayed in the bedroom. I didn't care about classes or a damn thing. I was waiting to be put into my grave so the pain in my chest from all the shit surrounding Fallon would end. When I thought about it, I realized it wasn't just Fallon. It was the fact that they had been prepared to *kill* me. That they had killed him.

"You need a bubble bath. It'll help you relax," Dom mumbled, coming into the bedroom and placing my dinner on the nightstand. He watched me for a moment before striding forward and kneeling in front of me. "You need to eat. You haven't eaten all day." He pushed my hair out of my face, his lips turned downward into a deep frown.

I remained quiet. Anything I said wouldn't be good.

He sighed, got to his feet, and walked away from me. The sound of flowing water came from the bathroom before Dom appeared once more.

"Levin and Vincent miss you." He kneeled in front of me again with a pudding cup in his hand. He spooned some chocolate out and offered it to me.

I didn't take it.

"Please eat," he whispered, his hand shaking.

He tried again, but I ignored him. He jammed the spoon back into the cup so forcefully it sent chocolate erupting over the sides. He rose, his body coiled with tension. I swallowed down the squeal as he trembled for a moment before he threw the entire cup of pudding against the wall, sending chocolate splattering everywhere. He breathed in and out deeply before finally turning to me. I clutched my blanket, worried I was about to meet the same demise as the pudding. Instead of being rough, he bent and scooped me into his arms. Dom took me into the bathroom where he placed me on my feet. He gently slipped my shirt off and then my sweatpants.

His green eyes lingered on my naked body briefly then he removed his clothes. His heavy cock brushed against me as he led me to the tub.

"I'll bathe you," he said softly, helping me into the water. He sank down and settled me between his muscular thighs. He worked silently, washing my hair and then my body, his hands lingering over my breasts before they trailed between my legs.

I flinched as he swept his finger through my folds and rubbed against my clit. His touch felt good, but I didn't want it to since I was furious.

"I miss you," he murmured in my ear as he caressed me.

My body trembled against his as he moved his finger to my entrance and pushed inside.

"So tight," he grunted, pressing his lips to my shoulder. "Do you like this?"

I said nothing, the tears burning my eyes as I stared straight ahead.

"I want to make love to you, wasp. Not *fuck* you. I just want to love you." He kissed my neck. "Let me. Let your husband make you feel good."

My throat tightened as the tears threatened to spill. I needed closure for Fallon. *How do you move on when you're still stuck?* I wanted freedom. I wanted ... God, I didn't even know what I wanted. Answers?

"Don't cry. Fuck." He withdrew his fingers. "What do I need to do? I don't know what the fuck to do." He slid me forward then stood from the tub and got out. He wrapped a towel around his waist. "I can't do shit right by you. This is killing me as much as it is you, Bianca. You're breaking my fucking heart."

He strode from the room then, his head down mournfully. I closed my eyes, a fat tear leaking out.

It was killing me too.

I LAY in bed beside Dominic, who slept soundly. The only way I'd be able to escape would be to kill him. I'd need to take out Vincent and Levin too before I left. The thought made my heart ache in all sorts of new ways, the confusion of my bitter love driving a stake right through the center of my soul.

I wanted my kings. I hated my kings. I loved my kings. I hated myself. I hated this fucked up life. I hated David for putting me here. I hated my mom for letting him.

I fumbled for the shard of glass beneath the mattress and pulled it out. The moonlight glinted off the white porcelain as I stared at it. If I didn't kill Dominic, he'd just end up killing me later. Or this new life without freedom would.

The idea of what I needed to do hurt so much. I swallowed down a sob before pulling myself together and sitting up. Slowly, I eased myself over Dominic, straddling his naked torso. He let out a soft grunt in his sleep, his long lashes resting on his cheeks, his lips parted.

He was beautiful. Like a fallen angel.

I adjusted the shard in my hand and pressed it against his throat.

Do it. Kill him. Run. Then just fucking run.

My hand shook as I pressed the glass to his neck, a tear falling from my eye onto his chest. And then another. I pressed harder. A bead of blood blossomed from his pulse point.

"If you mean to kill me, you're doing it right," Dominic's deep voice called out. He wrapped his hand around my wrist and moved the shard to his chest. "But this will get the job done faster."

I winced as he pushed my hand with the shard in it to a spot over his heart. It broke the skin, making blood pool out. I stared down at the thin crimson trail as it trickled from him.

I locked my eyes on his before releasing the shard. The moment it was out of my hand, he knocked it off the bed and rolled me onto my back, so he was looming over me, caging me in with his arms.

"Rule number one of killing someone, do it. Don't hesitate. If you hesitate, you lose. Rule number two, never play a game you'll lose."

I started to shove him off me, but he grabbed my wrists in one of his hands and pinned them over my head. He looked like a beautiful monster as he peered down at me, his cross necklace dangling in my face, his black hair a mess from sleep. Heat pooled between my legs, betraying me.

"I've been good to you, wasp, and this is what it gets me? Murdered in my sleep with a broken soup bowl?" His face darkened as he stared down at me.

A moment later, he ripped my panties off as I struggled beneath him.

I stiffened when he slid his fingers up my heat.

"You're wet for me," he husked out.

I squeezed my eyelids closed, my breathing coming in sharp gasps. *Damn this treacherous body of mine.*

I struggled to break free, embarrassed he was turning me on despite everything inside telling me the feeling was wrong.

But God, why did it feel so right?

Dom tightened his hold on me. He was strong. Way too strong for me to fight off. I was breathless from bucking by the time he managed to push up my t-shirt.

"Do me a favor, wasp," he said in a low, dangerous growl filled with dark promises. His lips curled up into a sinister smile. "Scream for me."

He pushed himself deep into my heat in one fluid motion, making me arch my back. I cried out, cursing his name with one breath while praising the devil for creating such a beautiful monster with the next.

I hated everything about him just as much as I loved him.

"No." I shoved against him.

"Yes." He thrust violently into my heat, making it hurt despite how wet he'd made me. "Take my cock like a good girl. You've been denying me long enough. If you can hurt me, then I can hurt you. We'll share the fucking pain."

"What happened to you just wanting to *love me*?"

"I still do. And I will. But sometimes pain is necessary."

"I hate you," I snarled at him, raking my nails down his back as the lie tumbled off my lips. "I fucking hate you!"

"Good. It makes this easier," he breathed out, continuing his onslaught as I tried to shred his back to ribbons. He groaned, moving faster, breathless as he fucked me into beautiful oblivion.

As much as I tried to stave off my impending orgasm, it surged through my body, making me cry out his name on repeat as my body strangled his thick cock.

"D-don't come in me. Please. I haven't taken my pill," I managed to stutter out as he pistoned in and out of me like he was drilling for fucking oil.

"Don't tell me what to do," he snipped, pressing me more firmly into the mattress.

I winced, heat sweeping through me again as another release built within me. Dominic De Santis could fuck like a god, and I'd be a lying bitch if I said I didn't enjoy the way he made me feel.

"Fuck," he groaned, moving faster and harder, his thrusts so violent they shook the bed.

The sound of slapping skin and his deep groan filled the room as he took out his anger on my pussy.

"Dominic. Stop. You're hurting me. Stop." I writhed against him as he continued. "Dominic." I cried out as he brought pain with the pleasure.

That sweet heat of release swept through my body again as I came hard.

Did I want him to stop?

Yes.

No.

Yes.

Never.

Fuck. Fuck. Fuck. YES. So good. He was so damn good.

"Don't. Don't come inside me," I choked out, digging into his skin with my nails. "Please."

He let out a low groan, his cock thickening inside me before his release jetted out, filling me.

His body trembled as he hovered over me, the blood from his chest painting my breasts red.

"I'm sorry, Bianca," he said softly, almost dazed, the monster he'd been now receding and giving way to his humanity. "I'm so fucking sorry."

He pulled out of me and rolled to sit on the edge of the bed where his body quivered for a moment as he cradled his head in his hands.

"I lose it sometimes," he whispered in a choked voice. "I'm a fucking monster. It doesn't matter what I do, I'll always be this monster. I-I tried to stop myself. I couldn't. *I'm sorry.*"

He rose to his feet and went to the bathroom. The sound of running water was the only noise as I lay in the puddle we'd made. I wasn't angry. I was sad. Heartbroken. I'd hated what we'd done but had loved it too. It scared me to have that thrill course through me. On the other hand, he hadn't stopped when I'd asked. I wasn't sure if I should be terrified of what he might really be capable of or pissed at myself for enjoying the excitement he'd made me feel or worried about the implications of him filling me while I was off my pill.

He came back into the room and cleaned me, the warm washcloth soothing the ache he'd left between my legs.

"I made you bleed," he said softly. "*Fuck.* I hurt you."

I stared up at the ceiling as he gently wiped the mess from me. With a second cloth, he washed his blood from my breasts before he lifted me into his arms and cradled me against him.

"I'll fix this," he said, kissing the top of my head fiercely. "Just promise not to hate me for my sins."

I said nothing because I couldn't promise a damn thing. Not when I secretly hated myself for mine.

SIXTEEN
DOMINIC

The next day, Bianca was still silent. I'd fucked up. Royally. Granted, she had tried to murder me in my sleep. I was at my breaking point and knew what had to be done to get her to at least talk to me like she once had, but doing it was killing me inside. We were down to the wire with our seventy-two-hour deadline for Ivanov. A decision needed to be made.

I'd told Vincent and Levin what had happened last night with Bianca. They'd exchanged looks but had remained quiet. Levin's expression had said he wanted to put a hole through my face. Vincent had seemed resigned.

I swallowed as I stared at the doorway to the basement where the root of all my fucking problems was. I needed to atone for my sins. I wanted my wife back, and I wanted her to forgive me.

"What are you doing?" Levin asked as I turned on my heel and went upstairs.

I said nothing. When I pushed my bedroom door open, I found Bianca sitting in that damn chair, wearing my long, white t-shirt and her panties. We needed to get shit back to normal. I was done with this.

I reached out and tugged her to her feet. Then I lifted her over my shoulder amid her soft protests and carried her downstairs.

Vincent sat up on the couch, and Levin took a cautious step toward us. But I kept moving.

"What's going on?" Vincent rose and headed toward us.

I opened the basement door and hauled a struggling Bianca down the steps. She bucked and kicked. When we reached the secret door, I opened it, taking her into the room. Levin and Vincent were right behind us.

"Here," I said, easing her to her feet. "Look."

Fallon scrambled forward, his lips parted. I released her arm. She darted forward before falling to her knees in front of the metal bars to Fallon's cell. My guts twisted as she reached inside and clung to him amid her tears.

"You're alive," Fallon choked out. "*Princess.* Oh God. Baby, I thought you were dead. I thought you were gone."

He let out a soft sob as her body shook. She blubbered out his name again, clinging to him.

"Well, ain't that some shit," Vincent muttered thickly.

I nodded, my throat tight. I hated it. *I fucking hated it.* But it was my wasp. I'd do anything for her. She deserved it. I knew that. She had to put up with my crazy ass. She had to deal with all of us. This was her prize.

I locked gazes with Levin. Storm clouds gathered in the depths of his blue eyes as he trembled. We'd discussed doing this already, but I guessed none of us were prepared to see how they'd actually react to one another.

Moving swiftly, I wrapped my arm around Bianca's tiny waist and dragged her away from him amid her protests.

"Listen," I said softly, lifting her and gripping her face so she'd look at me instead of him on his knees, quietly pleading her name. "You belong to me. *You're my wife.*"

She licked her lips, her blue-eyed gaze darting quickly over my face, her hand trying to force my fingers from her face.

"I don't want to let you go," I said so only she could hear me.

She paused her pawing at me, her brows crinkled.

"Promise you won't go, and I'll let him live. Promise me you're still mine. *Ours*." I paused, making sure I had her full attention. "If you run, I'll go to the ends of the world to find you and finish the job," my voice shook. "Do you understand?"

Her lips parted as she stared up at me.

"Swear it, wasp."

"I swear it, Dominic," she said, her eyes wide and pleading. "Just let him go."

I voiced the source of my biggest worry, "You don't hate him like you do us."

It wasn't a question, but she chose to answer anyway.

"I'm so mad at all of you that I can't separate my emotions. I hate him just as much as I hate you right now. You all deserve to pay for what you were going to do to me," her voice was so soft I had to lean in to hear her, but it was a satisfying answer.

Vasiliev wasn't out of danger from her wrath. I'd enjoy watching her make him squirm.

I studied her for a moment before I nodded to Vincent and Levin. I guided Bianca over to where there was a chair. Once I sat, I tugged her to my lap. Both my guys moved forward. Vincent unlocked the door as Levin reached inside and tugged Fallon out, throwing him on the floor in front of me.

Bianca leaned closer to him, but I yanked her back to me, my arm wrapped firmly around her waist so she couldn't leave.

"Behave," I growled in her ear.

She visibly swallowed before she nodded, her small body still tense.

I peered past her and stared down at Fallon.

"You have a choice," I said. "You can pledge your allegiance to the kings, *to me*, and I'll let you live. Or you can refuse and die right here and now."

"And my sister? What happens to Natalia?"

"I'll do whatever I can to save her on the condition you don't betray me. If you do, I'll let Levin and Vincent fuck her right in front of you before I cut her throat."

A muscle popped along Fallon's jaw, but he gave me a curt nod. "What about Bianca?"

I surveyed him for a moment, taking note of Levin's clenched fists and Vincent's fidgeting.

"Dominic—" Bianca started.

"Shh, *mia regina*," I murmured, tearing my gaze away from Fallon to press a kiss to her jaw. "Be patient."

I focused back on Fallon.

"What do you want with her?" I asked.

"I *want* her," he said evenly.

I ground my teeth for a moment. "No."

Bianca shifted on my lap, her body tensing. Pissed off or not, she still wanted the fucker. It gave me a little bit of hope for the rest of us considering what she'd said moments before.

"I won't betray anyone. Wherever Bianca is, that's where I want to be," Fallon said.

"How about this…" I ran my knuckles down Bianca's arm gently. "Tell me who killed Stefan Seeley."

Fallon paused, his eyes darting between me and Bianca. "Swear to me that I'll live, and I can be with Bianca if she'll have me, and I'll tell you what I know."

I swallowed and glanced to Levin since this was for him. His hands were still balled into tight fists.

"Levin decides." I deferred the decision to him.

Levin's eyes widened for a moment before he stepped forward.

"Bianca belongs to the kings first. You prove yourself worthy, you do what you're told, then yes. By rights as a king, Bianca will be yours too." His shoulders quivered as he said the words.

I knew it took a lot for Levin to agree to this. I inclined my head at him. It was a fair trade, even if I fucking hated Fallon's guts. Chances were, he'd fail, and we'd get to gut him before he got a chance at our girl. Or maybe Levin would be right, and the lords would do it for us.

"Stefan Seeley was dating my sister," Fallon started.

"What?" Levin growled as Vincent gave a low whistle.

I shook my head.

"Ivanov's men found out they were together. So Stefan and Natalia planned to run away and get as far from this life as possible. Sergio Ivanov put an order out on Stefan. They wanted him alive. He was delivered to Ivanov. I don't know what happened in that room, but I know he walked out alive because I was the one who drove him back to the bus stop on 53rd. He didn't say what was going on. He didn't say anything to me other than I had to take care of Nattie for him, and he'd be back for her. I left him, but I waited, watching from afar." Fallon's voice grew soft. "Klaus Seeley picked him up." He stared directly at Levin. "Your father was the last one to see him alive. That's what I know, and that's where you need to start."

The room fell silent before Levin let out a loud curse and began pacing.

Vincent frowned. "That doesn't make any sense. Klaus wouldn't hurt Stefan. He was his oldest son and his favorite, no offense to Levin."

"I don't know," Fallon said, shrugging. "I told you what I know. But I will say this, I think Hail knows the truth. Just like he probably knows about what happened to Bianca's father. I didn't push the subject with him, but I got the impression he was hiding a lot from me."

"Asshole," Vincent muttered, shaking his head.

Levin stopped pacing and looked at me.

"Your task will be to get us more information," I said. "Betray the lords for the kings. Prove your allegiance that way. Then, we'll welcome you to our kingdom. But you don't touch Bianca until we say so."

"Deal," Fallon said without hesitation, his gaze back to being locked on Bianca in my lap.

I dragged my fingers through her hair and lifted her delicate hand to my lips where I kissed the diamond on her finger.

"A few things you need to know. First, Bianca is my wife."

Fallon's brows crinkled before he darted his gaze around at Levin and Vincent, who both nodded. Then he looked to Bianca. "Princess?"

"We got married a few days ago," she said softly.

"Motherfucker," Fallon snarled, trying to get to his feet.

Levin kicked him, knocking him back down. Fallon groaned. Bianca struggled against me to go to him, but I held fast.

"Bianca needed my protection. No one within my circle would dare harm my wife," I said easily. "It was a simple enough choice because you were right. I do care about her, a fucking lot, and would've saved her. This is proof of that."

"You're a son of a bitch," Fallon cursed, glaring at me.

I clucked my tongue at him. "I'm a great many things, Vasiliev, but I'm the husband of the woman you've fallen in love with. You're going to want to be in my good graces if you ever want to feel my wife writhe beneath you again. I'm hers and she is mine. I choose if and when I share her. That brings us to number two. Here's what's going to happen. We're going to free you. I want you to go back to Ivanov and tell him you followed me for a few days and learned I took Bianca as my wife. You're returning now because you wanted to tell him."

He opened his mouth to speak, but I silenced him by continuing, "You're our inside man. I can save Bianca from my circle, but I need help saving her from yours. That's where you come in. I want to know their plans. Secrets. *Fucking sins*. Got it?"

He glanced at Bianca before licking his lips and nodding.

"You'll return to campus and go about your life like you don't give a piss about the kings except to talk shit like you fucks usually do in your little circle jerk with one another's dicks."

"And what the fuck am I supposed to say happened to my face?" he snapped, tearing his focus from Bianca and giving it back to me.

Vincent smirked. "Tell him Levin and I caught you trying to take Bianca like you'd planned and kicked your ass."

Fallon glowered at Vincent but gave a curt nod. "Fine."

"Vincent and Levin will drive you back to campus. I'll send for you when I need you. Until then, be a good little lord and get me every ounce of information you can." I leveled my gaze on him. "Do *not* seek me out. Do not seek out Vincent or Levin. And never fucking look twice at my queen. Not until you're told otherwise. Prove your fucking worth. Got it?"

He nodded again.

"Let him go," I said.

Vincent bent down and unlocked his cuffs then freed his legs. Fallon rose to his feet, wincing.

"Take Stella with you. She may as well sleep on campus since she's been going to classes. No sense in leaving her here with us," I continued.

Levin rolled his eyes.

"Bianca and I will be back the day after tomorrow. I want you two to stay on campus as well," I said, nodding to Vincent and Levin. "Make sure everything is going according to plan before I bring our queen home."

Bianca had been silent the entire time. I took her chin in my fingers and made her face me instead of Fallon.

"Look at me," I murmured, staring intently in her eyes. "Bid him goodbye. Make sure he does the right thing. I really don't want to have to kill him, but you know I will if he fucks this up."

"OK," she whispered.

I released her, my heart aching, as she scrambled up and approached Fallon. He stared at her hungrily. The moment she was close to him, he hauled her into his arms and held her, whispering in her ear as she buried her face in his chest, sobbing softly.

I hated it, but I loved her. And love, as I was learning, had a fuck of a lot of sacrifice.

SEVENTEEN
BIANCA

"I won't fail you, princess," Fallon whispered urgently in my ear. "We'll be together. I swear to you. You're so strong. *My* strong girl. We'll get through this. I'm so sorry for what I did to you. So fucking sorry. I know you're pissed, but I'll make things right. I swear I will. I'll prove my worth."

I nodded against his chest, my throat aching from trying to choke down my sobs. This was worlds better than thinking he was dead and feeling the agony of that. The guilt. The remorse. I knew there was hope for all of us now. Whether the kings realized it or not, they'd shown me what they were truly made of over the past few days.

Now it was my turn.

"Be careful," I said, peeking up at him. "Because there won't be a second time for us, Fallon. I haven't forgiven you. What you did…… what you were *going* to do to me…" I wanted to shout my fury at him but bit it back, not sure how to express it.

He nodded and thumbed my tears away. "I'm so sorry. I promise to make this right and prove it to you. I'll see you soon, baby." He placed a gentle kiss on my cheek before stepping away from me.

Dominic was quick to come from behind me and ease my back to his front, his arms encircling me as he held me.

"He'll be fine, B," Vincent said, leaning down and pressing a kiss to my other cheek. "I'll make sure of it."

I nodded and squeezed his hand. It seemed to make him happy because he gave me a lopsided smile and backed away.

Levin shifted awkwardly, catching my attention. He didn't come toward me. He didn't do anything other than stare at me. He and I had a lot to talk about and sort through. I was still so pissed at him after what happened. The same held true for Dominic. At least Vincent had shown some sort of remorse the night Levin and Dominic had decided I was supposed to die with Fallon. It didn't mean Vincent was off the hook. My rage flowed deep.

I watched as they led Fallon away before I spun in Dominic's arms to face him.

"Why didn't you tell me he was alive sooner?"

His lips twitched, but there was no hint of humor in his smile. "Because I wasn't sure if I was going to let him live."

I swallowed. It seemed like an honest answer.

"What changed your mind?"

"You did," he murmured. "I didn't want to lose you. The thought drove me insane. So I made a sacrifice, potentially endangering us, all in the name of love."

"You really love me?" I asked, disbelief in my tone.

I peered up at him, scrutinizing him, trying to find any semblance of a lie. Green eyes filled with sincerity were all I found.

He lifted my wedding-ring-clad finger to his warm lips and pressed a kiss to it. "Yes."

He didn't elaborate, and I didn't push.

"I'm still mad," I said with a pout.

"I know." He kissed the corner of my lips. "And I'm still hurt you were fucking Vasiliev behind my back. I figure we're even as long as you promise to be my good girl and stay in line."

"You know I can't promise that."

"I know. And oddly, I think it's what makes me eager for you to promise me and then break it so I can break you," he said, leaning in and biting my bottom lip.

"You're messed up."

"You don't know the half of it, wasp."

I didn't, but something told me I wouldn't have to wait long to find out.

"YOU SHOULD EAT." Dominic leveled his gaze on me as I sat cross-legged on his bed hours later, the food he'd brought earlier still untouched.

"And you should give me my phone back. I'd also like some pants."

He shook his head. "You're a De Santis now. My wife. We made a deal before that though, and that deal was you'd wear what I said you'd wear. And this"—he gestured to his t-shirt on me and my bare legs—"is what I want you in, wasp."

"Right." I licked my lips. "But happy wife, happy life. If you deny me my pants, I'll choke you to death with yours. Get me?"

His lips quirked up as he chuckled. "I'd love for you to try it." He pushed off the doorframe and stepped into the room. "Speaking of death threats, I'd really appreciate it if you didn't try to kill me in my sleep again."

"And I'd really appreciate it if you didn't stick your dick inside me and blow your load after you pissed me off," I retorted sourly. "Especially after I asked you not to."

He stalked toward me like a predator and shoved me flat onto my back, straddling me. My heart jumped into my throat as I stared up at him. His silver necklace hung down and tickled my skin, his glorious body doing things to me that pissed me off because I didn't want to feel them right then. I was still so mad at him and the kings for what they'd done. It would take a hell of a lot more than a few smiles to get me over it. But at least the pain in my chest at the thought of losing Fallon was gone. I knew he was safe and alive now. It helped my mood immensely.

"You're my wife. I'll stick my cock inside any part of your body any time I want. In return, you own me, Bianca *De Santis*. I am yours as much as you are mine."

I panted out, my heart racing. "What about Stella?"

"Stella who?" he murmured, leaning down and kissing along my jaw.

Fucking asshole knew how to work me, and I hated it. I wanted to give in, but I wanted to kick him in the dick too. My emotions warred with one another.

"The bitch who's been sleeping down the hall. The one you have a *history* with."

"The only history I have with her is one that means absolute shit, *mia regina*. She's a tool. I have her doing dirty work which could get her killed. If she dies, she dies. If she lives, she brings me valuable information. Past that, she's worthless to me. I care nothing for her. And my dick isn't going anywhere near her and hasn't since I realized I was in love with you. When are you going to realize my world revolves around you and has since the moment you ran into me in that hallway?"

I swallowed as he shifted and looked down at me again.

"I never lie, and I never break a promise," he murmured.

"You promised you'd kill me if I was with anyone else. You told Levin to kill me."

"*He* failed to follow through on my orders." He scowled at me before lowering his voice to say, "I knew he would. I was counting on it."

"So you would've killed me?" I crinkled my brows at him.

"If it had come to that, yes. Death would've been an easy escape compared to the hell that awaited you at the hands of my father. I would've been doing you a favor. I love you enough to kill you in order to save you. I couldn't let that happen to you. If killing you was the only way to protect you, I would've done it, even if it would've broken my heart."

"You're sick," I whispered.

"First and foremost, I'm a villain. *A monster.* I never expected a happy ending for my life. I doubt I'll get it. Knowing you would've been free from pain and torture would've been the happiest of endings. Anything else would've gutted me. So yes, maybe I am sick, but it's a sickness that only wants you to not suffer."

"Yet you made me marry you."

He chuckled humorlessly. "Like I said, Levin didn't listen. It was marry me or die in his mind. He chose your life."

"Are you happy with his choice?"

Dom licked his lips before closing in and placing a tender kiss on the corner of my mouth. "You, *mia regina*, are a dream come true to me. *Yes*. I will *never* regret vowing myself to you. Ever."

My body trembled beneath him. Damn him for his words and the look in his green eyes.

But really, damn me for feeling the same.

Maybe I was a monster too.

EIGHTEEN
FALLON

"Where the fuck have you been, and what happened to your face?" Hail shoved me hard in the chest.

I stumbled back. The kings hadn't exactly been accommodating during my stay in their palace of torture, so I was still tired and weak.

"I was trying to get Bianca as planned." I grunted, rubbing my eyes.

They burned from barely sleeping. I'd lain awake most nights with my mind on Bianca. I'd wanted to do so much more than hug her when I saw her, but Dominic had looked like he'd rip my head off if I'd tried. Levin looked like he'd dismember me. I supposed if Bianca were my wife, I'd act the same. *Fuck. Wife.* That son of a bitch…

"Where is she?" Hail scoffed. "Wait. Don't tell me. The fucking kings have her."

I nodded tightly. "They do, but I know what they were doing because I followed them."

Hail raised his brow and waited for me to continue.

I cleared my throat. It was showtime.

"Dominic took her the night of homecoming, and he married her. She's now Bianca De Santis."

Hail sucked in a sharp breath, his face turning a brilliant shade of red before I pushed on. "They found out I followed them." I pointed to my face. "And I paid for it. They also broke my phone."

"Fuck," Hail swore, buying into my lie right away.

It wasn't like he had any reason to not believe me. I'd never betrayed his trust before.

"They let me go and vowed to kill me the next time they caught me lurking anywhere near them," I finished.

"De Santis. *Kakashka,*" he swore in Russian. "*Ebanashka.*"

I waited for his tirade to end. He cursed some more, pacing like a caged lion, before he finally got his shit together and drew in a deep breath.

"Fine. We'll just have to come up with another plan. And because De Santis decided to up the ante, I'll play along." He let out a soft, sinister laugh which sent chills through my body. "We'll modify our plan and make him pay. Nothing worse for a man than another man touching his woman. Since they hurt you, I'll let *you* help me hurt them. Sound good, Vasiliev?"

I nodded tightly, my guts churning with the possibilities. "Sounds fucking amazing."

He clapped me on the shoulder. "Good. I knew you'd be onboard."

I chanced a look around the courtyard. On the way back to campus, Vincent had reminded me of the rules while I sat in the backseat with a bag over my head. Levin had remained silent. The guy was fucking insane. The night he'd almost killed me, he'd leaned in and told me I should pray the devil took me before I woke. Then he'd knocked my ass out with whatever drug he'd jammed into my neck with that needle. My head had spun immediately before everything had gone black.

Aside from throwing my ass in that sealed-off room in their basement, he hadn't done much to strike up a conversation with me.

Honestly, I didn't give a shit now. I wanted to do whatever I had to do in order to be with Bianca. I knew it meant I had to fall in with the kings, but there were worse things—like thinking she was dead. *That* had been hell.

"Where were you?" Tate looked me up and down as he approached with Drake.

"Fucking your sister," I said.

He scowled at me like I knew he would.

"Fallon got caught by the kings. He followed them the night of homecoming and found out De Santis married Bianca. Then they kicked his dick in." Hail gestured to me as he gave a short variation of the story I'd given him. "Now, Bianca really is the enemy. And what do we do to our enemies?"

"Well, this one in particular I'd like to sink my cock into so… " Tate let out a bark of laughter as Drake high-fived him.

I huffed out a quiet breath as I tried to keep my fist from embedding in the cackling dickheads' faces.

"I like that idea. In fact, I was just telling Fallon how I'm going to let him fuck her since the kings fucked him up. Seems fair, right?"

"Why does he get to?" Tate quieted down and glared openly at me.

It was no secret Tate had a thing for Bianca. He was an insane nutjob about her, even worse than Hail. Where Hail was bitter she didn't want him, Tate was obsessed. After the night Hail had made her suck our cocks, Tate had kept reminding us nearly every day about how his balls still tingled from the release she gave him. He'd been overly graphic in his descriptions. Once when Hail hadn't been around, Tate had confessed he'd do anything for a night alone with Bianca and had proceeded to describe all the twisted shit he'd do to her once he had her.

I'd left the room before I lost it and ripped his dick from his body. They'd made fun of me and called me soft. I called it being a decent fucking human.

"Fallon gets to because he clearly took a fucking beating and deserves retribution for it," Hail said as if it were the easiest thing in the world to understand.

Tate grumbled his discontent but didn't push it. I had a feeling he'd be looking for a way to appease Hail so he could get some time with Bianca. I'd never let it happen. I'd kill them myself before I'd let one of those fuckers touch her.

"We at least get to watch?" Drake demanded.

Hail rolled his eyes while I tried to keep my cool. "Of course. Like I'd deny you guys."

That seemed good enough for Drake, but Tate didn't look the least bit happy. He'd try to worm his way in because that was just how Tate was.

Fucking prick.

But at least things were good with Hail. For now, anyway. I hated I was forced to be someone's bitch though.

For Bianca, I'd do anything, even endure this bunch of bullshit because I knew she was worth it.

ALL NIGHT, I tossed and turned, not sleeping. I punched my pillow, wondering if Bianca was OK. I'd seen the way De Santis had looked at her. The way he'd held her and whispered to her. How she'd curled into him even after the shit he'd pulled.

And the other two kings… yeah, all three of them were head over heels for her, even Levin, the tough-as-nails dickhead.

But so was I.

I wasn't stupid enough to think things were going to be easy or that the kings weren't just using me to get to Hail. Hell, I wouldn't be surprised if this shit actually got me killed this time. Bianca was worth the risk. I felt it beyond my heart and into my soul. We just…*clicked*. My missing puzzle piece, even if she was pissed at me right now. It was no less than I deserved after the shit I'd done.

I rolled over, envisioning her smile. Her laughter. The way her body felt against mine. How my heart shattered into a million pieces as I was tied in that damn basement thinking she was dead.

When she'd walk into the room, my heart had nearly jumped out of my chest with joy.

De Santis had crushed my world when he'd said he'd married her. It was worlds better than Hail though. She wasn't exactly *safe* with De Santis—given his family's connections—but she was a hell of a lot safer there than if she were Hail's girl. At least the kings seemed to give a shit about her.

And I sure as hell did.

"Bianca," I murmured into my dark room.

I closed my eyes, keeping her face in my mind's eye. What I wouldn't give to hold her right then. My stomach turned, knowing that was exactly what De Santis was probably doing. Holding her. Kissing her. Touching her. Making her moan.

I ground my teeth and pushed the image of her writhing beneath *him* out of my head. I didn't know how the fuck I was going to deal with that whole mess, but De Santis swore to me that she'd be mine too if I complied.

If I became a king and was loyal.

I'd be anything they wanted me to be if it meant getting my princess back in my arms.

In the meantime, I'd have to learn to control myself whenever I saw her. I already wanted to haul her away from all this shit, and she wasn't even back on campus yet.

I licked my lips, hoping the kings gave me something to do so I could be that much closer to holding her again.

I thought about my sister, Natalia. In the morning, I'd ask De Santis for help with her. I knew they said they'd do what they could to save her. And I knew I was supposed to heel and be their bitch, but I wanted Nattie to be safe too. I wanted confirmation that De Santis was actually doing something to help her and not using her as a way to control me.

Something told me the big German fuck, Levin, wanted it too if it meant she loved his brother Stefan. I was banking on his feelings panning out because if they didn't, I'd be forced to step out of line and pray I didn't fuck things up worse than they already were.

Hell, it had worked last time.

NINETEEN
LEVIN

I sat on our table in the courtyard, my leg bouncing as I waited for Dom and Bianca to show up. She hadn't texted me, but then again, Dom probably had her phone on lockdown like Stella's.

"You look like shit," Vincent commented, collapsing beside me.

I glanced at him to find he wasn't faring much better.

"You heard from Dom?"

"Radio silence," he grumbled. "I did see Vasiliev trudging across the lawn this morning looking like he was dead on his ass."

"Guess we all have that in common," I muttered. I'd barely slept, worrying about what shit would go down once Dom and Bianca made it back to campus. I wasn't even sure what to do when she got back. I'd tried to comfort her back at the safe house, but she'd pretty much ignored my efforts, which didn't give me much hope for a future with her.

I hoped she could tell I cared. I did, after all, refuse to shoot her in the head like I was supposed to. That shit had to count for something at least.

"You OK?" Vincent asked.

I scoffed and continued glaring at a tree across the courtyard. Celeste Vander Veer giggled beneath it with her friends. Her old man owned one of the largest gun factories in the entire country. Old money. He was someone we'd been trying for ages to get close to.

"I'll take that as a no." Vincent shifted in his seat. "You know, she's going to forgive us."

"Why would she do that?" I murmured.

I'd planned on killing her. We'd made her believe Vasiliev was dead. We'd forced her into a marriage. She'd be crazy to forgive a single hair on our heads.

"We've talked about this before. Just relax. She'll come around." His gaze roamed the courtyard, probably looking for bumblebee and Dom like I was. I hated the silence from them.

"Whatever," I grunted, knowing damn well it was more than a *whatever* matter.

This was all my damn fault, and knowing that haunted me. If I'd kept my distance I wouldn't feel so fucked up inside. This was what I got for getting involved. *Everyone fucking leaves*. Even Stefan…It was the story of my life…

I sighed, trying to keep my shit together. Vasiliev's words about my brother had been weighing heavily on me. It was a surprise to find out Stefan had been dating Natalia. I knew there'd been someone, but a fucking Russian enforcer's daughter? Fucking idiot bit off more than he could chew. Imagining my old man being involved in Stefan's death made me sick. I knew what he was capable of, but I wanted to think he'd never do that to his own son. He would've killed me before laying a finger on Stefan. There was just no way.

"There they are." Vincent slapped my arm.

I followed his gaze to where Dom and Bianca were walking across the courtyard. They were close to each other but not touching.

Her head was down as she listened to him talk, her blonde waves tumbling around her.

I rubbed my chest as I took in every perfect facet of her. Those long legs. That blonde hair. Her full, pouty lips that made me want to bury my cock deep in her throat just so I could feel the brush of them against me. The thought of blowing my load into her warm mouth and making her swallow me down just so I'd always be a part of her had my cock growing hard in my pants.

I drew in a deep breath and forced myself to think about how awful the dumpsters on campus smelled on a hot summer day. It helped. Some.

"How are the newlyweds?" Vincent asked when they stopped in front of us. "B looks like she's walking all right."

She lifted her gaze and scowled at him, her lips pursed in irritation. It helped soothe my ego to know she hated all of us and not just me. At least, I wasn't drowning alone.

"Everything status quo?" Dom asked, ignoring the mention of his marriage. With a frown on his face, he reached out and tucked a lock of Bianca's hair behind her ear, his wedding ring glinting in the sunlight.

My guts tightened, nauseous for some fucked up reason. *Jealousy? Anger? Resentment?*

I wanted her too. At the rate we were going, she'd freeze our asses out before she warmed up to the idea of being with us all again. I'd seen her with Vasiliev though. She'd do anything for that son of a bitch. *But fuck it.* I was scraping rock bottom and would gladly eat shit with that piece of trash if it meant I got Bianca to care again.

"All's good. Vasiliev is being a good boy and doing what he's told," Vincent said.

"It's been one fucking day. Don't give him a halo yet," I grumbled.

"He won't disappoint you," Bianca cut in, surprisingly addressing me. She stared me down with so much certainty on her pretty face it made me sick. She believed in that little shit but hadn't had an ounce of faith in me.

I rose and peered right back at her. "I've taken pisses longer than you've known him. *We—*" I gestured to Dom and Vincent. "—have known him and his entire gang of shit stains since we could walk. Never trust an Ivanov, and by default, never trust anyone associated with them."

She visibly swallowed. "I trust him, d-despite…"

I scoffed, knowing she had her reservations. I wanted to twist the knife though because I really hated the guy. "He's the last person you should trust."

"As opposed to you?"

Low blow, but I had held a gun to her head.

"Enough," Dom snapped, getting between us as my fury over the entire situation took hold.

What the hell is the matter with me? I'd agreed to this shit. I could've said no, beat the piss out of Vasiliev, and shot him in the head like I was supposed to. Then I'd be free of this nightmare. But no, I'd found a spark of hope with Bianca and had clung to it like an idiot. I'd saved their lives, but it still wasn't good enough. Hell, I'd saved Vasiliev's life *twice* in a week. Apparently, it didn't matter to her.

"He's staying in line as far as we know," Vincent said, casting an uneasy glance between me and Bianca. "If B thinks this will work, then let's have a little faith too."

A muscle popped along Dom's jaw as I rolled my eyes. This was fucking stupid.

"Time will tell. For now, we play the game like we intended. Everyone." He looked pointedly at Bianca. "That means you too."

"Like I'd ever *dare* defy my dear husband," she said with a sneer.

"Oh, I hope you do so I can teach you a damn good lesson," he said in a silky voice as he hauled her body against his, his fingers threading through her soft locks.

I ground my teeth as that ugly bubble of jealousy inflated in my chest again. She didn't pull away from him. Not really. She simply rested her hands on his chest and gazed up at him. They seemed to share some sort of weird silent conversation with one another for a moment before he gave her a wicked smirk and leaned down to kiss her.

Or at least I *thought* he was going to kiss her. He bit her lip instead, making her hiss.

"Be good, wasp," was all he said as she glared up at him.

"Never."

"Then be bad. Either way, I win." He shoved her at Vincent, who caught her easily in his arms, immediately winding them around her so she couldn't escape. "Watch my wife. I have business to attend to with Vasiliev." And with that, Dom turned and left us with Bianca.

"You smell nice," Vincent said as he breathed her in.

"It's called *essence of fuck you*," she said, elbowing him in the ribs.

He let out a whoosh of air and released her.

I wrapped my hand around her wrist when she attempted to dart off and yanked her back despite her angry glare.

"Nothing has changed," I said. "You belong to us. We watch you. We'll continue to follow you. You'll have a bigger target on your head once word gets out that your last name changed."

"Let me go," she snarled at me, trying to wrench her arm free of my hold. She winced because I tightened my hand.

"You know the rules. Stick to them, and stop making this fucking miserable," I snapped at her.

"Or what? You'll take me out to the woods and really shoot me next time?"

I snarled and yanked her to me. "Yes. One less pain in my ass would be fucking heaven, bumblebee."

She visibly swallowed as she stared me down, her lips parting. I buried my emotions and continued to hold her gaze.

"I hate you all."

"Trust me, I feel the same," I said, pushing her into Vincent, who once again wrapped his arms around her.

"I don't feel that way at all," he said, giving her a squeeze. "I know you know how I feel."

She relaxed against him, her back flush with his front.

"And maybe later, I can show you," he continued.

I turned away, nausea twisting my guts again. I had to get my shit under control.

"You want me to cheat on my husband already?" she asked.

"Hell, I want your husband to join us."

She let out a soft laugh before she spun in his arms and stared up at him, her lips a fraction from his. "I'm not going to fuck any of you ever again, so feel free to go fuck yourself."

"Ouch, baby B. That's a little harsh. You know I love the shit out of you."

She scoffed and looked away, but Vincent took her by the chin and brought her focus back to him.

"I do. You know I do," he murmured, leaning into her. "So does Dom and Levin. Don't punish us for doing what we thought was right."

"It isn't right to do what you did," she said, her voice quaking with emotion. "None of you are without sin. Every single one of you hurt me in some way. Some more than others."

"This isn't the same world you're used to. We live differently here. Violently. Dangerously. If we didn't care, we would've killed you both."

"But it was the plan," she argued.

"We didn't want it to be. Whether you want to believe it or not, Levin saved your life."

"Why didn't you save me?"

I bit the inside of my jaw as I listened to them. She didn't give a shit that I'd stuck my neck out for her and her piece of shit lover boy.

"We already talked about this," Vince said, cradling her face in his hand. "I needed to help Levin find out who killed Stefan—"

"She doesn't give a shit. Stop trying to convince her," I snapped, shoving him in the shoulder and taking her away from him. I pushed her forward, causing her to stumble a bit. "Fucking walk so we can get this day over with."

"Easy, dick," Vincent said, nudging me aside to catch up to Bianca, who didn't even bother glaring at me as she took off, her ass swaying in her uniform.

I knew she wasn't doing it on purpose and was absolutely pissed off at me, but it didn't stop it from happening. It just made everything worse. She was the epitome of perfection and didn't even know it. At least to me she was. And the kings. And apparently that little shit nozzle Vasiliev.

I let out a sigh as Vincent fell in step with her and smacked her on the ass. She elbowed him, causing him to laugh.

Sometimes I wished I were more like Vincent. He lived a life where he found the good and humor in everything.

Even when our girl told us she hated us. In her hatred, he'd find the silver lining.

As for me, it looked like I'd just watch him do it since there wasn't shit else I could do but wait it out and try to bury any semblance of feelings I had in the meantime.

Life was a bitch like that.

TWENTY
DOMINIC

I leaned against a small alcove in the alley behind the science building as I stared down at my phone. Vasiliev was already five minutes late. I scrubbed my hand down my face, my irritation already at its peak for the day.

Dealing with Bianca was a nightmare sent from hell. She was sassy and fierce, making me want her even more. But she resisted my come-ons, shoving me away. And after me forcing my way between her legs —even though she'd enjoyed it—I swore I'd attempt to keep myself in check. I wasn't that guy, and I had no excuse for my actions other than I was a monster.

But I was a fucking monster who loved her just the same.

It was a strange world. I'd never felt anything quite like this before, and I wasn't sure how to navigate these new feelings. On one hand, I wanted to fuck her senseless, whether she wanted me to or not. On the other hand, I wanted to kiss her and whisper to her all the things I felt and have her tell me she loved and wanted me too. The two parts of me were battling with one another. And I was just rolling with whatever the fuck happened.

"You're late," I said as Vasiliev stepped into the hidden nook with me.

"Yeah, sorry," he grunted, his face still bruised and swollen. It was beginning to look better though. "Tate was up my ass about something."

"I hope not literally."

He scowled at me. "I'm here. What do you need?"

I let out a soft, dangerous laugh. "I need you to remember who the fuck you're talking to."

He glared at me. "How's Bianca?"

"My wife is fine," I said, surveying the anger and resentment on his busted face.

He nodded. "When can I see her?"

"You know." I leaned against the brick wall and lit a joint before taking a deep hit and blowing out the smoke. "You fucked my wife."

"More than once," he added.

I laughed at that. Vasiliev had balls, that was for sure. It didn't piss me off any less.

"Why'd you do it? What made you brave enough to fuck a king's girl?"

He stared me down for a moment before speaking, "Because I fell for her. I fell hard the moment I first laid eyes on her. I tried to protect her when she was with Hail. Bianca is… everything," he finished with a shrug.

I nodded, hating some other motherfucker was in love with her, but shit, what wasn't there to love about my little wasp?

"And yet you were going to hand her over to a life of fucking horror. What a way to demonstrate your love, but maybe it's different for you lords."

"It wasn't like that," he snarled. "I would've come back for her. It wouldn't have gotten that far—"

"Then that shows what you know. A tender, pretty girl like Bianca in my father's clutches wouldn't have lasted a day. Know your fucking enemy. That's a pro tip from me."

"I fucked up. I admit it. I was desperate and stupid. In a way, I'm grateful you tried to kill me. You saved the day just like I thought you would."

I scoffed at him. "You got lucky. That's it."

"Thank you," he said softly. "I know you didn't have to extend your mercy to me, but you did, and, for that, I'm grateful. I want this chance to prove my worth not only to Bianca, but to the kings."

I surveyed him. Nothing in the way he stared back at me made me doubt his sincerity. As much as I wanted to view him as a sneaky little weasel, I really couldn't. He loved her. I could see it. I could hear it. I could feel it coming off him in waves. Bianca had that effect on those under her spell.

"When can I see her?" he asked again.

"Are you asking to *see* her or *fuck* her?"

"Both."

I smirked at him, nothing humorous in the gesture. "Let me set you straight on something. Bianca is my wife. She belongs to the kings. You are not a king. Therefore, you have zero claim to anything pertaining to her. You're lucky we even let you live."

His throat bobbed as he stared at me. "Don't use me and then take her from me. I'm loyal to those I love, and I fucking love her. What do I need to do to become a king so I can have my girl?"

Tension corded through my body. Memories of the look on Bianca's face when she realized he was still alive flooded my mind. To keep her, I had to let him live. Maybe even join us.

"Every fucking thing I tell you to do. Without question. Right now, you aren't earning any points."

He pursed his lips and studied me for a moment before speaking, "Give me something. Anything. I need a sliver of hope. Just let me hold her for a moment—"

"She's not a fucking puppy, and you're not a child," I snapped at him. "She is *my wife,* so fall the fuck in line, or I'll kill you myself this time."

He glared at me, and his hands tightened into fists. "I want to know I'm not just a pawn and that you mean what you say."

"Are you questioning me?"

That muscle ticked along his jaw as he gritted his teeth.

"Because if you are, you're out. *No one* fucking questions me. Got it?"

"Got it," he ground out.

Fucking Christ. This was ridiculous. And not just the situation. The shit going on in my head. I understood where the asshole was coming from, and I knew I had to give Bianca something to cling to as well so she'd give me half a fucking chance. I knew just demanding it of her wouldn't fly, so I'd have to make some adjustments. But I worried if I made concessions, it would look like I was soft and giving in. The last thing I needed was anyone thinking I was a pushover when I wasn't. Except maybe for her.

"Have you seen Ivanov?" I took another hit of my joint, not wanting to waste the shit and needing the buzz.

"Yes," he mumbled.

"And?" I blew out the smoke.

He sighed. "He's a prick. I told him the story we cooked up. He's out for blood, not just for me, but for Bianca. He still wants to steal her from you and then…" He raked his fingers through his hair, a look of pure anguish on his face.

"What?"

He locked gazes with me. "He said the way to piss off a man is to take and touch what belongs to him. He means to get her from you and fuck her. He wants me to do it too and has told Tate and Drake he'd work something out with them as well."

I breathed in, taking in the information before speaking softly, "What's the plan exactly?"

"I don't know it yet. Nothing solid, but I'm sure he'll get it worked out soon enough."

"If anyone touches her, I'll kill them. You know this. Let them know that too. I'm not playing. When a trigger gets pulled this time, the target will be someone's head. Get me?"

"Yes," he said.

"So if any of you lords want to see the light of day, you'll stay the fuck away from what belongs to the kings. I'll set an example if I must, starting with your fucking disciples who follow you like loyal dogs. I'll work my way up your fucking chain of command, pulling the guts from each of you. Make sure Ivanov doesn't push me. War with me will not end well for the lords."

"I'll relay the message," he said without an ounce of emotion on his face.

I examined him closely for a moment. If he was lying about his feelings on any of this, he was a hell of an actor. Just the way he said Bianca's name made me believe he was all in for doing whatever he had to do for her.

"And my sister?" he pressed.

"I see my father this evening. I'll do what I can. My intel says your sister is still alive. I've made a request with my father, and he seems amenable to it. I'll message you once I get back."

He nodded once, his Adam's apple bobbing as he swallowed. I offered him my joint, wondering if he'd take it. He peered at it for a moment before he took it and inhaled deeply, holding the smoke for a beat before coughing and blowing it out.

"That's good shit," he choked out, handing it back.

"Everything I have is the best," I said. "Keep it. It's just a taste of the things you could have if you do what you're told." I stepped out of the alcove and left him there, needing to see what other bullshit had been happening in my absence.

TWENTY-ONE
VINCENT

I leaned against the lockers outside of Bianca's class, waiting for the bell to ring. I always left classes early. Sitting there listening to the droning of these assholes didn't do much for me. It wasn't like I needed to know shit about amoebas or what-the-fuck-ever they were trying to jam down our throats.

"Hey there," Stella called out as she approached me.

I gave her a half-hearted glance before going back to reading a poster announcing tryouts for some school musical.

She stopped in front of me, blocking off the list of requirements for auditioning. "Why didn't you come see me last night?"

"Why the fuck would I do that?" I raised a brow at her, wondering just how crazy she was.

She giggled and ran her hand up my chest. "Because I know Bianca isn't giving you any. Dom won't let her. Figured I could help you out while you wait."

I knocked her hand off my chest. "I'll fuck Levin before I fuck you."

She scoffed. "That's fine. Bring him too. I'd love to be the meat in that sandwich."

I wrinkled my nose at her. "The fuck is the matter with you?"

She shrugged. "I'd say the problem is with you, not me. What sort of man says no to sex?"

"The kind with some fucking decency."

She laughed again. "Stop your holier-than-thou act, Vincent. We both know how dirty and depraved you are. We've fucked before. I won't tell anyone if that makes it easier on you. I know how you are and just what you like." She reached forward and rubbed my dick through my pants. I tensed beneath her touch, rage flowing through me.

With as much control as I had, I grasped her wrist and pushed her hand firmly away. "No, Stella. Don't touch me. I'm a king, not a fucking lord. You come to me if I tell you to come to me, not the other way around. If you keep this up, I'll tie you to a train track and let the cops sort you out."

She snatched her wrist out of my hold, a sneer on her face. "You're all the same, you know that? Everyone wants Bianca, and for what? She doesn't want you back. Yet, you still pine for her. What the fuck is the matter with you?"

I raised my brows at her, cool and calm as could be. "Ask yourself that question. The kings don't want you, and yet you still try. Explain it to me, wise one, so I may understand."

"You're an asshole."

"Noted."

She rolled her eyes and crossed her arms over her chest. "Whatever. I don't even care. Dom has me fucking Hail again anyway. Dom changed his mind on his terms. He wants me to get as much information as I can. This morning was a nightmare. Do you know what I had to do to get back in Hail's good graces after I stormed out on him last time?"

"The same shit you always do? Drop to your knees and eat cock like a starved dog?"

"I did it to stay alive. If Hail knew what I was really doing, he'd kill me."

"Then why the fuck are you standing here talking to me like we're best friends?" I slid my gaze over to her. "Get lost."

"I don't have anyone else to talk to about this."

I shook my head at her. "This is what you get when you play with fire. Loads of burns. Just stay in your lane, and hope to fuck shit doesn't hit the fan. If Dom said we'd protect you, we will, but that doesn't mean any of us are going to fuck you or give a shit about you. If you want to stay alive, *then follow the fucking rules*. Now beat it. You're ruining my dream of starring in the school musical."

"Fuck you, Vincent." She turned on her heel and sashayed back the way she came.

"Fucking psycho," I muttered, going back to reading the poster.

I bet I could audition and get the lead. Who the fuck wouldn't want me to play Romeo? I was a shoo-in.

The bell rang, pulling me out of my weird thoughts, and I waited for Bianca to come out of her class. She appeared a moment later, looking just as beautiful as she had an hour ago when I'd left her here.

"Hey, baby B," I said, draping my arm over her slender shoulders. "Did I tell you how beautiful you are today?"

"It'll take a lot more than a few compliments to make me like you again, Vincent," she said, trying to shrug my arm off.

"I thought we were good. What happened?" I took her books out of her arms and tucked them beneath my other arm as we walked.

When I'd left her with Dom at the safe house, she'd given my hand a squeeze and acted like things might get back to normal. Now, I was confused.

"Nothing happened. I just haven't forgotten the shit you guys did to me. Add to it, the fact I'm now goddamn married—"

"You're married to a fucking legend, B. Dom isn't just some fuckboy. He's the big time. I mean, I wish it were my ring on your finger, but I'm sure we'll play house just the same."

"You're overly optimistic," she grumbled, stopping at her locker.

She twisted the combination and opened it. I placed her books on the shelf over her head as she stared into the open space.

"What's wrong?"

"Everything," she said softly.

"Come here," I instructed gently, not knowing if she was going to kick me in the dick but deciding I'd take my chances. I wrapped my arms around her, the tension leaving my body as she nestled against my chest.

"It's OK, baby. I know you're pissed, but I swear you're safe with us. No one is going to hurt you if we can help it."

"I don't believe you."

"I know, but I promise, OK?"

She pulled away and offered me a sad smile. My hands were still on her waist as Drake moved past and shoved her hard. I stopped her fall and shifted her against her locker. Within seconds, my fist connected with the back of his head.

People jumped out of the way, some of them crying out, others whooping. My fist cracked against his nose when he spun around, sending blood pouring down his face. I'd just finished telling B we'd protect her, and then this shit for brains came along and shoved her. *No fucking way*. I'd bury this asshole and make B a believer.

"Piece of shit," I snarled as I punched him in the ribs, causing him to double over and gasp for breath. "Don't fucking touch what belongs to the kings. That includes our girl."

"She's not *your* girl," he rasped, ramming his shoulder into me and sending me stumbling back. "She's De Santis's little fuck toy. We all know it. He married her. By the time you get to her, she's just sloppy seconds."

Motherfucker. I saw red. I punched him again as he laughed before I brought my knee up into his guts, sending him hunching over again. I was just about to bring it up once more and finish off his nose when B darted in front of me and pushed me away from the piece of shit.

"Don't," she said.

I stared down at her, my fury fading away. I noted Vasiliev and Tate had entered the fray and were now helping Drake stand. I caught Vasiliev's eye and noted the grim look on his bruised face. His gaze darted to B, a look of longing in his eyes, before he schooled it and focused on the shit stain in front of him.

I took B's hand and pulled her away, hating she ever had to see the ugly side of our lives. Truth be told, if she hadn't stepped in, I would've probably killed him on the spot, opting to stomp on his fucking head the moment I got it on the ground.

I let B lead the way without saying a word. We reached my dorm a few moments later.

"Sit," she instructed, pointing to my bed.

I did as she commanded and watched as she rummaged around in my bathroom before emerging with a first aid kit and a cloth.

"I'm fine," I said as she kneeled in front of me.

"You're not. You're bleeding." She dabbed my cheek with a warm rag and frowned at a cut I hadn't even known I had. I studied her face, in awe of her. She was a remarkable woman.

I winced as she cleaned my wound before moving to my hands, where I'd broken the skin on my knuckles punching him.

"You didn't need to fight," she said as she finished bandaging me.

"I'm not going to let someone push my girl around," I answered, flexing my hand. *Yeah, that shit would be sore tomorrow.*

She frowned. "Am I your girl? I'm married to Dom now."

"You're still my girl, B," I confirmed, reaching out and cradling her face in my hands. "You're also Dom's and Levin's."

"And Fallon's?" She looked up at me, her brow crinkled.

I sighed, not wanting to give her an outright *no* since she looked so damn hopeful. In the grand scheme of things, I doubted Vasiliev would become a king. It didn't take a rocket scientist to know we led dangerous lives, and he'd probably fuck up or die before he was sworn in as a king.

I said as much, "I don't know. Maybe if he doesn't fuck up."

"He won't. I know he won't."

"You really have faith in him. I admire that. I just want you to have that much faith in us too."

She scoffed and turned away.

I leaned in and cradled her cheek, bringing her focus back to me. "I'll prove you can trust the kings. If I'm being honest, you make me nervous."

"I do?" Her lips were a breath from my own.

"Yeah. I don't want you to break my fucking heart. You leaving us would gut me. The fact you're cutting Vasiliev slack wounds me. I think in this entire shitstorm, I'm the one who was by your side and didn't want *any* of this. I feel like my punishment is unjust. I just… want you, B." I didn't wait for her to answer. I closed the distance and pressed my lips to hers, relishing her cherry lip gloss and the soft, little sound she made as my tongue slid along hers.

After she kicked my ass all over the safe house, I didn't expect her to kiss me back. I figured she'd knock me out with a lamp or her high heel, but no, she fell into our kiss quickly, her fingers mussing my hair as she raked them through it.

Did I win her over? Were my words enough? Did fucking up Drake's face help?

"*What the fuck?*" Dom's voice called out.

Bianca was snatched away from me, leaving me with nothing but a raging hard-on and a glare on my face.

"Yeah. What the fuck?" I said, glowering at Dom as he held Bianca's arm.

She struggled against him, but he held tight.

"Let me go." She kicked his shin, which only made him growl and pull her struggling body against his.

"What did I just walk in on?" Dom demanded, staring down at her, both his hands holding her upper arms.

"*He* kissed *me*," she said.

"Hey, you kissed me back," I cut in, disbelieving she'd broken so easily and pinned the blame all on me.

She shot me a look which said what I'd assumed. *She liked it. She wanted it.*

"You know what I told you. If you're not giving it to me, then you're not giving it to anyone," Dom said, frowning down at her, clearly reading the look on her face.

"She's *our* girl, asshole," I snapped, anger rising in my chest.

He'd made a damn promise. There was no way in hell I'd let him back out of it.

"And she wasn't fucking me. We kissed."

Dom shot a glance in my direction, his eyes raking over me before he released Bianca. She had the balls to kick him again. He hissed and hauled her back to him once more.

For fuck's sake.

"Behave, wasp." He gave her a face a squeeze with one hand.

"Let me go," she shot back, glaring up at him. "You're not my damn boss, Dominic."

"You're driving me insane," he said as he stared down at her.

"Funny. I thought you were already there."

A smile curled his lips up in the slightest way. "Vincent."

"Yeah?"

"My wife is grating on my last nerve today. What would you do to teach her a lesson?"

Dom's gaze never left Bianca, who scoffed at him. The slight tremor in her body was unmistakable though.

"Deny her an orgasm?" I suggested, remembering how pissed that had made her before. Her eyes widened for a moment, and I knew it was the right answer.

Dom released her face and ran his knuckles along her jaw. "Did you hear that? Vincent thinks that might make you behave."

She said nothing as she shot a quick peek at me.

"I think he's right," Dom continued, shifting away from her. "Vincent. Hold her."

"No." She moved to dart around me, but I snagged her around the waist, enjoying her struggling in my arms.

"What the hell, Vinny?" she cried out as I hauled her to the bed.

The way she said my name made my dick harder, so if her plan was to woo me, she was doing a great job at it.

I brought her back against my front as we reclined on the bed, my legs hooking between hers to open them for Dom. I twisted my fingers with hers and held them down on the mattress as she squirmed against me.

"All you're doing is making me hard," I murmured, shifting against her. I knew she could feel my cock against her back.

"You're a Judas," she snarled, her chest heaving as she continued her useless battle.

I laughed. "How?"

"You know how."

Dom got onto the bed and positioned himself between her legs, his green eyes filled with storm clouds as he eased her skirt up.

"You are not allowed to kiss, touch, suck, or fuck anyone but me unless I tell you otherwise," Dom said in a soft, dangerous voice.

My hackles went up before he shot a look at me that made me simmer down. I knew that look. It was his *be patient* look. I gave him a slight nod.

"I hope to hell you're going to suck Vincent to near completion as punishment since he started it." She wiggled against me, my cock painfully hard.

I let out a soft grunt.

Dom cocked his head like he was considering her words. "You're right."

"What?" I said, wide-eyed, at the same time Bianca let out a soft gasp of surprise.

"Maybe this should be a punishment for both of you. On your knees, wasp."

I let her go, confused off my ass. Bianca hesitated for a second before Dom snapped his fingers at her. She quickly shifted to her knees and faced me. I stared at her, my heart in my throat. I had no idea what this lunatic had in mind.

"Take his cock out and suck it," Dom ordered.

"Dominic—" Bianca's eyes widened as they skirted over my face.

My heart pounded hard at the idea of her mouth on my dick.

Dom let out an exasperated sigh. "You wanted to play around, right? Both of you?"

"I just wanted a kiss," I muttered, clearly lying my ass off. If B had given me the green light, I would've railed her into next year without hesitation.

"Well, you're going to get one," Dom said. "Bianca. Now."

"You're such an asshole," she snapped at him, her fingers fumbling on my zipper.

I exhaled, more turned on than I should be considering I was about to be punished.

Bianca eased my cock out and stroked it, making me suck in a sharp breath.

"Suck it," Dom grunted, kneeling behind her. "Try to make him come in your mouth."

Bianca snarled obscenities before my cock sank deep into her mouth. My eyes rolled back at the warmth and perfect suction.

"*Fuck*," I hissed as she sucked me.

"Spread your legs," Dom instructed her.

She grunted along my cock but parted her legs for him. I tangled my fingers in her hair as Dom pushed her skirt up and pulled her panties down, his eyes dark. I could practically see a vein of cruelty and anger oozing from him as he stared down at her. A twinge of remorse ran through me for getting her in trouble, but I couldn't help myself when it came to her.

He raised his hand and brought it down on her pussy.

She yelped along my dick, making me groan.

He slapped her again and again until she was panting on my cock. He slid a finger deep inside her, making her back arch as she choked on my erection.

The sound of him finger fucking her drove me right to the edge.

I was set to blow as my balls drew up for what I knew would be the most intense orgasm of my life.

Dom withdrew his fingers and smacked her pussy three more times as she moaned. Just when she began to shake with an impending release, he stopped and twisted his fingers in her hair, hauling her away from my aching cock.

"Fuck, man. *Don't*," I cried out, desperate to blow my load.

Dom pushed Bianca down beside me, his chest heaving as he surveyed us.

He seized my cock in a tight grip and leaned over me. I winced at the pain he brought with his hold.

"Don't fucking do this shit again with her. She's being punished because she's punishing us. This is how she's doing it. Don't fucking give in to her until she submits."

I nodded tightly, understanding what he was saying. She kissed me because she knew she could throw it in Dom's face and piss him off, causing a fight between us. *Sneaky little minx.* Fuck me for not regretting kissing her though. I'd seen the look on her face. I was winning. Finally.

Dom released my dick, allowing me to relax against my pillows with the worst case of blue balls ever. My guts ached with the pain in my balls, and nausea twisted like a snake. He'd denied me my orgasm, and I would indeed suffer for the rest of the evening.

"Wasp," he said, moving to her and bringing her forward as he kneeled between her legs. "Don't play stupid games with me. You do shit like that again, and I'll tie you up to our bed and punish you on repeat. Neither of you is allowed to come. Neither of you gets your releases."

She visibly swallowed and nodded. I grunted.

"Use your words," he growled.

"Yes, Dominic," she said softly as I muttered my agreement.

"You fuck who I say you fuck, and you do it when I say you do it. You are my wife."

"I thought I belonged to all the kings, not just you—"

He ran his knuckles along her jaw. "You do, but not until you submit to me. If you want Vincent. Levin. You get them through me."

"You're so fucked up," she panted out, her voice shaking.

"I love you," he said thickly, his body corded with tension.

"You're ruining my life."

"Better than ending it, *mia regina*." He released her and got to his feet, sweeping his fingers through his black hair. "Put your dick away," he barked at me.

I grumbled and winced but pulled my pants up. Dom snagged B's panties off the floor and slid them back up her legs before he pressed a surprisingly gentle kiss to her forehead.

"Deny me what I want, and I'll deny you what you want," he murmured as he trailed his lips to her cheek. "Understand?"

"Yes, Dominic," she said tightly.

He held her for a moment before he broke away and looked at me. "What happened today?"

I rubbed my eyes, my hands aching from the beating I'd given Drake. I launched into what happened in the hall.

When I reached the end of my tale, Dom simply nodded. "He got what he deserved. If any of them do shit like that again, beat the piss out of them. We'll do it until they learn."

"I wouldn't have stopped if B hadn't made me."

Dom turned to her. "Never get between a lord and a king. You could've been hurt."

She snorted at him. "Pretty sure it wouldn't be as bad as being taken into the woods and shot."

"I don't think you've ever been taken to the woods and shot." He lifted a dark brow at her.

She gave him the finger.

I expected him to launch himself at her, but he only smirked. Fuck, he was even harder to figure out now than he used to be.

And my fucking dick and balls hurt.

I rubbed them gently, making a mental note to only kiss B when my door was locked.

I definitely liked learning the hard way, and judging by the tiny smile she gave me, she did too.

TWENTY-TWO
BIANCA

"Bianca!" Aubrey shouted as I walked across the courtyard later that evening.

Levin trailed behind me. He hadn't tried talking to me, seemingly as pissed at me as I was at him. I supposed he had a right to be mad too. I'd sworn I wasn't seeing Fallon when I really was. In the grand scheme of things, I probably would've been upset if my person had lied like that.

Of course, I wasn't exactly *his* person. I was more of a deal they'd struck if we were being technical. On the other hand, I loved Levin despite everything screaming for me to run the other way. I also hated him for all the shit happening around me. Vincent was the only one I wasn't seeing red over. His words earlier made me realize *maybe* I was being a bit of an annoying bitch over things. At least with respect to him. Giving in and kissing him had brought all my feelings tumbling back full force for him. And shit, I wanted him. *Bad.*

The rest of them? I was still pissed over the shit they'd all done. Whether it was rational or not.

I stopped and turned, waiting for Aubrey to catch up.

"Can you give us a minute?" I asked Levin.

He glanced at her then back to me and strode away to the king's table in the courtyard, making it a point to not look at me.

I sighed before fixing a smile on my face for my friend.

"Girl, is it true?" Her eyes widened as she stopped in front of me.

I knew what she was asking, but I feigned dumb anyway. "Is what true?"

She rolled her eyes. "You and Dominic De Santis. Did you really get married over the weekend?"

"Eh…" I started, but she snatched my hand and let out a garbled noise as she stared at the massive rock Dominic had slid onto my finger days before.

"Holy shit. That's bigger than Hail's," she said.

"Of course, it is," Dominic's smooth voice called out. "Everything I can offer Bianca is larger."

I whipped around to stare at him as Aubrey dropped my hand and took a nervous step away. Apparently, she hadn't seen him approach either, but if I had to guess, he'd come around the corner of the art building, so the large bushes had hidden him from view.

I peeked past him to see Vincent had settled next to Levin. Some senior, I recognized as Celeste, was talking to them, twirling her auburn hair around her finger. Pushing the sickness in my guts away, I focused on Dominic.

"What are you doing here?" I asked. "I thought you were busy, and that's why Levin was stalking me."

"I was busy, and now I'm not." He wound his arm around my waist and looked to Aubrey. "Aubrey McIntire. Did you notice you're down a neighbor today?"

"W-what?" she stammered as she looked between me and Dominic.

I frowned.

"I've had my wife's things moved to my room. It's larger than hers. It makes sense we live together."

"Dominic," I hissed, tensing as he tightened his hold on me like he knew I was about to bolt or kick him in the dick. Maybe both.

"No arguments," his voice held that note of authority to it which made others cower. But not me.

"I swear if you moved me without talking to me—"

"I did. Here's your key." He pressed the cool metal into my palm. "All your stuff has been moved to my place, minus your bed and a few things you won't need, of course. Clothes and things of that nature are in my—*our*—room now."

I was so furious with him I couldn't speak. *I can't believe I didn't see this coming.*

"That's beside the point. Aubrey, I was wondering if you could do me a favor," Dominic continued conversationally like he wasn't some cold-blooded killer who'd just squirreled all my shit into his room.

"Um, yeah. I mean, sure," she said, visibly paling as she twisted her fingers in front of her.

"My wife needs someone to hang around with for a few hours this evening. I was wondering if you'd do me the favor of staying with her in my room tonight. I'll have dinner delivered, and I have any streaming service you could want. I'll be out this evening and don't want her staying alone."

Aubrey nodded, her ponytail bouncing, relief washing over her face. "Y-yeah. I-I can do that. Wha-what time?"

"Seven would be good. I have somewhere I need to be. I do ask that you not leave my room though. It's important for both yours and Bianca's safety that you don't. If you do, there could be consequences. Do you understand?"

"Y-yes. Of course. We'll stay in your room," Aubrey sputtered, her cheeks darkening.

"Excellent." Dominic turned to me and gave me a Cheshire smile. "I expect you to do as you're told."

Or else.

He didn't need to say it. It was implied in the dark glint in his eyes which promised serious punishment. It'd be more than him denying me an orgasm. He'd probably break out his belt again and beat my flesh raw. And if I knew Dominic the way I thought I did, he'd extend his punishment to Aubrey.

"Where are you going?" I turned in his arms to fully look at him, seriously irritated that he thought he could dictate to my friend what we could do. It was one thing to boss me around, but it was really damn annoying he was extending it to Aubrey.

He cocked his head at me and tucked a strand of hair behind my ear. I swallowed thickly. *Damn, he was so beautiful it hurt.* For a moment, all my anger and frustration washed away as I stared up at him.

"We'll talk when we get to our room."

I snapped out of my stupor quickly and bit back a retort about him moving my stuff without my permission. I offered him a plastic smile instead. "And when will that be?"

"I have to meet with someone, so after that."

I was desperate to ask if the someone was Fallon, but I tightened my smile instead. "Great. I'll see you back at *your* room."

He leaned in and pressed a kiss to my lips that I didn't reciprocate before he nipped me, sending a course of goosebumps through my body. "*Our* room, wasp."

And with that, he turned and stalked away, nodding for Vincent to join him. I observed as Vincent got to his feet and shot me that disarming smile of his before following Dominic across the lawn. I turned my attention back to Levin, who was still talking to Celeste.

"I'll see you at seven," I grumbled to Aubrey while I watched Levin nod at something Celeste was saying.

"Just so you know, Celeste Vander Veer gets around. Her dad owns Rustic Rifles, the gun company. They're big money. Old money. *Really* important in the new world you're part of."

I swallowed. "Should I be worried about her?"

"Terrified," Aubrey answered. "If I were a girl who maybe liked a boy who was my mafia husband's best friend, I'd probably go intervene. Just an observation I've made recently."

Aubrey gave me a pointed look and waved goodbye. She was, in fact, too observant for my own good. I'd have to dial down my reactions to the guys back a bit if I were going to keep my feelings on lockdown.

I watched Celeste with Levin. It was no secret the kings had their share of women, but to blatantly flirt with them in front of me cut me deeply. Of course, he could just be talking, and it wasn't anything to worry about. But I trusted Aubrey. She knew more about these people than I did.

Drawing in a deep breath, I sauntered over to Levin and Celeste.

"Hi," I said, stepping to Levin's side and noting her hand on his knee.

She was pretty, I'd give her that. Long, auburn hair. Hazel eyes. A body I was sure got her everything her plump lips didn't.

She narrowed her eyes at me. "Hi?"

She was exactly the sort of snobby bitch Bolten seemed to like to churn out. *Whatever*. I was over the day and decided human interaction would not be a good thing considering I was pissed about the little trick Dominic just pulled with moving me to his room.

"Levin. I'd like to leave. Dominic moved all my things, and I'm sure he's made a mess."

"In a minute," Levin said, not bothering to glance at me as Celeste widened her smile at him.

He looked gorgeous sitting there in his uniform, his muscles bulging through the navy jacket, his tie partially undone and his blond hair a mess. I could see why Celeste was interested. I didn't like it. She had no right…

I silently fumed, my hands balled into tight fists.

"So. I was thinking why not, you know?" Celeste continued as if I weren't there. "It could be fun. It's only for the night, and Daddy would love it if you'd be able to come."

"Levin," I snarled softly.

He cast me a cursory glance before his attention went back to her.

"So, *anyway*," Celeste continued.

"Levin," I said, frustrated he wasn't paying attention.

He skated his heated gaze lazily over me, sending a torrent of goosebumps through my body as he paused at my chest before his eyes met mine.

"Do you need something?"

My gaze darted between him and Celeste as he made no motion to move and raised his brows at me.

"You're an asshole." I turned away from him, not in the mood to fight over a man who clearly wasn't interested anymore. Maybe he regretted not shooting me in the woods after all. He did say me being dead would've saved him a lot of trouble.

I was married to Dominic now anyway. As much as I wanted to believe he'd still let me be with the rest of the kings, I knew how jealous and possessive he was. Plus, I was still pissed at them, Fallon included. With the exception of Vincent, they could all kiss my ass.

So why does it hurt so much whenever I thought about losing them?

I stormed across the lawn in the direction of my dorm, my heart aching and my brain a jumbled mess of confusing thoughts. Even though Dominic said he'd had it cleaned out, it was still mine. If nothing else, I might be able to get some peace and quiet before I was forced into his lair.

But it wasn't peace and quiet I needed. What I needed was to curl up into a tight ball and cry. And maybe send a whispered prayer to whoever in the universe could hear me.

TWENTY-THREE
LEVIN

I jogged across campus to Dom's room. Bianca had split and hadn't even bothered to tell me where the hell she was going. Not that she would. She liked to piss me off like that. I knew she was upset about Celeste talking to me, but she needed to understand it was just business.

We'd been trying to find an in with her old man to secure a large supply of weapons and had been unsuccessful so far. Celeste approaching and showing interest in me and Vincent was a sure-fire way to slide our asses into her old man's good graces and get the deal I knew the Ivanovs were sniffing for.

When I reached Dom's door, I knocked and got no answer. I pounded on it, not wanting to burst in. When no one answered again, I sighed and pulled out the key. It was empty of people, but Bianca's stuff was everywhere. Seeing how seriously Dom was taking this made me sick deep in my soul. Stealing moments alone with Bianca would not be happening with her living with him. I loved Dom, but fuck was he irritating.

This whole moving thing must have been what he'd been talking to her about. I'd seen the angry look on her face when he'd approached her earlier. The little crease between her eyes. The pout to her lips. The way her shoulders had tensed.

None of that mattered though. She wasn't here, which meant I'd fucked up and lost her. *Again*. I slammed Dom's door shut and fired a message off to Vincent.

Me: Have you seen Bianca?

He answered seconds later.

Vincent: Don't tell me you lost her. Find her before we get back. We're going to see Snoopy.

I frowned at his message. *Who the fuck is Snoopy?*

I didn't have time to dwell on it. I pulled Bianca's number up on my phone and hit talk. It went straight to voicemail. Snarling, I ended the call and stuffed my phone into my pocket before heading off in the direction of her dorm. It was as good a guess as any, but I couldn't get the niggling thought out of my mind that she'd gone somewhere to meet up with Fallon.

Part of me wanted it to be true so we could finally just kill him. But another part of me prayed it wasn't true because it would hurt too damn much if she was kissing and touching him in a dark corner. Again.

I shook the thought off, hating how it made my chest ache. I was done dealing with her shit. She wanted to hate me, then fine. I wasn't going to kiss her ass. If she couldn't see how much I cared by sticking my neck out for her, then whatever. I'd move the fuck on.

At least that was what I kept telling myself in an attempt to dull the pain I felt over her withdrawing from me. It didn't matter that I'd earned it from her though.

I bounded up the stairs to her room and banged on her door. When she didn't answer, I inserted the key and threw the door open to find her curled up in a ball on her bed, weeping softly.

Relief flooded me before concern took the wheel. I hated that I fucking cared so much. It didn't make sense since she hated me regardless of anything good I did.

I shut the door softly and shuffled to the side of her bed, staring down at her.

Clearing my throat, I said, "You're supposed to be in Dom's room."

She remained silent except for her soft sniffles.

"Bianca, we need to go. Dom will be back soon. If we're not there, he'll get pissed. I don't feel like dealing with a pissed-off mob prince."

When she didn't react, I sighed and sank down beside her.

"What can I do?" The question had so many meanings to it. *How do I make this right? How do I earn your forgiveness? Do you even give a shit anymore? How do I get you to smile again?*

She sniffled for a moment longer before sitting up.

"Nothing," she finally whispered.

"You're not OK. Talk to me," I said, hating the desperate tone in my voice.

"There's nothing to say. You're right. I have to return to Dominic's before he gets back. I have to be the good, little wife and do as I'm told."

"Bianca—"

"It's fine, Levin. You don't have to fake it with me. I haven't forgotten what you said to me at the dance."

"I was trying to get you to run," I said sharply. "I didn't mean that shit."

She shrugged listlessly. "Doesn't matter, I guess. I listened in a way. The only problem was you guys decided to chase me down and shoot at us before putting me on my knees in the woods to murder me."

"When we were chasing you down, you weren't the target. We were trying to get you back from the prick who stole you from us."

"I was still a target because my heart would've been shattered if you'd killed him. You put me in danger with your anger. And even after firing at the car, you held a gun to my head," she choked out.

"I didn't pull the fucking trigger, did I?"

She wiped her eyes. "No. I guess you didn't. The idea of torturing me must have been far more appealing."

"How the hell am I torturing you?" I demanded. "What am I doing to you that's so fucking bad, Bianca? Tell me. I want to know."

"Nothing." She stood and grabbed the pink throw blanket she'd been lying with before going into her bathroom and rifling around in her cupboards.

I got up and leaned against the doorframe, watching her as she slammed cabinet doors.

"I told you how I felt about that shit in the woods. I didn't want you to die. Please fucking believe that. If I did, you wouldn't be slamming doors and acting like a spoiled brat right now."

"Spoiled? *Me?* Spoiled?" She approached and shoved me hard in the chest, sending me off the doorframe. "Go to hell, Levin. The last thing I am is spoiled. *Trapped. Broken. Angry.* Pissed off at you and your merry band of assholes…those are things I am. *Not* fucking spoiled!" her voice rose as she glared up at me, her chest heaving.

"What do you want me to do? I already asked, but you ignored me. How the fuck can I fix anything if you won't tell me?"

"You don't *need* to fix anything. Unless maybe you can go back in time and finish the job because then you could sit around and flirt in the courtyard with some bitch who has guns up her skirt."

I stared at her in disbelief. "You're jealous."

"I'm not jealous."

"You are. You're mad because I was talking to Celeste."

She shook her head. "I'm not. I'm mad because you're supposed to be watching over me, but you'd rather watch her tits than make sure I'm safe."

I let out a bark of bitter laughter. "You're ridiculous, you know that? You hate us trailing you. You've shaken me off more times than I can count. And that's just me. You've dipped on Vincent too. In fact, you ran off to fuck that piece of shit, so don't act like you're an angel, Bianca. You're not. You messed around with someone else behind our backs after you gave your word. So what if I talked to some chick in the courtyard? At least I didn't fuck her."

She glared at me, her body shaking. "At least Fallon wasn't scared to fuck me."

I snorted, trying to control my anger. "I wasn't ever *scared* to fuck you, Bianca. Don't get shit twisted in your head. I *chose* not to. That's called self-fucking-preservation. I knew you'd do this kind of shit. I was distancing myself so you couldn't fuck me up like you have Dom and Vincent." I shook my head at her. "Why do you care anyway? You hate me."

"You're right. I do hate you." Her bottom lip wobbled as she glared up at me.

I backed away, her words hitting me deeper than I wanted them to. "Then it doesn't matter who the fuck I talk to or what I do with them, does it?"

"It doesn't," she choked out. "If it came down to choosing one of the kings, I'd have chosen anyone but you. Every. Single. Fucking. Time. ANYONE but you. You and I will never happen again. I don't fucking want you. I'll *never* want you, Levin Seeley. As far as I'm concerned, I'm done with just the fucking thought of you!"

I swallowed, bile working its way up my throat at her words. "Good to know."

I wasn't about to stand there and be broken like that, so I turned on my heel and stormed out of her room, slamming the door behind me, but not before I heard her let out a choked sob, which completed breaking me.

Fuck it. If she didn't want me, that was fine. I deserved it. But I wasn't going to just stand back and be miserable because she wanted me to be.

If she didn't want me, then I was sure someone else would. I pulled my phone out and wiped at my eyes before hitting SEND on a number.

"Hey," a soft, sultry voice answered. "I didn't think you'd call so soon."

"Yeah. I, uh, I thought us going out might actually be a good idea. How about next Friday?"

Celeste giggled softly, the noise doing nothing for me, but I forced myself to focus.

"Friday is perfect."

"Great," I managed to say. "I'll text you."

"Sounds good."

I bid her goodbye and hung up the phone. Dejected, I leaned against the wall next to Bianca's room and sent a text off to Vincent.

Me: Please come watch Bianca in her room. I can't.

He replied immediately.

Vincent: Why?

Me: I just need you to come.

Vincent: Fine. Give me ten.

I shot off a thumbs up and darkened my screen, counting down the minutes until I could get the fuck away from there because even though there was an entire wall between us, I could still feel her presence.

And fuck if I didn't want to break the wall down and beg her to fucking love me.

But I wasn't that guy, and she clearly wasn't that girl, so I'd just let it go. Lesson learned. I was done too.

TWENTY-FOUR
FALLON

"**F**allon, get over here," Hail called from across his room. I sighed and got up from the chair in the corner, zigzagging through the large space and around the people he'd invited over. He was apparently feeling pretty morose after learning Bianca had married Dominic and needed to throw a party.

"This is my boy Fallon," Hail said, clapping me on the shoulder as two girls giggled at me, a third on his arm. "He's single and needs to get his dick wet."

I gave the girls a tight smile, not correcting Hail. *Was I single?* I supposed I was, but really, I was loyal to Bianca. The last thing I wanted to do was fuck things up more with her.

"The kings fucked him up because they're pieces of shit. He needs his wounds soothed," Hail continued.

"I'm fine," I said, holding my hand up. "Really."

"You're so brave and strong," one of the girls said, reaching for me. She caught my arm and sidled up against me. "I'm Pamela."

I offered her a nod and tried to untangle my arm from her clutches, but she tightened her hold and giggled again.

"And I'm Samantha," the other girl said, moving to my other side.

Hail winked at me. "You're welcome. Go have fun. Take them into my sitting room and get your dick sucked or eat some pussy. You look hungry."

I grimaced as the girls giggled again. I knew if I shook the girls off, I'd have to listen to Hail bitch. He was the sort of guy who'd stop the party, call me out, take my pants down in front of everyone, and make the girls suck me off. It wasn't like it hadn't happened before. The night with Bianca on her knees in front of me with tears in her eyes flashed in my mind. She'd been so scared that night when Hail had made her suck our dicks. I'd never been so fucking angry as I was that night.

"Come on," Pamela tittered, steering me through the crowded room back to my chair.

I sank down while she climbed onto my lap while Samantha kneeled beside us, her hand high on my thigh. I hadn't gone to the small sitting room Hail had suggested simply because I didn't want to fuck these girls. But it looked like having an audience didn't bother them.

"I'm fine," I repeated, leaning away from Pamela as she pressed closer to me.

Her hair was blonde and wavy, but she'd put so much hairspray in it to give it some weird wet look that I could taste the shit in my mouth. Rubbing her smallish tits against me, she let out a laugh. The girl wasn't attractive in the slightest, and the drunk, desperate vibe was a total turn off. Not to mention how large her cheeks were. She looked like a fucking squirrel who'd jammed too many nuts in her jowls.

I wasn't one to make fun of girls, but she seemed the sort who didn't take no for an answer, which pissed me the fuck off.

"Hey. Chill," I said.

"Ooh, he likes to play hard to get," Samantha purred as she ran her hand up to my groin and nudged my cock. "I like that."

"It's not hard to get," I said, looking around for an escape. "I'm not interested. It's been a long week."

"Let us help you relax," Pamela encouraged, skimming her lips along my jaw.

I clenched my teeth and let out a steadying breath. All I needed to do was play my part, let Hail see, then get the fuck out of there. I didn't want to be there anyway, although, Dominic wanted me up Hail's ass to collect information.

I peered across the room to find Hail snorting coke and knew he'd be fucked by the end of the night and nothing he did would be important. Usually, he ended up fucking whatever moved when he did coke before passing out until morning.

Stella caught my eye as she stood next to him in a tiny jean skirt and red tank top. She raised her brows at me when Samantha undid my belt. Stella tilted her head slightly like she wanted me to go to her.

I frowned. Stella and I had never been on great terms. I didn't *hate* her, and she mostly ignored me since it was Hail she was after. She tipped her head again. Samantha reached into my boxers at the same moment Pamela urged my hand under her skirt.

Fuck this. I'd risk Stella any day over this shit.

I rose to my feet and set Pamela on hers.

"Sorry, ladies. I need to go." I didn't offer an explanation as I refastened my pants and went to Stella.

"Tell Hail you want to fuck me," she whispered in my ear when I reached her.

"What?"

She backed away from me and gave me a wide-eyed look as Hail let out a cheer and slammed back a shot of whiskey.

If it got me the hell out of there, I'd say anything.

"Hail, hey, man," I said, clearing my throat.

He looked at me with glassy eyes and grinned. "I know you didn't fuck that fast. You like to take your time and get chicks off like you give a shit. Fucking ladies' man."

I gave him the laugh he was looking for. "Right. I was, uh, sitting over there and saw Stella. I was thinking I could, um…" I peeked at her, and she gave me a quick smile and nodded. "I was wondering if you'd be cool with me and her taking off."

Hail blinked at me several times before he cracked a smile. "You want to fuck Stella? *You?* Really?"

I nodded sheepishly and glanced at her.

"Tell you what. I'll let you fuck my whore if you do a line of coke with me. No line, then you go over there and fuck Sam and hamster face with me. Got it?"

I grimaced at that. Coke wasn't my thing, but I'd do it if it meant my freedom.

"Sure," I said apprehensively.

He let out a cheer. "Tate. Dole that shit out."

Tate got to work setting up the lines. I checked the rest of the room. Drake was getting a blow job from some random chick whose name I couldn't remember. He was messed up out of his mind and didn't seem to mind some guy was holding his cock while the girl sucked him.

I shook my head. Hail's parties were never my scene. My idea of a good time was reading a book and hiding from this shit.

"There you go, pussy. Do it up!" Hail shouted, thumping me on the back.

I bent down and took the rolled-up hundred Tate handed me, hoping Stella wasn't fucking with me, and snorted my line while Hail snorted his. Before I could get up all the way, he wrapped his hands around my head and pressed his forehead to mine. Rather than push him away and deal with any bullshit consequences, I waited for whatever he needed to say in his stoned stupor.

"Don't fuck up."

"Of course. I just want to see what the big deal with Stella is," I said tightly, knowing damn well this was out of character for me.

I had no idea what he meant about fucking it up. As far as he knew, it was simply sex.

"Fine. Go. Fuck my whore...*After* you take a drink!" He released me and pushed a shot into my hand then downed one of his own. Sighing, I swallowed the booze, my head spinning. He shoved another at me. And another. I downed six before I stumbled away, knowing I was about to regret being born.

"You'll have fun fucking him now, Stella," Hail slurred out. "I got him loosened up for you. Mostly." He winked at me with both eyes.

"Thanks," Stella said, taking my hand in hers and leading me out of the room.

The second we were in the hall, I fell back against the wall, my head a mess and my heart racing.

"Fuck," I groaned.

"Get your shit together," she instructed, adjusting her breasts in her top. "I'm taking you somewhere."

"I'm not really interested in fucking you, you know," I managed to say.

"That's too bad. I heard you're a good lay with a big dick." She held her hand out to me again. "I was thinking I could take you to see Bianca."

"What?" I blinked at her. "Dominic will fucking gut me."

"Dominic and the kings aren't on campus. She's with Aubrey McIntire in Dom's room right now. I just texted Dom and asked him when he'd be back because I don't like it when he's gone. He said it's still early, and he's with his father. He told me to meet him around midnight when he gets back. That gives you a solid two hours of alone time with Bianca."

"Why would you do this?" I asked, trying to keep my shit together.

My heart thudded hard against muscle and bone, and my vision swam. Coke wasn't my drug of choice. If I wanted to mellow out and get stoned, weed was my preferred method. Coke always made me feel like I was running a marathon. One I couldn't win.

"Because it's fun," she said, shrugging. "And Dom makes me furious sometimes. He ignores me for her."

I snorted at that. Of course he ignored her for Bianca. Who the hell wouldn't?

"It could get me killed."

"Me too." She shrugged again. "But life gets boring without a little spice."

I shook my head. She was certifiably insane. It was probably why she appealed to Hail so much. Not that he wouldn't throw her under the bus the first chance he got, but he was typically decent to his loyal piece of ass. And by decent, I meant he wouldn't kill her right out the gates. He'd let her live for a bit before he ditched her. It was, after all, the thrill in the torture which got him off.

"So you coming or what?" She took a few steps and looked back at me.

"I'm high and drunk as balls right now. My heart is trying to break through my chest."

She scoffed. "Bianca is married to Dominic De Santis and in love with Vincent and Levin. Do you think she's new to guys being stoned and drunk around her? Do you not know the kings at all?"

"You're right." I pushed myself off the wall and stumbled. "Take me to their queen."

She laughed. "Your death wish is my command."

TWENTY-FIVE
BIANCA

A soft knock on the door pulled me out of a fitful sleep. I sat up and peeked around the dark room. Aubrey had taken off about an hour ago. I'd told her I was too tired to hang out. She'd given me a hug and said she'd stay anyway. I knew she was terrified of Dominic, so I'd assured her I'd lock the door and be on my best behavior. Reluctantly, she'd left.

Vincent hadn't said much when he'd relieved Levin earlier in the day. Vincent had seemed preoccupied with whatever he was doing on his phone, so I'd taken a bubble bath and cried softly in the bathroom without him knowing. My argument with Levin had come out of nowhere and everywhere. I'd been so frustrated that I'd scream it all out at him. He'd already hurt me with the fiasco at the dance and the gun to my head in the woods. Then he'd had the audacity to outright flirt with Celeste in front of me.

I couldn't take it. I'd let it all out, and now my heart was cracking. The last thing I wanted was to hate him. Because really, I didn't *hate* any of them. I was just so livid over everything that was happening.

Another soft knock sounded out, and I shuffled to my feet. Nausea washed over me as I continued to think about Levin. Some tiny part of me hoped he was on the other side of the door. It wasn't possible though. He was with Dominic and Vincent.

Maybe Aubrey forgot something?

I cracked open the door, and my heart jumped in my throat as Fallon offered me a smile.

"Fallon?" I opened the door wider. "You can't be here—"

"Let me in?" he said, his words slurring. He shook his head as if to clear it. "Please, princess?"

"If Dominic comes back, he'll kill you," I hissed. "Go. If someone sees you here—"

"If you let me in, no one will see," he reasoned, swaying. He caught himself on the doorframe and groaned.

I shot a look up and down the hallway, noting it was empty. *But for how long?* Knowing we were treading in very dangerous territory, I grabbed his arm and hauled him into the room with me, closing the door behind him.

Immediately, I realized what a terrible idea it was because he gathered me to him and held on tightly, his face buried in my neck.

"I've missed you, princess. I was at this party at Hail's. I did coke and drank too much. I'm supposed to be fucking Stella right now because these other two chicks wanted to fuck me, but I couldn't do it. So Stella saved me and brought me to you. I just wanted to see you. She's nicer than I thought she was," he rambled.

I tensed and didn't hug him back.

"Fuck, I missed you. I've been living in this personal hell for days now. All I can think about is you. You're so mad at me. I know you are, but I meant it when I said I'd prove myself to you. I'm a good choice, Bianca. I promise I am."

"Fallon, you need to leave," I whispered, pushing him away.

His face fell, revealing his worry and fear. "You hate me."

"I-I don't," I said softly, untangling myself from him. "I'm just really upset with you. You were going to just hand me over to Dominic's dad and hope someone rescued me. Were you planning on running away on your own or something if someone else saved me?"

His Adam's apple bobbed as he stared at me. "I would've come back."

"Really?"

He blinked several times, and I sighed. He was way too messed up to be having this conversation with me right now.

"You need to go back to your room and sober up. Why were you doing coke?"

"Hail said I could fuck Stella if I did it with him." Fallon reached for me, but I pulled away in disgust.

That bitch...

"Not like that, baby. I wasn't going to fuck her, and she wasn't going to fuck me. She was trying to help me get away. So we pretended so I could come see you. Hail wanted me to stay so he and I could fuck these two chicks at the party. But that's not my scene. I mean, I want to be with you with the kings, so that's different. I'd make love to you while you sucked De Santis's dick or whatever you wanted to do. I only said I wanted Stella so I could get to you."

I wrinkled my nose. God, he was so high he couldn't even stand up. He leaned heavily against Dominic's dresser, sweat dotting his forehead.

"I'd do anything for you, Bianca," he said, shoving off the dresser and approaching me again after a moment of silence. "I'm risking my life right now for you."

"Well, don't," I said, staring up at him. "Go back to your room and rest. Please."

"Do you love me?" he whispered. "Please tell me. I need to hear it."

"I'm just really angry at you guys right now."

He nodded, his eyes so glassy I could see my reflection in them. "I understand. Just trust in me, OK? If I fail, I'll take my punishment from the kings, from the lords, without begging. I just want *you*. I love you, Bianca. I don't want to *not* be with you. It's driving me insane. I want to hold you right now and know I can't. I'm so sorry." He sank to his knees in front of me, sniffling softly. "I want to be a king so you can be my girl. So I can worship my queen."

"Fallon," I said gently when he reached for me. I didn't back away. I let him grasp my waist and rest his head against my stomach.

He pressed his warm lips to the sliver of skin which was exposed between my tank top and pajama shorts.

"Is Dominic being good to you, baby?"

"He's driving me nuts," I whispered, raking my fingers through his hair. "But he's not terrible. H-he's good to me. Really good, actually."

"Good. I've been so worried. So fucking jealous that he gets to love you while I can only watch from afar. Are Vincent and Levin being nice to my girl?"

I licked my lips. "Vincent is. He always is. He's just so… Vinny. Levin and I… we aren't talking right now."

"He's a dick. He's the one who beat my ass in the fucking basement. Thought he was going to kill me."

I clenched my teeth. Of course, Levin was the one who'd beaten him to near death. It sounded exactly what the giant prick would do.

"He doesn't hurt you, does he? I'll fucking kill him if he does."

"Not like that," I said, my heart hurting over what had happened between us earlier in the day.

I knew it was over with him. I'd seen the look on his face. Levin Seeley had shut down on me. He'd checked out just like I had. I'd been a bitch to him. He was right. I was jealous, but I was also prideful and refused to admit it. He'd let me live. But he'd also said some nasty things to me at the dance and had shot at me and Fallon.

Of course, I supposed I could see why, given what Fallon had been planning to do. I groaned inwardly. This was a disaster. I didn't know where to direct my frustration anymore.

"I'd kill them for you if you asked me to," Fallon mumbled. "But then we'd still have Hail to deal with. The kings love you. I saw it written all over them."

I knew they loved me. At least, Vincent and Dominic did. I couldn't bear the thought of losing them though whenever I thought about it. It didn't make me less pissed. And with Levin shutting down, I was hurting. Everything was so messed up and confusing. I just wanted to sleep. Sleep it all away and wake up when things were better.

But I knew the life I was in. Nothing would ever be better. Maybe this was as good as it got, and I'd have to learn to adjust to my new life. Maybe I needed to let go and let the chips fall where they may.

"I want to make you feel good," Fallon slurred. "Does Dominic make you feel good?"

I swallowed. "Yes."

When I let him.

"Fuck, I want to. I'm really fucked up right now though, baby."

"It's OK," I said, tilting his chin up so he was looking at me. "I don't want Dominic to catch you here, so I think you should go."

"But I miss you."

"I know, but you have a lot to do before we can even think about anything happening between us."

"You're really upset with me. I'm sorry. What can I do to prove to you?"

"You can start by going home and resting. Then tomorrow, just do whatever Dominic tells you to do."

He nodded, peering up at me. "I can do that."

I let out a breath of relief as he climbed to his feet. He swayed as he stared down at me.

"Can I kiss you before I go?"

I licked my lips, wanting to kiss him, but not like this. Not when he was so messed up. Not when I was still so angry with him. In fact, I wasn't so sure I should let him leave without an escort. Stella seemed to have wandered off, which pissed me off. I'd let that bitch hear about it tomorrow when I saw her. The alternative was her being here and going home with him. I knew how she was and how it would probably play out with a stoned Fallon. The thought disgusted me.

"We shouldn't," I said gently, cradling his face.

"Right. You're married." He crinkled his brows. "I hate that. You should be married to me. I would've taken you away and we could've gotten married. That was my end game. Guess De Santis is a better player, huh?"

I gave him a weak smile.

"Would you have said yes if I'd asked?"

"I-I think I would've," I answered honestly. "But in time. I'd have wanted time."

He beamed at me, the worry melting from his handsome face. "That would've made me happy, and I'd have waited for you."

My heart jumped in my chest at his words. *It would've made me happy too.* But then I wouldn't have my overbearing, possessive, jealous husband. I scoffed, hating that I knew I'd miss the asshole but secretly loving that Dominic wanted me.

I glanced at the clock. "You need to go. Dominic can't come home and find you here."

"I'll go but promise you won't forget about me?"

"I swear it," I said, still cradling his face. "Just please go rest, and don't do this again. I can't risk losing you. It hurt too much last time. Plus, you still need to make everything up to me."

He nodded tiredly. "I'll make it up. Promise." He gave my hands a squeeze before he stumbled to the door.

I moved around him and pulled it open so he didn't tumble into the hall. I peeked quickly into the corridor, letting the door open wider then allowing him to step out.

"I love you, princess."

"I love you too, Fallon," I said softly.

He gave me a smile that lit up my heart, even if it was colored by his drunken and stoned stupor.

He didn't say another word as he turned and staggered down the hall. I watched him go, my heart in my throat.

I hoped Dominic ended this soon. I wanted my life back, and that life included *all* my guys, even the drunk, stoned one and the angry, stubborn one.

Of course, a lot of that rested on me, and I just didn't see Levin coming back to me. Not after the shit I'd said to him.

And for that, I ached.

TWENTY-SIX
DOMINIC

"What's the plan?" Levin asked tightly as he strapped a nine to his side and stuffed a knife into his boot.

I twirled two blades in my hands before shoving them in the sheaths by my sides while Vincent loaded a magazine. We'd gone to my safe house to gear up. Leaving Bianca behind wore heavily on me. All I wanted to do was get back to her as fast as I could because I knew her. Threatening Aubrey had been a last-ditch effort to get my queen to stay in line while we went to deal with my father.

I figured since Fallon was still on campus, I'd test him. See if he'd come to her rescue if the lords decided to beat down my door. I also had Stella watching. Everything was a test for those two. The court, our ass-kissers on campus, had their ears to the ground, which offered me some reassurance Bianca would be safe for the evening.

"We go in. I inform my father Bianca is my wife. We hope he doesn't kill us in his rage," I grunted, shoving a Glock into the back of my waistband and a forty-five onto my hip. I straightened my black, wool jacket and cracked my neck.

This wouldn't be a good night. No visit to my father ever was, no matter the purpose. And tonight? I had to tell him I married into the enemy's family. It was the whole reason Vincent and Levin were going with me. If shit went down, we'd have to shoot our way out.

I already had the text message to Fallon typed out and ready to send.

If you're getting this, I'm dead or nearly dead. Take Bianca and run...

I'd added a list of instructions as well as the locations of my safe houses. No one knew where they were except me and my kings.

Would my father kill his only heir? Unlikely.

Was it out of the realm of possibility? Never.

He was insane, and what mood he was in would determine his next steps...and mine. If I could get him on board with this, then Bianca and I would be sitting really fucking pretty, at least for a bit until Daddy-dearest made his move.

"Did you tell Bianca you love her before you left?" Vincent asked, straightening his jacket. "Because I didn't get to."

"Yes," I said, remembering the look in her eyes.

She was worried, but my queen wouldn't say it. Instead, she'd straightened her shoulders and had given me a hug when I'd pulled her into my arms. I hadn't waited for her to say it back, but then I might not have left. So, I'd simply let her go and strode out the door. In retrospect, maybe I should've kissed her or made love to her, but she wasn't exactly in the mood for either. So I did what I did best—I went to work.

"How about you?" Vincent said to Levin, who was glaring at a spot on the wall.

"Didn't. Won't. I'm done."

"What?" Vincent crinkled his brows as he gaped at him. "Since when?"

"Since she told me to fuck off," he snapped. "I'm not waiting around for any fucking woman to get her shit together. I'm out."

"Is that why you called me to come watch her? You two had a fight?" Vincent's full attention was now on Levin.

I frowned. Levin had been quieter and more withdrawn lately. I hadn't asked why. I assumed it was a Bianca issue, but I didn't feel like pushing a dead subject around. We were all fucked when it came to her.

"Yeah. Doesn't matter. I'm going out with Celeste next Friday anyway."

"What?" Vincent and I asked in unison.

It was news to me. We'd been trying to get in bed with the Vander Veers for ages. Celeste had always had a boyfriend and never paid two shits to us. I'd heard her Ivy League toy had dumped her recently.

Levin clicked his tongue. "Yeah. I was talking to her after Vincent left today. She gave me her number. Since Bianca isn't interested, I figured I may as well get this shit over with."

"Are you fucking insane? You're done with B just because she's pissed off?" Vincent frowned.

"I'm done with Bianca because she told me she was done with me. Not a fucking hint of it. She said she didn't want me, and we'd never happen. I feel really fucking confident that means it's over before it started." Levin glared at Vincent, who shook his head in disbelief.

"She's Dom's problem now. I never wanted her to start with. I honestly don't give a shit anymore. I just want to get this over with so Dom can cut her ass loose, and we can go back to how shit was before she came along," his voice shook.

I sighed, my irritation with him rising. "Wasp is pissed at all of us right now. While I like the idea of you getting in with the Vander Veers, I'm also concerned about how it'll affect our relationship with Bianca—" I started, trying not to completely launch myself at him.

"There is no *relationship*," Levin snarled back. "There's a sham of a fucking marriage and her hating all of us. She's even pissed at that cunt Vasiliev. I've got too much shit going on in my life to deal with her too. I said I was done, and I meant it. She and I are *not* happening. I was stupid to even consider it." He turned away from me quickly, his Adam's apple bobbing. "I should've just fucking shot her in the head and been done with it."

I leapt forward and punched him in the face before wrapping my hand around his throat and shoving him against the wall. He stared me down, a trickle of blood dripping from his nose.

"You want out? Fine. More for me. I don't share well anyway. But don't ever fucking say shit like that about my wife ever again. Got it?"

He swallowed and nodded sharply at me. I knew he was hurting from whatever had gone down between them. But friend or not, I wasn't going to let anyone talk about my queen like that.

"If she were just a piece of ass to me, I wouldn't have married her and risked my own life or your lives for her. She's more than that. Either act the fuck like she is or get out of my sight," I hissed at him. "Now, I'll ask you again. Are you sure you're done?"

He stared at me, his blue eyes wavering. "I-I'm done."

Fucking liar.

"Fine. Then I want you balls deep in Celeste by the end of next week. Free men get to fuck new pussy. Congratulations. You just won." I released him and backed away.

"You're a fucking idiot," Vincent said to him, shaking his head sadly. "Hope you enjoy Celeste."

Levin wiped his nose before stomping past us to the car.

"What do we do?" Vincent asked once Levin was gone.

I grabbed another magazine out of the cupboard and stuffed it into my jacket. "We do what we always do. We take care of our own, especially when they can't take care of themselves."

"What if B and Levin never get along?"

"Then you and I are going to have to step up our game for her," I said, sending a silent prayer to the devil that shit would turn around. If it didn't, I feared for our future, especially hers.

"IS THE GIRL DEAD?" Father leveled his gaze on me as I sat across from him with Levin and Vincent standing behind me. Father lifted a cigar from the box on his desk as he awaited my answer.

I cleared my throat. "No."

"No?" He raised his dark brows at me, resting his elbows on the top of the polished mahogany. "Is she with you?"

"She is not. There's been a change in plans."

He dropped the cigar and steepled his fingers as he stared me down. "Enlighten me."

"In the spirit of fucking over the Bratva and pissing off D'Angelou, I opted for another route." I locked gazes with my father, taking in the controlled expression on his face. I knew the wrong answer would set him flying into a fit of rage. I felt the tension in Levin and Vincent behind me, ready to go out shooting if it came down to it.

"I married her."

The silence in the room was palpable as my father studied me. I stared back at him, refusing to allow him to intimidate me.

Finally, he let out a boom of laughter. "You *married* her?"

"I did," I said firmly, my voice strong.

He chortled again, his whole body shaking. When he finally seemed to calm down, he picked up his cigar and lit it. Casually, he sank back in his leather chair.

"Tell me, Domenico, are you in love with the girl?"

I knew better than admit to a weakness, so I answered in a strong voice, "I do not love her. She's a key which could prove fruitful. A potential bargaining chip. I see no reason why I'd throw her away when I could use her."

Father took a puff of his cigar and blew out the smoke, letting it circle his head like a tarnished halo. "You've taken me by surprise, boy. I thought you'd bring me her tits on a platter, but instead, you *bring me a key*. Clever. I hadn't considered it." He grew quiet for a moment before speaking again, "Did the girl fight you on the marriage?"

"She slapped me in the face and tried to escape."

He grinned, only wicked humor in the gesture. "I do love when they fight. Have you fucked her?"

The guys shifted behind me as I leaned forward, willing to play whatever the fuck game he wanted to play. "Yes. I painted her sheets red with her virginity."

His grin widened. "You're a wicked boy, Domenico. But I suppose maybe you are a man now. Your mother would hate your blackened soul. You're too much like me. Tell me, was she worth the slap to the face?"

I knew what he was doing. Testing me. Trying to find a chink in my armor. I steeled myself. "No woman slaps me and gets away with it. She was punished accordingly."

Father eased forward. "If she steps out of line, a night at your new palace could make her appreciate what she has with you."

I nodded tightly. "It would, but I prefer being able to dole out punishment to my wife on my own. I find it... *satisfying*."

"I like that." He wagged his cigar-laden finger at me. "Beat her. Train her to stay in line. Make her a better woman than your mother was. And if you can't, we can always be more creative with her punishments. So now, tell me your plan."

"I intend to break the news to D'Angelou. I assume we'll go to war for real now. Either because he's pissed I took her or pissed I've ruined his plans with the Ivanovs. Either way, there'll be blood in the streets, or they'll lie down like dogs at our feet. We'll rule as we're meant to."

Father grew contemplative for a moment before he pushed his box of cigars at me. I took one and lit it, inhaling the sweet taste.

"Then I suppose I should meet your queen, shouldn't I?"

I blew out smoke, remaining as calm as I could. The last fucking thing I wanted was him meeting Bianca. "Just say when."

He gave me a sinister smirk. "How about we do it at your wedding reception? We'll make an official announcement of your nuptials. It won't take long for word to reach the Ivanovs and D'Angelou."

"I'll make the arrangements." I puffed the cigar to mask my rage.

He relaxed in his seat again, a tiny smirk on his face which made chills race over my skin. "It's tradition in our family to allow the father to *sample* the bride. We do it before the marriage, but since this is a little out of order, I'll forgive the delay. Bring her to me before the reception so that I may have a taste."

I ground my teeth, knowing this was all part of the test. I rose to my feet, needing air before I completely lost it on him and shot him between the fucking eyes.

"Regardless of traditions, she's already my wife. I make the decisions on who samples her."

"Ah, protective, are we?" He let out a soft laugh and stood as I backed toward the door, Levin and Vincent moving with me.

They'd been quiet like they tended to be around my father.

Father approached me and clapped me on the shoulder.

"Congratulations," he said before leaning in and speaking into my ear, "But I sample the bride, or I kill her. That plan is still good as far as I'm concerned. I'd hate to make my son a widower so soon. If I kill her, I'll still fuck her. Understand that I *will* take what I want, Son." He stepped away from me, leaving me barely able to control my rage.

"Sir, what are we doing with the Vasiliev kid?" Levin asked, diverting the attention from me.

"Ah, yes. The littler traitor. Is he of any use?"

"Yes," I snarled. "I have a use for him."

"So be it. Make it worthwhile, or I'll make him suck your dick before I blow his head off. If I remember, you didn't much like all that blood on you." He went back to his seat and sat, giving me an even look. He wanted me to challenge him. Punishing me excited him.

"It'll be worthwhile." I drew in a deep breath before speaking again, "Natalia Vasiliev. I want her in my palace. I want her untouched. She's a bargaining chip in my plans. I need her safe, so when the time comes, I can unleash hell on her *and* her snake of a brother."

Father inclined his head. "Acceptable. The palace is your gem. Do as you see fit. We won't wait for long though. So make sure whatever plan you have in mind, you execute it sooner rather than later. The girl is rather tender. Tearing her apart appeals greatly to me." He peered past me to Levin. "I'm sure you'd love to watch your father fuck her ass until she bleeds. For Stefan."

I didn't need to look at Levin to know he was coiled and ready to pounce.

"The girl remains safe," I cut in.

"You have my word. For now. We're done here. Go." He swiveled his chair toward the window, dismissing me.

I marched from the room, my guys at my back.

Shit hadn't gone to plan, but at least Bianca would live. For now. But not without a little suffering first.

TWENTY-SEVEN
VINCENT

I followed Dom to his car and climbed into the passenger seat while Levin got in the back. Dom was eerily quiet the entire walk back to the car. Knowing he was pissed off, I kept my mouth shut. The thought of his father touching my baby B made me sick to my stomach. It took everything in me not to jump across his desk and beat the shit out of his psycho ass.

And if I'd nearly lost it, I couldn't imagine how close Dom was.

We left the estate, none of us speaking. I caught Levin's eye in the rearview mirror. His gaze was hard as he stared back at me.

He was pissed too, but he'd never admit it.

We drove for several miles in silence before Dom pulled off the road and slammed the car into park. He pounded his fists against the steering wheel, shaking the car in his fury as he cursed in Italian, his body trembling and his black hair a wild mess.

"Fuck. Fuck. Fuck!" he snarled.

Levin and I remained quiet as he continued his assault on the helpless steering wheel. Finally, he stopped and tugged his phone out. He hit call on a number and pressed the phone to his ear.

"Wasp, are you well?" he asked in a thick voice.

I heard her faint voice come through the line but couldn't make out what she was saying.

"That's fine," he said, raking his fingers through his hair, appearing to calm down.

I could still see the tension in his body. His shoulders were drawn up, and his hands trembled.

"I'll be home soon. We need to talk." He listened for a moment before blowing out a breath and casting a quick look at Levin in the rearview mirror. "Yes…It's important….He'll be there."

I heard her rattle something off again, and Dom let out a soft chuckle.

"You know I won't allow that. Wear the nightgown I placed on the nightstand for you. I'll see you soon." He hung up and let his head fall back against the headrest. He puffed out a breath.

"What are we going to do?" I ventured carefully, not interested in having to call a tow truck to drive us back to Bolten because he tore the car apart in a fit of rage.

"What we must," he answered in monotone, shifting the car into drive.

Knowing it was far better to keep my mouth shut, I did so, wondering what the hell the mob prince had up his tailored, designer sleeve.

B WAS SITTING on the edge of the bed when we arrived at Dom's room. The moment we stepped inside, she rose, her blue eyes sparkling in the light cast by the bedside lamp. Dom stalked toward her and hauled her against him. He murmured something in her ear I couldn't hear. She remained tense against him and didn't return his hug, but she didn't pull away either.

I peeked at Levin. His jaw clenched as he watched Dom's hands tighten on B's tiny waist. The red, silk gown he'd insisted she wear rode up to display the bottom of her ass in a delicious way. I had to bite back a groan. I was certain Dom knew what game he was playing with

Levin. Dom might be the jealous, possessive asshole, but he'd set those feelings aside for me and Levin, even if it were a struggle for him. He wanted us to be with B but on his terms, and Levin was throwing a man-size wrench into the plans.

"Sit," Dom instructed, nodding back to the bed.

Instead of telling him to eat shit like I expected, B sank to the mattress and slid to the center of it, her blue eyes roving from Dom, who stood beside the bed, to me. They flicked quickly to Levin, her mouth pursing, before she cleared her throat and focused on Dom.

"What's going on? Did you tell your father?"

"I did." He strode to the small bar in his room and poured himself a whiskey.

"And?"

"And he accepted it."

"Why does that sound like a bad thing?" She glanced at me again.

"Because it is," I said, sighing and moving to sit on the edge of the bed as Levin leaned against Dom's dresser, his eyes fixed on a point over B's head. "He's requiring something completely fucked and disgusting."

B wet her lips. "What is it?"

Dom slammed back his drink and focused his green eyes on her. "You."

"*Me?*"

"Yes. He wants to fuck with you," Dom continued, barely suppressed rage rolling off him. "Or fuck you. Either way, my answer is no." His hands shook as he poured another glass of whiskey.

B's gaze moved to me. "I don't understand."

"Matteo is sick," I said gently. "He's trying to break Dom, to test him. He needs Dom to have a weakness. It's hard to control someone if they don't. Matteo likes to exploit things which can cause someone pain. And in Dom's case, that might be you since Dom chose to marry you rather than kill you."

"I thought you were going to tell him the truth?" B demanded, leaning forward. "That I didn't want to fucking marry you. That you forced me to!"

Dom finished his drink and poured a third. "I did. And I told him I don't give a fuck about you. It didn't stop him from demanding to get between your legs to fucking *taste* you," he spat out as if the words left a terrible taste in his mouth. He stared down at the glass in his hands for a moment. "He knew I was lying. Despite forcing you into this, I *do* give a shit. He had to have sensed it."

B shot to her feet, her hands curling into fists. "I don't want this. I don't want any of it! I didn't want to come to you in the beginning and beg for help. I didn't want to be on my knees in the woods with a gun pointed to my head. And I certainly didn't want to be married to you! Now look! You didn't have to take things this far. You could've let me leave or just fucking killed me a long time ago when I first arrived at Bolten. Isn't that what you said? You said you'd kill me to save me?" Her chest heaved as she glared at him.

I chanced a look at Levin, who was staring at her, a hard glint in his eyes.

When Dom didn't say anything, she moved to Levin and stood in front of him.

"Do it," she hissed at him. "You wanted me dead. *So fucking do it.*"

He glared down at her, not moving a muscle. She snarled and grabbed the nine tucked in his waistband and shoved it into his hand. With a sob, she fell to her knees in front of him.

"Kill me. You want me out of your life so bad, then fucking do it. Here's your chance. You know what hell awaits me if Dom's dad gets me."

My heart thudded hard as Levin raised the gun and pressed the barrel to her forehead. I scrambled to my feet, panic alive and well within me. I gaped at Dom, who watched the scene silent as midnight.

"You'd be doing us both a favor," she choked out, her small body trembling as Levin scowled at her. "Please, Levin. Do it."

Levin's hand shook for a moment before he let his arm drop. "I'm not in the business of doing you any fucking favors," he said in a quaking voice. "You wanna fucking die? Then kill yourself. Don't look to me for help."

She crumpled into herself, her shoulders sagging forward as she wept softly.

I started to step forward, but Dom shoved past me and scooped her into his arms, carrying her to the bed. He cradled her in his arms, whispering to her in Italian as he comforted her.

Seeing Dom give a shit like that was intense to watch. I knew him well enough to know he'd *never* been with a woman like he was with B. Hell, if anyone else had been on their knees begging for death, Dom would've taken the gun and shot them himself. Not with B though.

"I know you don't want this, but I'm what you have. Getting on your knees and begging for death won't fix anything," he murmured as he raked his fingers through her blonde waves. "We'll figure this out. I won't let him touch you. I fucking swear to you I won't let him harm you, *mia regina*."

She sniffled and buried her head in his chest, her fingers twisted in the fabric of his shirt.

"Vincent," he called out, not looking to me.

"Yeah?"

"There's a bottle of pills in my medicine cabinet. Bring them to me."

I hesitated a moment before going into the bathroom and grabbing the bottle out of his cabinet, hating the idea of him drugging B but knowing better than to say shit about it when he was clearly teetering on the edge of completely losing his shit.

"Here." I grabbed a bottle of water as I stepped in front of Dom.

He held his hand out as I unscrewed the bottle and sprinkled a pill onto his palm.

"Open," he commanded softly to B.

Her face was soaked with tears as she parted her lips for him. He placed the small pill on her tongue, and I tipped the water bottle against her lips. She swallowed the medicine down without question and rested her head against Dom's chest again.

The room was silent. If I didn't know Levin was still standing by the dresser I would've thought he'd left.

Within minutes, Dom was shifting B from his lap onto the pillows.

She was completely out.

I watched as he gently adjusted her on the bed before he covered her. He stared down at her for a moment before he rose and marched to Levin. Dom snatched the gun from Levin's limp fingers and pressed it beneath Levin's jaw. He didn't flinch as they stared one another down.

"You're really pissing me off today," Dom snarled at him.

Levin said nothing as he swallowed.

I stared between them before glancing back at B to make sure she was still OK. She remained sleeping, her long, dark lashes resting on her cheeks. I swiveled my attention back to Levin and Dom.

"You ever do anything more than fucking smile at her, and I'll shoot you," Dom continued in a dangerous voice. "Get your shit together. We're all fucking hurting here. Don't make it worse by dying over it." Dom pulled the gun away and slammed it against Levin's chest. "Get the fuck out of here and have a better attitude tomorrow."

Dom stepped away from Levin and went back to B's side.

"I need to meet with Stella. Vincent, stay with Bianca while I'm gone."

"Sure," I said.

He leaned down and pressed a kiss to her forehead. "Call me if you need anything."

Levin hadn't moved an inch. He simply stood there staring at B in bed.

"Levin. Out," Dom snapped, straightening and moving toward the door. He jerked it open.

Levin pushed off the dresser and left without a backward glance.

"Talk to him, man," I said softly. "You're right. We're all hurting here."

Dom sighed and shut the door without another word, leaving me alone with B. I let out my own sigh, took my jacket off, and placed it on the chair before crawling in bed beside B.

I pushed a strand of her hair away from her face before whispering, "I love you to pieces, baby B. Don't worry. We'll figure this out. I swear it, or I'll kill everyone my damn self."

And I would. Without. A. Fucking. Doubt. I would.

TWENTY-EIGHT
BIANCA

A week later, life had pretty much returned to normal. I was still sullen toward the kings. I was worried too because I had no idea what was going on with Dominic's dad. Dom had gone radio silent on the subject. With the upcoming celebration upon us, I was getting sick to my stomach. Last night, I had a panic attack, and Dominic had given me something which had knocked me out. It had to be the same thing as before because now I woke with the same hangover headache.

Dominic's arm tightened around my waist, where he was cuddled against my back. I'd all but given up on having my own space. Dominic didn't allow me to stray far from him. Vincent was always just a step away as well, offering me his calming smile and reassuring looks. Levin kept his distance on all accounts. I'd only seen him once since the night Dominic had come home from his father's to tell me about his dad being a sick fuck. Thankfully, Levin had been alone when I'd glimpsed him, but I'd heard the rumors of him and Celeste floating around. He spent most of his time with her. No official *dating* status had been proclaimed yet, and Dominic and Vincent didn't speak about it at all to me.

"How do you feel?" Dominic's deep voice greeted me as I rolled over beside him. I squeezed my eyelids closed and groaned. I hated waking up to the same feeling every day. "Like I could go back to sleep."

He let out a soft huff of laughter and hauled me closer to his large, warm body. "I wish we could. Unfortunately, wife, we must keep up appearances."

We'd been getting along better because I'd stopped fighting him as much on things. I was learning that picking my battles was important. I still hadn't given in and had sex with him again though, which had been a challenge on a few occasions because Dominic really was a force to be reckoned with.

I stiffened as he leaned in to press his lips to mine. He caught me by the chin before I could pull away too far.

"Stop," he growled, squeezing my face. "I want to taste you, wasp."

"Dominic—" I let out a gasp of surprise when he released me and pushed me onto my back so he could level his hard body over mine.

His shirt was off, displaying planes of muscle and smooth skin.

"Why do you punish me so?" he murmured as he stared down at me, his weight supported on his elbows.

"Because you punished me first." I locked gazes with him, butterflies flapping wildly in my chest.

"Mm, wasp, I haven't even begun to punish you." He ran his lips along my jaw.

I tensed beneath him, my breath held. This was one of those moments I knew if he persisted, I'd cave in.

"Please stop fighting me and let go." He nipped at the sensitive skin of my neck. "Let me love my wife how I want to love her."

I swallowed, my breath whooshing out softly.

"Let me bury myself deep inside your heat so I can hear you scream my name." He ground his hard length against my aching pussy as I trembled with desire beneath him.

"I need my birth control refilled," I managed to choke out as he captured my face with his hand.

"You really don't," he said softly, forcing me to keep looking at him.

"I didn't want to get married let alone have a baby."

A soft chuckle escaped his lips as he released my face and pushed my panties aside. My breath hitched when the warmth from his dick slid through my folds and threatened my entrance.

"You'll learn soon enough that in this life, we don't always get a choice."

Before he could take things further, a knock sounded against his door. He let out an angry snarl.

"Case in point." He hefted off me.

I scrambled to haul the blankets up to my chin. I was moments from giving into anything he wanted, that old anger be damned.

He yanked his pants on and went to the door, jerking it open.

"What the fuck are you doing here?" he demanded.

"I need to talk to you," Fallon said in a rush. "You didn't answer my calls. What choice did I fucking have?"

Dominic grabbed Fallon by his shirt and yanked him into the room. Fallon stumbled before righting himself quickly. His eyes found me immediately in bed, and he took a step forward. Dominic was fast to intercept him and stood in front of him.

"What the hell do you need?" Dominic snapped. "Don't fucking look at her. Look at me."

"No offense, but she's way better to look at," Fallon mumbled, peeking back at me.

"What did I tell you about coming to see me? I recall telling you I'd shoot you in the fucking face if you didn't listen."

"You were supposed to let me know what's going on with Natalia. I haven't heard about it. I had a rough night last night. The last thing I want to do is get bitched at, OK?"

Dominic leveled a glare on him and folded his arms across his chest. "Why was last night rough?"

"Because I was doing your bidding," Fallon shot back. "Do you have any idea what it's like trying to come up with creative ways to ask Hail questions? He's an inquisitive fuck and assumes every inquiry has a hidden motive. In this case, he's right."

"So did you get any information?" Dominic demanded.

"I did, so what about my sister?"

I watched the two of them face off, wondering what the hell Dominic had Fallon fishing for.

"Your sister is under my protection. I've seen to it myself and now she's separated from harm and is comfortable. I ensured she was."

"How do I know she's even alive?"

Dominic stepped to the bedside table and scooped his phone up, pulling up something on the screen and shoving it in Fallon's face.

"See? This was taken two nights ago. She's literally watching TV on a ten-thousand-dollar sofa. She's fine."

Fallon nodded, seemingly accepting what Dominic showed him.

"Now. My information?" Dominic asked.

"Levin's father met with Hail's two days before Stefan was killed. Hail said he didn't know the details though. I tried to encourage him to find out so we can use it against old man Seeley."

Dominic nodded and placed his phone back on the bedside table. It took him a moment to speak again. "OK. It's not just for Levin at this point. *I* want to know why the hell his old man was meeting with the enemy."

"If I had to guess, I'd say he's not exactly loyal to your father."

Tension corded through Dominic's bare back as he shifted, blocking my view of Fallon.

"Anything on Nathan Walker?" Dominic continued, his voice low.

I leaned forward at the mention of my father's name. I had no idea Dominic was still looking into it for me. He hadn't mentioned it to me, and I hadn't pushed, deciding I'd just do the sleuthing on my own somehow.

"I didn't get that far in my questioning. I felt like it might make him more suspicious if I kept poking around. There's a party tomorrow at the dip. I'll try to see what I can get out of him then. He talks more when he's hammered."

"Come straight to me when you get the info. Got it?"

"Yes," Fallon said tightly.

Dominic grew quiet for a moment before he called out to me.

"Bianca, come here."

Nervously, I rose to my feet and approached, clad in the too-short, red silk gown he'd wanted me to wear again. Fallon's gaze immediately dipped to me, his pupils dilating. I swallowed and stood beside Dominic. His arm snaked around my waist, and he shifted me between them.

"Do you like looking at my wife?" Dominic asked, his hand sliding up the side of my thigh, making me draw in a shaky breath.

I had no idea what he was up to.

Fallon swallowed. "I came here to ask about my sister and to deliver what I knew."

Dominic let out a soft, sinister laugh which sent goosebumps racing across my skin. "Then why were you trying to look at what belongs to me when you came in?"

"Because she's beautiful, and I love her," Fallon answered in a thick voice. His words made my heart jolt. "I'm doing what you asked, De Santis. I'm not here to fuck you over. I'm here for her. I want to be a king."

"Do you hear that, *mia regina*? Fallon wants to be a king. What do you think?" Dominic skimmed his lips along my jaw.

"Why do you want to be a king?" I asked as I tried to stay focused.

Dominic kissed my collarbone, making focus really damn hard.

"Aside from you?" Fallon asked, his eyes drinking me in. "I'm not some fucked in the head piece of shit. I actually have a conscience. Don't let this go to your head, De Santis, but I've always seen the kings as fairer and more on the straight and narrow than the lords. I was just shoved into their group because of my father. Had I gotten to choose, I wouldn't have picked the lords. I fucking hate them."

Dominic let out his signature soft laugh. "That a fact? You're sure it has nothing to do with our queen? Because you could've come to me long ago and tried to join up. Yet you didn't. You see where I'm coming from?"

"Status quo," Fallon said evenly. "My plan was to break free and get the fuck out as soon as I graduated. I would've gone underground to never be found again if Bianca hadn't come into my life and shit didn't get fucked the way it did. Yes, it's true. She's a motivating factor, but if

I can't escape this life, then I at least want to live it on my own terms. I feel like the kings would gift me that option if I'm loyal."

Dominic was quiet as his hand lingered on my waist. Finally, he spoke. "Do you want more motivation to get things done?"

Fallon said nothing, his gaze darting between me and Dominic.

"Because if you need more motivation to hurry things along, I can offer it to you," Dominic continued, gently easing the thin, silk strap of my nightgown down my arm. He moved to the other side and slid that strap aside. The gown whispered down my body, pooling around my feet and leaving me in nothing but the red, lace panties he'd gotten me.

Fallon swallowed, his Adam's apple bobbing as he took me in. I stood still as stone, not sure where Dominic was taking this, but unabashedly interested in the journey.

"Here's the thing," Dominic said. "My wife is very upset with me. She thinks I'm a bad man who wanted to hurt her. She's been struggling with her anger at the kings ever since she woke up. Things did get better when we told her we didn't kill you, so that means she probably doesn't hate you as much as she says she does."

Fallon listened, not moving a muscle, his gaze continuing to volley from Dominic to me like he was doing all he could to keep from launching himself on me.

"I'd really like her to stop hating me, and the kings as well, so how about a small offering to help all of us out?"

"I'm listening," Fallon said in a throaty voice.

I remained quiet, my heart in my throat.

"What would you like from her—and me— that you think will motivate you?"

"I-I'd like your permission to kiss her," Fallon said softly, his eyes completely on me.

Heat rose in my body until it settled low in my belly.

"*Mia regina*, would you like that? Would it make you happy if I let him kiss you?" Dominic whispered in my ear.

I swallowed, my head spinning. *Was I ready to get over this and try to live a decent life? Could I forgive just a little? Did I want to kiss Fallon?*

The answer came easily. *Yes.* I wanted all of it and then some. I was getting tired of feeling so shitty all the time. Truth be told, I was even missing Levin, although a kiss probably wouldn't sort out our issues.

I could still be upset with them all, but I didn't have to be miserable about it. Life was going to get a hell of a lot harder before it got better. This I knew. It would be easier to get through it as a team than with me hating the four guys who were just doing what they thought they had to do. Holding onto my anger wasn't doing me any good.

"Y-yes," I said, my voice shaking.

"Would it... make you love me again?" Dominic's question was so soft I was sure Fallon couldn't hear it.

"I already love you," I answered back just as quietly, the words making my heart race.

He let out a soft grunt before he swept my long, blonde waves around from the front of my body and tangled his fingers in them behind my back.

"Make my wife happy with a kiss. If you get me more information, I'll share more of her. Deal?"

"Yes," Fallon said.

The way Fallon looked at me made the heat boil in my body.

"For you, wasp," Dominic murmured, turning me so he could kiss me first.

I didn't fight him. I parted my lips for him, letting him kiss me hard and deep, turning the boiling heat into sweeping flame. He broke our kiss off just as quickly and stepped away from me, his green eyes filled with an emotion I'd never seen on him before.

Is that... worry?

I didn't get to contemplate it because Fallon turned me around and cradled my face.

"I've missed you, princess," he said before his lips met mine in a soft, delicious kiss.

The flame Dominic built within me burst through, a wildfire engulfing me as Fallon deepened the kiss, his hands cradling me against his body. His erection pressed against my belly as he devoured me.

I fell into the kiss, knowing damn well Dominic was watching us. The idea turned me on, and I raked my fingers through Fallon's hair, earning a soft groan from him. Fallon's mouth moved to my neck where he sucked the sensitive flesh. I gasped and wiggled against him, forgetting his betrayal for just a moment so I could feel him again like I used to. He cupped my ass, squeezing. His warm breath on my skin made me pant. I hadn't had an orgasm since Dominic had pushed himself into me back at the safe house.

I was desperate for one.

Fallon's lips shifted back to mine, his kiss turning frantic. In the past, this would've been the turning point where he'd hitch my legs around his waist and thrust into me, ending my torment.

Instead, Dominic's warm arms wound their way around me, and he eased me away amid mine and Fallon's protests.

"No," Fallon whispered hoarsely.

"Sorry. That was the bargain," Dominic said. "Of course, you're welcome to stay and watch me take care of my wife."

Fallon visibly swallowed but made no move to leave.

Dominic chuckled softly and pulled me back to his chair. After he pushed my panties off, he sat down, bringing me onto his lap. My back rested against his chest. He lifted my feet onto his thighs, baring me to Fallon, whose lips parted.

Dominic's hands moved between my legs, and he skimmed his fingers along my drenched pussy.

"Did he do this to you?" Dominic growled in my ear.

"Both of you," I managed to choke out as he swept his fingers up me again.

Dominic gave a grunt in my ear. "Tell him you like him watching while your husband fingers you."

"F-Fallon," I rasped.

He took a step forward.

"I-I like you watching Dominic finger me."

Fallon licked his lips, his body trembling.

"Ask him if he wants to do this to you." Dominic flicked his thumb over my aching clit, making me moan desperately.

"D-do you want to do this to me?"

"Yes," Fallon said immediately.

"Tell him to get me more information, and I'll let him join us next time. I'll fuck your tight, wet pussy while he sucks your sweet, little clit."

"Oh God," I groaned as Dominic drove his fingers deep into me, the wet squelching sound echoing in the room.

He was going to have me falling apart before I could get the words out.

"M-more information, Fallon," I whimpered. "G-get Dominic more information."

Fallon nodded, keeping his eyes locked on everything Dominic was doing to me.

"Fallon, tell her it's OK for her to come," Dominic said as he continued his brutal, delicious fucking, his thumb hitting my clit in perfect rhythm.

"Come, princess," Fallon said thickly. "Please, I want to see you come on his fingers. Do it for me. Let me hear you."

His words were my undoing as I clenched around Dominic's fingers and came so hard I saw stars. I cried out, my fingers digging into Dominic's forearms. I trembled as I came down from my high, noting the mess I'd made on Dominic's hands and pants.

"Good girl, wasp," Dominic purred in my ear. "My very good girl."

Fallon was breathing hard as I collapsed against Dominic's chest, my body too boneless and weak to do much else.

Dominic traced his fingers lightly across my bare breasts as he addressed Fallon. "You want this, then get me what I want," he said in his deep, commanding voice. "Bring me more information, and we'll move this forward. Start listening. Don't fucking come back until you have what I need. If you do, the deal's off. We stick to the plan. Got it?"

"Yes," Fallon said, our gazes locked on each other's. "I won't fuck this up."

"Good. Now get to work. I need to give my wife a bath."

Fallon backed away while Dominic began kissing along my neck, his hands cradling my breasts as he rolled my nipples between his index fingers and thumbs. My body was still overly sensitive. I whimpered as he nipped at the sensitive skin of my throat.

Fallon finally made it to the door and left, leaving Dominic and me alone in the room.

"You play a dangerous game," I said softly.

He let out a soft laugh. "It'll be beneficial for all of us."

"Did you mean it? You'll let him join?"

"I meant every word of it. You're my queen, Bianca. I want your happiness. I want your forgiveness. I want your love. I'd risk everything for those things. So if Vasiliev is what will help, then who I am to throw it away? He may be exactly what the kings need."

Dominic lifted me, and I wrapped my arms around his neck as he brought us to the bathroom. He really was going to bathe me.

Maybe Dominic *was* playing a dangerous game, but maybe the danger wasn't *to* us. Maybe the danger would be to everyone else once we were united the way I knew we should be. But we had a hell of a lot of work ahead of us.

I'd start with the bath.

TWENTY-NINE
BIANCA

"I hate economics class," Aubrey grumbled as we walked through the courtyard. "Is Anderson making your life miserable too? Tell me he is and I'm not just a dumb shit."

"B has a four-oh," Vincent said from beside me.

Aubrey groaned again.

"How did you know?" I asked, frowning at him.

"I know everything about you, baby B," he said easily, giving me a smile. "You didn't think we took you on without doing our research, did you?"

I sighed. That didn't surprise me.

"Well, you're lucky. I'm riding the struggle bus." Aubrey stopped with us at the vending machine.

I got an apple juice after Vincent slid some money in before I could. He shot me a wink.

"I can probably help you if you need it," I offered as Vincent snagged my juice from me and opened it before handing it back.

"No," she said. "Lance Larkin is in my hour. He's a super brain and super hot. Maybe I can get him to tutor me in my room."

"Suck his dick," Vincent said.

Aubrey laughed.

"Vinny," I said, rolling my eyes at him.

Aubrey was more at ease with Vincent than she was with Levin or Dominic. I knew Dominic scared the shit out of her, and Levin put her on edge because he was always pissed off. When Vincent was my guard, she laughed and chattered more.

"What?" Vincent grinned. "I'd do anything you wanted if you sucked my dick, B. You know that."

"I'll keep that in my arsenal for when I ask him," Aubrey said with a laugh before she bid us goodbye and went to sit with Emy.

We reached our table and plopped down. I looked around the courtyard and saw Fallon sitting with the lords. He was staring off into space as Blair, one of Stella's friends, talked to him. He nodded occasionally, but I knew he wasn't listening. His gaze caught mine. The impassive look on his face didn't change, but his stare did sweep over me before he turned away like I was just another girl.

I knew he was playing his part. My cheeks heated when I thought about him kissing me and then watching while Dominic got me off. Fallon's face turned back in my direction, and a tiny, knowing smirk cut his lips upward before he looked away again.

"Wasp," Dominic's deep voice greeted my ears.

He held his hand out to me. I took it, letting him pull me to my feet. He slid his tray onto the table as he sat. Once he was situated, he tugged me across his lap and turned my face to his for a kiss.

When I pressed my mouth to his, I earned a deep growl of approval from him. He nipped my bottom lip before he pulled away.

I leaned into him. He gave me a squeeze before he released me and handed me a fork for the salad he'd gotten me.

"Thank you," I said.

He said nothing. He just nodded to my salad as a way to tell me to eat. I dug in, listening as he engaged Vincent in conversation.

"How's the day going?"

"Nothing incredibly interesting happening," Vincent said. "Wish I liked salad like B does though."

"Why don't you get something to eat?" I asked after swallowing my lettuce.

"It's spaghetti day, and that shit isn't real spaghetti," Vincent muttered.

Dominic nodded in agreement. "I wouldn't feed that slop to Ivanov."

"Looks like you don't have to," I said.

Hail was chewing a forkful of his spaghetti lunch as he listened to Tate. I quickly looked away, hating those assholes.

"Trash consuming trash," Vincent muttered.

"Hey," Levin said, sliding into his seat.

I peeked up as Celeste stopped next to him.

Dominic tensed against me. Even Vincent looked confused. No one sat at the kings' table but me and them. Even Aubrey wasn't allowed to sit with us.

"Not eating?" Vincent asked as Celeste stood awkwardly beside Levin with her tray in her hands.

"Fucking spaghetti. Even my German ass knows that doesn't count as spaghetti." Levin paused and looked to Celeste. "You can sit."

She set her tray, containing a bowl of fruit and milk, down as she slid into the spot beside him. I chewed my bite of salad slowly then put my fork down, my appetite disappearing. Dominic picked my fork up and speared more lettuce onto it.

"Open," he commanded.

I let him feed me. Levin stared at us for a moment before he looked away. I waited for Dominic to say something to Celeste about sitting with us. When he didn't, I leaned into him and buried my face in his neck.

Vincent and Levin talked as Celeste poked at her fruit.

"Why is she sitting here?" I asked softly in Dominic's ear.

His hand slid up and down my back.

"Because the alternative is her sitting at her own table and taking Levin with her. The kings look weak if we don't remain together," he answered back in my ear, his lips skimming gently. "So play nice."

"Make me." I nipped at his earlobe.

He ran his fingers up my leg and beneath my skirt. "Gladly."

"Aren't you guys cute," Celeste broke in.

I pulled away from Dominic and glared at her as his hand stopped its dangerous trek.

"Who would've thought Dominic would ever fall for someone? It's all over school. Your marriage. Did you guys really get married?" Celeste continued, eyeing my ring.

"Yes," Dominic said before I could answer.

"It was a beautiful wedding. They got married at sunset," Vincent said, winking at me.

I sneered back at him which only made him grin wider.

"My boy, Levin, was his best man," Vincent continued.

"I wasn't. You were," Levin grunted, glancing at me before looking to Celeste. "Come here."

I tensed as he patted his thighs. She eagerly rose and climbed onto his lap.

That son of a bitch.

"I'm surprised Levin is going out with you," I spoke up, glaring at him.

Her eyes widened. "Why would you say that?"

"Because he was seeing someone else just before you."

She narrowed her eyes at me as Dominic leaned in and whispered, "Play nice."

"I wasn't with anyone," Levin snorted. "No one that mattered anyway."

I was on my feet, and before I could think it through, I pitched my salad at him. It covered him in bits of dressing, lettuce, and croutons. Some even hit Celeste. Not that I cared. In fact, I'd been aiming for her a bit too.

I knew he was mad at me, but that was a low blow. It made my heart hurt to hear I didn't matter. I may not matter to him now, but I at least thought he'd given a shit then. He had saved my life. He had lain with me in bed after and whispered all those things to me. I hadn't forgotten.

Maybe it was his anger and bitterness talking, but it didn't matter. It was messed up and cruel. It made my feelings for him retract further.

"What the fuck?" Levin snarled, shifting Celeste off his lap.

She let out a hiss of anger, her cheeks red. People stared at us. I'd made a scene after all. I caught Fallon watching. All the lords were craning around to get a look. *Great.*

"Yeah, what the fuck?" I snapped back at him. "You're such an asshole."

"For telling the truth? That's what you're mad about?" He let out a bitter laugh.

I quivered as I glared at him.

He sneered at me. "I thought we were all about being truthful."

"You're right. She *didn't* matter. I'll make sure she gets the message." I stepped away from the table as Dominic snagged my hand.

Vincent looked between Levin and me uneasily. A piece of lettuce fell off Levin's navy blazer as he glared back at me.

"Levy, are you going to let her get away with this?" Celeste whined, brushing lettuce off her arm. "Do something!"

"Yeah, Levy. Do something," I snarled at him.

"He will do *nothing*," Dominic said, getting to his feet. "Except clean this fucking mess up."

Dominic took me by the arm and hauled me away from our table. The moment we were away from everyone, he slammed me against a brick wall. I cried out as he grabbed my face and squeezed it.

"What the hell was that?" he demanded.

"He was being an asshole."

"And you were no better," he snapped back. "I'm getting tired of your temper tantrums, Bianca."

I swallowed as I stared up at him.

"It hurt," I whispered.

He released my face and let out a sigh before he ran his fingers through my hair. "I know. But you need to understand displays like that threaten us. We deal with our differences behind closed doors. Not in front of the entire student body. We can't appear as if we have any issues between any of us. It makes us look weak. We're not in a position to look weak, wasp."

"I'm sorry," I breathed out.

"I know it hurts, but you did this. You need to learn to live with the consequences."

I swallowed and stared straight ahead.

"Look at me when I speak to you," he said softly.

I shifted my gaze to his.

"You're beautiful, and I love your fierceness."

"Then why do you try to hold me back?"

He ran his knuckles along my jaw. "It won't always be like that. Just for now."

I nodded. My jaw clenched as I looked at a spot over his shoulder.

"Look at me," he commanded again.

I did, noting the glint in his green eyes.

"*Sei tutto il mio mondo*," he murmured. "Always, Bianca."

I crinkled my brows, unsure of what he said. But his tone was incredibly sweet and reverent.

"And someday I'll let you sting. For now, please listen to what I tell you. You're my good girl, right?"

"Yes," I said.

"Yes, what?"

"Yes, *husband*," I rasped.

He smiled and placed a kiss on my lips. "Mm, my very good girl. Come."

I had no idea where he wanted to go. But I was grateful when I put my hand in his, and he led me further from the courtyard.

He smirked at me as we walked. My heart jumped as I smiled back at him.

God, he was the perfect monster.

But so was Levin. And he wasn't mine anymore. Hell, maybe he never was.

THIRTY
LEVIN

I adjusted my black tie and swallowed my irritation. I'd been in the Vander Veer mansion for over an hour and still hadn't seen Celeste's old man. Instead, I'd been hit on by at least six cougars doused in overpowering, powdery perfume that burned the shit out of my nose and with tits which were so plastic I could recycle them and build a self-sustaining, off-the-grid hut. There was also one very suspect maître d' who I was certain had grabbed my ass.

I threw back a glass of champagne and grabbed two fresh ones off a tray that passed by. I wasn't one for schmoozing and ass kissing. Playing the part of some uptight, rich bitch wasn't my scene. I was always the muscle, not the fucking show. Dom was the one needed for this kind of job. Having been raised in this world and having Dom as my friend, one would think I'd have gotten the hang of this shit over the years, but I always tended to grab a bottle of booze and disappear. Even Vincent was better at this shit than me.

If Bianca hadn't told me to go fuck myself, I wouldn't be surrounded by all these pricks. Vincent was better suited for this. He was the one who could woo the panties off a chick. Not me. I was on the edge of fucking this up because I wanted to leave so I could go get high and drunk and forget about the shit in my life.

After Bianca's outburst at lunch, shit had gotten way worse. The moment the words had left my mouth, I'd regretted them and had been kicking my ass ever since. I knew taking Celeste to our table had been a bad idea. But fuck, did Bianca have any idea what it was like to see her loving my two best friends and my fucking enemy while hating me? I got that I was going to kill her, but damn. Get over it.

She and Dom had left and hadn't come back. But I'd imagined what he did to her knowing him.

Fuck my life. I wished I could bury my fucking thoughts and feelings. They were overwhelming me. Making the hurt turn to anger. This was why I didn't fuck with people. I knew what it was like when they left. *Fuck.*

"You look so handsome." Celeste giggled, running her hand down the arm of my suit, pulling me out of my thoughts. "Come. I want to introduce you to my mother."

I groaned inwardly. I hated meeting fucking parents. My smile was brittle, but Celeste accepted it and steered me like a prized show dog toward a woman who looked a lot like her—stacked and regal, great tits, but most likely fake like her nose, and a face that said *lick my shoes, bitch.*

Great.

"Mother," Celeste said in a breathy voice as we approached.

Her mother raised a perfectly painted-on eyebrow.

"I want you to meet Levin Seeley. Levin, this is my mother, Katherine."

"Ah." Her mother gave me her hand to kiss. At least it wasn't her ass.

I took her hand and pressed my lips to it. She beamed at me.

"A pleasure to meet you," I said, fixing the smile on my face.

"Celeste has been so excited about bringing you home to meet us," Katherine said. "She tells me you're friends with the De Santis family."

"Mother." Celeste's laugh was fake as hell as she clung to my arm.

"I suppose it depends on who's asking," I said, desperate to hurry this shit along. "But I am familiar with the family." I offered her a grin. When she smirked back at me, I continued, "I'd love to meet Mr. Vander Veer. Is he available?"

"He's here somewhere." Katherine waved me off, her flowery perfume just as bad as all the old cougars' fragrances. "I'd recommend having something to eat and getting to know everyone. My husband has a tendency to bound about and is often hard to find."

A young woman touched Katherine's arm, drawing her attention. She must have been the party planner because Katherine wrinkled her nose and started snarling obscenities at her about running out of something.

"Oh, Levy. I see Selene Abrams. Her father owns ICW, this company that makes microchips for computers or something. Daddy is friends with her father. Honestly, I've never seen the appeal in the friendship. He doesn't even make a fraction of what Daddy does."

"Well, any amount is a fraction," I said.

"What?" She frowned. "I didn't take you for an intellectual. That just makes you so much hotter." She licked her lips.

"Yeah," I said, rolling my eyes. "I'm a scholar."

"You seem smart to me. I *love* smart men." She giggled again.

Fuck. Get me out of here.

I followed Celeste through the crowded mansion and half-assed listened to her do her fake laugh and converse with a few other heiresses while I nodded politely when it seemed appropriate. My phone buzzed halfway through a conversation about some bitch getting a botched nose job.

"I need to take this," I said, not waiting for Celeste to respond.

It could've been a telemarketer trying to sell me an extended warranty for something I didn't own and I still would've answered.

"Hello?"

"How's it going?" Vincent's voice came over the line.

"Fuck, get me out of here." I cast a quick look around to make sure no one was close by.

Vincent laughed loudly. "You did this to yourself, man. Dom just wanted me to check in on you. See how you and that big cock of yours were doing. Dom said to get your dick wet and get that deal."

"The only way my dick is getting wet is if I jump into the pool in an attempt to drown myself," I muttered.

"Hey, that's good enough as long as Celeste is with you. She seemed really into you."

"She is, I guess. I'm just… not." I sighed, glancing around again.

"Baby B, huh?" he said knowingly.

"No," I snapped, hating the fucking lie.

"Whatever. Do what you need to do. But just so you know, Fallon was in the room with Dom and B early this morning. I didn't get a chance to tell you because Celeste was clinging to you, but, boy, you might be getting replaced. Vasiliev looked pretty fucking lovestruck when he left. I ran into him on my way to see Dom."

I tensed at this information.

"Did he…"

"Touch Baby B?" Vincent asked. "He definitely did something. I didn't ask. Laying low and all that. He just smiled and winked as he passed by, the cocky prick. And Dom was bathing B when I got to his room. You don't bathe clean girls."

"Fucking prick," I snarled, dragging my fingers through my hair in frustration. *I should've shot that cocksucker when I had the chance.*

"But you're not mad, right? You said it was over between you and B. And we all heard what you said at lunch—"

"It is," I snapped at him. "He can fucking have her. You all can."

"Right. Because you have Celeste. Way to go, man. But hurry up and get the deal before you pussy out with her, OK? We need those weapons. Dom said for you to let Vander Veer know we'll more than double what the Ivanovs are willing to pay. Also, there's a party at the dip tomorrow night. Your presence is requested."

"Of course, it is," I muttered, catching Celeste's eye as she blew me a kiss. I acted like I'd caught it, which made her giggle. *Chick was dumb.* I cleared my throat. "What are you up to tonight?"

"I'm on my way to Dom and B's. B texted me to come hang out

with them. Being I'm pretty sure they let the F-word in, I should be able to get some from baby B no problem. Or at least, get really damn close. I hope I'm not in for a night of watching chick flicks with a dry cock."

"Who the hell is the F-word?" I asked.

"Fallon. That'll be his new code name in case someone hears me."

I snorted. It was a good name for the fucking weasel.

"Who's Snoopy then?" I asked, recalling a previous message.

"Stella. She has her nose in everyone's business."

I nodded like he could see me. "Well, have fun."

"Oh, I intend to. B was in a good mood earlier. So was Dom. Netflix and chill, know what I mean? Keep your fingers crossed for me."

I did and hated it. It pissed me off. *How the hell could Bianca blow so hot and cold?* Vasiliev did just as bad of shit to her as we had, but she was all about forgiveness for him. Sure, she was still pissed at him, but if she was already on her knees for his cock, then it was fucked up because I'd saved them both. It didn't count for shit though in the grand scheme of things.

Fuck it. I said I was done. I had to be. Fuck feeling the pain of rejection again.

"Levy, I saw Daddy. Come on," Celeste said, taking my hand.

"Gotta go," I grunted into the phone.

"Wet dick, *Levy!*" Vincent shouted before I disconnected the call.

I adjusted the plastic smile on my face and played the part of someone who gave a shit as I let her lead me through the room again. Seeing all these assholes made me hate everything so much more. Knowing I was in this a little deeper than I wanted to be, made me sick. I could be Netflix and chilling too, but no. I'd been cut loose, or maybe I'd broken loose, and now here I was—hating every fucking thing about my life.

And if Dom was letting Vasiliev in with Bianca...

I shoved the thought out of my head. Thinking about her would only piss me off more, and I had a job to do.

"Daddy," Celeste simpered.

A tall man in a pressed suit which probably cost more than his wife's tits turned and faced us, his dark eyes sweeping over me quickly. I knew that look. He was sizing me up.

"This is Levin Seeley. Do you remember me telling you he was coming tonight?"

"Yes. Levin, hello," Mr. Vander Veer said, a steely glint in his eyes as he shook my hand.

"Hello. A pleasure to meet you." I gave him a nod and released his hand.

"I'm glad you could make it tonight. The party is a bit dull right now, and for that, you have my apologies. I do recommend trying to catch one of these waiters and getting yourself a drink. It makes it better."

Celeste laughed. "Levin is having a good time, aren't you?"

"The best," I said, putting some inflection into my voice so I sounded like I was having more fun than a pig in shit.

"Well, I suppose that's good. Makes the evening better."

"It does." I grabbed a flute of champagne as a waiter moved past me.

Vander Veer smirked as I downed it and dropped the glass on the next waiter's tray.

"Say, Levin, you're good friends with the De Santis family, aren't you?" Vander Veer picked up a flute of champagne and sipped it, frowning.

"Depends," I said, wishing I'd grabbed another drink. "Are there cops here?"

Vander Veer let out a hearty chuckle. "I like you. Celeste, why don't you go talk to the ladies? I'd like to speak to Levin alone for a bit."

"OK." Celeste went up on her toes and pressed a kiss to my cheek before sashaying away to greet another group of girls I hadn't had the misfortune of meeting yet.

"Let's get something that doesn't taste like piss," Vander Veer said the moment Celeste was out of earshot. "I hate the properness of these parties." He gestured for me to follow him.

We moved down the hall outside, away from the party.

"Nice place," I said, not enjoying the awkwardness of the moment.

"It serves its purpose," he said, entering a study.

I followed and sat in the leather armchair he gestured to. He strode over to a small bar and poured two drinks.

"Scotch good?"

"Great," I said, taking the glass from him when he approached.

He sat behind his desk and sipped his drink. I followed suit, enjoying the delicious burn as it traversed my throat.

"So...De Santis," he said.

"Guilty."

He chuckled. "I'll get to the point. Are you here with Celeste because you need weapons?"

I raised my brows at him. "I'll save the bullshit and say yes... and no. I do find her captivating. The weapons are just a bonus."

It wasn't a complete lie. Celeste was hot as hell. She was no Bianca, but I doubted I'd ever meet anyone like bumblebee.

I pushed her out of my head again and focused on the task at hand.

He smiled knowingly. "Then you know the Ivanovs have already approached me with an offer."

"We'll double it."

He cocked his head at me. "You don't even know what their offer is."

"Doesn't matter. Dominic is prepared to do double whatever they offered."

"I see." Vander Veer leaned back in his seat and surveyed me with keen eyes.

I didn't take him for a stupid man. Stupid men didn't accumulate millions and enemies. Vander Veer knew he had what we needed.

"I'll tell you what. I'll give De Santis the weapons and my word he'll have priority *if* he pays double and you date my daughter."

"What?" I couldn't have heard him correctly.

He sighed and swirled his drink. "Celeste likes to date men I'd rather she stayed away from. None of them want her for more than a few nights. The last one was sleeping with someone he met on campus. I'd like for her to experience a real relationship. One that'll make her fall in love and then break her to strengthen her. Give that to her, and you'll have your contract with me. But your relationship needs to last for a decent, believable stretch of time. A few weeks. Four. Six. More if you're enjoying yourself. I'll let you decide."

I swallowed, sickness roiling deep in my guts. I hadn't planned on making this a long-term thing.

"You'll get your weapons. You'll get my word to be exclusive to De Santis. And you'll get a decent enough girl."

"And how long will the contract and your word last?" I said, dreading his answer.

"For as long as you make Celeste happy. I realize you're a young man who has needs. I also realize my daughter isn't some innocent princess. I'd like for you to remain faithful to her. When you need to leave, do it in such a way she'll feel it. Teach her to be...smarter. Make better choices. As of late, she hasn't impressed me, and she's going to be out on her own soon. She won't survive the way she is now. She needs to toughen up. You strike me as someone who can harden her a bit."

I breathed out, trying to stop the burning in my throat from the rising bile. *What choice did I have?* Dom—*we*—needed these weapons. It would fuck the Bratva. We'd have more than them. They'd be scrambling to fill their weapon void. And wars were fought with weapons in my world.

I had no choice. Bianca had already told me to fuck off. Me continuing to cling to any sort of hope was stupid. I came here to get this deal. Here it was, dangling like a carrot in front of my face.

"Deal," I said. "But don't come for me when shit goes south with her. I'm not good with women."

He laughed. "None of us really are. You're perfect for the job." He threw back his drink, and I did the same, washing down the sickness.

"I'll send over the contracts. Dominic De Santis is who I presume I'll be dealing with? Not his father?"

"No. We don't even want Matteo to know of this."

"Understood." He rose to his feet. "Shall we return?"

I nodded and stood. My legs felt like lead as I followed him out of the room. But my job had always been to do the shit no one else wanted to do.

Looked like that wouldn't change any time soon.

THIRTY-ONE
BIANCA

"Why do you always get to pick what she wears?" Vincent asked as he crossed his arms over his chest and stared at Dominic. He'd come over last night and watched movies with us, his eyes more glued to me than the screen.

I'd almost wished Dominic had made a move then, but he hadn't. Instead, the guys had ended up drinking and talking about stupid shit, like cars and guns, while I'd fallen asleep to the sounds of some cheesy chick flick playing in the background.

"Because you'd have her dressed like a princess when she's a queen," Dominic muttered as he pulled a black, lace dress from his closet and studied it.

I shook my head at him. He treated me like a doll. I dressed in a pair of skinny jeans and an old, ripped-up Alice Cooper band tee this morning, and the vein in Dominic's neck looked like it was near bursting as his face reddened.

I'd changed into a cashmere sweater and a baby pink skirt to get him to relax and stop bitching so much. If I were being honest though, Dominic was growing on me. I enjoyed pissing him off as much as I enjoyed when he hauled me into his arms and forced me to submit.

I still hadn't given in on having sex though. When he'd bathed me yesterday, I nearly did. His touch was so gentle and sweet as he washed me. But he hadn't pushed for more, even though I was practically panting for it. Maybe that was his plan. To entice me. He was doing a damn good job of it.

"At least she'd be comfortable," Vincent returned. "We're going to the dip. She's going to be in the woods. You can't possibly want her in heels and a dress."

"Then you underestimate me," Dominic grunted, putting the black dress back into the closet and grabbing out a red one.

"I want to pick her clothes."

"Unlikely."

I could sense an argument brewing, so I spoke up, "I don't mind if Vinny wants to pick out something for me this time."

Dominic paused and looked over at me as Vincent grinned widely.

"No."

"Dominic," I said, sighing. I got up and approached him. "Please? Maybe a compromise?"

He narrowed his eyes at me. "I'm listening."

I took it as a good sign. Dominic De Santis didn't negotiate. *Ever*. I seized the opportunity.

"How about you each pick something for me to wear? Then you both get to have me in what you want." My desire to live what was left of my life peacefully motivated me to give in more than I would have a week ago.

Dominic stared over my head to nod to Vincent. "Fine. I'm agreeable."

"Excellent. Where are the clown shoes?" Vincent called out, pushing past Dominic and going into the closet.

I moved in to drag Dominic's attention from Vincent, who was excitedly rummaging through the closet. Placing my hands on his face, I brought his focus to me.

"Thank you."

His hard glare softened as he surveyed me. I took the opportunity to go up on my tiptoes and place a soft kiss on his lips. He came to life beneath me and wrapped his arms around me, the red dress falling to the floor.

"Hey!" Vincent said, coming out of the closet with a skirt in his hands. "If he gets to kiss you then so do I."

"No," Dom growled, nipping at my bottom lip.

"Listen, fucker—"

I laughed and eased away from Dominic, feeling more at ease than I had in the last two weeks. I went to Vincent. Before Dominic could reprimand me and tell me no, I kissed Vincent. It happened so fast he didn't have time to react as I snagged the skirt out of his fingers and danced away.

"Tease," Vincent said, all sulky.

Dominic smiled and went back in the closet to dig around. I tossed the skirt on the bed and moved to sit in front of the small vanity. With a practiced touch, I dotted on moisturizer and began my makeup since I knew Dominic would want me to do it. He was much easier to get along with when I complied.

And right now, I wanted a little peace. I'd piss him off some other time. The last thing I wanted was to kneel on the hard patio like he'd made me do last time there was a party at the dip.

"Perfect," Dominic said, coming out of the closet with a black, off-the-shoulder top and a pair of black boots.

"Why do you get to pick two things?" Vincent demanded, frowning as Dominic dropped the items on the bed next to the skirt.

"Because you weren't smart enough to? Snooze you lose."

"Man—"

"Vinny, you can pick out my underwear," I called out, knowing damn well that would please him.

He immediately shut up and went to the dresser drawer.

Instead of arguing, Dominic approached me and rested his hands on my shoulders, his gaze locked on mine in the mirror.

My heart jumped in my chest as we stared at one another. *Damn, he was beautiful. And maddening. God, was he maddening.*

Dominic leaned down and whispered, "You're a sneaky little thing, aren't you, wasp?" His lips brushed against my ear.

Goosebumps flittered over my skin. "Is that a problem?"

"Not for me," he said, his breath feathering over my skin. "But it will be for you later."

I swallowed hard but didn't get to pursue questioning him because Vincent came over and showed me the lacy, black panties he'd picked out.

"I want these when you're done," he said coyly, winking at me.

"What for?" I stared down at the scrap in his hands.

He shrugged. "The nights get lonely with Dom hogging you."

I suppressed a laugh and went back to doing my makeup. I tuned out the guys as they chatted. It wasn't until I heard Levin's name mentioned that I perked up and began listening.

"Has he said anything?" Vincent asked.

"He said we'd talk tonight. He's been…busy."

Vincent snorted. "Balls deep in Celeste, you mean."

My heart jumped at Vincent's words, hurt radiating through me. I dropped my tube of mascara, causing the guys to look over at me. I quickly picked it up.

"Don't worry, baby B. He's an idiot," Vincent said gently.

Dominic said nothing, simply opting to watch me with no emotion on his face.

I forced a smile onto my lips. "It's fine. I told him I was done. He said he was too. He's free to do whatever he wants. Or whoever he wants," I muttered.

It didn't make my heart hurt any less. I'd been so furious before. Not that I wasn't still mad, but I knew I needed to get my shit sorted if I was going to get through any of this. My dad used to tell me to look on the bright side, so that was what I was trying to do. I had food. Shelter. A husband who seemed to care about me despite the earlier shit. Vinny… and even Fallon in a weird way. Instead of fighting those things, no matter how despicable they'd been, I had to be grateful. I was still alive. If anyone deserved my anger, it was Fallon anyway. He was the one who'd been intent on handing me over, while the kings hadn't pulled the trigger. But I was so sick of being angry. I really did want my peace and sanity back.

I shoved all the angry thoughts away. Not tonight. I wanted—no, I *needed*—to let go so I could feel something good again. So I could move past everything. And if I was doing it without Levin, so be it. The fact he'd decided so quickly Celeste was who he wanted made it easier for me to let him go, even if it did hurt like a bitch.

The guys didn't say anything else, but based on Vincent's face, he shared my pain too.

And that was good. At least I wasn't alone.

MUSIC AND SHOUTS of partygoers sounded out loudly as I leaned against the railing of the old dip house. Bonfires blazed while people danced and had a good time, drinks in hand. Despite the cool fall air, I wasn't too cold in the short pleated skirt.

"Got you a drink," Vincent said, sidling up beside me and handing me a cup of alcohol.

I took it and sniffed. "Did you poison it?"

He grinned. "Well, I drugged it if that's what you mean. Figured I'd get you wasted then fuck you silly when you couldn't fight back."

I lifted a brow at him. "You'd really do that?"

He snorted. "No, baby B, I really wouldn't. Well, I mean, I might if you don't give me something soon. I still have the worst case of blue balls imaginable."

I sipped my drink and glanced to where Dominic stood with a few of their court. He seemed to be in a decent mood, but I had a feeling he was plotting like always. If I had to wager a guess, I'd bet he was directing his loyal followers on what he needed done. He was always all work.

I licked the alcohol from my lips and leaned into Vincent. His hand immediately moved to rest on my lower back as I whispered in his ear, "I'd like to pick up where we left off," I said softly.

He shifted closer as I angled my face to stare up at him. His dark hair was a mess, but like always, he was dressed to kill. His eyes glinted in the light from the bonfire.

"Just say when," he answered back. "My cock has been hard since I got to rifle through your panty drawer earlier."

I started to lean in to kiss him, unsure how Dominic would take to the display of affection in front of others since I was pretty sure he wanted the world to think I belonged to him exclusively, when something caught my eye.

Or rather *someone*.

Levin had arrived. Celeste's hand was wrapped firmly around his as they made their way to Dominic.

Sensing my hesitation, Vincent turned to see what I was staring at.

"B, come on—"

"Are they... *really* together now?" I asked, my voice shaking.

"B, it's just business, you know? Besides, you both said you were done—"

"I know what I said," I snapped.

He frowned. The fact Levin had moved on so quickly hurt. Maybe he was doing it just to cause me pain since I hadn't been kind to him when I'd needed to be. Or maybe it was business. In the grand scheme of things, it didn't matter why, it just mattered that he was.

And that really fucking broke my heart.

Levin approached Dominic whose gaze flitted over the pair before he excused himself from the group and nodded for Levin to follow him. The kiss Levin quickly pressed to Celeste's temple made bile rise in my throat. His gaze locked on me as he pulled away with no emotion on his face.

"Perfect timing. Levin did us a favor. Come on." Vincent took me by the arm and led me around the patio to a darkened corner out of sight of everyone.

The moment we were away, his lips crashed against mine, and his hands tightened on my hips. My mind was still with Levin as Vincent's mouth moved with mine.

"B, don't tell me I really should've drugged you," Vincent whispered.

I shook myself out of my stupor and kissed him back. He let out a soft groan before his tongue slid along mine.

"How fast can I get you off?" he asked breathlessly as his hands traversed beneath my top and skimmed my breasts.

As furious as I was, I went for it. An anger fuck might soothe my wounded soul.

"Try me and find out," I answered back.

That was all he needed to hear because a moment later, he lifted me and pinned me to the side of the house, his dick already out of his pants and his fingers pushing my panties aside.

"I-I'm not on the pill right now—"

"I'll fuck you for a bit, and then you can suck me off, baby," he said, guiding his dick through my folds.

I was good with that.

He pushed forward, filling me as I cried out against his lips.

"Shh. We don't want to get caught," he choked out, thrusting hard into me.

I raked my fingers through his hair, causing him to hiss.

"Fuck, I hope you're OK with a good time and not a long time," he grunted as he thrust into me once more. "Your pussy is strangling my cock so good."

I nipped his neck making him growl and rail into me harder. His lips kissed and sucked any place he pressed them.

"Vinny," I choked out as the heat grew low in my belly. "Faster."

He obliged, spearing me hard and fast, the sounds of our dirty, rough fucking echoing in the cool night air.

It was exactly what my wounded heart needed. I came with a cry, which he swallowed down.

Breathless and weak, I pushed him away and dropped to my knees. I took his length in my hand and stroked him. His head fell back, and a groan slipped from his lips. I slid my tongue along him, tasting the mess we'd made before sucking him deeply into my mouth.

His fingers tangled through my hair as he fucked my mouth with wild abandon, his dick hitting the back of my throat with every thrust.

"Fuck, baby. That's it. God, you're fucking amazing," he rasped as he held me still so he could continue his onslaught.

Moments later, he let out a low, erotic groan that made electric shocks dance between my legs. He came hard and fast in my mouth as his legs trembled.

"Fuuuck," he moaned softly.

When his cock stopped twitching, I pulled away and swallowed. He held his hand out to me and helped me to my feet a moment later.

"You're the fucking dream, baby B," he said, zipping his pants and giving me a lazy smile beneath the moon.

He leaned in, his lips brushing mine as he caged me against the side of the house between his arms. "How'd we taste?"

Before I could answer, someone cleared their throat from behind Vincent.

Slowly, Vincent turned his head, and I peeked over his shoulder. Levin stood a few feet from us, looking so pissed I thought he was going to take out his gun and shoot someone.

"Dom is looking for you," he said with a grunt.

"Just in time, huh, baby?" Vincent said, backing up and wrapping his arm around my waist.

"You shouldn't be sneaking off with her," Levin said tightly as Vincent led me along the side of the house.

"Dom knows she's with me," Vincent shot back. "And she was completely safe, right, B?"

"Yeah," I said, casting a quick peek at Levin, who still wore a deep frown.

He yanked Vincent to a stop. "Listen, I don't give a fuck what you do with her, but I do care if my ass gets ripped into because of it. So the next time you feel like fucking off with Dom's *wife*, make sure he knows. I just got chewed out because he couldn't find her."

"I'm sure Celeste will lick your wounds." The words tumbled out of my mouth before I could stop them.

Levin glared at me. "Yeah, she will. You got a problem with that?"

My bottom lip quivered as I scowled back. "No. She can have you."

"Easy, B," Vincent said softly, giving me a squeeze.

I shoved away from him, all the happiness and calmness evaporating. I was right back to feeling like shit over the giant asshole in front of me.

"Seems like you're mad," Levin continued. "But why wouldn't you be? I did replace you."

"R-*replace* me?" I stepped forward and jabbed him hard in the chest with my finger. "You didn't replace me, Levin Seeley. Why would I want a boy who's too scared to fuck me? Celeste is a little lower tier, so she's probably more your style."

He balled his hands into fists, a muscle popping along his jaw.

"B, go find Dom, OK? Enough of this." Vincent stepped between me and Levin. He leaned in and swept his lips against mine. "Go, baby."

I glared at Levin for another second before I gave him the finger and spun on my heel, leaving him standing there.

Whatever. Celeste could have him. At least that was what my brain said. My heart said something else entirely, and for that, I hated it.

THIRTY-TWO
DOMINIC

I sat in my chair and looked out over the party. I'd sent Levin to find Vincent and Bianca after he'd told me he was successful in securing the weapons deal with Vander Veer. The terms weren't terrible on my end, but they seemed rough on Levin's.

"You don't have to do it," I said, eyeing him for a response. "I'll find another way to get what we need. Other dealers. Other avenues."

He straightened his shoulders. "I already agreed. There are no others who can provide what we need like Vander Veer can."

"And Bianca?"

"We're over. I've got shit to do now."

And so that was it. Levin was with Celeste, as per the terms of the arrangement, and my wife was now most likely fucking one of my best friends.

I sighed and rubbed my eyes.

I eased my hand from my face as Bianca slid onto my lap and nuzzled my neck.

It was a strange thing for her to do, but I wasn't going to question it. She'd been a lot more affectionate the past few days. Either she was starting to give a damn again, or she'd just accepted this would be her life now.

I draped her legs over mine and cradled her against me.

"Hello, wasp," I said softly, kissing her forehead.

She rested her hand on my cheek and urged me closer for a kiss. I did so, needing to make sure she knew this meant something to me as I held her tightly against me.

"What's wrong?" I murmured, my forehead pressed to hers.

"Nothing," she answered in a thick voice that let me know she was lying.

I let it go. I knew it had to be Levin's appearance with Celeste.

"Where were you?"

"With Vinny," she mumbled.

I ran my fingers through her blonde hair. "Did you fuck him?"

She hesitated for a moment before nodding.

"Did he come in you?" I hated the possibility of anyone but me getting my wife pregnant. I'd have to deal with it if it happened, and just hope my dad wouldn't question it since she was married to me.

"He came in my mouth," she said.

I sighed in relief. "You do realize I'm going to punish both of you again, right?"

"Or you could just fuck me, and we could forget about punishment." She licked her lips as her hand drifted between us, and she tugged at the button on my pants.

I let out a soft laugh at the enticing idea. "You want me to fuck you as punishment?"

She nodded. "Yes, Dominic. I want you to fuck me hard."

I loved when she submitted, but part of me loved it even more when she resisted. I'd been starved of her long enough.

"I think something can be arranged," I said, gripping her chin and pulling her into my kiss.

Her lips parted immediately for me, allowing me to sweep into her mouth and devour her.

I was lost in her, my hands roaming all over as she allowed me free rein of her body.

"Hey, um, Dominic?" a voice called out uncertainly.

I snarled and reluctantly broke away from Bianca, spearing the intruder with a glare. Jason Manning. One of my court members.

"What?" I snapped at him as he fidgeted.

"I was told to give you a message. Um, Stella said you have an appointment with a god later. Midnight. That's all I was told. She's over there making out with Ivanov though."

I chuckled at her coded message. I followed the direction he nodded and saw she was practically fucking Ivanov against a tree. *Little slut.* I knew she was good for something. So far she was proving more useful than Vasiliev was. At least, she did what I told her to do—keep tabs on the lords and don't get caught. That meant doing whatever it took. Maybe Fallon would finally come through at midnight tonight.

I gave him a nod. "Message delivered. Find somewhere else to be."

He scurried away like his feet were on fire.

I turned back to Bianca. "Where were we, *mia regina*?"

"Dom," Vincent called out, interrupting my bid for pussy.

My plan to put my baby in her hadn't changed. In fact, I was practically clawing at the walls to sink deep into her tight heat and plant my seed. But I was trying to give her fun, love, and proof of my feelings before I took everything away. I wanted her to understand she was more than a warm hole to hide in or a pawn in this twisted game.

I sighed and pulled back from Bianca to stare at him. "What?"

"Are you aware of what this asshole has done?" He jerked his thumb to Levin.

"I'm aware," I said as Bianca nuzzled deeper into my neck. I wanted to think it was affection, but I knew it was more likely her trying not to see Levin.

"And you're OK with it?"

"Levin knows what he's doing. He likes Celeste enough. Let him do it."

"But baby B—"

"Levin made his choice. Let it go," Bianca snapped, sitting up and glaring at Levin. "We're over."

"You're fucking ridiculous," Levin said, shaking his head.

Bianca let out a snarl of frustration at him but didn't bite back. It didn't stop Levin from surging forward with more words for her.

"*You* made that choice, bumblebee. Not me. I only reacted to it. So if you're pissed about me being with someone new, then that's all on you because *you* said you were done. Don't play the fucking victim. Besides, you're married to Dom now. How about focusing on your husband and not on all the cock you can get like some dick-deprived whore."

"Fuck you, Levin," she shouted, jumping to her feet.

I could've stopped her, but I let her rush forward. Her palm connected with Levin's face with a loud crack that echoed around us. His head snapped to the side before he straightened himself and glowered down at her, his blue eyes flashing with fury.

"Don't ever call me a fucking whore again," she hissed at him. "Or I swear, I'll gut you in your sleep."

I rose to my feet as Vincent stepped forward. Based on past experience, I knew Bianca wasn't giving Levin an empty threat. I reached her before Vincent did and wrapped my arm around her waist, hauling her against me. Anger vibrated through her small frame.

Levin stepped back, his body trembling. He turned on his heel and stalked toward Celeste, who stood at the top of the stairs with her mouth open. I knew she hadn't heard a word since she'd only just appeared with a drink in her hand, but she'd definitely seen Bianca slap him.

"It's OK, wasp," I murmured.

She spun in my arms and clung to me. I wound my arms fully around her and peeked at Vincent.

He sighed and shook his head, his gaze following Levin with Celeste. If I knew Levin like I thought I did, he'd soon be angry-fucking Celeste as he tried to bury his pain. He was stubborn and violent. There wasn't anything I could do for him. It had to come from Bianca. I accepted it would take some time. They'd been at one another's throats since the beginning. It made sense the animosity between them wouldn't go away.

Levin getting this deal for me had only made shit worse though.

We all knew it. But Levin did whatever he wanted, whenever he wanted. Nothing would change his mind once it was made up.

And Bianca… that woman was fire and brimstone on a good day. On a bad? No comparison.

"I'll go get her a drink," Vincent said, his gaze raking over her.

I nodded. I needed to get her more pliable. Getting her wasted would hopefully work in my favor in more ways than one.

He went down the stairs to the keg. I brought Bianca with me back to my seat and pulled her onto my lap.

"Look at me," I commanded softly, tilting her head up.

Her eyes were bloodshot as she stared back at me.

"That can't happen again. Either you get over your anger and pain and tell Levin how you feel, or you let him go and stop making fucking scenes in front of people. You can't have it both ways—"

She started to turn her head, but I grabbed her face and forced her gaze back to mine.

"*You can't have it both ways.* If you're not going to tell him you still care, then I don't want to see you behave that way again. Do you understand me?"

"You can fuck off with him," she snarled, moving to get off my lap.

I let out a growl and hauled her back down.

"*Be-fucking-have*, wasp. I'm trying to get you to understand this isn't just affecting you and him. It's fucking with both Vincent and me. There's a lot of heavy shit going on right now. We have to deal with my father in a week's time. I don't even know how I'm going to get us out of that mess without shooting him in the fucking head. We need to tread carefully with Vasiliev. The scales are tipping, and we don't need it fucked up because you throw a temper tantrum. I love your fire but quell it for now."

"You think I'm overreacting?" She stared at me, her big blue eyes wide and filled with disbelief.

"I think given what Vasiliev was going to do to you, yes."

"*You* were going to kill me, Dominic. Levin pressed a gun to my head—"

"I don't need the fucking details. I was there," I snapped at her. I hated the memory of her sobbing on her knees, her life on the cusp of a fucking shallow grave. Although, if Levin had pulled the trigger on her, I'd have given her a proper burial in a place of my choosing. My connections ran far and deep.

She flinched away from me, making me hate the snarling monster I constantly tried to keep on lockdown within me.

Reaching out, I brushed her hair from her face as I tried to reel in my frustration. "The point is, you should hate Vasiliev the most. Yet he was the one you wept for. It broke us all to see that. Levin saved your life and Vasiliev's. And Vincent… he never wanted you harmed. None of us did. You didn't hear the way he sobbed for you when he thought you were gone. You didn't see me broken and praying Levin would defy me and save you. I know I'm asking a lot of you for you to believe me when I say I will fucking *die* to save you. So will Vincent and Levin, even if you think Levin hates you. But believe me. Now, we have more important shit to worry about than this bullshit between you and Levin. Figure it out, sort it quietly, but fucking sort it. Got it?"

She nodded mutely, a sour expression on her face.

"Wasp…" I warned.

"Yes, Dominic," she grunted, her bottom lip jutting out.

"Good girl," I praised. "Now let's drink some shitty alcohol and have a decent enough time, OK?"

"OK," she said, her body still tense.

I knew the urge to fight me was there, but I saw the hesitation in her eyes. She knew we had a lot at stake in the coming weeks.

"Shit tastes like piss," Vincent said.

I took one of the cups and pressed it to Bianca's lips.

"Open," I commanded.

She hesitated for a second before parting her lips. I poured the liquid into her mouth. Her eyes widened at me as I held the back of her head and forced her to drink the entire cup. She coughed once she finished, and I nodded to Vincent to hand me another.

"Dominic—" she started.

"Shh," I tutted, pressing the second glass to her lips. I got the second glass down her throat when she opened her mouth again.

"Light it up," I called to Vincent as I stared into Bianca's eyes.

Soon, he handed me a lit joint. I took a deep hit and held it, relishing in the surge of calmness before leaning in to kiss my wife.

"No," she mumbled.

I fisted her hair and forced her mouth to mine. She gasped, and I blew the smoke into her mouth. She fought me until she had no choice but to inhale.

She sputtered when I released her.

"It wasn't a request," I said, giving her a pointed look before I took another deep hit. I offered her the joint.

She parted her lips again, and I let her take a hit of the weed.

"Deeper," I instructed.

She sucked in more and held it before she coughed and blew it out. I smiled at her, noticing how she was beginning to sway on my lap. A calm wasp was a pliable wasp.

I took a few more hits before handing the joint back to Vincent. He finished it off as he sucked down his beer.

We sat in comfortable silence for quite some time, Vincent leaving and returning with more alcohol as the night wore on. Bianca drank another two glasses and smoked more weed before I was satisfied she was feeling good enough.

"Weed gets old," Vincent grunted, staring down at the joint he'd been toking.

"It makes us lots of money."

"Ivanov banks on heroin and coke."

"I'm not Ivanov. If I find a better drug, I'll push it. I'm not in the business of getting people addicted to bullshit habits that could kill them. Dead customers aren't returning customers," I said, eyeing Celeste rubbing against Levin.

He looked stiff and unnatural as he stood there, not touching her. He'd have to try harder if he wanted to make that shit look real.

Vincent nodded. "I see your point, but there's gotta be something else out there we can do. Don't get me wrong, I love getting high on weed, but it's missing something for me."

I nodded. I got it. It didn't blow my mind the way I wanted either, but it was better than nothing. Bianca shifted in my arms. Her lips met my neck, making me tighten my hold on her. If she wasn't careful, I was going to fuck her right there in front of everyone. Claim her so these fuckers knew who she belonged to. I'd seen some of the guys gawking at her when we'd arrived. One glare from me was all it took to get them scampering off, which probably saved their pathetic lives.

"Can I go with you at midnight?" she asked softly in my ear.

"Yes," I answered immediately.

Whether Vasiliev had good news or bad news, I'd need her there. I wanted her to be part of everything where he was concerned so that when he fucked up or betrayed us, she'd see it firsthand. Not that I thought he'd fuck up or betray us. I'd seen the way he looked at my wife. The asshole really did care about her. But he was still a loose cannon as far as I was concerned.

"Mmm," she purred in my ear as she reached down and rubbed my cock through my pants.

I liked I'd pleased her. Getting her wasted had been a good idea.

"Does this mean you aren't mad anymore?"

"No, I'm definitely mad," she slurred out softly. "But a girl has needs."

"Didn't Vincent fuck you hard enough?"

She giggled softly. "He did, but we had to cut it short since I'm not on the pill anymore."

I breathed out and glanced to Vincent, who was watching us, his eyes dark.

"Do you want both of us?" I asked, eyes locked on Vincent's.

His eyes widened, his eagerness plain to see.

"Yes. I want to feel good, but I don't want you to get me pregnant."

"*Mia regina*, I'm going to come so deep inside you once I'm in, that you'll have no choice but to carry my baby. Your belly swollen with my heir makes me unbelievably excited."

"Not too soon, Dominic," she said breathlessly, fumbling with the button on my pants.

I didn't stop her as she unfastened them and tugged my zipper down. She dipped her hand beneath my waistband and grasped my cock. Alcohol and weed had made my queen... looser, less inhibited. I could work with that.

I ran my fingers through her hair as she gave my dick quick strokes beneath the fabric.

"Vincent, what time is it?" I asked, desperate to fuck her breathless.

"Time for me to join in," he said, eyeing her hungrily as she sucked on my neck and continued to stroke me. "But it's just after eleven if you need numbers."

Fuck. I had to meet Vasiliev.

"Baby," I murmured as I ran my hand up her bare thigh. "You're making me so fucking hard, but we have to stop. I have to meet Vasiliev so I don't have time to give you a proper fucking like you deserve."

She slowed her movements on my dick. It was agony as she removed her hand.

"How about you smoke and drink a little more for me?" I asked.

She pouted, completely wasted off her ass already. "Will you and Vinny do it too?"

Vincent nodded eagerly. He took off to get more drinks.

"Yes. We'll have fun tonight."

"All of us?" she asked, sitting up and swaying as she focused on my face. "Fallon too?"

"Maybe if you're a good girl," was all I said right when Vincent returned with glasses of alcohol for us.

I peered past Vincent and noticed Levin standing not far from the patio, Celeste still clinging to him as her friends giggled around them. He'd been watching Bianca on me. I smirked and inclined my head to him. Tipping my cup, I drank deeply while Vincent helped B. Levin's gaze darted to Vincent and Bianca.

Levin would cave eventually. I'd make sure of it. Because if my queen wasn't happy, then no one was happy.

THIRTY-THREE
BIANCA

I clung to Vincent as he gave me a piggyback ride through the darkened campus. We passed two security guards, who quickly looked away like they hadn't seen us. Or maybe there was only one. I was seeing double after everything I'd consumed earlier.

"Where—" Vincent nipped at my fingers when I tried to pinch his lips together, making me giggle. "—we going?" he finished.

"I'm thinking Bianca's vacant dorm. Everyone in her building is probably still at the dip, so it makes it easier," Dominic said as he sent a text message from beside us.

I reached out for him. His fingers immediately twined through mine as he gazed at me through the darkness.

"Be careful," he warned, pressing a kiss to my knuckles. "I don't need you falling and getting hurt. Hold onto Vincent."

"I won't drop her," Vincent promised as he hefted me higher above his hips and kept moving. "She weighs nothing. I could probably run all the way to her dorm and not be out of breath."

"That's because you're so delicious," I said, pulling my hand from Dominic's to rub Vincent's washboard abs beneath his shirt.

He let out a grunt.

"I can go lower," I slurred, my head spinning.

Dominic and Vincent had force-fed me alcohol and weed all night. I was lucky I could remember my own name.

"Wasp," Dominic reprimanded from beside me.

There wasn't any bite to his tone though which only made me eager to push for more.

"You know," I murmured, looking over to the two blurry Dominics walking beside us. "I'm baby B. I'm wasp. I'm... bum-bumblebee," I said the last part with a quake to the word. "You should be, like, hornet ass or something."

Vincent let out a burst of laughter as Dominic closed his eyes briefly before yanking open the door to my building without a word.

"Come on, hornet ass," Vincent chortled as we stepped into the elevator. "Get your key out."

"Hornet ass?" Dominic asked, raising his brows at me. "Really?"

I blinked innocently at him. "You don't like it?"

He snorted and shook his head as the elevator dinged on my floor. We walked to my door. I slid off Vincent's back and stumbled, nearly hitting the wall before he caught and dragged me against his body.

"Easy, baby B. Can't let you get hurt. Hornet ass would get pissed."

"Get in the fucking room," Dominic grumbled, shaking his head again and letting out a sigh like he was a fed-up parent ready to kick our asses.

That was just encouragement as far as I was concerned.

I eased away from Vincent and danced into my room, singing some made-up song about Dominic's hornet ass. Inside, I flopped back onto my bed and stared at the ceiling, the spins taking hold and making me groan.

"Dizzy?" Vincent asked, sitting beside me.

I nodded. "But I like it. I feel good."

"Good," he said softly, leaning down to kiss me. His warm lips met mine briefly before he pulled away, leaving me wanting.

I figured Dominic would've swooped in and stopped the kiss, so I peeked to see what he was doing. Once more, he was frowning at his phone, not paying us a bit of attention.

"He's trying to get through to Vasiliev." Vincent raked his fingers through my hair affectionately. "Then he'll yell at us."

"I can hear you," Dominic muttered, not bothering to look at us. "Don't worry. You'll both be taught a lesson soon enough."

"Sounds like an invitation to make it worth the punishment." Vincent grinned down at me. "Right, baby?"

"Definitely," I mumbled, eager to take whatever they wanted to the next level.

His fingers traced down my throat and across my collarbone. A knock on the door stopped Vincent's hand halfway to my breast. He dropped his hand back onto his lap and offered me an apologetic wink. "Later, B."

I curled against him as Dominic opened the door and Fallon quickly stepped inside looking windswept.

"You're late," Dominic said.

"Sorry. I was dealing with Tate," he mumbled. "He wanted me to do this shit called sugar with him before I left and wouldn't take no for an answer."

"Sugar?" Vincent asked.

Fallon glanced at Vincent then me, a smile softening his features. I sat up and swayed. Vincent wrapped his arm around my waist to keep me from toppling over.

Fallon's lips shook before he cleared his throat and spoke, "It's some new street drug. There's a new guy in town. Goes by the name De Luca. Old money. Old ties. Guess he and his crew are really expanding. Tate got hold of some of his product, and he and Drake were tasked with trying it out. Guess they wanted me in on it too."

"I see," Dominic said, frowning.

I wish he'd smile more was the first thought that popped into my head.

"It's good shit," Fallon continued, standing awkwardly in the room.

"You tried it?" Dominic strode to my overstuffed chair and sank onto it.

"It's why I'm late."

Dominic nodded for a moment before saying what was apparently on his mind, "This De Luca guy... what else do you know about him?"

"Just that he's the heir to some big organization that doesn't fuck around. They say he's pretty ruthless and his right-hand man is fucking insane. They're running the east side. They're leaking into Bratva territory and yours," he said the last words softer.

Vincent shot a look to Dominic, who leaned forward and steepled his fingers.

"That might be a bit of a problem," Dominic said in a voice which sent chills down my spine.

"Hail feels the same way."

"And the product?" Vincent broke in. "How does it make you feel?"

"I feel like I'm fucking flying. It comes in these intense waves which I can't seem to get enough of," Fallon said, his eyes wide. "It's the best drug I've ever tried, and trust me, hanging out with Hail all these years, I can say I've used a fair amount. The crazy thing about it though, is my head is clear. I'm focused. I feel like God without a drug problem. This shit is something to worry about. Weed, coke, heroin, addy... nothing will touch this if they start pushing. And I really think they're going to start pushing."

Dominic's face darkened as Fallon continued.

"De Luca is going to take over. From both sides. Hail is a narcissistic prick who thinks it won't matter and our customers will stay loyal to us. But he hasn't tried this. This shit is legit, man. It's the next best thing to heaven."

"Thank you for the information," Dominic said softly.

It was like his good mood dissipated the moment the words left Fallon's mouth. I stared between them, the spins making me wince. It looked like Mr. De Luca might be in some trouble if I had to guess.

Dominic cleared his throat. "What news do you have for me on Hail's plans? Bianca's father? Stefan's death? Anything on that stuff?"

Fallon swallowed. "I-I don't have any info."

"So you failed?" Dominic raised his brows at him.

"I didn't fail," Fallon seethed. "I still brought you information. I gave you a head's up even."

"I could've learned this through my court," Dominic said, slipping a joint from his shirt pocket and lighting it.

I watched as the cherry bobbed in the dim light and he inhaled deeply.

"But you learned it faster through me," Fallon shot back.

"I was already aware De Luca was becoming a problem. You only confirmed it."

"Man, what do you want from me? I know you want to make me suffer for fucking your girl, but she was my girl too!"

"You were going to betray her and set her loose in a sex trafficking ring. I hardly call that love," Vincent said conversationally. There was a bite to his voice which made my stomach tighten. He was right though.

"I was going to come back for her," Fallon snarled. "You pricks were going to put a bullet in her head in the woods and then bury her where no one would find her."

"But we didn't," Dominic said easily. "Had you had your way, you'd have finished what you started."

"And if Seeley hadn't pussied out, she'd be dead. We both would be! You keep fucking punishing me for a situation where there was no good way to handle!"

"Let's not split hairs here. Bianca," Dominic snapped.

I glanced at him with wide eyes as I tried to focus on his two faces.

"Come." Dominic patted his thigh.

I shuffled over to him, aware Fallon's eyes were locked on every step. When I got to Dominic, he pulled me onto his lap.

"Wasp, tell Fallon how you feel."

I swallowed. "I'm really drunk. And pretty high."

Vincent let out a huff of soft laughter as Dominic sighed.

"I meant about him. About the shit he put you through. About how he deserves to pay just a little bit."

"You hurt me," I whispered, trying to keep my words from slurring. "I-I love you like I love my kings, but I'm mad at you. I want you to join us. I-I want you to prove yourself, so I don't feel like a total idiot for letting you in again."

"I know, princess," he choked out. "I know, and I will."

"We don't deal in dead promises. Don't tell us what you *will* do. Show us," Dominic said, running his fingers through my hair. "The good, the faithful, the *fucking loyal*, get rewarded when you're a king. Was the incentive I gave you already not enough?"

Fallon swallowed, his Adam's apple bobbing.

"I want her," Fallon rasped. "Please. This is fucking torture. Enough, De Santis!"

"It's enough when I say it is," Dominic snapped back. "Maybe I didn't give you enough fucking motivation before. Maybe you need to see us in action."

I turned to Dominic, confused about what he was talking about or what his demented plans were.

"Wasp. Knees. Now."

I swallowed and looked from Dominic to Vincent, who gave me a slight nod. I slid off Dominic's lap and faced him on my knees.

"Suck my cock," Dominic breathed out. "Show this fucking lord how you reward those you forgive. Those who fucking prove they're worth your time."

I blinked at him. He raised his eyebrows.

With shaky hands, I reached out and unbuttoned his pants. I pulled his thick length out. He was already hard.

"Suck it, my good girl," he cooed softly.

I felt like I was beneath a microscope, being examined by every male in the room. But I wanted to do this. I wanted to feel in control again.

Dominic let out a soft breath as I ran my tongue along his dick. I locked my eyes on his. He took a deep hit from the joint he still held in one hand. So much desire and affection simmered in his green pools that I sucked him deep into my throat, willing to do anything for him at the moment. Maybe I'd gone crazy. Maybe the weed and alcohol made me lower my guard. Maybe I was simply just the slut Levin insinuated I was.

Whatever it was, I felt empowered and desperate to prove to these men that I was worth it. All of it. Life. Death. Hope. Love. I'd earned it. I wanted it. It was mine, and I was going to take it.

"There you go, wasp," Dominic breathed out as he guided my head at the pace he wanted. "My perfect queen."

"Why are you making me watch this?" Fallon called out in a throaty whisper. "She's fucking wasted. You're *making* her do this."

"Am I?" Dominic asked as I slurped along his length. He put his joint out and set it on the arm of the chair. "She seems like she's enjoying herself, right, *mia regina*?"

Knowing I was being watched turned me on more than I thought possible. Memories of being with Vincent and Levin together spurred me on. Dominic was here now. My heart ached as Levin's face flashed in my head. He should be here too. But he'd made his choice. And I made him think I'd made mine.

I sucked Dominic harder, making him hiss.

"That's right, baby," he grunted, thrusting up into my mouth so his thick cock struck the back of my throat. "Good answer."

"My punishment is watching her suck your cock?" Fallon asked, his voice quivering.

"No," Dominic said, tangling his fingers into my hair and forcing my face farther down on his dick.

I coughed and choked when he let me up for air. He liked his dick sucked like Levin did. Rough. Violent. I should've figured as much. Everything Dominic did was rough and violent.

"Vincent, let's reward our good girl. Show this asshole what he's missing out on by not finishing his fucking job."

Vincent moved forward, and a moment later his warm hands squeezed my waist.

He fumbled with the button on my skirt for a moment before he undid it and tugged it down my thighs, my panties following soon after.

Dominic pushed my mouth off his dick. With impatient moves, he removed my shirt and bra. He reached down and grabbed my panties from the floor, wadding them in his hand. He gripped my chin and forced my eyes to his. His fingers softly caressed my cheek.

"We're going to fuck you until you're screaming. I promise, it's going to hurt so good, wasp. You're going to love it. Now, open your mouth like a good girl."

I parted my lips, and he shoved my panties into my mouth.

Vincent was already on his feet when Dominic lifted me into his arms and carried me to the bed. My heart thudded hard in anticipation of what was going to happen.

"Fallon, take a seat, and enjoy the show," Vincent said, nodding to the spot Dominic had vacated.

Fallon moved to the chair, his features twisted into an expression I couldn't read.

Vincent lay on his back and smiled up at me, his clothes completely gone.

"Bury his cock inside your pussy," Dominic commanded as he undressed.

I swallowed hard and straddled Vincent as he dragged his fingers along my slit.

"Fuck, you're dripping for us," he groaned.

Dominic's fingers joined Vincent's. "Is my good girl ready for us?" he rasped.

I peeked over my shoulder at him and nodded, watching as he coated his dick with my arousal. Then he spat in his palm, stroking himself more. My insides clenched with need.

Vincent stole my attention as guided his length into me. I breathed out through my nose and forced down a whimper as he quickly shoved deep inside. I wanted this so much I couldn't think of anything else. Dominic's warm hand moved to the center of my bare back. He pushed my chest down onto Vincent's as he lined himself up where Vincent was already buried to the hilt.

I whimpered as he prodded the tightness with his cock.

"This might hurt a bit," he said softly. "Scream for me, wasp."

My scream came out muffled by my panties as he forced his way in, his cock sliding against Vincent's inside me.

I'd never felt so full in my entire life. My heart thrashed violently in my chest as I realized I had both of them inside the same small space.

Vincent thrust up into me, making my eyes roll back. A panty-muffled groan sounded out as Dominic shoved in deeper.

Then they moved together. A well-oiled machine made of cocks, abs, and violence pounded into my aching heat in tandem, each thrust in sync, loaded with both pain and pleasure.

I panted and cried out against the panties as Dominic fisted my hair and pulled hard, his cock slamming into me at the same time Vincent's did.

Slapping skin. Grunts. Groans. Whimpers.

"Fucking B," Vincent moaned breathlessly. "God, baby. Fuck. Your pussy is golden."

Dominic slapped my ass so hard, I cried out again. Then they were fucking me hard. Fast. Ruthless. Brutal. Cock against cock. Skin against skin. My moans muffled by the panties as Vincent groaned softly beneath me and Dominic's breathing puffed out in soft pants against my ear. It felt like forever and yet not long enough.

"Fuck, I'm going to come," Vincent choked out, his body trembling beneath mine as Dominic continued to slam into me faster and harder.

Dominic released my hair and gripped my hips, pushing me off of their cocks. Then he pressed my torso tight against Vincent's, trapping Vincent's throbbing cock against my belly. Dominic reached down and fisted Vincent's hair as he shoved his own dick back inside my pussy. Vincent cried out a moment later, his cock twitching against me as he spilled his release on our stomachs. It was messy, but so hot.

Dominic let go of him, then he thrust hard and deep. My eyes rolled back, and I clawed at Vincent's chest as an orgasm slammed into me.

I came with a choked wail as Dominic's cock painted my insides white with his hot release. He pressed his lips to my bare shoulder.

"My perfect girl," he murmured, nipping at my skin.

We stayed plastered together for a moment before Dominic pulled out. Vincent removed the panties from my mouth and gave me a lazy, sated smile.

Dominic rolled me onto my back and swirled his fingers through the sticky mess on my belly, drawing designs in it before swiping his index finger up my wet center, pushing his come back into me, his gaze locked on mine.

"Do you want to be included?" Dominic called out to Fallon, not bothering to tear his stare from mine.

"Yes," Fallon whispered, his voice shaking.

"Come here."

Fallon got to his feet and joined us on the bed.

"Clean up the fucking mess Vincent and I made," Dominic commanded, moving away from me. "Taste what you're missing. Then get the hell out of here and get me my fucking information. If you do a good enough job, it might be you buried in her next time."

Fallon's bottom lip trembled for a moment before he took Dominic's spot and looked down at me.

"I'd do anything for you, princess." Moments later, he was lapping at the mess my kings had left behind, cleaning my abdomen and core.

I arched my back at the wicked thrashing he gave my sensitive pussy.

He gripped my hips hard enough to make me wince and pulled me to his mouth.

I nearly sobbed at the pleasure I was being tormented with.

I squirmed and bucked until Vincent and Dominic sat on either side of my head so they could hold my arms down.

"Easy, baby B," Vincent said. "You're going to give him a concussion with those sexy as fuck hips."

I moaned, but Dominic quickly silenced me with a scorching kiss, eating down my groans of euphoria as the heat swept low and hot. A rush of anticipation coursed through me as the threat of another orgasm gripped me.

"Make her come," Dominic commanded as Vincent pressed his lips to mine in a searing kiss which made me buck harder against Fallon's mouth.

Fallon devoured me, his fingers digging into my flesh, creating enough pain to spur me on for more.

Dominic fisted Fallon's hair and forced his face deeper into my folds.

Fallon let out a muffled snarl and sucked harder on my clit.

My orgasm exploded through me, making starlight dance in my eyes.

"Eat it. All of it," Dominic growled, rubbing Fallon's face against my pussy.

Fallon didn't fight the demand. He simply licked and sucked me clean of the pretty little sins we'd just experienced together.

I lay like a puddle in my bed, panting hard, my body covered in a sheen of sweat.

"Look at that beautiful mess." Vincent chuckled, brushing my hair away from my face as I panted.

I reached for Fallon, who immediately glanced at Dominic for direction.

"Give her what she wants," Dominic said in a soft voice.

Fallon eased forward, pressing his lips to mine. His clothed body rested lightly over mine, and his hard cock put pressure on that perfect spot.

I kissed him deeply, tasting Dominic, Vincent and myself on his lips. I was exhausted by what I'd just been put through. When Fallon broke away, we were both breathless.

"I'm worth it, princess. I am. I'm just trying to be safe. That's all. I'll get the information."

"Tell Dominic," I murmured sleepily. "He's in charge."

Fallon nodded. "I know."

He moved away from me and faced Dominic, who was now dressed. Even Vincent had put his pants back on.

"I'm not a fucking failure. I'm loyal to Bianca and whatever comes with her. That's you and the kings. I'm not ever leaving. You could put a bullet in my head, and I'd still come back because I love her. I'll spend my entire life making things up to her. Please don't keep torturing me with my shortcomings. I did what I thought I had to do. I would've come back. I swear I'd have come back for her."

Dominic surveyed him for a moment before speaking, "Get me my information. This isn't a power move on my part. Her life fucking depends on it. If Ivanov is planning to hurt her, I need to know about it. I need all the details I can get about Ivanov's next moves. I want to know *everything* he knows. I don't care if you have to suck his cock to get me the info, you drop to your knees and open your pretty fucking mouth. And get me more intel on the De Luca prick. Got it?"

A muscle thrummed along Fallon's jaw before he nodded. "And then?"

"And then I'll consider what comes next. Fucking *wow me*, Vasiliev. Your life depends on it because if you don't get me what I want, I really will put a bullet in your head. Get me?"

"I get you," Fallon growled before turning back to me with longing.

"Now get the fuck out of here and go back to the dip. See what you can get out of your drunken comrades. *Mi capisci?*"

Fallon nodded and gave my hand a squeeze. "I love you, Bianca."

I said nothing, watching as he got to his feet and shuffled to the door before pulling it open. He disappeared without a backward glance, his head held high in determination.

"Think he's going to come through?" Vincent asked.

"He has no choice but to come through," Dominic murmured, his gaze on the closed door Fallon had disappeared through.

I closed my eyes as a pair of warm lips met my forehead. I wasn't sure which of the kings was kissing me, but it didn't matter. I loved them all. Even that asshole Levin.

He was the missing piece I had to get over though. And that was the worst feeling in the world.

"Everything will be OK, B," Vincent murmured, sliding into bed against me and covering us both with one of my extra blankets. "I promise."

"And if it's not?"

"Then we'll fucking make it be," Dominic answered, slipping in on my other side and placing a kiss on my temple.

I believed him. *What choice did I have?*

THIRTY-FOUR
LEVIN

"Come on," Celeste breathed out as she rubbed my cock through my jeans.

I slammed back my drink and ignored her. I'd seen Bianca and Dominic all over one another. Apparently, she'd gotten over being pissed off at him.

Good for him.

It didn't hurt any less. Watching her suck Vincent off earlier in the dark had my rage bubbling over. The vision of her on her knees, eating his cock like a starved dog lingered in my mind, causing my fury to rise still. And not because one of my best friends had gotten off.

But because it wasn't me. I wanted to be involved. But now, I was an outsider to something I should've been part of.

Fallon had left soon after Dom and Vincent had taken Bianca away. Shit was going down, and I wasn't invited. I had no idea the status of any of that, but I vowed I'd find out the first chance I got.

I imagined they were all fucking her in Dom's room. I pictured her on her knees, gazing up at Dom with those too-blue fucking eyes as he slid his cock deep into her mouth. Her hand stroking Vincent's dick as he let out a groan, his head falling back.

Is she thinking about me while they take turns on her? Does she wish I was there to help? Wish I was there to feed her my cock—

"Levy!" Celeste jutted her bottom lip out at me. "You're not paying attention to me."

"Sorry," I grunted, shoving the thought of Fallon fucking her out of my head. *Of course the asshole had to pop up and ruin everything.* "Guess I'm tired."

"We can leave," she said, biting her bottom lip.

I nodded, wanting to see if I'd run into Dom. Our dorm rooms were on the same floor.

"Let's go." I nudged her forward as she giggled like a fucking airhead.

We left the dip and walked to the dorms. She giggled and clung to me the entire time. As far as conversations went, she wasn't great. Everything came out sounding fake and overly inflated.

"I can't wait to see your room," she said, twining her fingers with mine.

I snorted and shoved open the door to my building. Silently, we rode the elevator to the top floor where mine, Dom's, and Vincent's rooms were—where even Ivanov's room was. Luckily, his room was around the corner, so his stupid ass wasn't something I saw a lot of up here. He was always with his boys or holed up snorting coke with his disciples and their whores.

I strolled slowly past Dom's room, straining to see if I could hear him fucking Bianca.

Nothing.

Maybe they'd gone to Vincent's room. His was farther down the hall than mine but to hell with it. I led Celeste to Vincent's room and stood outside it, listening intently.

Again, nothing.

Fuck.

"Are you going to open the door?" Celeste asked, twirling a piece of hair around her finger.

"Wrong room. I'm really wasted," I muttered, turning and moving back to my room. I pushed the key into the handle, unlocked the door, and stepped inside with Celeste on my heels.

"Ooh, it's really clean," she said, stepping deeper into my space.

My heart pounded. I hated having chicks in my room. I'd always preferred being in theirs where I could fuck them and leave.

She stopped in front of my record collection and slid my Rolling Stones album out, wrinkling her nose.

"What's this?"

"One of the greatest bands in the world," I said, going to my little fridge and taking out a beer. I downed the entire can in one go and then opened another.

"Can we listen to it?" She looked at me with hopeful eyes.

" No," I said quickly.

That was bumblebee's band. *Our band.* Ridiculous fucking thought, but I wasn't going to share it with Celeste.

I took another deep drink of my beer and slid out my phone as Celeste pouted and put my album back onto the shelf. She sauntered over to my bed and settled on the edge as I leaned against my dresser.

I thumbed out a message to Dom.

Me: Where are you?

I stared at the screen until my eyes burned, but no reply came. I didn't need to ask where he was. I knew where the fuck he was. He was with bumblebee. So was Vincent. And probably that fucking weasel Vasiliev. *The F-Word.* The cunt who was taking my girl.

Should've just fucking shot him.

"Come here, Levy," Celeste called out, patting the spot next to her on my bed.

I finished my beer and grabbed a bottle of whiskey before I marched over to sit beside her.

"You know, you're my boyfriend now. I don't think it's a good idea for you to drink so much." She took my whiskey slowly from my hands.

I ground my teeth as I stared at her. Purposefully, I reached into my front pocket and pulled out a joint. Staring at her, I sparked it up with the lighter from my pants pocket.

She watched me with narrowed eyes, her lips turned into a deep frown.

I took a long drag and let the burn fill me.

Then I took another.

She snatched the joint out of my hands and put it out before tossing it into the trash.

"You definitely shouldn't be getting high as my boyfriend."

I stared back at her blearily and let out a soft laugh. *Boyfriend.* Fuck my life.

"And I was thinking, maybe we could get you some new clothes so you don't look so...scary. You wear a lot of black."

"I like black. Bianca likes black."

Wrong thing to say in my stoned stupor.

"Bianca D'Angelou?" Celeste snorted, pure fury on her face.

"De Santis," I corrected in a soft voice. "She's married to Dom."

"I don't care who she married. Why are you even talking about her? You shouldn't even be *thinking* about her after what she did to us at lunch. She embarrassed me."

I shrugged. "I would be smoking and drinking, but you took them."

She scoffed. "Listen, I saw her slap you tonight. She clearly doesn't like you, so whatever weird thing you might have with or for her needs to end. She's married to Dominic. I'm sure he wouldn't like knowing his best friend keeps staring at his wife."

I scoffed and shook my head. She had no clue how our trio worked. Hell, if Bianca weren't in the picture I would've probably offered up Celeste's pussy to them.

"I wanted to-to *beat her* for touching you," she continued "No one touches my Levy."

I smirked at that thought. If she would've raised her hand to bumblebee, she'd have gotten one hell of a surprise. I wouldn't have been the only one getting hit. Plus, Dominic would've put Celeste to the ground for even approaching Bianca. Woman or not, Dominic didn't fuck around. Any threat was enough to put a bullet in it, especially when it came to Bianca.

"Why are you smiling?"

"Oh, I just like the thought of you wanting to defend me," I lied, giving her a half-assed grin.

I'd been in this sham of a relationship for only a few days and was already wanting to get the hell out.

She smiled at me, buying my bullshit.

"You're so sweet, Levy," she sighed, stroking my cock through my pants again.

I forced the grimace from my face.

She eased to her knees in front of me and stared up at me as she tugged on my pants button. I swallowed hard, my heart aching as I thought about bumblebee.

It's not cheating. She's not yours. She never was. She said she was done. She said she didn't want you. That she never would. You were never a choice.

My mind went to ugly thoughts of Vasiliev touching her with Dom and Vincent.

Celeste pulled my dick out. My lip wobbled as she sucked along my length.

I'm doing this for Dom. For the deal. I fucking hate this. Fuck. Fuck. Someone save me from this nightmare. God, help me...

"Your dick is so big." Celeste giggled before she licked up my shaft.

I swallowed and tried not to jump up and run from the room. I didn't know what the fuck was the matter with me. Any other time, I'd have welcomed a blow job and some good, sloppy drunk fucking.

Then Bianca came into my life and changed every fucking thing I thought I knew, myself included. Now, there I was with some chick who wasn't my bumblebee, slobbing my knob.

Celeste sucked me deep into her mouth and gagged. I winced as she caught me with her teeth. And again.

Fuck, is she a goddamn beaver gnawing on my log?

She scraped me again. I sucked in a sharp breath she must have taken as a sound of pleasure because she sucked harder, dragging her teeth more as she bobbed up and down.

Unable to bear more, I pushed her away by the shoulders. She released my cock with a loud popping noise.

"What's wrong?" she asked, wiping at her lips.

"Nothing," I said, breathing out. "Uh, how about we just…talk?"

"Talk?" She frowned. "Really?"

"Yeah." I cleared my throat. "Let's get to know one another."

"O-OK." She stood up and sat next to me as I tucked my dick away, the confusion evident on her face. "Um, what's your favorite color?"

"Blue," I said, thinking about bumblebee's eyes. "Yours?"

"Mm, pink."

Figured.

"Uh… what do you plan on doing after Bolten?"

She bumped her shoulder against mine and smiled. "Marriage. Kids. I'll probably do some time at college because Daddy thinks I need to be able to support myself and learn the business side of things in case I don't get married, but really, what an absurd idea. Of course, I'll marry. What are you going to do?"

"My life is planned out for me. Probably Mayfair after Bolten. It's where Dominic and Vincent will probably go as well. Then I'll work for Dom."

She wrinkled her nose. "Are you sure you want to do that? Work for Dominic doing… whatever really bad things you do?"

I nodded. "Yeah. Dom and Vincent are my best friends. I was born and bred to work with them."

"You said with. Don't you mean *for*? I mean, Dominic is the son of a mob boss. He's the heir to, like, everything. You're not his equal, Levy. I think you should try to break away from that life. You and I could go off to Mayfair or Princeton or Harvard together. We could get married someday, and you could take over Daddy's company. You're much better than some henchman. You know that, right?"

"I'm not a henchman. I'm Dom's equal." I tried to keep the snarl out of my voice, but it was damn hard.

"You aren't," she murmured, cradling my face and giving me a look of sympathy that made my guts churn. "And you never will be."

I gritted my teeth and forced a smile onto my face. "Guess that's my problem then, huh?"

"Really, it's our problem," she said softly. "You're my boyfriend. We both come from powerful families. Although I'd say mine is a bit more than yours. It doesn't mean we can't rule this campus. I mean, people worship Bianca, and she's nothing. She came in here engaged to Hail. Then she cheated on him with Dominic, and now they're married. It's like she's trying to get clout for being a whore."

"Bianca is not a whore," I snapped at her. I'd pretty much called her one earlier, but I hadn't meant that shit. I was just pissed off and regretted the words the moment they were out of my mouth.

"*Whatever*. I heard she's cheating on Dominic with Vincent."

"Where did you hear that?" I tried to keep the humor out of my voice, wondering if maybe I'd been part of that rumor at some point.

It wasn't like she and I hadn't done stuff together. Good stuff. Fucking *amazing* stuff.

She shrugged. "*Everyone*. Honestly, don't you pay attention?"

"Guess not."

"Besides, I heard her dad was involved in this money laundering scheme with her stepdad, David D'Angelou. I guess her dad was playing both sides with the Ivanovs and De Santis family. That's how he came up missing. And Bianca was the payment to David D'Angelou for her dad messing up. Like, it was basically give up his family or die, so he gave them up. David needed a way into Ivanov's good graces more than he already was. So he wanted to secure it with a marriage. That's why Hail was engaged to her."

"How...where did you hear this?" I asked, frowning.

"Promise you won't get mad?"

I stared back at her not ready to promise a damn thing.

"Please, Levy?" She pouted, pushing her cashmere-clad breasts out to me.

Fuck it.

"Promise."

She smiled triumphantly. "I was seeing Drake for a little bit over the summer. It wasn't serious," she rushed on when she saw the look on my face. "I was going through a rough patch with my boyfriend and wanted to get back at him, so I messed around with Drake. I regret it now because he definitely wasn't someone I should've associated with, but he told me things when we were together."

"Did he tell you anything else? Like where Bianca's dad is?"

"Mm, I don't really remember."

I clenched my fists. "Did he tell you anything else? Maybe about my brother Stefan?"

She cocked her head at me, her eyes narrowed. "I know a few things."

"Like?" I was losing my patience.

"You of all people should know nothing in this world is free, Levy," she murmured, leaning in and brushing her lips against my stiff ones. "If you want information, make me believe it. Make me believe I'm the only girl in your world. I saw the way you stared at Bianca tonight. I want you to look at me like that. I want to own you how she owns you. I want you to be mine and me to be yours. Me and you, Levy. Say it. Prove it."

I swallowed hard, my pulse thundering in my ears.

But I wanted information. I needed it.

"Me and you," I choked out, the words like acid on my tongue. "Us."

She let out a soft giggle, her bottom lip pulled between her teeth. "Now prove it."

Nausea twisted in my guts like a snake. I had to do this. I was in charge of getting this deal for Dom, and I needed any information Celeste had for me. I leaned in and kissed her, ready to pay whatever the cost was. *What choice did I even have?* For Bianca. For my brother. For Dom and Vincent.

This was for them.

I pushed her back onto the bed and undid my pants.

THIRTY-FIVE
BIANCA

"You'll need something white," Dominic said as he picked a cheesy nacho off his plate during lunch a few days after I'd woken up between him and Vincent.

My pussy ached like no tomorrow the next day, but if memory served me correctly, they'd both done a number on it at the same time. Whenever I thought about it, I blushed.

God, I'd changed.

I'd gone from no sex to being pounded by two dicks in the same hole seemingly overnight.

"I don't think white suits me, husband," I said, feeling the heat in my cheeks.

He smirked at me, clearly having the same image in his head I'd just had in mine.

"You're an angel, B," Vincent said, leaning in. "You took us to heaven that night. You should definitely wear white."

My face grew hotter at his words.

"Open," Dominic said.

I opened my mouth without pushing his buttons, and he slid the nacho into my mouth. Over the last few weeks, I'd noticed a change in Dominic. He was still possessive, jealous, and violent like always. But he also had this overwhelming caring streak that made me stumble a bit emotionally whenever we were near one another, which was often since Levin was spending all of his time with Celeste. Levin and I hadn't spoken since the night at the dip. I'd seen him talk to the guys when I wasn't nearby, but whenever I'd approach, he'd glare and storm away.

I'd be lying if I said it didn't hurt my heart a little, but Vincent had summed it up perfectly for me the day before while we sat in the commons waiting for Dominic.

"You made your bed, B. Now, you gotta lie in it. It doesn't mean it's forever, you know?"

"But he's with Celeste," I said, frowning.

Vincent nodded but said nothing, so I plowed on, letting the words tumble off my lips before I could stop them, "Do you think they're sleeping together?"

Vincent winced at the question and leaned back in his seat. "Why does it matter? Like, what will knowing do? Make things worse? Is that what you want? To feel more miserable? Baby, don't do that to yourself. You both said you were done. He's just doing what he has to now."

I swallowed, knowing Levin was sleeping with her. I'd overheard Maria Vance talking to Lacy Morse about it in the bathroom on Monday. Naturally, I'd stayed in my stall, listening. Apparently, Celeste had gushed to them about how incredible Levin was in bed.

I'd thrown up after they'd left, the knowledge making me sick.

"What's wrong? Your little posse split up?" Hail asked as he loomed over our table with the lords flanking him. "I heard you were all on the outs. Didn't realize Bianca's pussy could work up so many men at once."

Immediately, I curled against Dominic, my heart thudding hard.

"Who the fuck said you could come over here and speak?" Dominic snarled, rising to his feet, Vincent following.

I reached out and tugged at Dominic's hand. He twined his fingers through mine and gave them a gentle squeeze which was a stark contrast to the look on his face and the stance he'd taken.

"I just wanted to check out how my girl was doing," Hail said innocently. His gaze snapped to me. "How are you? You sucking the kings' cocks as good as you sucked the lords' or were you holding out on us? I heard Levin thought your pussy was so sloppy he ran off to fuck Celeste."

One moment Dominic was holding my hand, and the next that hand turned into a fist and connected with Hail's face in a sickening *crack*.

Then it became an all-out free-for-all. The lords snapped into action, attacking Dominic and Vincent. I gasped when Fallon's fist connected with Dominic's face. Fallon ducked away as Dominic lunged for him with so much fury on his face it took my breath away. Before he could get to Fallon, Hail intercepted him and took a swing. Dominic blocked it and punched him in the gut. Fallon swung at Vincent, who dipped away.

It was still an unfair fight. Four on two always was. *And really, what the hell was Fallon doing? Did he really need to play along so violently?*

Vincent had Tate and Drake on him. Dominic dealt with Hail and Fallon, the three of them going blow for blow with one another. Dominic was definitely not pulling punches like Fallon seemed to be doing now.

Hail's elbow came up and caught me in the jaw as I tried to scramble away. The hit sent me tumbling to my ass, blood seeping in my mouth from where I'd bitten my lip when I fell.

Warm arms wrapped around me and hauled me to my feet as students screamed and dove away amid the hurricane of gang warfare.

I glanced up to find myself staring into Levin's blue eyes. His gaze swept over my face, zeroing in on my lip. His thumb brushed against it, his eyes darkening. My heart skipped.

"Get her the fuck out of here," Levin snarled to Aubrey who'd rushed over to me. "Take her to Dom's room. Now." He shoved me back and jumped into the fray, punching Fallon in the face.

Fallon cursed and punched him back, both of them toppling to the floor in a heap of fists and fury.

"Bianca, come on," Aubrey said urgently as Stella shot up from her seat and rushed to the door.

I didn't know what that bitch was up to, but she'd been lying low lately. It was probably on Dominic's orders, but who knew with her.

I cast one last look at the chaos behind me, noting the teachers didn't even try to break things up. The security guards just stood around looking dumbfounded.

I followed Aubrey out of the cafeteria and to the grounds.

"Bianca," Stella called out as we rounded a corner to walk to Dominic's dorm.

I paused and stared back at her as she strode forward. "What?"

"I'm coming with you."

"Why?" I snorted at her, wondering who the hell she thought she was.

"I think we both know why," she shot back. "Aubrey, you can go."

"She's not going anywhere but with me. *You* can go," I snapped.

Stella rolled her eyes. "Whatever. I'm not leaving. Dominic would have my ass if I did."

"Trust me, I won't tell."

"I would," Aubrey muttered.

Stella sneered at her. Before the two could argue, I threw my hands up and started my trek back to Dominic's. I'd deal with this shit later. Right now, I needed ice on my lip.

The girls fell in step beside me and remained silent the entire way to the room, something I was immensely grateful for. My heart was still thrashing from the look in Levin's eyes and the way his fingers had brushed against my lip.

We entered Dominic's—*our*—room. I went to the small fridge and found an ice pack in the freezer. Gently, I pressed it to my lip before flopping down in the overstuffed chair. Aubrey perched beside me on the arm of the chair.

"Hail really got you," Aubrey murmured, her brows crinkled.

I grunted, hating that prick.

"Too bad he probably doesn't realize he did because I'm sure he'd be gloating about it," Stella said.

I gave her the finger, and she replied with an eye roll.

"I just mean he'd feel good about it. I didn't say *I* felt good he did. Get a grip."

"Why are you here?" I demanded. "Like, why did you come with us?"

Stella licked her lips and sat on the edge of the bed, smoothing the duvet as Aubrey shot me a confused look.

"I wanted to help."

I scoffed. "What's the real reason?"

"I just told you." She sighed and went silent for a moment before speaking. "Listen, Bianca, I know we don't get along, but I know some stuff, OK? Stuff I'm *not* OK with. We have a chance to be alone, so I thought I'd take the opportunity to actually talk to you."

I narrowed my eyes at her. "About what?"

"Are you having sex with Dominic?"

I swallowed but didn't answer.

She nodded and reached into her bag and pulled out packets of pills. "Here. Take these."

I took them and frowned. "Birth control?"

"Yeah. Listen, I know Dominic's plan is to get you pregnant, and I know he threw out your pills. Not only would you be tied to him for, like, *ever*, but it's also just not right. And if you're fucking Vincent and Levin as I suspect you are or will be, then you're going to need these."

Aubrey shot me a surprised look. "You're trying to protect her?"

"I think you should get to choose if you want a baby. Not have some asshole force it on you."

"I already had sex with Dominic a couple of times without anything," I admitted softly, the heat rising in my cheeks. "I was really wasted, and I-I—"

Stella wrinkled her nose as Aubrey gave my hand a squeeze.

"I don't need the details. I've fucked them before, you know. I mean, not together, but I do remember how things work with them."

Nausea rolled in my guts. I tried not to think about all the women they'd been with, and I definitely didn't want to think about Stella being with any of my kings.

"My point is, take the pills. Don't let Dominic know I gave them to you, or we're both dead, OK? Take a pregnancy test. If it's negative, you can start the pack right away. It might make you skip a period though."

"It should start Monday," I muttered.

"Good. So starting the pills now won't alter your schedule too much," Stella said.

"Where am I going to keep these? Especially here," I said, glancing around.

If Dominic found them, he'd beat my ass raw.

"I could keep them," Aubrey said softly. "I could hand one off to you every morning. We'll make it a habit that we hang out before classes start. We'll eat breakfast together or something."

I nodded. That could work. If we were discreet enough, Dominic would never know she was slipping me birth control.

"And on weekends, we'll see each other. I'll bring you guys food or something," she continued. "We'll make it work."

"Thank you." I looked up at her and smiled.

She was a good friend. One of the best. She grinned back and patted my hand.

"*Excuse* me. I'm the one giving them to you," Stella called out. "Where's my thanks?"

"Right here." I gave her the finger again.

She rolled her eyes. "I still don't know what Dominic sees in you. You're so uncultured."

"Maybe he likes me dirty and unpredictable."

She grunted. "Whatever. Anyway, it would be better for you to find somewhere to keep them yourself that way if something comes up and you're not on campus in the morning or something, you'll still have them. Do you have a secret zipper in your purse?" Stella asked.

I did have a teeny zipper in the inside of my purse that I might be able to slip them in.

"Aside from girl code or whatever you're labeling it, why are you helping Bianca?" Aubrey asked.

Stella smirked. "I have my reasons."

"What are they?" I frowned, knowing damn well she had some ulterior motive.

"Well, if he can't get you pregnant, he might find solace elsewhere. He might realize he needs someone a little more refined and... useful."

"Someone like you?" I asked dryly.

She grinned. "Maybe. Can't hurt a girl to try."

"You really are a slimy, little bitch, aren't you?"

"The rule of thumb is to go after what you want, even if it might kill you or break your heart," Stella said, smiling broadly. "And Dominic would certainly kill me if he knew, so let's just keep this between us. It'll be beneficial to both of us."

While I wasn't in the market to give up my kings, and certainly not my husband, who I was growing rather fond of again, I also wasn't ready for everything Dominic was forcing on me so soon. So I'd take the double-edged sword with the hopes Dominic wouldn't leave if I didn't give him an heir right away.

"By the way, Fallon *really was* wasted that night, wasn't he?" She rose to her feet, her eyes twinkling.

"You better not have touched him," I snarled, standing up.

Her smile trembled, but she quickly righted it. Before she could answer, the door to Dominic's room swung open. Aubrey snatched the pill packets from me and jumped up, shoving them into her blazer pocket and moving away from me as Dominic stormed into the room.

In one swoop, he had me in his arms, his lips peppering kisses along my face. When he reached my lips, I whimpered, pulling away.

"What's wrong? Are you hurt, *mia regina*?" He frowned as he spotted my swollen lip and let out a snarl.

"It's nothing," I mumbled. "Hail's elbow caught me when I was trying to move away." I noted the cut over his brow and frowned. "You're hurt."

He shook his head. "I don't even feel it." He pressed the ice pack back to my lip. "Keep that there."

He released me and looked at Aubrey, standing nervously to the side, then to Stella, who was now standing beside Vincent. Levin propped himself against Dominic's dresser, looking like he was trying to not be noticed.

But I noticed him. I saw the look in his eyes when he stared back at me. The hurt. The fear. It broke my heart. I didn't know how to fix this mess with us. *Could it be fixed?*

He was dating Celeste now. Maybe I just needed to let go and let the chips fall where they may. It was my fault, after all.

"Um, I'm, uh, going to go," Aubrey called out nervously as she skittered to the door. "Bianca, let's do breakfast tomorrow."

"OK," I said, forgiving her for rushing away.

If I'd been in her place, I probably would've run too. She opened the door and disappeared moments later, leaving me with the kings and Stella.

"I'll get something for your eye," I murmured to Dominic.

He sank into the chair, but instead of letting me go, he wrapped his arms around my waist and pulled me to his lap.

"I got something for my eye," he answered softly in my ear so only I could hear him. He gave me a squeeze, and I relaxed against him, my head fitting into the crook at his neck. He eased the ice pack back to my lip.

"You'll be happy to know, I broke Tate's nose, and I'm pretty sure I cracked Drake's ribs," Vincent said, moving to sit on the bed, looking like he hadn't just fought guys rivaling him in size.

Stella followed him and sat entirely too close. I tensed when she reached out and brushed his dark hair out of his eyes.

He swatted at her hand before continuing, "And Levin punched Fallon in the face too hard."

"I was going for realism," Levin muttered, glancing at me before quickly turning away.

"He's never going to heal at this rate. What's wrong with you, Levin?" Stella demanded.

"Why the fuck are you even here?" Levin snapped back. "Last I heard, you were Dominic's lapdog and fucking Ivanov. Shouldn't you be licking Ivanov's wounds right now? Judging by his face, he has quite a few."

Stella started to protest, but Dominic spoke up, "Levin's right. Stella, go. Now is a great time to listen in."

"Dominic, he'll be pissed right now. He'll probably hurt me—"

"Then brace yourself," Dominic said in an icy voice. "Fallon is there. He'll make sure you're OK. Then report back to me."

Her bottom lip wobbled for a moment. "You said you'd protect me, but you're sending me into danger. He'll hurt me if Fallon can't stop him—"

Dominic lifted me easily and stood, sliding me back onto the chair. He went to his dresser and rummaged around in it. He produced a handgun and stalked toward her. She flinched, her eyes wide with fear. He gripped her face tight with one hand and held the gun to her head with the other.

"*I'll* fucking hurt you. He'll just fuck you harder than he usually does and bruise your pussy," his slightly accented voice held a promise of danger as he pressed the gun to her forehead. "Now get the fuck out of here and do as you're told."

She visibly swallowed as he released her, her eyes darting to me quickly before she rushed from the room without another word.

"We'll be lucky if she doesn't betray us," Vincent said as Dominic put the gun back into his drawer.

"Then she'll die. It's pretty fucking simple," Dominic said. He let out a deep breath and turned to Levin. "Status?"

Levin glanced at me before he focused back on Dominic. "I'm in fucking love. What can I say?"

My chest tightened at his words, and I stared down at my lap, wishing I could just vanish.

"Pussy that good?" Dominic pressed.

Levin grunted but didn't elaborate.

"Baby B, you want to come with me to get some lunch? You didn't get to eat much," Vincent said.

I shot him a grateful look and got up. He held his hand out to me. I slid mine in his and let him lead me to the door.

"She's the best I've had in a long time," Levin said softly, his voice shaking.

Vincent squeezed my hand when I paused at the door. My broken heart shattered completely in my chest.

Don't cry. Don't cry. Don't cry. Be the bigger person. Wish him well and move on.

Slowly, I turned to face Levin and choked out words that burned like acid on my tongue. "I'm so happy for you, Boo Bear."

He winced but said nothing back.

"Get her something to eat and take her back to class," Dominic said.

Vincent tugged me through the open door, my misery still alive and well in my chest.

Levin was the master at heartbreak, but I was probably a close second. We did this to each other.

THIRTY-SIX
DOMINIC

With the tidbits of info Levin had been able to get from Celeste so far, I decided I should look deeper into things, which was why I was sitting at the palace a couple days after my fight with Hail to talk with my father.

"You haven't been doing much with this place," Father barked as we strode to the dungeon area. "Are you even trying to get women in here?"

"I'm considering running this as a legit, full-service business where the women actually want to be here," I answered as we stopped at the bottom of the stairs.

I could already hear soft sobs in the darkness. I hated the way it made me feel. Before Bianca, I may have overlooked this shit, but now I felt everything—always putting her in these women's places in my head and hating the thought of it.

Father glared at me. "Explain to me the revenue if you're paying these women. What I have set up here is absolutely free. *Everything* is profit."

"Except the sins," I said evenly. "Those have a price to pay."

"I daresay the devil would enjoy our kind, Son. We'd be rewarded, so where's the sin in that?" He turned back and marched into the dimly lit room.

A few things had changed since I'd been here last. I'd stayed out of here since he'd shot a girl named Macy on my lap after she'd sucked my dick. I'd tried to calm her, and he'd viewed it as weakness and had sprayed her brains all over me.

Now, there was a decked-out stage with various BDSM contraptions on it and small tables around it so sick fucks like him could watch the torture. Because it would be torture. None of these girls were consenting. Consenting girls didn't cry.

"What are we doing down here?" I asked as he settled at a table and gestured for me to sit.

I pulled the chair out and sat, watching him.

"You've agreed to everything the party planner has sent. She seemed surprised when I spoke to her on the phone, claiming she'd never had a bride and groom be so agreeable before."

I nodded tightly. "The reception doesn't matter to me. It's all fluff. None of it makes a difference."

"So you haven't let *your wife* make any decisions regarding your celebration?"

"No," I said. "*I* make the decisions. Not her. She's not in a place to offer a say. She's simply my prize, a piece to my empire."

Father sat back and studied me, trying to see through my damn lie.

Fuck, when had she become more than a piece of the puzzle? The answer was easy. The first fucking moment my eyes locked on hers. I hadn't realized it at the time, but thinking back, it was definitely then.

"Will she wear white despite the fact you've *defiled* her... first?" There was a note of poison in his words. He was still pissed I'd fucked her before he could *taste* her.

The men in my family had absurd traditions, that was for sure.

"She'll wear white," I confirmed.

He nodded. "It's all a lie."

I swallowed and remained calm. "What's all a lie?"

"This life." He gestured around us. "We aren't human, you and me. We're monsters cut from the same cloth. The same fabric that's been cutting out sinners for centuries. You know, your grandfather fucked your mother in front of me before I married her. Moments before. He made me watch. She wept, pleading for it to stop. His men stood observing with me. My men. He fucked her so hard she bled. Luckily, he'd lifted her dress so as to not ruin the material."

My guts churned with the knowledge of my mother's defilement. I remained still, not revealing an ounce of my anger.

"Then she got up, dried her tears, and said *I do* at the altar. I got what was left, which wasn't much. She was a good woman...until she wasn't. Always trying to run and find a way out. It took over her mind. She fought me every chance she could." He grew quiet as a soft sob sounded out in the distance.

What a fucked-up heart-to-heart.

"I wasn't prepared for how I felt watching my father fuck her. In a way, I wondered if she secretly enjoyed it. In fact, I oftentimes believe she had. He'd made her come for him. I wasn't much older than you when we married, so I didn't know as much about a woman's body then as my father did. But I learned."

I stared at the monster in front of me, wondering when he'd drop the bomb he was setting the stage for.

"Our traditions make us stronger, Dominic. You may see it as foul and immoral, but I promise you, it'll make you stronger." He set his dark gaze on me.

"This is you telling me you're going to fuck my wife."

"Yes."

"And this is me telling you that you're not."

We glared at one another, the soft cries from the imprisoned girls around us.

Father clicked his tongue. "Are you sure about that?"

"Without a fucking doubt. She's already my wife. I already tore her virginity out and left it bloody on her sheets. There's nothing you need to help me with, Father. I have it covered. I definitely don't need you to teach me how to make my woman come."

His stare hardened, something dark and ugly flashing in his eyes before he schooled his face and rapped his knuckles on the table.

"Then maybe we'll start a new tradition," he said.

"Maybe we will."

He nodded. "So be it."

We stared one another down before I spoke again, "I am curious about Nathan Walker though, Bianca's father. I've heard rumors."

Father raised his brows at me. "What rumors have you heard?"

"That he worked for you."

Father smirked and looked down at his lap before he fixed his gaze on me. "He did some books for us. Stole lots of money from me."

"Did you kill him?" I waited, holding my breath.

When it came to murder, he'd never lied to me about those he ended. Their names were trophies to him. He'd never deny a trophy.

"I did not," he said, sneering. "He disappeared before I could, taking my money with him. You marrying his daughter is like a gift from the devil, dropped right into my lap."

"So you wanting to fuck my wife is a revenge thing?"

He gave me a wicked smile. "It's a De Santis thing."

I swallowed, nodding.

"Someday you'll have a son, and he'll take a wife. You'll carry on our traditions by fucking her until she begs for mercy in front of him and your men. It makes no difference if he loves her or hates her. It matters not what name she has or the amount of begging she does. What matters is that you do what you need to do because it's who the fuck we are." He surveyed me, leaning in. "I did not raise you to be soft, Domenico. You are a De Santis. We fuck who and what we want without guilt. We let go when we need to let go. We *never* love. Love is a weakness. Your wife is flesh and bone. A nice, warm hole to bury yourself in when you're not busy fucking someone else. Don't forget it."

"I don't love her," I said softly, hating the lie as it left my mouth.

"Then me spreading her legs shouldn't matter." He stood and smoothed down his suit.

I got up and locked gazes with him. "It changes nothing. That tradition ended with my mother."

"We'll see," he said coolly. "As much as I'd like to continue this conversation, I have some things that need to be tended to."

"As do I."

His gaze swept over me before he nodded and walked ahead of me up the stairs, his body still stiff. I knew he was pissed off. And I knew I should be concerned about it. Part of me wanted to believe he wouldn't do anything stupid, but the other part knew him. Evil didn't just back down. It simply grew a second head and started destroying shit.

"I'll see you at six tomorrow night," he said, turning to me at the door. "Start considering your business plan. You've yet to impress me with your current one. I'd hate to think I raised a coward." And with those sweet words, he pivoted on his heel and disappeared to his waiting car.

"Prick," I muttered under my breath the moment he was gone.

Haley bustled out in a skimpy, red dress and offered me a quick smile. There were guards all over this place—all my father's men ready to rain hell down on anyone who stepped out of line. It was probably why Haley hadn't broken free and run the fuck out of there. They'd shoot her in the back before she made it to the eight-foot-high, wrought iron fence.

"Do you need anything, Mr. De Santis?" she asked nervously.

"Yes." I turned to her. "I want you to inform me if my father comes back. I'll be upstairs tending to something." I handed her a card with my cell number on it.

She licked her lips. "Should I log it in the book that you received services from one of the girls—"

"No," I snapped at her.

She flinched like I'd struck her. I blew out a breath.

"No, that won't be necessary."

"Your father doesn't log his time either," she said softly.

I nodded. Of course he didn't. I wasn't too keen on anyone thinking I, a married man, was upstairs fucking the imprisoned pussy we kept on the grounds, but whatever.

"Text me if he shows up or anyone comes to disturb me."

She nodded quickly, and I strode to the stairs, grateful none of the guards tried to stop me. They stared straight ahead as I passed by.

The moment I reached room twenty-seven on the third floor, I slid my key in and cracked the door open.

Natalia Vasiliev bounded off the leather sofa, her eyes wide, when I stepped into the room.

"I-I'm not supposed to have visitors," she sputtered out. "I'm not for sale."

"You're already bought and paid for, Vasiliev. Sit down," I said, closing the door behind me.

Her slender body shook, but she held her ground, her glare hardening as I approached her.

"I swear I'll scream—"

I pulled out the gun hidden in my jacket, which my father's fuckwits had been too dumb to check for and pointed it at her. She stepped back, her hands up like they could stop a bullet.

"I'll shoot you before the sound leaves your mouth. Sit." I pointed to the sofa with my gun.

She sat down, her sweatpants hanging low on her hips, her white tank top crooked.

"What do you want?" she whispered. "I'll do anything. Just don't hurt me."

"I'm glad to hear that," I said, taking a seat on the sofa. "I'm Dominic De Santis."

She sucked in a sharp breath, her eyes widening.

"I'm the one who bargained for your safety. Of course, I can revoke that at any time."

She visibly relaxed. "What do you want?"

"I want to know what you know about Stefan's murder."

She swallowed and rubbed her palms along her sweats before the words flowed easily from her mouth. "I don't know much. I fell in love with Stefan at college. Like a Romeo and Juliet thing, you know?" She looked wistful as she took the trip down memory lane.

I liked the fact I didn't need to press her for information.

"Stefan was perfect. Beautiful. He wanted out of this life just like me. We planned on running away together, but he-he didn't make it."

"Do you know what happened?"

She shook her head, a tear sliding down her cheek. "No. He went to meet with someone. He said they were going to help us. I don't even know if that's true. Then he texted me to tell me Fallon dropped him off at 53rd. He said his dad was coming. I was scared because his father found out we were together days before and he threatened Stefan. Told him he'd kill him. They fought. Stefan made me go to the car, so I did."

"Did you hear any of the argument?"

She shook her head. "Nothing really. It was just him telling Stefan he'd disown him if he ran off with me. He threatened to kill me too." She sniffled and wiped at her nose. "That's when Stefan told me to go to the car and lock the doors. That's all I heard."

She drew in a deep breath. "Stefan came out like ten minutes later really upset and said we'd be leaving the next day. I went to say goodbye to Fallon. I didn't want to give anything away because my father would've killed Stefan too if he knew I was leaving. Fallon promised he wouldn't say anything. I went to where I was supposed to meet Stefan, but he never came back for me. I-I thought it was maybe because his dad had won, and Stefan had given in and was done with me. I waited in my apartment and then got the news S-Stefan was murdered. Fallon came to tell me."

She cried softly, her body trembling. "Someone killed him. I wish...I wish I knew who. He was taken from me! And for what? Because of some stupid rivalry? It's not fair. *It's not fair.*"

I swallowed. "For what it's worth, I'm sorry."

She nodded miserably. "Thank you."

I studied her as she cried for a moment. Then she gathered herself and let out a slow, shaky breath.

"Am I going to die too? Because I want to. Without Stefan..."

"You're not going to die. I knew Stefan. He'd want you to live. I know he would."

"I know," she said softly, her dark hair falling over her shoulders.

"I just miss him so much. I've been a prisoner since I tried to leave town."

"How did it happen? How were you taken?"

She licked her lips. "I was trying to leave in the middle of the night. You know, when most of the world is sleeping. I figured I'd slip out of town with the money Stefan and I had saved up. I didn't even make it out of town before I was run off the road. These men in masks put a bag over my head and knocked me out. I've been under Matteo's thumb ever since."

"You're wrong. You're my property now," I said, gesturing around to the room. "I negotiated it as part of an agreement with my father. Your safety so I could use you as I see fit."

She immediately tensed and slid away from me, fear in her eyes. "Stefan said you-you were better than Matteo. H-he said I-I could trust you, V-Vincent, and L-Levin—"

"I'd have already fucked you if I were intent on causing you harm," I said, cutting her off. "I mean that in more ways than one."

Her hands shook as she twisted them on the leg of her sweatpants.

"Your brother. Fallon."

"Don't hurt him. He's a good man. My brother isn't like the others. He's stuck like me. Please." She got up and approached me, dropping to her knees in front of me. Her hands rested on my thighs. "I'll do anything to keep him safe. He's all I have left."

I reached out and tilted her chin up. "That wasn't me propositioning you, Natalia."

"Then what do you want from me?" she whispered, tears in her eyes.

"Your cooperation. You know you're the enemy to us, right?"

She nodded miserably.

"I made a deal with your brother to save you. I intend on following through as long as he follows through on his end."

"He won't let you down. I know my brother. If he says he's going to do something, he does it."

I nodded. "I hope that's true. But if he fails me, he fails you. So just know, no hard feelings."

"I know."

I released her face and studied her. She was a pretty girl. She was no wasp, but no one else was. I could see the family resemblance between her and Fallon. Same hair color. Same high cheekbones.

"If you can think of anything you didn't tell me, let Haley know. I'll be sure she gets you better clothes and food in here."

"And soap?" she pleaded softly, her cheeks flushing at the request.

"I hadn't realized you were without necessities. I'll see to it that everything's taken care of."

"Thank you, Dominic. Really."

"Don't thank me yet," I said, getting to my feet and stepping around her. "I still own you and have no immediate plans to release you. But I will take care of you. Better than the treatment my father gave you."

I strode to the door and paused before I opened it. "Did he hurt you?" I looked back to see her trembling again.

"He's not a nice man. He-he tried to get information out of me. So did Stefan's father. I think he was worse if I had to say. Even after I broke and begged for death, they kept the punishments coming. Months after."

She rose and lifted her tank top, turning so I could see the deep scars on her back. A roadmap of her pain. Some were still healing.

I tightened my jaw. "I'll see to it that those wounds are treated, and you have proper supplies. For what it's worth, I'm sorry for this shit. In a different world, you'd be with Stefan, and no one would've hurt either of you."

"Too bad we live in this world, huh?" She gave me a sad smile.

"Too bad," I answered back, stepping out of the room and locking her in.

I thought of the nightmare that awaited me and Bianca tomorrow night at our reception because I knew there would be one. My father would see to it. Tomorrow may very well be the day I put a bullet between my old man's eyes.

"*Way too fucking bad,*" I muttered.

THIRTY-SEVEN
FALLON

"If there's one thing I hate, it's a fucking king," Hail said as he sank in a chair in his room and snorted a line of coke from the table.

"Why you doing coke, man?" Drake called out. "I got more sugar. I thought you wanted to try this shit."

"I do," Hail grunted, adjusting his dick in his pants and then rubbing his nose but missing some of the powder. "But later."

"You're missing out," Tate said as Drake shook his head and pulled out a small baggie.

I sat forward, watching as he took the items out.

"What's this?" I gestured to the paraphernalia on the small table.

"What's it look like?" Drake asked, smirking. "It's drugs."

I rolled my eyes at him. "No shit." I moved forward and picked up a syringe and small vial, examining them. "Injectable?"

"Yeah, guy I got it from said it hits faster and offers a more intense high. He said the injectable has hallucinogenic effects with it. Different strain or some shit."

"You want to take hallucinogens?" I looked back to Hail, who shrugged.

"I want to know who the fuck this De Luca guy is, thinking he can come onto our turf and push his drugs. I need to know what we're dealing with. So if I have to see little, green men, I'll do it," Hail said, sniffing and wiping at his nose again.

The fucker was already feeling his coke high.

"I think you should hold off a bit before trying it," I said. "I think we need to know how this shit interacts with the shit you're taking."

Hail waved me off but didn't argue.

"I think fucking Valentino broke a rib," Drake said, wincing as he raised his arm. "Shit hurts, man."

"Pretty sure you broke one back," Tate said, high-fiving him.

"You got a good hit in on De Santis." Drake grinned at me before grimacing again. "Thought he might lose it and shoot you in the face though."

I nodded. I'd lost it myself for a minute and taken my frustrations out on him when I'd known damn well I shouldn't have.

It had been days since that night in Bianca's room when Dominic had made me lick his and Vincent's come off her body and out of her pussy. I wasn't complaining about eating out my girl, but I wasn't overjoyed about having to clean up after the assholes. It had made me feel like a little bitch on my knees begging for scraps.

But I knew I'd do it again and again because Bianca was worth it to me. I'd do anything for her. I wanted to prove to her I was someone she could trust and love. I wanted her to see my loyalty. Shit, if De Santis told me to drop to my knees and suck his dick, I'd do it just to prove my fucking point. Dudes didn't do it for me, but she did. I wanted her to know *nothing* would stop me when it came to her.

"I'm jealous. I wanted to punch him in the face," Tate grumbled, setting up lines of sugar. "But I wanted to grab Bianca more. I should have." He looked angry that he hadn't, and that shit pissed me off.

"What would you have done?" Drake teased. "Come in your hand? Because we all know you'd cream yourself before your dick even touched her. You lasted all of two minutes when she sucked your dick that time."

"Fallon is the MVP for that." Hail laughed. "He got all *holier than thou*, trying to guard his virtue. Motherfucker has had his cock buried in so many pussies that hers terrified him into chastity."

"Eat shit," I muttered. "It wasn't like that. I'd fucked Maria Vance earlier that day. I wasn't in the mood."

The guys guffawed loudly, further irritating me. I hadn't fucked Maria Vance. We'd made out in the locker room, but I hadn't taken it as far as I could have.

As for my princess, I wasn't one to enjoy a woman being forced to do anything for me. I'd been captivated by Bianca from the beginning and having her on her knees for me with everyone watching while she cried had rubbed me wrong. So I'd taken the opportunity to show her early on that I cared about her.

But man, what a nightmare it had been, wanting her so much and not being able to have her. That was all it had taken. I'd been teetering on the edge of falling, but the moment her soft lips had wrapped around my shaft, I had taken the plunge. Her strength, her resilience to the bullshit, the way she'd looked at me… yeah, there had been no going back. She was all I'd wanted.

Sounded fucked up, but it had been more than the blow job. I'd wanted to protect her like a national fucking treasure from that moment on.

I'd failed so hard though.

"Whatever. I've fucked Maria Vance before. The last thing anyone would want is not having sex after because her pussy is so chewed up it's like fucking a bag of air," Hail called amid the guys' laughter.

I shook my head, ignoring them.

"Listen. When Bianca was sucking your cock that night, did you get the feeling she was enjoying herself?" Tate asked.

Drake snorted, and Hail laughed.

"She wasn't enjoying herself. She didn't want to suck our cocks," I said, disgusted he even thought anything close to that.

"The way she stroked my dick definitely didn't seem that way to me," Tate continued. "But hey, you're lucky, Fallon. Hail already said when we grab her, you'll get to fuck her. You should be proud."

I grunted. *Fuck that.* I'd *never* let that shit happen, but I played along anyway because the last damn thing I needed was to fuck this up too.

"Seriously, though," Tate pressed. "You're going to do it, right? When we snatch her?"

I swallowed, knowing I had to answer. "Yes."

Drake raised a brow at me and nodded. The look on his face confused me. While I knew Tate was into being a fuck-up, Drake's reaction wasn't what I was expecting. He looked like he was trying to hide his anger over the situation without giving himself away. Or maybe I was just hoping he was.

"We at least get to watch, right?" Tate asked.

"Of course. For one thing, seeing Fallon finally give in to his baser needs will be something we all should witness. Locking him in a room and telling him he can fuck her won't have quite the same effect," Hail said, raking his fingers through his blond hair.

"Think she'll fight back?" Tate turned to Hail like it was story time.

"Absolutely. She's a little hellcat," Hail said.

"Can we not talk about me forcing my dick into some chick?" I snapped, trying to make shit sound like I didn't care.

Drake nodded. "I agree. Shit's premeditated, and I ain't burning for it, so let's just get high and have a good night."

"Drake's right." Hail stretched out and reached into his pocket for his phone. "Let's get some chicks over here. Tate needs to get off before he decides to go find Bianca and do all the fucked-up shit in his head to her."

Tate shot him a wicked smirk, which made me want to punch walls. I remained cool and calm and watched as Drake pulled out some blunts.

"Powdered sugar. Sugar cubes. Sugar straws. Sugar blow. Sugar rush." Drake nodded to the stash in front of him. "You can smoke, drink, eat, snort, or inject this shit. I'm told each does something different. I may have the names wrong. Just know sugar gets you fucked up."

"Who's the guy who made this? Was it De Luca?" I picked up one of the blunts and took a sniff. It smelled like vanilla ice cream.

"Nah. I heard it's one of his men. There are four of them. *The horsemen.* They call the dude who created it Masters. He must be a fucking rocket scientist to come up with this shit though," Drake said.

"Heard he's an addict," Tate added.

"Recovering," Drake pointed out. "At least that's what one of my sources said."

"Dead if I get my fucking hands on him or anything he loves," Hail mumbled from his chair. "Tate, find out if this Masters or De Luca have a girl or something. I'd like to pay her a visit."

My guts boiled. There was never a reason to involve someone's loved ones, but these assholes thrived on it.

"Dibs on her pussy first." Tate laughed.

"Find me the information, and she's yours," Hail agreed.

What the fuck?

Tate seemed happy at the potential screams he could earn and proceeded to pull his phone out, thumbing through it. If I had to guess, he was already looking up these horsemen and trying to get info on them.

"When are we snatching Bianca?" I asked, wanting to get to the heart of shit.

Hail shrugged. "I don't know. Soon. When the timing is right. I'm waiting on a few things. Figured we'd stir the pot in the meantime."

And that was all he'd say, so I sat in silence, waiting for later when we'd be high on sugar and maybe he'd talk.

I needed information. Anything. I was tired of being the guy who sat on the sidelines and watched the kings with my girl. I wanted to play the field with her too.

I WAS FUCKED UP.

My head spun, but I felt incredible, like a superhero.

"Stella sucks cock decent enough," Hail called out to the room.

He'd invited people over again, and everyone was wasted. As much as I'd wanted to remain in control of my head and body, I knew it was over the moment I'd smoked the sugar straw or whatever bullshit it was.

"Inject it. Fucking elite," Drake mumbled, staggering over to me and sitting down. "I think there are fucking rainbows coming out of that chick's tits."

I laughed and looked to where he was pointing at some cheerleader named Dara.

"You gotta see it, man. It's intense as hell."

"I've had enough, man. I need to stop." I tried to push him away, but he snickered. I'd already drunk my weight in alcohol and smoked enough to last me a good week.

"Seriously, Hail is going to make you do it. You know he will. Just hold out your arm and get it over with."

I sighed, knowing he was right.

"They say you can't overdose on this?" I asked as I rolled up my sleeve.

"That's the word on the street. It's all about the sugar rush."

"What about the crash?"

"What goes up, must come down," he said as he flicked the new needle, making the white liquid even out. He wrapped a band around my arm and felt for a vein before he shoved the needle in.

I closed my eyes, waiting for the rainbows or goats or whatever the hell I was supposed to see.

"All done. Have fun," Drake said seconds later, clapping me on the back.

I kept my eyes closed as heat swept slowly up my body. I felt light. Free. It added to what I was already feeling, making me want to giggle and try out my new wings.

I had wings, right?

I shook the ridiculous thought out of my head and opened my eyes. My breath caught in my chest as Bianca walked toward me in her tiny jean skirt, her tits pushed up so high all I could think about was burying my face in them and never coming out.

"What are you doing here?" I called out, fucked out of my brain. My voice didn't sound like mine as I blinked rapidly.

She had wings. My princess was an angel.

"Hail said you needed some help." She giggled, lowering herself onto my lap and raking her nails through my hair.

I practically purred beneath her touch. "You're going to get into trouble being here with me. A lord. If he finds out, we're both fucked, baby."

She laughed again. "He's the one who told me to come."

"Mm, good," I mumbled, burying my face in her neck and kissing the sensitive skin.

She curled into me as I gripped her ass.

"Our secret, princess."

"Yes. Our secret," she said, her voice not sounding like Bianca's but whatever.

I was high. Maybe my hearing was off. Maybe she was nervous to be in the lords' lair. She should be. We were fucking animals.

"Want me to fuck your cunt?" I slurred out, the ceiling strobing with stars and flying sheep. *When the fuck did sheep get wings? And was that a cat with horns?* Fuck, this shit was strong.

"You're so dirty, Fallon." She nipped at my earlobe.

Another wave of intense heat hit me. I needed to take my fucking clothes off.

"Suck my dick? I've been good. I've been doing everything I'm told," I said, slowly blinking at her.

Now she had a crown. *Well, she should. She's a queen.* Why was it made of turtles though? *That's fucking weird.*

"I thought you'd never ask. I've liked you forever," she said all breathy as she shifted on my lap, shoving her tits in my face.

I reached out and cradled them, eager to give them a suck. She let out a sharp gasp as I tore her shirt, sending the buttons flying across the room. Hail let out a whoop and a few goat laughed, but I was too far gone with my princess—no, *queen*—to stop now.

I pushed her bra down, freeing her tits, and wrapped my lips around a pebbled bud, sucking the flesh into my mouth. She moaned, her fingers in my hair as I nipped and sucked. I hauled her closer, and she ground her pussy along my aching cock.

I popped my lips off one tit and moved to the other, sucking harder this time. I wanted to mark her, so Dominic would remember I was part of their little clan too.

She cried out when I bit down, her body thrashing against me as she moaned like a whore in church.

"I'm going to come," she gasped as I squeezed her ass and rocked her along my jean-covered cock.

There was cheering somewhere in the background, but I kept my pace, desperate to get her off.

It didn't take long. She came with the sweetest moan, her body going limp as I continued to thrust against her. I closed my eyes, desperate to have my own finish, but I wouldn't do that until I was buried in her heat.

I pushed her skirt up and swept my fingers along her wet pussy.

"Fallon." Someone tapped my shoulder. "Fallon."

"Mm?" I mumbled as Bianca's fingers tugged at the button of my jeans.

"Wake the hell up before you ruin everything," a voice hissed at me.

"You want to threesome with Fallon?" Hail called out. "Stella, I'm insulted. I have perfectly good pussy you can share with me if you want."

Stella laughed. "You're right." Her voice was tight.

Something was wrong.

I popped my eyelids open to see Bianca was gone, and the girl on my lap was someone I didn't even recognize. She looked like a girl in my econ class, but fuck if I knew.

Horror set in as I realized what I'd done.

I pushed her off my lap, and she fell to the floor with a cry, her lips twisted in an embarrassed scowl as her tits bounced. There were those rainbows.

Stella widened her eyes while Hail stared at me like I'd lost my damn mind. I had. I had lost my mind.

Fuck.

I staggered to my feet, my head spinning. Colors flashed around me. The goats kept fucking singing, and the turtles raced up the wall. And the fucking bugs... *When did Hail get such an infestation?*

"I-I gotta get out of here," I shouted, fisting my hair. "I fucked up. Fuck. *Fuck!*"

"Easy, man. It's just some pussy. We aren't judging you for getting off in front of everyone," Hail said with a laugh.

I shoved past him and stumbled to the door, ready to vomit.

"Here, kitty, kitty, kitty," I called out, pulling the door open and falling into the hall. I crashed against the opposite wall as Drake called out to see if I was OK.

"The cats! The fucking cats can drive! I'm going insane. I fucked up!" I rushed away to the confused cackle of the goats and a suspicious looking leopard.

God, I hated cats.

THIRTY-EIGHT
LEVIN

"What's the plan?" I asked, settling on my bed as Dom took up residence in my computer chair.

Vincent propped himself up against my pillows and folded his hands over his head.

"I don't know. I might have to kill him," Dom said softly. He was wearing his black-rimmed glasses tonight. He must have been reading before he came over and had forgotten to take them off.

I glanced at Vincent, who wore a look of worry on his face. Killing Dom's dad would be a hell of a battle. His men would probably kill us all before we got out of there. And bumblebee would be caught in the crossfire regardless of our desire to protect her from his fucked up old man.

"We'll die," I said, cracking my knuckles. "You do realize that, right?"

"I know." Dominic downed his glass of whiskey. He and Vincent had arrived a few minutes ago with news of a potential issue with Matteo.

That issue was a big, fucked up one that made me see red.

"If we die, who saves B?" Vincent asked, sitting up.

"We might make it out," Dominic said, not sounding very convincing.

I snorted at his answer.

"*Might* isn't a strong enough word for me, buddy. Try again. If we do this, we're dead, whether it happens then or days later, especially if he fucking *lives* through the attempt. He's been shot how many times now and still comes back?" I rubbed my eyes.

Five. The answer was five times he'd been shot and had lived through them all. I swore he came back more fucked up in the head each time too.

Dominic sparked up a joint and inhaled deeply, sprawling out in the chair with his head resting against the back. He stared up at the ceiling, remaining was silent for a beat before he spoke.

"Her dress is beautiful," he said softly. "I don't want it soiled by his hands or an ugly fucking memory. I don't want her hurt."

I swallowed, my throat tight. I didn't want her hurt either. But shit, we were stuck between a rock and Matteo De Santis. Not to mention my father, who was hell with a gun on his own. Add in Vincent's old man? Definitely fucked, but I knew Vincent's father was a decent guy. He'd probably shoot around us as long as he thought we were in the right.

"Here's what we'll do. One of us will create a distraction. Set off the fire alarm or light something on fire. Everyone will have to leave. We snatch our queen and make a run for it," Vincent said.

"If my father decides to create a new tradition, or adhere to the old one, he'll want the three of us there. We can't create a distraction if we're all watching my wife get fucked by that prick."

I balled my hands into fists at the mention of Matteo De Santis laying his hands on Bianca. She was sleeping peacefully in Dom's room at the moment. It pissed me off to think it would be the last night of good sleep she'd get if Matteo got his hands on her. Bile burned my throat at the thought of her screaming for help as he pushed into her.

"Vasiliev," Vincent said suddenly, snapping his fingers. "He's the distraction."

Dom lifted his head off the back of the chair and looked at Vincent.

"He wants to prove himself. Let this be the way he does it. Let him be the distraction." Vincent looked between Dom and me with wide eyes.

I nodded. "It's a good idea. It might even get him killed and out of our way."

"Don't say that shit." Vincent sighed. "B would be devastated if he died. She may be upset with him, but the night he ate her out with us—"

"What?" I snarled, leaping to my feet, my body vibrating with rage. I wasn't stupid enough to believe nothing had happened with the three of them while I was out in the cold with dry pussy.... Maybe I was stupid. I was delusional, thinking Dom wasn't serious about The F-Word becoming part of our crew.

"It's not a big deal," Vincent said in a voice that suggested I was being a little too hot-headed. "We fucked her in front of him, and then Dom made him clean up our mess. He did. B came all over the damn place. I mean, I'd like to think I can eat pussy like a champ, but Fallon really had her back arching off the mattress—"

I put my fist through my wall.

"Why are you pissed off?" Vincent demanded, giving me a sour look as I rested my forearms against my wall, my head down as I tried to suck in slow, even breaths to control the rage bubbling within me. "He's going to be one of us. B loves him—"

"Stop fucking talking, Vin," Dominic called out, finally speaking up.

Vincent went quiet, and the only noises left were the ticking of the clock and my breathing.

When I finally calmed down enough, I shuffled back to the bed and sat on the edge again. *Why was I upset?* I knew this was the plan. Let the prick onboard. Convert him if he didn't die and managed to prove himself. Hell, I'd even thought it was a good idea. I mean, I'd hoped he'd get killed in the process, but at least I'd been onboard for the damn effort.

"Vincent is right. Bianca loves him. As much as I fucking hate it, she does. But she loves us too. Just as much. If Vasiliev can be of use, we'll use him," Dom continued.

"You've gone soft," I muttered, swallowing.

"It's not being soft," Vincent said when Dom didn't answer. "It's about giving the woman we love what she wants. You should know that, Levin. You were there the night we gave her what she wanted. Remember? We own her. But she owns us too. To make this work, we need to be able to give a little more than we take. Vasiliev isn't so bad. I can learn to like the guy. Hell, I might already like him. You just need to pull your head out of your ass and join us. Then you'd see how happy she is now."

"She's happy because I'm gone," I muttered.

"Stop with your pity party," Dom snapped. "I'm tired of it. Fuck Celeste if you want. I don't give a shit. But if you're done with Bianca, be done."

"I'm fucking Celeste so we"—I gestured angrily between us—"get the weapons deal from her old man."

"*Fuck the deal.* I don't care about the weapons. I'll figure out some other way if it falls apart. If you want to come back, then fucking come back," Dom said, staring intently at me. "If not, then just knock the shit off. We have more important things to worry about right now than your fucking emotions. Get a teddy bear if you need a hug, but shut the fuck up already."

I ground my teeth and didn't reply. Maybe he was right. *But what if I put myself back out there again, and she told me to fuck off again? Then what? Do I fuck off for good then? Would that be it?*

I shook the thoughts away. *Fuck it.* I was going to finish the weapons deal, keep Celeste happy, and make sure we had a plan for tomorrow night. Past that, I'd wing it. Alone, if I had to.

I was just about to say all that when there was a loud bang on my door. I looked quickly to Dom and Vincent, who both frowned. No one visited me but them. Ever. I had my doubts Bianca would come over.

Rising to my feet, I went to the door and cracked it open to find Vasiliev standing there looking like birds had been fucking in his hair.

It was standing straight up, his pants were unbuttoned and hanging low, and he was missing his shirt.

"What the fuck?" I called out.

"S-Seeley. I-I fucked up, man. I really fucked up." He fisted his hair and let out a snarl like a wild animal. "Can you let me in before the fucking leopard gets me? He followed me the whole way here." He jerked his thumb down the hall, and I peered out, confused off my ass but knowing I couldn't let the nutbag stand out in the hallway talking to me.

I stepped aside, and he stumbled into the room, not bothering to look around. I closed the door and crossed my arms over my chest as I surveyed him.

"I fucked up, man. De Santis is going to kill me. Bianca...Oh, God. Bianca." He tugged more on his hair.

"What about Bianca?" Dom called out in a sharp voice, getting up and moving to block the door with me.

Vincent quickly joined us as we stared down Vasiliev.

"Oh-oh that's just fucking...you know what, you oversized fucking German shitbrain? You could've told me the king of kings was hiding in the shadows. But *no*. It's like you're trying to get me murdered."

"What?" I asked, still confused. "Why is your half-naked, crazy ass here, you Russian fuck-cheese?"

Vasiliev widened his eyes at me. "That's nice. Real nice. You're friends with the fucking leopard in the hall, aren't you?" He moved forward and jabbed me in the chest. "I fucking knew it. You're not on team B. You're on team A. Asshole." He poked me again.

"He's blitzed out of his mind," Vincent said. "What are you on, man?"

"Fu-fucking sugar rush. Fuck, these pants are made of protein!"

We stared in shock as he took his pants off and threw them across the room, leaving only his boxers on.

"He eat a box of Lemonheads or some shit?" I shook my head at his unhinged ass. "Is he diabetic or something having a sugar rush?"

Vincent quickly stepped forward and led Vasiliev to my bed and sat him down.

"Don't put that shit brick in my bed—"

Dom tapped me on the arm to shut me up. I sighed in frustration and dropped into my computer chair, making a mental note to wash the lord fungus off my bed tomorrow as Dom moved to Vasiliev and stared down at him.

"What's going on with my wife?"

"What? Fuck, you invited him?" Vasiliev groaned and closed his eyes.

Vincent lifted a brow at Dom. "He's really fucked up."

Dom grunted and slapped Vasiliev across the face. "Wake the fuck up and answer my question."

"I can't," he moaned. "You fucking piranha."

"You better," I said, sitting forward.

"I thought you could relate, fuck-face, because you've been smashing pissers with Celeste for too long now."

Dom rubbed his eyes as Vincent smirked at me.

Smashing pissers? What the fuck?

"I'll go check on B," Vincent said, backing away. He didn't wait for an answer. He opened the door and left.

"Dominic. Man. You gotta know. I thought it was her." Vasiliev sat up quickly, his eyes wild. "I'd *never* touch another woman. Cut my dick off. Feed it to the leopard. I'm done."

"Get that F-Word out of my bed," I grunted. "Ain't no one cutting dicks off in my sheets."

"I don't deserve my cock. I failed. Fucking goats, man. They kept laughing at me. Ugh, her tits. You know how great princess's tits are, right?" Vasiliev reached out and grabbed Dom's hands as he continued to babble. "You know, right? Of course, you know. You get to touch them every night. The fucking rainbows were so beautiful, man. Like… like… beautiful rainbows, you know?"

"I do know. Now tell me what drug you're on so I can try to help you come down," Dom said.

Vasiliev shook his head, his lips pursed in a duck face. "No. Nope. Can't do that, king fuck because if I told you that, the fucking leopard would get me. He's with you guys, isn't he?"

I raked my hand over my face and got up and poured a drink. This was just too much. I slammed back two glasses while Vasiliev continued to ramble about shit that wasn't here. He even screamed about the leprechauns in my closet and asked me why I had such a bug infestation.

"B is fine. She's sleeping," Vincent said, coming back a few minutes later. "Figure out what his issue is yet?"

"He's batshit crazy," I said, throwing back my third drink. "Probably bad coke or heroin. He's on a bad trip. If he dies in my room, I'm going to be pissed."

"People might think you two were fucking," Vincent called out with a grin.

I flipped him off.

"I'll fuck you," Vasiliev said morosely. "I don't want to. But I will. I can close my eyes and pretend. I'll totally do it." He started to push his boxers down, but Dom threw my blanket over his body.

"Keep your cock locked up," Dom said, shaking his head.

"His cock better not be out and touching my sheets," I snapped. "Throw his ass out into the hall and be done with this. Let the lords deal with him in the morning. Or the janitor."

A quick knock sounded on my door again, and I let out a snarl as I stomped over to it, actually hoping Ivanov was here to collect his trash. Instead, Stella stood in the hallway.

"What the hell do you want? Come to get the fucking leopard?" I grumbled, opening the door and letting her in.

She pushed past me and went to stand beside Dom.

"He took too much sugar. The new drug on the market. Drake overdosed him I think. One of the disciples said he can't die from it, but he'll be really messed up for a while." Stella wrinkled her nose as she stared down at him. "Fallon? Are you OK?"

"Oh, thank God, you're here. You can help me with these guys. Take my boxers off. They want me to fuck—"

"—ing shut up," Dom finished for him. "Before I push you out the window."

"I'm sorry I punched you," Fallon mumbled. "During the fight. I let myself go there for a minute. I was really upset with you for keeping my princess from me. You're like Bowser, hoarding the princess. What a fucker."

"How long is this supposed to last?" I asked.

Stella shrugged. "I'm not sure. Trent said he heard it could be several hours until he comes down. That's why it's called a sugar rush. And then the crash."

"Does Ivanov know you're gone?" Dom asked.

She nodded. "He told me to go find him."

"Now take him back to your place." I stared at the barely conscious pussy in my bed.

"Absolutely not," Stella sniffed. "I can't possibly deal with him the way he is. Or carry him."

"Then leave him in the hall but get him out of my bed," I snapped.

Dom held up a hand to silence us. "Just tell me what happened and why he's upset about Bianca."

Stella blew out a breath as Vasiliev let out a pitiful whimper at Bianca's name.

"Drake shot him up with the rush. Fallon had already smoked some, so he was already messed up. After Drake shot him up, Fallon got all goofy. He thought Bianca was making out with him. It clearly wasn't her. It was some slut named Abby. She has blonde hair and big boobs, so I guess I can see how he got confused since he was so wasted. Anyway, he put on this big show with her in the middle of the room. Like he made her orgasm, and I'm pretty sure they were going to fuck if I hadn't interrupted."

"Buzzkill," I muttered.

She stuck her tongue out at me before continuing, "Normally, I wouldn't have bothered to stop him, but he was talking about you—not saying your name of course—but really weird, random things and calling her princess and stuff. I knew what he was saying. Luckily, I don't think anyone else did. It was only a matter of time before he said your name or hers though. So, I intervened."

Dom nodded tightly. "I see."

"Listen, king shit. I'm sorry, OK? I had these fucking turtles all over the place, man, and I miss my girl. The turtles had teeth. Like, big ones. Then she was there, you know? I just wanted her. So I made her come in front of everyone, but she wasn't my girl. She was just a cat from my class or something. God, I'm fucked up. Can you tell the horns to stop playing the piano?"

Dom blinked several times while Vincent gaped at me in disbelief.

"OK. Thanks for the information," Dom finally said. "I, uh, guess he'll stay here tonight."

"The fuck he will!" I shot to my feet.

"Easy. Vincent can stay to help you. It'll be fine. Just watch him. Make sure he doesn't die or something." Dom nodded to Stella. "You're a hero tonight."

"What's my reward?" she teased, biting her lip and raising her brows at him.

"What do you want?" he asked.

"A date with you," she said coyly, batting her lashes.

"How about you give me a favor?" Dom countered.

She raised her brows, clearly intrigued. "I'll owe you a favor? What kind of favor?"

"Anything I want, when I want it." He winked at her. "It'll be a good favor for me and a reward for you. Something we *both* can enjoy."

Her eyes lit up, and she nodded. "Deal."

I glanced at Vincent. He smirked.

Whatever. Dom could do whatever shady dealings he had to with Stella. I had my own issues to worry about, and they started with the asshole in my bed.

THIRTY-NINE
VINCENT

"Fuck," Fallon groaned from the floor.

I cracked my lids open. He was rubbing his face, his eyelids squeezed tightly together. He let out a gasp when Levin chucked a pillow full force at his face.

"Shut the fuck up, Vasiliev. I've had to listen to your whimpering ass all night," Levin snapped from beneath his blanket. He'd changed his sheets and bedding before he lay down last night much to my amusement.

Fallon whipped the pillow back at him, causing Levin to grunt when it bounced off his head.

"Why the hell am I in here? And where the hell is here?" Fallon grumbled, sitting up, his hair sticking up in different directions.

"Levin's room," I called from my spot on the chair. "You're here because you were balls deep in sugar and high off your ass. You came pounding on Levin's door and interrupted our meeting with talk of a leopard chasing you or something."

"Damn it." Fallon pushed the thin blanket off and quickly replaced it when he realized he was naked.

"You took your boxers off and refused to put them on," I added, smirking at him. "That's when Levin threw you out of his bed and why you're sleeping on the floor."

"Lucky I didn't tear your cock off and choke you with it," Levin grumbled from beneath his blanket.

Fallon visibly swallowed. "I feel... off."

I sat forward and ran my fingers through my dark hair. "Like maybe you almost fucked some chick in front of the lords and disciples? That maybe you had her tits in your mouth and got her off with, like, twenty people watching you do it?"

Fallon visibly paled and froze before he managed a choked *fuck* from his mouth.

"Nice job, shitlips," Levin said, sitting up and glaring at him. "You cheated on Bianca."

"I-I did not," Fallon shot back, his eyes wide and filled with fear. "I was fucked up. I-I'd never do that to her. *Shit.*"

He was on his feet in an instant, spinning a circle with his dick out while he tried to find his boxers. I pointed to the floor by my feet. He rushed over, making a feeble attempt to cover his junk with his hand.

A knock sounded on the door before it was opening and Dom stepped into the room. His green eyes swept quickly from a bare-assed Fallon to a sour looking Levin to my grin.

"You all look like you had a good time," Dom called out.

Fallon yanked his boxers on quickly and turned to face Dom.

"Man, last night I fucked up. I'd never do that shit sober—"

Dom held his hand up and gave a quick shake of his head. A second later, the door opened again, and Bianca stepped inside. Her blue eyes quickly took in the scene, her face expressionless.

"Bianca. Princess," Fallon called out thickly, taking a step toward her.

Dom shifted in front of her and gave Fallon a look that said he'd kill him if he tried to get closer.

"Get your fucking clothes on. We need to talk," Dom said.

Fallon cast a mournful look to Bianca, who stood with her head down, before he nodded and backed away, grabbing his clothes as he went. Within moments, he was dressed from the waist down and sitting on the edge of Levin's bed.

Levin scoffed and got up in nothing but his black pajama bottoms. Bianca's eyes immediately zeroed in on him as he went to his dresser and tugged out a white t-shirt. Her eyes didn't deviate from him. I watched curiously as Levin paused, catching her eye. He hesitated for a moment before he dragged the shirt over his head, covering his tattooed torso.

Bianca's cheeks reddened.

We'd all seen it. I offered her a gentle smile. She came to me immediately, and I opened my arms for her as she crawled onto my lap like a sweet, little kitten and nuzzled against me.

"How's my favorite girl?" I murmured, kissing her cheek.

"Tired," she answered softly, her fingers twining with mine. "Dominic wouldn't let me sleep in."

"He fuck you?" I asked. I was aware all eyes were on us, but I had my doubts they could hear what we were saying.

"No," she answered back.

"Too bad." I kissed the tip of her nose. "You look like you need to come. I can help with that."

She let out a soft laugh and kissed me.

"Enough," Dom called out, his voice thick with jealousy. "We have things we need to do this morning."

"Yeah, B," I said, winking at her as she shook her head at me, a tiny grin on her lips.

Dom liked to direct who, what, when, and where. I got it. I'd fall in line.

Levin turned away from us, a muscle popping along his jaw as he leaned against the small countertop in his kitchenette.

"Bianca received a phone call this morning from D'Angelou," Dom said.

All playfulness left me at those words.

"What did that prick want?"

"To see how things were," Bianca muttered. "He said my mom wanted to talk to me since I never call home. I think he put her up to it because all she wanted to talk about was Hail and how we were doing and the wedding plans. I didn't tell her anything."

"And that needs to change. I expect after tonight's events, the entire fucking country is going to know Bianca is married to me," Dom said, staring at each of us. "Everything is going to go from bad to worse in just a few hours. We need to be ready. We're already facing the *tradition* with my father tonight. Once the Ivanovs and D'Angelou hear about what's gone down, we're all in some shit. We wanted a war. I think we're about to have one worth fighting."

"What tradition?" Fallon asked, frowning. "Why does that sound bad?"

"Because it is," I said, giving B a squeeze. "Dom's family has a tradition. Each time an heir marries, the head of the family gets to fuck the bride before the groom does."

"What?" Fallon screeched, leaping up, his hands tightened into fists as his chest heaved. "What the fuck? Don't tell me you're letting that happen. I swear to fucking god, if anyone touches her, I'll kill them—"

"That's the attitude we need," Levin spoke up.

Dom nodded. "We need a distraction tonight. When shit goes down with my father, which it will, we need to be able to get the fuck out of there. That's where you come in."

"What do you need me to do?" Fallon didn't hesitate.

I gave B another squeeze, grateful he wasn't bailing on us and really did seem intent on keeping B in his life. As much as I disliked the lords, I wanted Fallon to succeed. Not because I loved the guy, but because B did, and I wanted her happiness. If it meant the F-Word became a king, so be it.

"Whatever it takes," Dom said. "I need you to be waiting, ready to do what you have to do to break the party up. Set something on fire. Smash up cars. Molotov the fucking house. I don't care. Don't get fucking caught and don't get killed."

"Or *do* get killed," Levin muttered.

"Shut up, Levin," B snapped, sitting forward. "You always have a shitty attitude. Everything is *fucked* right now. We don't need you adding to it."

"Me adding to it?" Levin immediately bristled.

Here we go.

"I'm not adding to shit. You've got *a lord* here learning our shit. Finding out when we'll be vulnerable. The fact you aren't even a little worried doesn't surprise me though because why would you be? We're all busting our asses here to keep you safe while you sit around and make us feel like we need to kiss your ass. Like we aren't good enough for you." He glared at her as the room fell silent.

"My thoughts on whether you're good enough for me don't really matter, do they? You have Celeste. So maybe we don't need you to help us. Maybe you should go fuck your new girlfriend since we're—*I'm*—taking up so much of your precious time!"

"B—" I started.

"Are you saying you don't want me at your fucking wedding reception? You don't want my help tonight?" Levin snarled, his eyes flashing with fury.

"You're officially uninvited," B snapped back. "I don't want your help. I don't need your help. You proved your feelings when you ran off with Celeste. I don't want you to come tonight. You aren't wanted, Levin."

B trembled in my arms as Levin stared at her, his chest heaving and his Adam's apple bobbing.

"She's just upset," I started, but Dom silenced me.

"We aren't going to do this right now. Levin's right. We're trying to keep you safe, wasp—"

"If he goes, I won't." B crossed her arms over her chest. "I'm serious. I will throw a fucking fit and make the biggest scene you've ever witnessed. *I'd rather die* than have him there. He should just stay here. He can fuck his new toy instead," her voice wobbled.

I glanced at Fallon to see him staring down at his hands, wordless.

"Bianca," Dom shouted, getting to his feet. He hauled her out of my lap and gave her a shake. "Knock your shit off. What did I tell you?"

Tears trickled from her eyes before a soft cry left her lips. She shoved Dom away from her and stormed to the door. Without a backward glance, she jerked it open and stalked out, the door slamming so hard behind her it knocked a few of Levin's records off his shelf.

We sat in silence for a moment. Dom dragged his fingers through his hair as he grumbled in Italian.

"I-I can go check on her," Fallon said, clearing his throat. "If you guys need to discuss some stuff."

"Just go back to your place. Make sure everything is good with the lords." Dom looked to the door like he wanted to leave and tear B a new one.

"What about needing my help? What do you want me to do?"

"I'll text you the address. Come up with something and don't get yourself killed. We'll handle the rest," Dom said.

Fallon got to his feet. "OK. Well, here's to hoping we don't all die in a few hours. Just know if it comes down to saving you guys or Bianca, I'm choosing her."

"It's what I expect from you," Dom said gruffly with a nod. "Her first. We'll manage."

He and Fallon shared a look before Fallon left, leaving just Levin and me with Dom.

"Levin," Dom started.

"It's fine. I don't think I should go. We're trying to make this as smooth as possible. If she's pissed off and doesn't want me there—"

"I want you there. I *need* you there. If shit goes down, Vin and I could end up fucked. I don't know that I can trust Vasiliev just yet. There's always a chance he'll fuck us over. Bianca is hurting right now and clearly doesn't know how to deal with her anger. She will fall in line."

Levin shook his head. "I know, but you *know* Bianca. She'll make it worse if I show up, hurting or not." His phone buzzed, and he snagged it off the dresser, frowning. "I need to go. I have to meet with Celeste this morning."

"You're fucking kidding, right?" Dom's face morphed into the one he wore right before he shot someone in the head.

I cast an uneasy glance between them and got to my feet, the very real thought of having to potentially stop a murder in my mind.

"Look, I can't do this shit anymore, all right? I'm fucking tired of it. I can't do anything right by her, but I can do this. I can fucking walk away and give her what she wants. As long as you guys are with her and I'm here, shit's just going to get worse. I need to be done with all of it."

"You don't fucking walk away from this life," Dom growled, advancing on him. "The only time you leave is in a body bag."

"Then shoot me, Dominic. Fucking put a bullet in my head. I've done all I could for her. I saved her fucking life and the life of that piece of shit she was fucking behind our backs. What more can I do? If I show up tonight, she could end up dead or worse. You fucking know it. You know how she is. She cannot be controlled, man. Stop trying. Stop trying to control everything. Everything fell apart when she got here. She's going to get herself killed. She's going to get *you* killed. I can't be the reason for it. We have a lord trying to worm in with us now. I don't know what the fuck you expect me to do—"

"I expect you to stick by the kings through thick and thin. Through heartache and love. I don't expect you to walk out on us when we need you. You love her. *You fucking love her*, but you're stubborn and refuse to just say the words to her. You refuse to make her believe them." Dom let out a loud breath. "Maybe you're right. Maybe this isn't going to work. But here's the deal. Tonight, I'm taking my wife to my father's to celebrate our nuptials. She's probably going to be forced to fuck my father. And I'm probably going to be forced to watch with Vincent beside me. I'm probably going to kill some people tonight, and I might even fucking die myself. Tonight I might lose everything. But you know what I'm *not* going to do? Be a fucking scared pussy about it." He shook his head and backed away from Levin. "Vincent, let's go."

I followed Dom to the door. He didn't stop. He slipped through without a goodbye.

"Do you remember when you and me were with B that night? Do you remember what it felt like?" I asked, turning to look at Levin as I paused in the doorway.

He stared back at me with his brows crinkled and his lips parted.

"Do you remember never wanting to leave her side? Do you remember wanting to do anything to make her happy? And then we did?"

His bottom lip trembled.

"If you walk away, it's gone. All of it. Break things off with Celeste. Forget the fucking weapons deal. Forget making her old man happy. Tell B you love her. You know you do. Don't live in anger, man. You're going to regret it. Come be where you know you belong."

He stared back at me, unmoving. Sighing, I left him there, really fucking hoping he'd make the right decision.

Our lives probably depended on it.

FORTY
BIANCA

I stayed in our room all day on Saturday. I'd gotten my birth control pills from Aubrey and started them right away. I hoped they'd be safe in my purse, and I hoped they kicked in quickly so I was protected. A few days of pills had to be better than no days, right?

I still didn't like Stella, but I couldn't deny she'd been rather helpful, even if it was for her own gain.

My heart hurt. Even sweet Vincent couldn't get me out of my funk despite him trying everything from gentle kisses to soft words of affection. Dominic barely looked at me. He'd left sometime around one in the afternoon, and Vincent had followed soon after he'd received a text from him.

I had promised to stay in the bedroom with the door locked. Now, I stared out the window to the grounds below, watching as students passed by. My stomach twisted into knots when I saw Levin and Celeste approach. She smiled as she pulled him to a stop and pressed her lips against his. He kissed him back, his arms around her.

They looked good together. I hated it, but I hated myself more for being unrelenting. He made me so mad, and I'd been so pissed off the day I'd said those hateful words to him. My fury wouldn't go away either, and his being with Celeste now only made things worse. Seeing them kissing and touching on campus. Of knowing that sometimes he didn't come back to his dorm at night because he was with her doing things that made me want to scream at the top of lungs in rage.

I'd let him go and could only blame myself.

I swallowed as her hand shifted to his groin and rubbed. He didn't pull away from her. Instead, he clasped her hand as she laughed and tugged her toward our building.

As if sensing me standing in the window, he looked up at me. His expression darkened, and I stepped back, my heart in my throat. I hated the feelings clawing at my heart. They were suffocating me. Killing me.

You let him go. It's what you get.

"Wasp," Dominic called out as he came into the room.

I spun around quickly, my face hot. I wiped at my eyes. His brows crinkled, and he closed the distance between us quickly.

"*Mia regina*," he murmured, cradling my face. "What's wrong?"

"Just nervous," I answered softly.

It wasn't a lie. I knew things had the potential to get terrible in just a few short hours.

Dominic frowned and peered past me out the window and sighed. "Come here."

He led me to the bed and urged me down beside him. Tenderly, he tilted my chin up so we were looking into one another's eyes.

"I need to be honest with you," he said.

"OK." I licked my lips, nervous about where this was going.

"I know your heart mourns Levin's absence—"

"It doesn't," I protested weakly.

He pressed his finger to my lips. "It does. His mourns yours too." He brushed a strand of hair away from my face. "The thing is, Levin is only with Celeste because he's closing a deal for me with her father for weapons. He'd never tell you that."

I stared at him in confusion. "What? You mean…"

He let out a sigh. "I mean, it started as him closing the deal for me.

He needed to get close to her so her father would give me the contract. We needed the weapons. I paid a lot of money to get them, and Levin made a big sacrifice. He also sacrificed when he saved you and Fallon that night in the woods. He saved your lives even though it could've cost him his own life because he loves you."

"Then why is he still with her if he loves me?"

He thumbed my bottom lip. "He doesn't need to be, that much is true. I already told him to fuck the deal and come back, but he's a stubborn prick. I can't answer your question, but I'm sure he has his reasons. Maybe he'll break it off once the weapons are delivered. It shouldn't be long now." He paused and studied me for a moment. "He's not coming tonight. I don't know what that means for us. He made his choice. He didn't choose us. Although, I think if he weren't hurting as much as he is he would have. This is his way of trying to save you, I suppose. Since he knows you'll be unruly. He's not going to be the one to make the first move. While he did all those terrible things in the woods that night, he also spared you. Levin has done nothing wrong. This is all on you, wasp. You need to take the first step."

"I-I can't," I whispered. "Not if he's still with her. And he must want to be or he would've listened to you when you said to drop the act with her."

"Bianca." Dominic leaned in and kissed the corner of my lips. "We didn't kill you. You're still here. I don't want my crew torn apart over this. Fix it. Only you can."

"I-I don't know if I can. But I want to," I said, giving in because, honestly, I did want to. I wanted Levin back. I was terrified of what the night would bring. When I considered that, I realized he'd probably be safer on campus. Maybe I'd be saving his life this time like he'd once saved mine. And if I survived tonight, I'd do whatever I had to do to fix everything. If it even could be fixed.

"Good girl." Dominic shifted forward until I had no choice but to lie on my back and stare up at him. He trailed his lips along my jaw, his hand moving to cradle my breast over my shirt.

"What are you doing?" I asked softly.

"I thought it was obvious. I'm going to make love to my wife in case it's the last time I get to." He nipped at my bottom lip. "And maybe I'll even put my baby inside you so you can carry on my legacy if I'm not here."

My heart banged hard. He still hadn't given up on that. For a moment, I felt like a complete bitch taking the birth control, but then I reminded myself how I was in no way prepared to have a baby, regardless of what Dominic thought he needed. Or *we* needed. Bringing a baby into our world would keep me sleepless because I'd always be worried about who might be plotting to hurt it.

I didn't need that stress. Not right now. I had too much other stuff to sort out in my life without adding a baby to it. Even if that baby would be part me and part Dominic.

He pushed my top up. I shifted so he could remove it along with my bra. Moments later, the rest of my clothes were in a pile on the floor next to Dominic's.

I'd been resisting having sex just the two of us since we'd gotten married, but I recognized a losing battle when I saw one. Giving in felt right.

Dominic's fingers slid through my folds, teasing me, making me gasp softly.

"Does my girl like when I touch her?"

"Y-yes."

He pushed a digit into my wet center. I moaned quietly at the rough intrusion as I grasped his rock-hard cock and rubbed him. A bead of excitement made stroking his thickness easier. He groaned into my mouth as he kissed me. Another finger pushed deep within me as his thumb worked delicious circles on my clit.

"D-Dominic," I gasped as the heat grew within me.

He picked up his pace, his fingers working magic inside of me until I cried out against his lips, euphoria pumping through me as I rode the delicious waves.

With his eyes locked on mine, he removed his fingers from me and sucked them into his mouth. I swallowed, ready to go again because damn, he was hot as hell.

He shifted and pushed my legs apart so he could settle between them. My husband stared down at me, so much emotion in his expression.

Without a word he shoved forward, filling me in one dangerously violent thrust, making me cry out. I raked my nails down his back, causing him to hiss in pain. His cock throbbed within me as he pistoned in and out. His tongue wrestled mine as we both struggled to take control.

I came with another cry, my body trembling beneath Dominic's weight. He didn't relent. He picked up his pace, bringing pain with his pleasure.

Breathless, he lay atop me, his forehead pressed to mine before I could find my release again.

"You're so good," he murmured, kissing the corner of my mouth. "The fucking best."

I dragged my nails gently down his back as he shuddered against me. His lips met mine again in one of the sweetest kisses he'd ever given me. He took his time, tasting, licking, sucking. His finger and thumb expertly tweaked my nipple as he began to move slowly inside me again. Shoving in hard and pulling out slowly. Each deep stroke made me pant and shift my hips up to match his rhythm.

"You're going to have my babies, *mia regina*," he rasped against my lips. He thrust hard, over and over, jostling me beneath him as my breath caught in my chest. "I want one inside you right now. Fuck, baby, I'm going to do it."

He let out a feral groan, his cock twitching deep in my heat as he filled me with his release. He didn't know I was on birth control. As much as I hated to admit it, I liked the way he spoke about wanting to put his baby in me. There was something hot about thinking of belonging to him that way. Being tied to him irrevocably.

He slowed when I was climbing high enough to tumble helplessly into bliss, his words on repeat in my head.

"No," I gasped when he pulled out of me completely.

"Greedy girl." He lifted me easily, putting me on my hands and knees, his hands firmly on my hips as he jerked my ass up.

I swallowed hard as he collected our combined releases and pushed it back into me, stroking my insides with his finger. I exhaled when he pulled out and to swirl his thumb in our juices before pressing it to my ass.

I jerked at the touch, but he gripped my hip tighter with his other hand and leaned forward, his body over mine, kissing the space between my shoulder blades.

"I'm going to fuck your ass, *mia regina*. I will own every single first before we leave this room. Every piece of you is mine. No one will take it from me, from us. You're going to give me all of you whether you want to or not." He pushed his thumb in, making me arch my back and whimper out a soft protest which wasn't all that believable.

"Dominic—"

He replaced his thumb with his index finger, pushing past the first knuckle until he breached the tight ring of muscle. His lips sucked the skin along the nape of my neck sending shivers over my body.

"That's my good girl," he whispered as he added another finger into my tight opening.

I gasped at the intrusion.

"Shh. Relax. I'll make it feel good. I promise."

He scissored his fingers as he stroked them in and out of my ass. Just when I started to get used to the feeling, he added a third finger, stretching me to the point a whimper slipped out.

"I have to stretch your tight virgin ass so my cock won't rip you open. I want you to enjoy me owning you. And while a little bit of pain mixed with your pleasure makes me harder, I don't want to hurt you. Too much."

As his fingers moved slowly, his other thumb circled my clit, making my pleasure build again. A few moments later, he kissed my neck and removed his fingers. He sat back up and pressed his cock to my ass. I tightened up, afraid of the pain.

"Don't. Please. I'm not ready—" The words faltered on my lips as he pushed forward, breeching me.

I gasped, clawing at the sheets over the pain he brought with the small movement.

"It hurts," I panted out, wincing. "Please—"

"Good. It'll only hurt for a minute. I promise," he answered breathlessly, forcing his way deeper into me as I scrambled to get away from him. But Dominic was strong and held tight, drilling slowly into my ass until he was fully seated.

Tears slipped down my cheeks as he pulled out and pushed slowly back in.

"Don't cry," he murmured as he pressed me into the mattress. "You're doing a good job, *mia regina*. So good. You make me so fucking happy."

My heart jumped at his words. Dominic was a hard-ass, but hearing him admit his feelings made me breathe harder, suddenly eager to please the monster buried inside me.

He wrapped his hand firmly around my throat as he thrust in harder. He squeezed, making me rasp out strangled breath after strangled breath.

"That's my good girl. My strong girl," he praised. "You take my cock so good, don't you, baby?"

"Y-yes, Dominic," I managed to whimper as he snapped his hips forward, hitting some spot inside me that made my eyes roll back.

Could I come like this?

The answer came moments later as the rush took hold. I sobbed out my release, my fingers twisting in our sheets, my hair a wild mess as he continued to squeeze my throat.

My orgasm rushed through me like a typhoon. Dominic bit the tender flesh of my shoulder as he picked up his pace, fucking me hard and fast, oblivion swirling around us as I cried out his name over and over like a prayer to the devil.

His hold on my throat tightened until stars dotted my vision and I was gasping for air. More pleasure rained down on me with each snap of his hips, his cock claiming every last bit of me until he grunted loudly, his body trembling as he spilled his second release into my ass.

I collapsed on the mattress as he released my throat, him dropping on top of me and staying inside. He peppered kisses along my shoulders and neck as we both came down from our high. When our breathing evened out, he pulled himself free of me and went into our bathroom.

Water splashing into the tub greeted my ears, and a moment later, he returned and swept me into his arms, carrying me into the bathroom where he deposited me on my feet and helped me into the tub.

I sat between his legs, my back to his front as he gently massaged my breasts and kissed my neck.

"Are you OK?" he asked softly as he placed a kiss on my collarbone.

I nodded. Every hole he'd slammed into was tender. But I felt good. Great even. Hell, I could probably go again if he gave me a few minutes.

"Good." He turned my face toward his and kissed me sweetly.

"I love you," I whispered against his soft lips. I cracked my eyelids to peer at him.

His eyes were already open as he stared back at me.

"*Ti amo*, wasp. So fucking much."

I DREW in a deep breath as I settled into the backseat of a black stretch limo in my white dress. It wasn't a traditional wedding dress, but it was damn pretty with an A-line, beaded skirt that hit at my knees and a sweetheart neckline. Vincent said it was his idea, and he'd had to argue with Dominic to get him to buy it because Dom had wanted me in a long, body-hugging silk gown.

"You're breathtaking," Vincent said the moment he slid onto the leather seat across from me, his dark eyes glittering as he took me in.

The crown necklace he'd given me was around my neck, and Dominic's diamond adorned my finger.

"I could just eat you up," Vincent continued, his dark gaze raking up my body, sending a torrent of goosebumps through me.

His black suit looked amazing on him. I leaned forward a bit, noting the twinkle in his eye at the movement.

Before I could entice him to make good on his comment, Dominic slid in beside me and told the driver to go.

I frowned, my guts churning as I thought of the reasons Levin wasn't with us. He was probably buried inside Celeste right now. The image did nothing to comfort me unless I could count the fact he'd at least be safe tonight.

And then there was Fallon. Dominic said Fallon was going to be the distraction. I didn't want him hurt either. But Fallon needed to prove himself to the kings, so there wasn't much I could do about it other than whisper a prayer he'd make it out safely and be inducted into the kings.

"Stella said Ivanov was up to something tonight but didn't know what," Dominic said as he ran his hand down the front of his black bespoke suit. "She said she heard him cursing De Luca's name but that he also mentioned me. So he's coming for one of us tonight I assume. I'm hoping it's De Luca's gang because tonight is not the night for us to deal with the lords' shit."

Vincent hadn't taken his eyes off me. "I'm not worried."

Dominic sighed. "I couldn't reach Fallon. I assume whatever Ivanov is up to is keeping him away from his phone."

"I'm sure if we're in danger, Fallon will let us know," Vincent continued, his gaze darting to my cleavage.

"If you want to fuck her, just ask," Dominic snapped.

Vincent blinked and gaped at him.

"You heard me. You're not focused because you're too busy eye-fucking my wife. Let me help you." Roughly, Dominic grabbed me and shifted me onto his lap, forcing my legs apart. "Fuck her if you need to. I want your head in the game tonight. Our lives depend on it. Her life depends on it," he rasped, emotion betraying him for a second.

I glanced toward the driver, but the dark partition was already up. Dominic reached into the neckline of my dress and slipped my breasts out. He rubbed my nipples between his fingers and thumbs. I gasped, heat flooding the apex of my thighs.

Vincent unfastened his belt and pants then pushed them down his thighs. He tossed his jacket aside before losing his shirt without a bit of protest or shame.

In all his glorious nakedness, he moved between my legs.

He didn't ask me if I wanted it. Instead, he lined up with my pussy and pushed inside me, groaning as his cock filled me.

I hissed against the rough intrusion as Dominic held me flush against him. I was the meat in this sexy as hell sandwich. Dominic's dick poked me hard in the back through his pants while Vincent slid in and out of me.

I moved to reach for Vincent, but Dominic grabbed my arms and held them tight as Vincent railed into me.

"You're going to let him fuck you," Dominic purred in my ear. "Don't touch him. Let him use you, so he can focus tonight. I'm going to let him do anything he wants to you, and you're going to take it like my good girl, *capisci*?"

"Y-yes, Dominic," I gasped as my eyes rolled back.

Vincent was working magic on my already sore pussy.

"Fuck her hard," Dominic called out softly as Vincent jostled me against Dominic's hard body. "I want *us* to be her only memory of tonight if my father gets her."

Vincent grunted, the wet sound of him thrusting hard and fast into me echoing in the car. "I want to fuck her ass."

"I fucked it earlier," Dominic said.

"Her ass was supposed to be mine first." Vincent slowed, making me let out a whimper of protest.

His thumb pressed against my clit with deliciously soft movements which sent a zing of electricity through my body.

"What can I say? I'm greedy, and she's my wife," Dominic said without an ounce of remorse.

Vincent's jaw muscle twitched as he clenched his teeth before he pulled out and thrust violently back into me. I cried out at the roughness of his movements.

He did it over and over until my body clenched around him, my release rushing hard and fast through me.

"I love watching you come," Dominic murmured in my ear. "Look how fucking beautiful you are taking his big cock. Tell your Vinny you want him to fuck your ass. He's upset that I owned it first. Make him happy by sharing it with him."

I swallowed as my euphoria faded, knowing this was going to hurt. "Vinny, please… fuck my ass."

He pulled out of me immediately and pressed his cock to my tight hole, his dark gaze locking on mine. Dominic shifted, leaning me back and easing my legs over his thighs, opening me wider for what was about to happen. He laced my fingers with his, anchoring me to him.

"Vincent," he said softly, tearing Vincent's attention away from me.

Vincent looked to him.

"It's OK. Let go," Dominic whispered. "She can take it, and you want it."

Vincent's eyes darkened as he looked back to me, a monster emerging I'd never seen in him. My heart thudded hard as he thrust forward into me. I cried out at the painful intrusion, struggling to shift away from him, but Dominic held fast as Vincent stroked in and out of my ass.

"Ah," I cried out again, knowing the driver had to be able to hear me. "S-slow down—"

Dominic let go of my hands so he could cover my mouth and pin me in place with his other arm.

"Take it, *mia regina*. Take Vinny's cock like a good girl. He might not make it past tonight. Let the monster within him fuck you," Dominic cooed like the devil in my ear as Vincent gripped my hips hard and fucked me into oblivion.

My chest heaved as I came again, my body trembling. I thought I was going to pass out from the intensity. Vincent didn't stop, his hips snapping roughly against me as he buried himself over and over inside me.

Vincent leaned closer to me, and Dominic uncovered my mouth. Vincent's lips crashed against mine as he moved his hips in quick bursts. His warm tongue wrestled with mine until I couldn't breathe, then he broke off the kiss, looking over my shoulder at Dominic.

"Good," Dominic murmured, reaching out and raking his fingers through Vincent's hair.

Vincent let out a soft groan when Dominic gave a tug and brought him closer, smashing me between their hard bodies.

"You're good," Dominic breathed out in his soft, sexy accent. "Do you like fucking my wife?"

"Yes," Vincent gasped as Dominic adjusted his grip on his hair.

My heart jumped into my throat as Dominic leaned over my shoulder and brushed his lips along Vincent's jaw until he got to his ear and growled into it.

"Prove it." Dominic released him.

Vincent's eyes darkened more as Dominic settled back again and turned my face to his. He captured my lips against his while Vincent pushed deep inside me. Dominic swallowed my wail, his hands on my breasts, caressing and squeezing.

"Please," I choked out against his lips. "I can't take any more. I need—"

"To open wider so Vinny can fuck you deeper," Dominic murmured, his hand moving to my throat.

I knew he was going to choke me. I sucked in a sharp breath right before the pressure started.

"Fuck," Vincent panted, letting his head fall back. He rocked my body against Dominic's.

I twisted my fingers into Dominic's pants as I tried to keep my sanity.

"If she's not coming again in thirty fucking seconds you'll be sorry," Dominic snarled, tightening his hold until my breath stalled in my chest.

I struggled against him, scared I really would pass out this time.

Vincent fucked me harder as I continued to struggle, desperate for a breath.

"Calm down, *mia regina*," Dominic cooed in my ear, his grip still tight. "The more you struggle the less air you'll have."

I immediately relaxed against him, my head spinning, my body shaking as the impending heat from the orgasm began to take hold.

"Now scream, baby." Dominic released my throat, and I moaned like a whore in church as I came hard, my body spasming from Vincent's onslaught.

I sucked in as much air as I could.

Vincent groaned, his thrusts uneven now. In seconds, he pulled out of my ass and gripped his length. His release spurted out, covering my pussy.

"Fuck, baby B," he called out.

His release spilled in long, thick, white ropes. His head was back. His muscles glistened from the rough fucking he'd given me. When he was finished, he shifted forward, collapsing on me, his forehead against mine.

"You're so good. Fuck, baby." He kissed me deeply.

When he broke off the kiss, Dominic cradled his face.

"You did good, Vin," he murmured.

"You liked it?" Vincent asked, his eyes wide as he sought Dominic's approval.

"I did. Now, we need to clean this mess up." He patted Vincent's cheek.

Vincent pulled away from me, his seed running down my pussy in a warm stream.

"Help me?" Vincent asked softly, a slight plea to his voice as he stared at Dominic.

Dominic chuckled and shifted my limp body off his lap. Tenderly, he lay me where he'd been sitting, my legs still open. He kneeled on the floorboards with Vincent and locked his gaze on me.

My breath caught when he leaned down, staring at me with so much love and adoration as he licked up my wet center, swallowing everything he raked up with his tongue. Vincent joined in, both of them cleaning me with their tongues like I was a weak kitten.

With each lick, each suck, my clit throbbed. Sometimes their tongues would touch, but they never stopped their perfect rhythm on me and never pursued tasting one another past that. It was all about me. I knew I was all they saw as I watched them work me over.

When I came one final time, it was with two mouths on my trembling core, eating up everything I had left to give them.

And greedy me could only wish there were two more mouths on my body to help.

FORTY-ONE
FALLON

My phone buzzed for the third time as I stuffed my gun into my waistband. I knew without a doubt it was De Santis. He needed me to create a distraction. *How the hell was I going to create a distraction at his father's place?* The whole three-mile area around his dad's place was locked down on an easy day for fuck's sake. I could only imagine what it would be like at Dom's wedding reception.

Busting in there, if I even made it past the guards, would get my ass killed. I was still working on a plan though. My issue was Hail had decided we had work to do with the De Luca guy in town. It was putting a serious damper on what I'd be able to pull off for Dominic and my princess.

I was stressed out and almost to the point of giving Stella a gun and sending her in. She'd probably be all for it if she thought it would gain her brownie points with Dom. God knew she'd break her back for him. I'd thought she had it bad for Hail, but it was nothing compared to Dominic. I knew where her loyalty was, that was for sure. She'd probably lie down and die for the kings with a smile on her face.

"You're quiet tonight," Hail said, loading his gun beside me.

We were at one of the warehouses his family owned in the city. Lots of bad business went down inside it, from chopping cars to drugs to murders. If Hell had a location on the map, this would be its headquarters.

"Just trying to get my head in the game," I muttered, grabbing a blade and sliding it into my boot.

I was good with knives. I preferred them over guns, honestly. It was an ugly part of my personality I liked to keep quiet. Blood was so much prettier when it was coaxed slowly from the body with a single, precise slice. It mesmerized me. It made me feel like a complete fucking monster.

Everyone already thought I was fucked up as a lord. I didn't need to let my lust over blood out of the cage and add to it. I wanted to be a normal guy, but that ship seemed to have sailed long ago. The best I could muster was keeping what was left of my dark soul on lockdown.

"Me too." He crammed the gun into his jacket and grabbed another while Tate and Drake loaded up across the room. "I'm pissed we got a bad batch of sugar. That shit fucked you up. I can't believe you woke up naked in the damn woods."

I'd lied and said that was what had happened. The last thing the lords needed to know was that I'd slept naked on Seeley's bedroom floor. Stella had run back to Hail, saying she couldn't find me.

"It was dangerous. The kings could've fucking killed you if they'd found you alone like that. I'm not happy. Whether De Luca realizes it or not, he fucked up. He came into my territory. He's stealing my customers. He's taking what the fuck belongs to me, and he could've cost me one of my men. Not fucking happening. He and his whole crew dies tonight, or they survive with the knowledge of who they're fucking with."

I nodded as I stared at him. His mouth was set in a thin slit, his eyes devoid of any warmth. He was a son of a bitch when he was pissed. My rough experience with sugar may cost a few people their lives tonight.

"What's the plan?" I asked.

"We leave a calling card. Shoot the piss out of De Luca's crew. If there are any stragglers, they can blame the kings."

I swallowed. "So we're pinning it on the kings and starting a war between them and the horsemen?"

"Yep. If there are any left to start a war with when we're done."

For fuck's sake. This was going to be a shit show.

"De Santis and Bianca are having their wedding reception tonight," I said carefully, changing the subject.

Hail grunted. "I'm fucking aware. My father will hear about their nuptials soon enough. If I take out De Luca as a gift to him, I might be able to not get fucked too hard. So really, killing this horsemen crew is a damn good idea for a few reasons."

I licked my lips, an idea forming. "If we're going all out and you need to save your ass, we could hit De Luca and then hit the De Santis party. We might be able to kill De Santis or one of the kings, maybe all, plus his old man. Less of their crew would have to be a win. And it might buy you some goodwill with your old man. De Santis would never see it coming. Not tonight."

Hail's brows crinkled as he stared at me. "And Bianca?"

"We bring her back, and you do what you have to. If we kill De Santis, she won't be married anymore. No one has to know. And if they do find out, we'll tell them he forced her into it and you were saving your bride. You'd be seen as a hero. We won't catch shit for it if your old man decides to flip his lid on us for attacking without notifying him first."

Hail said nothing as he rolled my plan over in his head. He glanced at Tate and Drake for a moment before he finally called out, "Get our best disciples and our most loyal men on the phone. Tell them to meet us here in twenty. We have a change of plans."

My heart jumped. I might be able to be in two places at once now. It was a shady, dangerous, fucked up thing to do, but De Santis said he needed a distraction. My hands were tied. I had to do what I had to do.

Drake and Tate got on their phones, and, within twenty minutes, six of the best disciples were standing in front of us and a whole slew of Bratva, who'd suck Hail's dick if he demanded it because that was just how fucking dedicated to him they were.

"I need a hit on De Luca carried out tonight. I want him and his crew dead by morning. Trent," Hail called out to the dark-haired guy standing in the ranks. "I want you to lead this. Pick your men. You got me the inside track on De Luca and his crew. If you can take De Luca alive, do it. There's a sexy redhead he fucks. I want her alive too. He's going to watch me fuck her bloody before I kill him."

"But you want the rest of his crew killed, not taken alive?" Trent asked.

"Dead. I want no one left alive. I don't care how many motherfuckers you have to kill to get to him. His crew dies. Bring him and his whore to me. I'll take it from there."

Trent nodded.

"Tate, Drake, Fallon, and the rest of us will be paying the De Santis clan a visit tonight. I need to congratulate him on really fucking up." Hail's eyes darkened as he glanced at us. "You boys ready?"

There was a loud chorus of whoops, excitement and danger palpable in the air. I'd done a lot of bad shit in my life, but this might be the worst because it could get a few people I'd just started to be OK with killed.

She was worth it though. Bianca was worth everything.

I had faith De Santis knew what he was doing, so it helped soothe my worries. The last thing I wanted was to hurt her again by getting the ones she loved killed. This was the only plan I had though.

I'm coming, princess. Hold on.

FORTY-TWO
LEVIN

Celeste's moans died down as I pulled away from her. I was knuckles deep in her pussy, trying to take my mind off shit. This wasn't the way to do it though, because all I kept thinking about was bumblebee. The way her eyes had locked on mine when she'd seen me with Celeste outside our building. The way Bianca had quickly looked away and disappeared. How Dom had seen me, a grim expression on his face.

He probably fucked her to soothe her anger.

It's what I would've done.

My mind was all sorts of fucked up. It didn't help I knew Dom's dad was a piece of shit and Bianca was in for a world of hurt tonight while I made Celeste moan like a little slut. The idea of anyone but a king touching Bianca made me want to put bullets inside some skulls.

God, if any of them die tonight…

"What's wrong, Levy?" Celeste cooed in my ear as she stroked my cock. "You're usually more into our alone time."

I stared down at her hand on my dick, deciding that I hated the shade of pink her nails were. Bianca's nails would be black. The thought of her hand on my cock made my heart jolt. Those black as night nails digging into my thighs while I fucked her warm mouth. I'd hiss with the pain her claws brought as she tore into my skin...

Fuck, I missed her.

Celeste shifted her nearly naked body and dropped to her knees in front of me, sucking my dick into her mouth. I winced as she caught me with her teeth.

Bianca had never gotten me with her teeth unless I wanted her to. She'd been so careful with my dick. And God, could she suck cock. I could choke her with it until her face was my favorite shade of blue, and she'd take it like a fucking champ. Celeste gagged every two fucking seconds. I couldn't fuck her mouth like I could with Bianca. Bumblebee would swallow my cock and my load then come back for more.

Celeste spat.

Fuck, what am I doing?

My friends could be killed any moment. My girl... fuck, someone else's cock could be buried in her right now, and she could be screaming for help. It would break Dom. I knew it would. He loved her like I did. And Vincent? I didn't even want to think about the damage it would do to him to see his precious B being fucked by someone who wasn't us.

I shoved Celeste off my dick and stood, hauling my pants up.

"What's wrong?" she asked, scurrying to her feet.

I tossed her shirt at her. "I've got shit to do. Get dressed."

"What?" She held her shirt and gave me a look of confusion.

"I didn't stutter. Dom and Vincent need me. Bianca needs me."

Celeste's face darkened as I slipped my shirt on and buttoned it. It had taken me less than a second to decide where I needed to be tonight. Hell, I knew it before I'd even watched Vincent leave my room earlier. I wasn't going to abandon my crew when they needed me most and for a girl I wasn't in love with. I didn't give a shit if Bianca did throw a fit. I'd shut her ass up with my dick in her mouth if it came down to it.

"*Bianca?* Are you kidding me?"

"I'm not." I snatched my keys off my dresser as I put on my shoes.

"You're leaving *me* to go to her?" Her tits were still out. "What is it about her that you can't leave alone? I see the way you stare at her. When you think I'm not looking, I see you, Levy. What's really going on?"

"*Nothing* is going on," I snapped.

She blocked the door, still naked from the waist up. "I'm not moving until you tell me what the big deal with her is."

"There isn't a big deal. She's my best friend's wife," I lied.

Well, fuck. *Why was I lying?* I could just tell her I'd fucked Bianca's mouth and fed her my come after Vincent had stroked my cock and kissed me. I could tell her all I can fucking think about is Bianca whenever Celeste had my cock in her mouth. Or that I blew my load in the shower every morning to the memory of my dick sliding through the valley of her tits as I fucked them, my fingers twisted in her hair. How Bianca was the only one able to make me let go and feel something.

Fuck, just thinking about the shit we'd done that night made my dick hard.

I blew out a breath, my patience waning. "I'm leaving to get to my crew. We have shit we're doing tonight, and I'm late."

Celeste put her bra and shirt on, sighing far too much for my liking, before she approached me. I was already reaching past her to the doorknob.

"I love you, Levy. I don't like Bianca though. You're always worried about her. I hate it. She's not nice to you."

"She's my best friend's wife," I repeated evenly, like it had any bearing on my desperate need to sink my dick inside her and regretting I never had.

Even when she was pissed at me, all I wanted to do was fuck her into submission. Fuck the fight from her body. *God, that body...*

"Are you sure that's all?"

"Yes," my voice came out in a low snarl.

"I want you to stop talking to her. Stop looking at her." She rubbed my dick over my pants. "Stop *thinking* about her. I want all of you, Levy. Whatever thought you have in your head about her needs to leave. She doesn't want you. If she did, she'd be with you right now, not with Dominic. *She chose Dominic.* Not you. I chose you though. Please, understand who really loves you. If you have some sort of childish crush on her, you need to let it go. She's not like us. She's just something pretty for Dominic to screw until he finds someone more worthy. He'll throw her aside eventually because she's trash. You don't need to ever consider picking up the trash. Not when you have someone like me. Someone who really cares about you and is worthy."

"You need to shut up," I said, gripping her by the shoulders and pushing her away from me. "You don't talk about her like that. Bianca is not trash. If you ever fucking call her that again, I'll bury you in a place no one will find your fucking body."

Her gaze hardened as she glared at me. "*This* is what I'm talking about. You're threatening me over her!" Her voice grew shrill.

I closed my eyes, willing her to just go the fuck away. I needed to get out of there.

"Tonight is supposed to be *our* night, but you're shoving me aside to go do God knows what with the kings and *her.* I want you out of the kings. I want you to stay away from all of them, including Bianca."

"I'm done having this fucking conversation," I snapped, pushing past her. "You don't tell me what the hell to do or who the hell I can associate with. We haven't been together long enough for you to even think about bossing me around. You're not my fucking mother, and even she wasn't stupid enough to tell me what the fuck to do."

"I love you," she repeated, her voice pleading as she reached out for me, tears in her eyes. "I don't want to lose you, Levy. Please. Just promise me—"

"Celeste, I need to go."

"Why don't you ever say you love me too?" She peered up at me with wide, earnest eyes, her hands wrapped around my wrists as I tried to pull the door open.

I ground my teeth. "I'm going to be late. We'll talk later."

"Really?" She studied me, worry clear in her eyes.

"Yes," I said softly. "I'll see you when I get back."

Her bottom lip trembled, the damn tears still in her eyes. "OK. I'll leave my door unlocked. We can pick up where we left off. I-I'll swallow this time if you want. I-I won't complain."

I only grunted as I jerked the door open and led her out, not giving a shit about walking her back to her room.

As for picking up where we'd left off, I very fucking much doubted it.

FORTY-THREE
BIANCA

Dominic's dad knew how to throw a party. I hadn't had much say in any of it, so everything was a complete surprise. Dominic pretty much approved it all. The only thing he'd asked me was if I wanted lobster, salmon, or steak.

So that meant chicken tenders were off the menu. He'd laughed and kissed me when I'd asked and had put me down for lobster. I'd cringed. Eating sea scorpions wasn't on my to do list, but hopefully we'd be out of there before I had to.

And if we weren't out of there, maybe I could eat a salad instead. The thought of seafood made me want to vomit. But hey, maybe throwing up would get me out of it too. Always have a plan B.

"Is this where you grew up?" I asked in a hushed tone as we stepped through the door where four large men in black suits stood guard.

Dominic's and Vincent's weapons had been taken at the door, meaning they were armed with just fists and fury up in this bitch if things went bad.

"Mostly," Dominic answered, his hand on the small of my back as he led me through the massive foyer. Marble floors. A sweeping staircase. A ballroom down the hall to our left. A sitting room to our right.

Even David's house wasn't like this. This mansion screamed power and money from the polished floors to the crystal chandeliers. The place was a castle. A fortress. I'd get lost trying to find the bathroom.

"Most of my time was spent between here and our home in Italy," he continued.

"And at Bolten," Vincent added, winking at me.

The smile wasn't on his face like normal. We'd had an incredible time in the limo, but now his game face was on. I couldn't tell if he was nervous, but if I had to guess, I'd say he was prepared for the worst.

So was I.

"Dominic?" I stopped and turned to him.

"*Mia regina?*"

"Everything is going to be OK, right?" I stared up at him, my heart racing, needing his reassurance.

He brushed his knuckles along my jaw. "We may have to do some bad things tonight, but it's all in the name of survival. Just know that no matter what I say or do in this house, it is all to protect you. I love you and will do what I have to. I'll probably need some forgiveness when the night is over."

Seemed like a Dominic answer if I ever heard one.

"I'll do everything in my power to keep you safe, wasp. *Everything.*" He placed an uncharacteristically gentle kiss on my lips before he pulled away, all stern looking.

"Things are different here though," he said. "Here, I own you. You *will* behave. Do not speak unless it's required. Understood?"

I nodded tightly. *There was the domineering mafia prince I knew and loved.*

"No hard feelings, baby B," Vincent said as we walked forward to the ballroom. More guards waited at the door. "It's all business behind these doors. You'll get used to it."

I grunted, hating how things were done. I despised I couldn't have both my guys show me how much they cared about me and vice versa without some asshole using it for power and control. I knew tonight would be bad. The only saving grace was that Levin would be safe no matter what went down. I kept repeating that in my head. I sent a silent prayer that Fallon would manage to make it out alive too. Even Dominic said he didn't know what Fallon had planned.

"Remember," Dominic continued softly to me as I twined my arm through his as one of the guards spoke into an earpiece. "Whatever happens, if I tell you to go, I want you to fucking run if you can. Don't look back. Don't try to save us if it comes down to it. Find Vasiliev. He'll know what to do."

"Did you guys work something out?" I asked, staring straight ahead, my back stiff.

"Don't worry about it," he answered right before the doors opened and our name was announced.

I felt like royalty strolling into that room on Dom's arm. There were hundreds of people I didn't know, all staring and whispering as they sipped expensive champagne. Their clothes alone had to cost more than my entire life was worth.

This was the big leagues, and I didn't know how to play. It was the first thought that crossed my mind as we stepped into the room to the ripple of soft applause. My second thought was to say to hell with it and run now. I was a meal in a tank of hungry piranhas.

The men stared at me like I was dessert. The women smiled, a glint of malevolence in their eyes.

Dominic ushered me through the room, nodding curtly to people until we reached a man dressed in black, who bore a startling resemblance to my husband. The older man's eyes were dark while Dominic's were green. The sides of his hair sparkled with the silver which was taking shape, displaying his age. He was fit too. I'd say he was in his late forties if I had to guess. He was handsome just like my Dominic. But he was wicked. I could see it in his dark eyes as they raked over me for the first time and in the way his lips curved up into a ruthless smile.

Chills ran down my spine when we stopped in front of him. This man was pure evil.

"Domenico," he said in a rich Italian accent. He reached out and gave Dominic a hug.

Dominic was stiff and only released me when he had to, clapping his father on the back quickly.

"And his beautiful bride, Bianca *D'Angelou*," his dad said, turning to me and taking my hand.

Dominic tensed beside me, a small tell of his anger and jealousy.

Dominic's father pressed his lips to the back of my hand, his gaze locked on mine. I tried not to tremble beneath his piercing stare. Dominic didn't reach out to offer me comfort, and Vincent had disappeared into the crowd after we'd entered the ballroom.

"This is my father, Matteo De Santis," Dominic introduced us in a strong voice that made me shake in my shoes. It was his no nonsense voice. The one that spelled trouble if you stepped out of line.

"It's nice to meet you," I lied, fixing a smile on my face and forcing my voice not to waver.

Matteo let out a soft chuckle. "Indeed it is. I had no idea what a beauty you were. Dominic failed to elaborate on that. Tell me, how do you like being married to my son?"

The guests had gone back to schmoozing as we stood in front of Matteo. I swallowed, glancing around for Vincent. He was at the edge of the room, watching us with narrowed eyes.

"I-it's good," I managed to say.

Matteo laughed that sinister laugh of his. "That's *interesting*. Would you say it's good because you're afraid to say otherwise or good because it really is good?"

What the hell?

"I-it's hard," I said as Dominic stared straight ahead, not helping me out at all. "Dominic can be overbearing."

"Truly?" Matteo smirked. "How was the proposal?"

"There wasn't one," I answered honestly. "I-I didn't get a choice."

Matteo raised his brows. "You were forced?"

"Yes," I said. "He had Levin knock me out, and then he forced me to marry him when I woke."

Matteo's eyes glittered as he looked to Dominic. "She speaks truthfully."

"She speaks too much," Dominic snarled, turning to pin me with an ice-cold glare.

I shrank away from him, confused about what I'd done wrong.

"I'll deal with you later," he continued, his scowl hardening further.

I swallowed and cowered away from him more, forcing myself to not bite back or tell him to kiss my ass. I didn't know if this was part of his act or not, but I could only assume he was turning on the cruelty to prove to his father I meant very little to him. I knew we had to convince this man of that, so if I had to be docile and timid, I would be. For now.

"I'm sorry, Dominic," I whispered, amping it up and hoping Matteo bought it. "Please—"

Dominic reached out, gripping my chin painfully as he scowled down at me. "Shut the fuck up. What did I tell you? Huh? I said for you to keep your fucking mouth closed. I'll do the talking."

"Yes, Dominic," I choked out, making a mental note to slap him when we were out of there.

He didn't need to be so damn rough. He released me and turned to his father. "Can we get this party over with? I have more important things to do than celebrate this sham of a marriage."

Matteo winked at me before he led us to the head table. I sat beside Dominic. A moment later, Vincent joined us. He didn't cast me a second look as he settled in.

Matteo paused and pulled his phone out of his pocket. He didn't say a word to us as he strode away, which was fine by me. I could breathe again.

The tension in Dom's shoulders didn't release.

"Do *not* overshare with my father," Dominic said tightly, looking out over the people.

"I didn't know what to do—"

"Stop speaking." His gaze slid over to me. "You need to look like you submit, and I can't stand you. Our marriage can't look like I love you. He will weaponize it. Bow your head. *Submit*."

I swallowed and tucked my head down.

"Elbows off the table."

I slid my them off the table.

"Fold your hands in your lap. Ankles crossed. Do not make eye contact with anyone in this room, not even Vincent. I should've gone over this with you before. I'm sorry." He let out a sigh. "I'm hoping this ends quickly. In the meantime, behave yourself."

I ground my teeth but kept my head down.

I sat stiffly, not looking around as people came to greet Dominic, none addressing me. Apparently, they knew the rules better than I did. Within the hour, my ass and back were sore from remaining so still in my seat.

"My father is here," Vincent said a few moments after a large man had cackled endlessly about some guy getting shot they must have all known.

Vincent nodded his head at someone as I tried to side-eye him.

Great. More assholes to meet.

A dark shadow loomed over us moments later. Vincent and Dominic both rose to their feet.

"*Padré,*" Vincent said as the man clasped his hand. *"Come va?"*

"*Sto bene,*" the man's deep voice rumbled out.

Vincent pulled away, and Dominic greeted him.

"*È bello vederti,*" Dominic said in his rich Italian.

I kept my head down and strained to figure out what they were saying. It sounded like a warm greeting.

"*È bello vedere anche te,*" the man replied.

"This is my wife, Bianca," Dominic said, nodding to me still in my seat.

The man took my hand. I peeked up at him quickly as he smiled down at me.

"Congratulations on your marriage. It's a pleasure to meet you, Bianca."

"Thank you," I said softly, not knowing what I was supposed to say. Social norms dictated I be kind in my reply and not silent.

"This is my father, Alessio Valentino." Vincent settled back in his seat as Dominic took his.

Alessio sat beside Vincent, still grinning at me. He didn't strike me as nasty and cruel like Dominic's father did. Alessio was a tall, broad man in his late forties with kind, dark eyes. He reminded me of an older Vincent.

Alessio inclined his head to me. "How are you enjoying married life, *tesoro*?"

I glanced at Dominic quickly. He gave a slight nod.

"It's... different."

"I imagine it would be, having to be married to a De Santis," Alessio said with a hearty laugh, winking at Dominic, who gave him a tight smile. "You'll do well. If it doesn't kill you."

I shot a look to Dominic, but he wasn't paying attention. It wasn't long until I knew why.

"Domenico," Matteo greeted him. "Everyone is dancing. Dinner will be served soon. You should dance with your bride."

"I'm not dancing tonight," Dominic said sternly.

"Then I suppose I'll dance with your bride. Bianca, would you be so kind as to share a dance with me?" Matteo asked, his eyes glittering with some sort of madness I wanted no part in.

Once again, I checked with Dominic for the right response, but Matteo reached out and tilted my chin in his direction, his touch cold and rough. "You look to *me* when I speak to you. Not him, *daughter*."

Chills rushed through me as I wordlessly got to my feet and slid my hand in his, noting Dominic seemed like he was barely holding it together. Vincent cleared his throat as Alessio watched Matteo lead me away, a peculiar look on his face.

The moment we were on the dance floor, Matteo spun me and pressed his hands to the small of my back. Unable to do much else, I rested my palms on his shoulders as he led me in time to the five-piece ensemble playing in the background.

"Are you having fun?" he asked.

"Yes sir," I answered thickly.

"I see my son has been training you well. Tell me, does he make you happy?"

"I'm a bird with clipped wings trapped in a gilded cage," I said, hoping it would take the spotlight off Dominic's relationship with me.

"Ah, but to be such a bird. Adored by all. Envied. Beautiful. A true goddess." He leaned in, his lips brushing against my ear, "I bet you fuck like a porn star, don't you, *passerotta?*"

My breath hitched, panic taking flight in my chest.

"A pretty, little captured sparrow, taking my son's cock every night. Tell me, does my son make you come?"

I trembled against him, making him laugh softly.

"It's no matter to me. As long as he plants his seed in your womb to carry on our legacy. And if he cannot, there are other options for getting an heir into you."

Cold rushed through me. I wanted to leave. Now. My instincts shouted for me to run and never look back.

"You shake so, my pretty little *principessa*. Tell me, do you think you could take my cock like you take my son's? Hmm?" Matteo's hand shifted to my ass, making me stiffen. He cackled softly, sending goosebumps across my skin.

"We have a tradition in our family. Dominic isn't too keen on it, and it makes me wonder if perhaps there's more to your relationship than he lets on. I suppose we'll find out, won't we?"

"What do you want?" I choked out, trying to find Dominic in the room.

He was chatting with Vincent, Alessio, and another man. Dominic caught my panicked expression and quickly got to his feet, excusing himself. I let out a breath of relief, knowing he was coming to my rescue.

"What do I want? To have what's mine, of course. That's you. Our tradition demands it. I will see it fulfilled," Matteo answered in a dangerous voice before he released me and stepped away.

I stood there, breathing hard as Dominic approached. Matteo turned to him and pressed his hand to Dominic's chest.

"Come. We need to talk," Matteo said.

Dominic stared at me for a moment, so much turmoil in his eyes.

Then he schooled his features, nodded, and turned on his heel, following his father.

"You OK?" Vincent asked, taking my hand to dance with me.

I watched as the man who'd been standing with Dominic and Vincent followed Matteo. Alessio brought up the rear.

"What's happening?" I asked, clinging to Vincent as we spun on the dance floor.

"Pieces are in play. Shit's about to go down. We should go."

"We can't leave Dominic," I hissed, locking eyes on him.

"Baby B, this is our chance. I can get you the fuck out of here right now. Dom can deal with his old man. No one has to get hurt."

I hesitated for all of one second before I nodded. Vincent gripped my hand and hauled me toward the exit. We'd nearly made it to the door when four guards stopped us.

"Valentino, boss wants to see you. Bring the girl," one said gruffly as they blocked our path.

Vincent's hold on my hand tightened. Two of the guards grabbed me by the arms, making me cry out.

But there wasn't shit we could do. I saw the look in Vincent's eyes. The game had started, and we had to play.

FORTY-FOUR
DOMINIC

I glared at my father as he sat behind his desk, smoking a cigar. I'd seen his hands travel to Bianca's ass. I'd nearly lost it and launched myself on him, not giving a fuck if he tried to have me killed for it.

"Your wife is very beautiful," he said, blowing out smoke.

I grunted. "She'll do."

He smirked and leaned forward. "You know why you're in here, yes?" He handed me a cigar.

I puffed as he lit it for me, inhaling deeply before blowing out the smoke.

"I assume you wish to discuss our family *traditions*," I said.

"Indeed."

"As you already know, I'm not interested in *sharing* my wife. I've taken her virginity. The deal is done and sealed. She bears my last name and soon my child."

"But no child yet."

"*Soon*," I said tightly. "I'm working on it."

"What if you stopped working on it and let me take over?"

My guts twisted at his words. "You wish to impregnate *my* wife? So that I might raise my half-brother, and he could call me both stepfather and brother? I'm sorry, Father, but I thought we were more civilized than some hillbilly family from the Deep South."

"Your wife is truly beautiful, Dominic. Created by the gods for men to lust upon," he said, ignoring me. "You're young. Getting tied down so soon wasn't one of your best ideas."

"What aren't you saying?"

He sneered at me and stubbed out his cigar. "Just that we have traditions."

"Not interested."

He nodded. "Then, as I've said before, we make new ones. Give your wife to me. I can have your marriage annulled. I'll take her and make her a mother. She'll want for nothing. It's no secret you hate our way of life. With a new heir, you could be free when he comes of age."

I swallowed hard. It wasn't that I hated our way of life exactly. I hated him. Big fucking difference. I adored fucking shit up.

"No," I snarled.

"You don't love the girl. That's what you said."

"She is *my wife*," I said in a clipped voice. "She's my responsibility regardless of my feelings. I don't back away from my duties, Father. You know that."

He nodded thoughtfully and grew quiet. "Then I propose a new tradition. If you agree, I'll let this go. If you don't, you'll pay."

"What is it?" I demanded, growing more impatient. I hoped to fuck Vincent was able to get Bianca out of here in the small window of time there had been.

He pressed a button on his desk, and a moment later his door opened. Some of his men strode in, Bianca held tightly between two of them. Vincent brought up the rear. I caught the worried expression on his face as I rose to my feet.

Shit.

"Ah, my darling new daughter. We were just discussing your marriage to my son. I'm so glad you could join us." My father stood and marched to the bar so he could pour himself a glass of whiskey. He handed me one. I slammed it back, needing it to numb my rage as Bianca trembled in the center of the room.

Before I could say anything, four more of his men entered the room, followed by Alessio and Klaus, Levin's father. As far as men went, Alessio was decent. But Klaus was a fucking nightmare with a heartbeat.

"Here's what's going to happen." Father crossed the room to Bianca, who stared back at him with wide, terrified eyes.

My heart ached as I watched her with him. He'd fucking break her. The very outcome I had been trying to save her from when I'd ordered Levin to kill her and when I'd married her instead of letting her die. And now the nightmare was staring my wasp in the face, ready to destroy her.

"I'm going to make an offer. If Domenico refuses it, we'll start a new tradition tonight." He nodded to his men, who moved behind me.

I tensed. "What is this?" I snarled when they latched onto my arms.

Vincent's worried gaze darted from me to Bianca then back to me. We had no fucking weapons. It didn't mean I wouldn't snag one off a dead body after I fucking killed someone with my bare hands.

One of the guards grabbed my chair and moved it to the center of the room. I was pushed down into it.

"Here's the deal. I'm going to fuck your wife. You watch. Jerk off. Whatever you want. When I'm good and done with her, you can take her and go. Our tradition is fulfilled and over. I'll let it go. You continue to do your fucking job and make an heir for our legacy if I fail to impregnate her tonight myself. Easy, right?"

Bianca wasn't on birth control. I'd taken it from her. If he came inside her, he could get her pregnant. The possibility of her carrying his baby crushed my fucking soul. I didn't mind if one of my guys got her pregnant—not that it made me happy—but I'd prefer it over this shit. It was supposed to be me. She was *my* wife. I owned her, and that included her fucking womb.

Not his. Not. Fucking. His.

"No," I growled, tightening my hands into fists.

He sneered. "I thought you'd say that."

A small cry left Bianca's lips as one of the guards pulled a gun and pointed it at her head while the other pushed her to her knees. My heart lodged in my throat.

Not again. Not fucking again.

I shifted to rise from my chair, ready to kill some motherfuckers. But a fist caught me in the face, sending me toppling backward. Arms laced around mine, holding me back as I struggled to clear the room of all the fucking monsters in it.

"Relax. She doesn't have to die," Father said calmly as if we were discussing the weather.

Bianca stared back at me with terror in her eyes. And she should be scared. She was in a den of vipers with no escape.

Father snapped his fingers. One of the guards went to the door and opened it. A man entered, holding a struggling Natalia. I stared at her, sickness washing through my guts.

The guard threw her roughly to the floor in front of me. She stared up at me, tears staining her pretty face, the sleeve of her blue cotton dress falling off her shoulder.

"What's this?" I demanded, trying to jerk away from the assholes behind me. I made a mental note of who they were—Darwin Adams and Malcom Sims. When I took over, I'd fucking kill them. Or maybe I'd do it tonight. It depended on a few factors, but I'd make a fucking effort.

"This is your little friend. Natalia, isn't it, love?" My father looked down at a sobbing Natalia and grinned. "I figured since you care about her so much this next part would be easy for you."

I watched as Father tilted Bianca's chin up. "Let me have your wife. Same terms as before. You can walk away when we're done."

"What's the other option?" I snarled.

"You fuck the Vasiliev girl, who you care about so much, in front of us all. We'll do a little reversal in our tradition."

"You fucking monster!" I shouted, losing my cool on him and jerking hard against the assholes who held me in my chair.

They could barely hold onto me. One clubbed me in the back of the head with the butt of his gun, making my ears ring. I stopped struggling as my vision blurred. It was still long enough for them to adjust their holds on me.

Father clicked his tongue at me. "It's not a difficult job. You went out on a limb to keep the Vasiliev whore safe. You've visited her. You promised me we'd use her... but we haven't. I figured tonight she could finally be of some use to us."

"I'm not doing it."

He nodded, lacing his fingers together. "I thought you'd say that too," Father said, giving Bianca a fond look. "But here's the catch. You either fuck the Vasiliev whore, or I kill your pretty, little wife. The one you claim to not love or care about. It should be OK since you lack any emotional attachment to her, right? When her heart stops beating, I'll fuck her dead body just so you can remember who the fuck is really in charge around here."

I shook, glaring at the man who created me, hating him with every ounce of my being.

"What happens if I do it?" I asked after a tense moment, unable to look at Bianca as I said the bitter words.

"Then you get to take your wife home."

"And Natalia?"

"Still safe. At least for now."

I chanced a glance at Bianca, fear clinging to my heart. She stared back at me with wild eyes, her lips parted. Both options would hurt her, wreck her. I had to choose the lesser of two evils. It was her or me. I'd never let it be her.

She must have known my decision because she let out a wail that broke my fucking heart.

"I'll do it. Natalia. For my wife's safety."

A sinister smile spread over my father's face as Natalia cried softly. I knew what happened the last time a woman was forced to her knees in front of me. I wouldn't let it happen again. I'd made a promise to Fallon that I'd keep his sister safe. There was a catch to everything though.

"Get to work or both whores will die," Father said, fisting Bianca's hair and jerking her head back.

I snarled as he forced her to remain kneeling in front of him with his gun pointed at her head. She sobbed softly as he gripped her hair.

"If you fuck up, she dies. I won't hesitate," Father said in a deadly whisper. He nodded to his men who released me.

I shook as I stared at Bianca. The pain and misery on her face ground the shattered pieces of my heart into dust. I wasn't sure how I'd come back from this, how we'd come back from this. She'd have to watch me fuck another woman. And not just *any* woman. Fallon's sister. I'd promised to keep Bianca safe. Any other circumstances, and I would've fucked like a king to save my wife without giving a shit who was watching. But it was *her*—my fucking wasp—watching me with heartbreak in her gaze.

Where the fuck was a lord when you needed him?

Reaching out, I took Natalia's hands and pulled her closer to me.

"Make me believe it," Father warned.

I brushed her hair away from her face as she stared up at me with tear-soaked eyes.

"Please. Please. Pl-please," she choked out, her fingers digging into my forearms as she gripped me with shaky hands. "Don't do this to me. Please."

"Shh," I said softly, leaning down and brushing my lips along her jaw before moving to her ear. "They'll kill you if I don't. I'm sorry."

Her body quaked against me, her fate sealed. She sobbed softly as I continued to speak into her ear. "You need to suck my dick, because I need some help from you right now."

I eased back, my chest aching as she reached out with fumbling fingers and undid my belt and pants. I freed my soft cock and urged her forward as her wails grew louder.

I nudged her lips with the head of my dick as I eased her face into my lap.

"No," she whimpered, her cries loud.

I shoved my dick between her lips, silencing her protests. She choked and gagged as I thrust into her soft, warm mouth, her fingers digging into my thighs. She tried to pull away, but I gripped her hair tighter and forced her mouth deeper onto my cock.

I turned to Bianca as she squeezed her eyes closed. My heart broke a little more.

"Don't close your eyes," Father snarled as I reached out and pushed Natalia's dress down her shoulders. "Watch how he enjoys it."

I twisted my fingers through Natalia's hair so she was choking on my cock as I moved her up and down at a speed I could handle.

"Look at your wife," Father ordered with a dark laugh.

Bianca's face was damp with tears, her body still trembling, as she stared at me.

All I wanted to do was go to her and erase her pain. But I couldn't. Not the way I wanted. Keeping my eyes on her made keeping my dick up easier, so I did it despite the agony for us both.

"You have about five seconds to fuck her, or I'm going to fuck your wife," Father threatened.

I ground my teeth and tugged Natalia's head up. My hard cock slipped from her lips as I met her gaze with my own.

"Dominic. Don't," she choked out. "Please."

"I'm sorry," I murmured, really fucking meaning it.

She fell on her ass as she tried to scramble away from me. I had to stand up with my dick out to grab her and even then she slid from my hold.

Fuck. I tucked my dick in my pants as she crawled on her hands and knees through the room. Father's laughter boomed out as I caught her by his desk.

She squealed and sobbed as I hauled her to her feet. Then she clocked me in the face. Usually, I'd be pissed, but I understood she was scared and didn't want this. So I accepted the hit without losing my cool.

I turned her around and forced her face down onto my father's desk while she begged for me to stop, her small body thrashing. My father turned Bianca around to watch.

Fucking prick.

"Your husband is going to rape her," Father said in a deep, sinister voice. "He's going to fuck her pussy and come inside it. How do you feel knowing her pussy will make him come just like yours? That he enjoys it? You'll replay this in your head every time he touches you. You'll know he fucked a sobbing girl while you watched."

"Stop. D-don't," Bianca choked out. "Dominic, I'll do it. Your father. Don't be like him. Don't do this."

I ignored Bianca's pleas, shoved Natalia's skirt up, and tugged her panties down, exposing her pussy to me. I locked gazes with Bianca again. She'd gone deathly quiet and appeared like she'd checked out with her blank stare and silent tears. I caught a glimpse of Vincent out of the corner of my eye. He looked like he was going to be sick.

I wanted this over with, so I pushed my cock through Natalia's folds while she struggled against me. My dick was at her entrance when a loud bang sounded beyond the closed doors.

Gunshots. Screams.

Everyone snapped into action as weapons were drawn. I backed away from Natalia and fastened my pants. I lunged at my father as he aimed his gun at the door. The impact sent him sideways, freeing Bianca. My fist connected with his face, knocking him off-kilter. The gun skittered across the floor. Bianca snapped back to reality and pounced on it. Vincent punched Malcom in the face and took his gun from him then put a bullet in him.

"Ungrateful," Father snarled at me when I punched him again. "You've fucked up, boy."

Vincent grabbed Natalia and Bianca and dashed from the room. I couldn't blame him. I would've done the same damn thing if I were him. Bianca was the only thing that mattered. Natalia was a close second because as far as I was concerned she was innocent. I didn't want another Macy on my hands.

Father slugged me in the guts, but I held fast, hitting him again and again. He wheezed as I stood and kicked him in the ribs, but he didn't stay down for long. He was on his feet and punching me in the face again, forcing me back.

He pulled a second gun from his suit. It took a moment for me to realize he was going to shoot me. I dove away as it went off. I managed to get out of the room, going from one war zone to another.

The gunfire was too close for comfort. I needed to get to Bianca. The acrid scent of smoke was in the air. Something was on fire.

I'd deal with my father's ass another day. For now, I only had one thing on my mind, and that was saving my queen.

FORTY-FIVE
LEVIN

I dove behind an overturned table as Hail shot at me, cursing everything that was a lord.

Mother fucking Vasiliev.

I returned fire. I'd only just arrived, and a fucking war was underway, which meant Vasiliev was here, creating a distraction. A damn good one based on the screams, blood, and the few bodies scattered around. Not to mention all the fucking smoke. Damn, the curtains were on fire.

How the fuck…

Hail had brought friends by the looks of it. It wasn't just the lords. Some of his father's crew were there too, which meant he'd probably grabbed the loyal to him groupies and promised them riches if they came to a gun fight.

I shot at one, hitting him in the chest. He toppled over as Hail darted away. I caught sight of my father shooting at one of the lords' men, his face a mask of wickedness. I said a silent prayer he'd catch a bullet to the brain, then I ran to an open doorway. Any death for that evil bastard was already too late. My grandmother should've swallowed my grandfather's load instead of letting it impregnate her. The world would've been a better place without the lot of us.

I peered around. The house was too fucking big. I'd never bothered to learn the layout. In retrospect, I wish I had because I had no clue how the hell to get anywhere in this damn mess. I coughed as I ran through a low hanging cloud of smoke.

Unable to take the main route to Matteo's office, I had to go around. Not that it mattered at this point. The house was overrun with the lords' cockroaches, their guns blazing.

I shot, taking down two more guys before I caught sight of Fallon. He fired at my father and missed before he dove behind the wall opposite of me.

"Hey, you Russian shitbrain," I called out to him.

He did a doubletake as he reloaded. His dark hair was a wild mess, and he had blood on his shirt. "Hey, you German cocksucker."

I snorted and shook my head before pointing my gun around the corner and pulling the trigger. A body thudded to the floor.

"Nice distraction. Maybe next time you should bring a fucking army."

"I didn't have much of a choice. I couldn't be at two places at once tonight, so I had to modify shit to make it work. I'm sorry if my distraction isn't good enough for you." He fired around the corner and took down one of Matteo's men before sending a slew of Russian swear words out as wood splintered next to his head.

"You do realize you're shooting the wrong people, right?"

Vasiliev cursed again and shot one of the lords' men. "Eat shit, Seeley. Are there any *right* men here tonight?"

"Jesus, you're a fucking mess. Do you even know what the hell you're doing?"

"Nope." He fired at someone else. "I'm improvising."

I didn't even know which side the guy was on since it was such a damn disaster around us. Matteo would be paying hella money to fix this mess. Looked like he'd be hiring a decorator too.

"We need to find Dom and Vincent. They'll be wherever Bianca is, and I suspect that'll be Matteo's office," I said, searching for an escape. I spotted one and motioned for Vasiliev to follow me.

He darted off behind me as I rushed forward, ducking and dodging as bullets flew around us. Glass shattered, and there were more screams.

We made it to a hallway which was relatively quiet.

Something was eating at me, so I glanced at him as I surveyed the area around us so we didn't get blasted. "Why did you really bring the whole of the lords' B team to fight tonight?"

"Isn't it obvious?"

"Clearly not."

He rolled his eyes at me as we pressed against a wall where the hallway formed a T. "Hail wanted to shoot up De Luca and his men. We were ready to go. I couldn't do that and do this. Decisions needed to be made. I put a bug in Hail's ear about this and how his father would praise him. It worked. Ta-da. Here I fucking am."

"You'd risk your life for Bianca?"

He spun toward me, his eyes widening. He lifted his gun and fired in my direction. I thought he was going to shoot me. I let out a shout and slid down the wall right as a body toppled behind me.

"I'd risk my life for her and anyone she loved," he said, offering his hand to me to help me up.

My ears were ringing as I took his hand and let him tug me upright. I turned to see a dead guy from the lords' side in the hall, blood pooling around him.

I looked back to Fallon. "You love her."

"Just as much as you do, I suspect. Now stop trying to sweet talk me, Seeley. I have to find our girl."

I grinned at him and shook my head. Maybe I wouldn't kill him.

Today, anyway.

FORTY-SIX
BIANCA

My chest burned as we ran. Vincent grabbed my arm and jerked me back before I caught a bullet to the head.

"Be careful," he called out, worry covering his face. "You know how to use that thing?" He nodded to the gun I clutched.

"I-I don't know."

Natalia clung to Vincent's back, her eyes wide with fear. She looked as rough as I felt. Seeing her and Dominic had gutted me. It hurt to the point I was certain I'd vomit. I knew he'd done it to save us, and fortunately, it hadn't progressed as far as it could have. I despised his father. I prayed Dominic had killed him and was on his way back to us. I'd fought with Vincent as he'd dragged me away, but I knew I had to go. I promised I'd behave. This was me doing that.

"Do this," Vincent said, taking the gun from me as bullets pinged past us in the hall.

He peeked out the door and quickly ducked back, swearing. Smoke hung in the air, making my eyes and lungs burn.

"Look. It's ready to fire. Here's a magazine. Drop this one like this." He pushed a button on the side of the gun, and the magazine dropped out. "Put this one in like this." He pushed the new one into the gun and handed me the old one.

I tucked it into the front of my dress as he readied the gun to fire. "Got it?"

"Then what?"

"Then you point and shoot, baby. You don't need to kill them, but it'd be real nice if you did." He glanced at Natalia. "Stay close, OK? B, cover me."

Natalia nodded mutely. I tightened my hand on the gun.

Vincent pressed his mouth to mine, kissing me fast and hard. "Just in case."

He darted out and shot at someone, sending them to the ground. He put another bullet into them as we followed. I tried to not look at the dead guy, but I did. I'd never seen him before, so at least he wasn't someone I'd feel bad for.

"These are lords' men," Natalia said, her voice quaking. "An attack by the Bratva."

Vincent nodded grimly. "This is the work of your brother."

"Fallon? I-I don't understand."

"We'll explain later," Vincent said, leading us through the house, shooting at anyone who crossed our path.

We'd just reached another hall, when a man darted from another room and punched Vincent in the head, sending him toppling to the ground, his gun falling away.

The man quickly grabbed the weapon and pointed it at Vincent. I watched in horror as the man wiped at his nose.

"Hell yeah, I'll be rewarded nicely for killing the great Vincent Valentino," the man guffawed as he tightened his hold on the weapon.

My pulse roared in my ears as I left my hiding spot, my pistol raised. I didn't even hesitate. I squeezed the trigger as Vincent covered his head. The man dropped to the ground. I pulled the trigger again and again until he stopped moving, crimson pooling around his body.

I stood holding the gun, my body quaking.

I didn't see Vincent get to his feet, but I felt him as his warm body pressed to mine.

"Give me the gun, baby," he coaxed gently.

I shook, clutching it tighter. *I just killed someone. Someone was dead because I shot them.*

"Baby, come on," Vincent said again, wrapping his hand around mine. "Let go."

I gasped and let him take the gun. He pulled me back into the room and wrapped me in his arms, holding me tightly.

A sob ripped from my throat.

"I-I killed that man. He-he's dead. I-I've never killed anyone before. I'll go to jail. I won't find my dad. Dominic will miss me. You. Fallon. Levin—"

"Easy, sweetheart. It's OK. You're not in trouble. No one gives a shit about some lord prick. He was going to kill me. You saved me, B. You're my hero, baby."

I shook against him, the urge to vomit real.

"Breathe, B. Come on," Vincent said, giving me a shake as I tried to suck in a breath that just didn't want to come. "We need to get the fuck out of here. I need you to pull yourself together, OK? Can you do that for me?" He eased back and tilted my face up, pressing a kiss to my lips. "Come on, pretty girl. We need to find Dom and Fallon. They need us."

I nodded, gathering myself. "OK."

"Here. I'm giving you the gun back. Don't hesitate if it happens again, OK? It's fine to kill these fuckers. They would've killed us without batting a lash." He swiped the tears off my cheek and kissed me again. "I love you."

"Love you too," I said hoarsely.

He smiled and pulled away. "Natalia? You good?"

"No," she answered weakly. "But I really need to get out of here."

"Good enough." Vincent peeked out into the hallway again. He gestured for us to follow. "B, just look straight ahead. Don't look down."

I swallowed and did as he instructed, trying to ignore the man I'd killed on the floor. We made it out to another corridor. This place was a damn maze. I hated it here and vowed to never return.

Vincent poked his head out at the T in the hall and ducked back as gunshots rang out. He fired back before shoving us away.

"Go. Go. Go!"

Footsteps rushed at us with the gunfire as we tried to go back the way we'd come.

"B, you're going to have to run. I'll hold these guys off. You're going to have to go back that way. Take the back hall. Just be careful, OK? Shoot anyone who crosses you, and keep fucking going. Got it?"

"What about you?"

"I'll be fine. This isn't my first rodeo." He gave my hand a squeeze before shoving me away.

Bullets pinged off the wall as I turned and ran, Natalia right behind me. I didn't know where I was going. I ran blindly, ducking and dodging gunshots as much as I could. I leaped over bodies, hoping Natalia could keep up because I didn't want to slow down. I coughed as I inhaled smoke from whatever was burning. I wanted to go home and wash the *what the fuck* off my body. This had to be the worst wedding reception in history.

I skidded to a door and let out a snarl when I realized it was locked. I glanced behind me to find Natalia was gone. I'd somehow lost her in the smoke and confusion. I said a silent prayer she didn't get killed in all the gunfire and smoke.

Damnit! I had to go back for her.

I turned to race back down the hall and slammed into a hard body as I rounded a corner. Warm arms wrapped around me before I stumbled back.

"L-Levin?" I choked out, staring up at him in shock.

"Hey, bumblebee," he answered gruffly as he hauled me back against the wall.

"Wha-what are you doing here? Where's Fallon?"

"We split up to find you. I'm here because this is where I belong."

I nodded, not questioning him further. Shouts sounded out in the distance, followed by more gunfire. I winced as Levin looked down at me.

"There should be a window in that room. It should lead to the back gardens if my memory of this place serves me correctly. If we break it out, I can get you out of here. My car is parked at the property line. If we stick to the trees, we'll be safe."

"OK," I said thickly.

"You're not hurt right? He didn't hurt you, did he?" his voice trembled as he took me in.

I shook my head. "I'm OK."

His gaze skirted over my face before he nodded and gestured for me to follow him. He went back to the locked door and shot the handle. The door banged open when he kicked it. We rushed to the window, which he shot out.

I turned just as a man dressed in black entered the room, his gun raised.

It happened in slow motion. One moment I was staring death in the face, and the next my head smashed against a desk as I toppled to the floor. Levin dove in front of me, blocking me from view of the gunman. A gunshot rang out. Levin jerked and staggered back, wetness blossoming on his dark shirt.

I reached for him, screaming his name. Fallon swept into the room and shot the man in the back of the head, his blood and brains splatting all over the place. Fallon stepped over the body and rushed at us with Natalia on his heels.

"Levin? Levin!" I screamed as I leaned over him, his blood staining the white material of my dress.

He blinked at me and groaned. My head swam from smacking it so hard. Stars dotted my vision. I shook it off as I pressed my hand to the dark spot on his shirt by his abdomen.

He reached out and cradled my face for a moment as his eyelids fluttered.

"No," I sobbed. "Come on, Boo Bear. Stay with me."

He gave me a tired smile. "I hate that name."

I wailed and tried to stay conscious. Blood dribbled down my jaw from my head wound.

"Help him, Fallon. Please. Don't let him die."

"We need to get you out of here. This place is on fire. Drake molotoved it. We'll be dead if we don't get going. The entire ballroom is in flames. We can't get to the front door, and the other half of the place is filled with fuckers." He tried to drag me away from Levin, but I let out a snarl and pushed him away.

"Don't touch me! We can't leave him! We can't!"

"They're coming," Natalia choked out, glancing fearfully over her shoulder as the gunfire got closer.

"Car is on the edge of the property through the trees," Levin said breathlessly, his voice strained. "Keys are in the middle console. G-get her out of here. Save her. Please. Get her to safety."

Fallon nodded and grabbed my hand. I tugged away from him as I tried to stop Levin's bleeding.

He wrapped his hand around mine. "Bumblebee, go. Please. Go with Fallon."

"I'm not going. Fallon, help me. We need to get him out the window."

"Bianca, princess, we can't carry him—"

"Fucking help me, or I swear to God," I snarled at him, swaying as I tried to lift Levin, who fought me weakly.

Fallon growled and grabbed Levin's arm, hefting him up amid a groan of agony from Levin. Blood trickled from his body, leaving red dots on the floor. Natalia helped me with his other side. We pushed him through the window with a hell of a lot of effort. He fell forward and hit the lawn with a moan, his shirt soaked with blood. I went out next, followed by Natalia then Fallon. I stumbled and fell, my knees hitting the edge of a concrete patio hard and making me hiss in pain.

"We need to go. Levin, you big German fuck, you need to wake up long enough to help me carry you." Fallon grunted as he helped Levin to his feet with Natalia.

With every ounce of energy we had, we managed to get through the trees with Fallon only having to kill two stragglers along the way. We made it to Levin's car. Fallon slid him into the backseat. I got in with him and held onto him, ripping off part of my dress to place over his wound, so I could try to slow the bleeding. Natalia got into the front with Fallon and grabbed the keys for him.

Fallon started the car and peeled out of the trees.

"We need a hospital," I called out as Levin let out a rough, garbled breath. "He's dying!"

"We can't go to the hospital. I need to call Dom. Fuck!" Fallon pounded the steering wheel as we hit eighty on the desolate stretch of highway outside of town.

"Where are we going then?" I demanded. "He needs a doctor!"

"Dom sent me a safe house address. We're going there. Nattie, call Dom and pray to fuck he answers." He tossed her his phone.

She quickly thumbed through his contacts before she put the phone to her ear. "No one is answering," she cried out.

"Try Vincent," Fallon shouted.

She dialed again and again to nothing before she tried once more. She straightened in her seat.

"D-Dominic? I-it's Natalia. W-we're going to a safe house. We need help. L-Levin's been shot. H-he's bleeding so much," her voice cracked. "Yes. She's with us... OK.... Yes.... OK.... OK." She hung up. "He said he's on the way with Vincent and will send someone to help."

Fallon gripped the steering wheel tighter. A wave of dizziness washed over me.

I stared down at Levin. His breathing was shallow, his eyes closed.

"Don't leave me," I whimpered, leaning down and pressing my forehead to his. "Don't go. I didn't even get to say I was sorry. I was an idiot. Stay, Levin. Please stay with me. I love you. I love you so-so much."

My head spun again, and this time I couldn't stop the fall. Darkness blotted out the light, and I let go, Levin's name on my lips.

FORTY-SEVEN
FALLON

Bianca wouldn't wake up despite Natalia shaking her. Seeley was barely breathing. I wheeled his car down the two-track road and raced to the end of the road through the dark forest as Natalia leaned in the back and took on Bianca's job of applying pressure to Levin's wound. When I reached the large, log cabin, there was a middle-aged man standing in the driveway. I got out with my gun raised. I knew this fucking place. This was where I'd been held captive in the basement when I'd thought Bianca was dead. They'd led me out and stuffed my head in a bag before we'd left. Call it PTSD or whatever, but I was on high alert.

The man immediately lifted his hands. "Dominic sent me. I'm a doctor. Name's Alan."

I lowered my gun and nodded for him to help me.

"We have two. He's been shot in the stomach. She's hurt. Head injury. Neither can die."

"I've been told as much." Alan grunted, helping me get Levin out first.

It was a struggle, but the doc, Natalia, and I managed to get him inside. The doctor led us to a room off the living room filled with medical equipment.

I guessed this wasn't a first for De Santis. I had to admire his preparedness.

I helped heave Levin onto a bed and ran back out to grab Bianca out of the car while Natalia stayed to help the doc. Bianca's small body was easy enough to carry. Her head lolled against my chest as I carried her in her blood-soaked, white dress into the house.

"You're OK, princess," I murmured, rushing her inside. "You're going to be OK. I fucking swear it. God, please."

I lay her on the couch since there wasn't another bed in the room Levin was in. Natalia came in with an ice pack and a damp rag.

"I-I don't know what else to do," she whispered. "I'm sorry, Fal."

"It's OK," I said, swallowing hard as I dabbed at the ugly, purple mark marring the side of Bianca's face and head. It was swollen pretty badly. I wrapped the ice pack with the rag and pressed it to the side of her head. "Stay with her. I'm going to go see if the doc needs help with Seeley."

I got up, and Natalia kneeled beside Bianca, holding the cold pack to her head and face. My mind raced with worry. Maybe my distraction had been too much. At least they hadn't died. *God, please don't fucking die.* If Seeley snuffed it, I definitely wouldn't get my girl back. I needed that German fuck to pull through.

"How is he?" I asked, going to Levin's beside and staring down at the pale, shirtless fucker in front of me on the cot.

I glanced around. There was even an x-ray machine in the room. Fucking De Santis really was locked and stocked. An x-ray of Seeley's abdomen was on display, the bullet clearly still inside.

"Missed all the vital bits mostly. He's lost a lot of blood." Doc moved to a small refrigerator and removed a bag of blood.

I watched as he set everything up, truly impressed with the small hospital in the cabin. Hail didn't have anything nearly as elaborate. If someone got shot, there was a pretty good chance he'd die if Hail didn't get to dump him in front of a hospital in time. Or he'd bring you to the old guy on Ninth, who ran a questionable restaurant I wouldn't feed my enemies in. Sometimes he'd patch people up if the restaurant wasn't too busy.

I watched as Dominic's doc finished hooking up the blood and IV.

"Can you hand me that?" He gestured to a pair of plier-looking things.

I grabbed them and handed them over, watching as he peered down at the bullet hole in Seeley's abdomen.

"Aren't you going to give him pain meds or something?" I asked.

"Already did. Hand me some gauze."

I handed it to him. He dug the pliers into the wound and searched around for a moment before he unearthed a bullet and dropped it into the bowl I held. Then he cleaned and stitched the wound with insane speed and precision. Satisfied, he adjusted the oxygen mask on Seeley's face and pulled a blanket up over him. The monitors beeped, claiming the big bastard was still alive.

"He's stable. I've given him enough meds to keep him under for a few hours. Let's go get a look at this girl now," Doc said, bustling from the room and tossing his gloves into the trash on the way out.

I followed him to where Natalia still held the ice pack to Bianca's face. Doc kneeled beside her and gave her a once over.

"She needs stitches. Grab the tray and needle." He grunted, checking her pulse. "It's in a package on the metal tray beside his bed."

I rushed back to Seeley's room and grabbed the tray with all the stitch shit on it and brought it back out. Doc took it and began cleaning Bianca up. He gave her a shot before he stitched along her hairline. My guts wobbled. She'd be scarred from this fucking shit.

The front door banged open. Dominic and Vincent rushed into the room, both looking like they'd just survived a plane crash. Disheveled hair, torn clothes, bloody as hell, faces dark with smoke residue.

Dom dropped to his knees beside Bianca as I shuffled aside for him. He gripped her hand, bringing it to his lips and kissing it.

"How is she?" he asked tightly, his green eyes raking over her as Valentino loomed nearby, looking like he was going to throw up.

"She's going to need her head scanned. You don't have one of those here. It looks like she hit it pretty hard. She may have some bleeding on her brain. I won't know until I look. I'm hopeful everything is just superficial, but she did have a large wound I stitched up."

A muscle thrummed along Dom's jaw. "Can you get it done?"

"Yes. I'll need you to bring her around back of the hospital. I'll let Jackie know we're coming."

"How's Levin?" Dom asked, staring down at Bianca, her hand still in his.

"Stable for the moment. I'll come back in a few hours to check on him. In the meantime, let's get this young lady checked out."

Dom didn't need to be told twice. He scooped Bianca into his arms and looked over at me.

"Thank you. For saving them."

I nodded, my throat tight as I gazed at Bianca. "Please make sure she's OK."

"I will." And with those words, he left, following the doc outside.

"I'm going to check on Levin," Vincent mumbled, leaving Natalia and me alone in the living room.

We sat in silence for a long time before I finally spoke. I looked over at her. "I missed you, Nattie."

"Missed you too."

Her eyes misted over, and I pulled her into a hug, clinging to her. She was the only family I had. We'd always been close. We only had one another. When I'd spotted her at Matteo's, I'd killed two people trying to get to her while she cowered behind a large potted plant like she was lost.

"Are you OK?" I asked, shifting back so I could examine her face.

Tears brimmed her eyes as she shook her head. "No."

"Do you want to talk about it?"

"N-not right now," she said softly, wincing.

I nodded and released her. Nattie was always quiet about her feelings. She didn't like to be pushed. I'd give her the time she needed.

"I was so worried about you. I tried everything."

"I know." She squeezed my hand. "I'm here now though. We're together."

"For how long? Tonight was a shit show. Matteo De Santis is going to retaliate. He's not going to accept this. There's going to be hell to pay."

"I know. I'm scared," she said softly. "We're in a war, Fal. We're as good as dead."

"Shh," I said, quieting her before she went into a panic. "We've always made it through, right? This time will be no different. I promise you, OK? I'll do whatever I have to do to keep you safe."

"Do you love her?"

I licked my lips, Bianca's face flashing in my mind. "I do. With everything I am, I do. You know me, Nat. I wouldn't be here if I didn't."

"And Dominic knows? He's not... mad?" Worry clouded her eyes as she stared back at me.

"He was. In fact, he almost killed me. We made a deal though. I'm hoping he comes through on it. He's done good so far. You're still safe."

She gave me a shaky smile, a tear trickling from her eye. She hastily wiped at it and sniffled. "How will it work with you and him and her?"

"And Levin and Vincent?" I let out a soft laugh.

Her eyes widened, and I smirked.

"Yeah. Four of us. We all fell for her when we shouldn't have. What was it Mom always said? That strength is measured in love, not hate? If that's true, we'll take out the damn world in the name of love for her. She's everything, Nattie. I can't wait for you to get to know her. I've never felt this way in my life for anyone before. She's it, you know?"

Nattie gave me a sad, gentle smile. "Yeah. I know the feeling."

I took her back into my arms and held her. I wasn't sure what to say, so I remained quiet, letting her weep softly on my shoulder until her breathing turned deep and even.

"There's a room with an attached bath upstairs if she needs it," Vincent's voice broke in as he came into the room. "I'll show you. She could probably use a bath."

Nearly thirty minutes had passed, and I was nearly asleep with her. I nodded and roused her.

"Nattie. Hey. Wake up. Let's get you upstairs, OK? Vincent says there's a bath and bed for you up there."

She blinked and nodded. I got to my feet and helped her to hers, watching as she winced. Vincent started for the stairs, so I followed with Nattie between us. He opened the third door on the left and led us inside.

The place was nice. Surprisingly modern considering it was a log cabin in the middle of nowhere. De Santis didn't spare a dime on this place.

"I'll run you a bath," Vincent said, not bothering to ask.

I watched as he disappeared into the attached bathroom, the sound of running water meeting my ears.

"We should be safe here," I said, observing as she looked out the window nervously.

"For how long?" She cast me a sad glance over her shoulder.

"I don't know," I answered honestly. "I trust the kings. De Santis knows what he's doing."

"Water's ready. I put out a towel and soaps for you," Vincent said, coming back. He walked to a dresser and removed a pair of blue sweatpants and a t-shirt. He handed them to her. "It's not perfect, but it'll do. You'll be comfortable. We rarely have females here."

"Thanks." She took the items from him and disappeared into the bathroom, closing the door behind her.

The moment she was out of earshot, Vincent turned to me.

"We need to talk."

I swallowed hard. Vincent was the nicest of the kings. The way he was looking at me though made me think he was about to hand me my death sentence.

I nodded and got to my feet. As I followed him out, I wondered if he would lead me back to the fucking dungeon in the basement for setting the fire and bringing an army to the De Santis estate.

Either way, I didn't regret it. A few less of Matteo's men in the world wasn't a bad thing. And a few less of Ivanov's wasn't either.

FORTY-EIGHT
BIANCA

I awoke with a groan, feeling stiff. I'd been in and out of it for what felt like forever.

I pried my eyes open and gazed up at a familiar ceiling.

The safe house in the woods.

I jerked up in bed, immediately regretting it as my head pounded.

"Shit," I hissed, wincing as I gripped my head.

It felt like a marching band was banging against my skull. I sat for a moment, trying to get my bearings about me. When the ache died down a bit, I shifted and placed my feet on the cool polished floor and stood, my body trembling.

Slowly, I made my way to the bathroom and did my business. Then I studied myself in the mirror. The side of my face was an ugly shade of purple, and stitches ran along my hairline. I touched it gingerly and whimpered. It was swollen, and my eye wasn't opening all the way.

I backed away, cringing.

I needed to get downstairs. I had to see Levin and my kings. And Fallon. I sent up a silent prayer he was still here, and that I wouldn't get bad news about Levin.

My stomach roiled with worry as I stood at the top of the landing. A wave of dizziness washed over me, making me feel weak.

"D-Dominic?" I called out, knowing I couldn't get down the stairs safely with my head spinning. "Vinny? Fallon?" I winced again, calling out to them making my head pound.

I was just about to drop to my butt and attempt to slide down the stairs when Vincent appeared at the bottom. He shot up to me, taking the stairs two at a time.

"Hey, baby B," he greeted me gently when he got to me. He took my hand and led me away from the stairs. "I wasn't expecting you to be up so soon. I thought you'd sleep a few more hours."

"Where's Levin? Is he OK?"

"He's out cold. He needs the rest. I'm sure he'll be waking up soon too. Doc has him on some meds to keep him comfortable."

"But he's OK, right?"

We'd reached the bedroom. He ushered me inside and sat me on the bed.

"He is. Doc said he just needs to rest and regain his strength. He lost a lot of blood."

My throat tightened at the memory of it, but as long as he was still breathing, I could handle that.

"Where's Dominic?"

"He's, uh, dealing with something right now—him and Fallon."

I nodded tightly, relieved both were OK. I reached for Vincent. He took my hand and sat down beside me.

"What's wrong, baby?" he asked gently.

"I'm tired and hungry. I need a bath. I feel gross," I said softly.

"I'll run you a bath." He kissed my forehead. "And I'll get you something to eat." He got up and went to the bathroom to run water in the tub.

He returned a few moments later and helped me to it, peeling my red nightie off me gently, his fingers gently brushing against my skin. Goosebumps flitted over my flesh as I looked up at him.

"I'm sorry," he said in a soft voice. "For everything that's happened." He cradled my face.

I nodded silently, tears biting my eyes.

"Listen," he continued gently. "All the shit that went down in

Matteo's office, you know Dom did it for you, right? He doesn't feel anything for Natalia other than he made a promise to not let her die. He was stuck in a really shitty position. I told Fallon what happened with Dom and Natalia. He was upset but understood the reasoning."

I said nothing for a moment, hating it was even something he had to tell someone about. Another tear slipped down my cheek.

"I know. I'm not mad because he did it. I'm upset because he had to. His father is a monster. I-I hate him. I wish he were dead. Tell me Dominic killed him."

"I wish I could say that. Dominic busted him up pretty good. I think it's safe to say he's on the outs with his old man, so that leaves us in a bit of an ugly spot."

My stomach fell. "What now?"

"Let's get you in the bath and get some food in you, OK? We'll talk about everything else in a bit. You've been in and out of it for the last day and a half. Dominic hasn't left your side since he got here. But then he had no choice when word came in about the horsemen."

"The drug guys?"

Vincent brushed my hair away from my face. "M-hm."

"Is it bad?"

His Adam's apple bobbed. "Bath. Food. Rest. In that order. Come on."

I knew he shut down, so I let him help me into the tub. I sank beneath the warm bubbles and let out a sigh of relief.

"Can I see Levin? After?"

"You're going to eat and rest. Levin is slumped, baby. When he wakes *and* you're feeling better, then yes. You can see him." He pressed a kiss to my forehead and left the room, leaving no room for argument.

Sighing, I rested my head against the back of the massive tub and closed my eyes, worry creeping through me.

It seemed like things had gone from bad to worse.

Wasn't that the story of our lives?

I AWOKE HOURS LATER, dressed once more in the red, silky nightie Dominic had added to the safe house. Yelling came from downstairs. It must have been what woke me. Groaning, I sat up, noting it was dark outside.

"I did what you wanted! If you don't like the fucking outcome, then that's your fault!" Fallon bellowed, his voice carrying.

Dominic swore in Italian, and something broke.

I staggered out of bed and gingerly made my way to the top of the stairs. I'd felt a little better after the soup Vincent had made me. My stomach growled at the thought of food. I took the first step down and then another, definitely feeling stronger.

Dominic and Fallon were facing off in the living room when my feet touched the bottom floor.

"What's going on?" I called out.

All attention in the room snapped to me. Dominic hissed and moved toward me in quick strides, closing the space between us.

He ran his fingers through my hair as he tilted my chin up. "*Mia regina*, you should be resting."

"It's hard to rest when all I can hear is you guys down here fighting. What's going on?" I peered past Dominic to see Fallon staring at the floor and Vincent looking pained.

"Go back upstairs and rest—"

"Dominic, stop," I said, cutting him off. "I want to know what's going on. Is Levin OK?"

"Levin is fine. We gave him another dose of morphine. He's out." Vincent stepped away from Fallon and flopped onto the couch, rubbing his face. He let out a groan. "Dom, man. Just tell her. She needs to know."

Dominic sighed and took my hand in his to lead me to the couch where he sat me down. He took up a spot on the coffee table and faced me while Fallon settled in the overstuffed chair beside us.

"What's going on?" I asked again.

"The lords did a hit on De Luca and his horsemen. It was bad."

"Did people get killed?" I glanced from Dominic to Fallon.

"Yeah," Fallon said. "Trent hit up a club where De Luca was known to hang. Shot the shit out of it. Bunch of innocent people were killed and injured."

"Did they get the guy they were after?" I turned back to Dominic, who swallowed.

"We don't know. It was a sloppy, amateur job."

"I don't understand."

"They left a calling card. A *king* calling card." Vincent tossed a black card with a skull and crown onto the table. "These are used to send a message sometimes. If you get one of these, it means you've pissed us off. We rarely use them, but people know what they are. Apparently, the lords made up a stash of them when we took you from Hail. They planned on fucking us over. Looks like they did because now De Luca is after us."

My heart skipped. "We're in danger? Again? What are we going to do?"

"We're in a bad spot," Dominic murmured. "Especially now. I don't have the manpower to fight three wars right now."

"*Three*? Who the hell are the three?" My heart beat harder.

"De Luca, the lords, and now, my father," Dominic said in a soft, flat voice. "I've been cut off. I guess beating the shit out of him didn't go over too well."

"Oh my God," I whispered. "Is there one of those hit things on you?"

Dominic abruptly stood and tugged his hair as he let out a snarl. He punched a wall, putting a hole in it.

"Not for him, but it's expected there'll be one for you," Vincent said softly. "We think he'll put the hit on you. Matteo will pay a fuck ton to make it happen if it goes down the way we think it will. My father said he's pissed. He's been talking about paying for you either dead or alive."

"How much is a fuck ton?" my voice shook.

"Millions," Fallon said softly.

My heart stopped as the blood rushed from my head.

"Millions?" I finally squeaked out.

Dominic turned to me, his eyes bloodshot and furious. "It's so he can torture you in front of me before he kills you. It's the only reason he'd want you alive. He knows if he gets you, I'll be close behind. It's about him showing power and control. If I come to heel, he wins."

"Wh-what are we going to do?" I looked at each of them. "Are we even safe here if he calls this in?"

"This is my place. No one knows of its existence except a select few that I trust with my life. We're safe here. For now." Dominic breathed out and came back to sit in front of me. He took my hands in his. "I'm sorry I got you into this. I fucked up."

"I came to you, remember?" I said, my voice shaky. "And he hasn't ordered it yet. So there's that."

He sighed. "I didn't have to agree when you approached me, but I was greedy and wanted you. In fact, at this point in time, you may have actually been safer with Ivanov."

"I wasn't safer with him," I seethed, pointing at Fallon. "Ask Fallon. He was there for a hell of a lot of it. He knows what I went through. He knows what it was like for me."

"She would've been safer if she'd never met any of us," Fallon said with a grunt, staring down at his hands.

"Let's get a few things straight." I turned back to Dominic.

He looked like he hadn't been sleeping. His hair was a mess, and his eyelids were heavy. We needed to do this though.

"Is Fallon a king yet, or did he risk his life for nothing?"

Vincent's dark gaze darted from Fallon to Dominic as he leaned forward. Fallon looked up, his brows crinkled.

"It's fine. Everything is a mess right now. I haven't done much to earn the title," Fallon started, but I got up and went to him.

Dominic didn't try to stop me. I fell to my knees in front of Fallon and cradled his face. He stared back at me, so much emotion in his eyes it made my heart beat harder.

"You saved Levin. You saved us all. If it weren't for you, things could have gotten really bad. You helped get Levin and me out of there. You did what Dominic told you to do. You deserve to be part of the kings."

"I appreciate the sentiment, princess, but that was all you. You fought me on it and won. I was prepared to leave, remember? I was going to leave Levin."

"But you didn't," I said.

He gave me a sad smile. "I guess."

"He's alive because of you. You know it. So am I. So is Natalia."

"I agree," Vincent called out.

I looked over my shoulder at him and then to Dominic, who was staring at Fallon.

"Dominic?" I asked. "We need Fallon. You know we do. He came through. He saved even you. You almost had to *rape* Natalia. He stopped that too. His distraction stopped it from happening to me."

A muscle thrummed along Dominic's jaw. "He's in."

"What?" Fallon whispered, his voice shaking, his eyes widening. "I'm in?"

"You're in," Dominic repeated in a stronger voice. "But if you so much as step out of line, you're out. You're dead. There are still rules you need to follow. You're in, but I need you to stick with the lords. We need the inside track."

"OK," Fallon said without hesitating. "I'll pull double duty."

"So that's it?" I asked, breathing out and getting to my feet.

Dominic nodded. Vincent let out a whoop. I rushed to Dominic and threw my arms around his neck. His arms immediately snaked around me and held me tightly.

"Thank you," I choked out, pulling away.

He smiled down at me, sadness and worry in his green eyes. *"Qualsiasi cosa per te, mia regina.* Anything for you, my queen.*"* He cradled my face, his brows crinkled. "Are you feeling OK? Your face is so bruised." He sounded physically pained by the observation.

"I'm fine," I said, placing a kiss on his lips. "Just a little sore."

He nodded, his Adam's apple bobbing. "Go to him." He released me and stepped away.

I studied him for a moment. He visibly swallowed, a muscle

twitching in his jaw. I backed away from him and turned to Fallon, who was on his feet. Vincent looked from Dominic to me to Fallon then back to me.

Fallon approached and dragged me into his arms. His lips found mine, and he kissed me deeply, stealing my breath and sealing our fate.

He was in. He was a king.

FORTY-NINE
BIANCA

I stared at Levin while he slept. The monitor beeped a slow and steady sound. He had an IV in his arm, and his face was pale. After Dominic let me go to Fallon, we'd kissed and I'd cuddled with him in his chair while he, Vincent, and Dominic went through a list of things we had to do, including Fallon remaining within the lords. I'd fallen asleep at some point in Fallon's lap. I'd woken up in Dominic's bed with the sun shining in on me. I immediately went downstairs to check on Levin's status.

Vincent had said Levin had only woke long enough to groan before they gave him more pain medication.

I took Levin's large hand in mine and held it. I dragged my fingertips along the tattoos on his fingers, wishing he'd wake up and feel better. He'd taken a bullet for me. Had nearly died for me. Maybe it was nothing. Maybe it was everything.

I had no way of knowing because he was unconscious.

"Still sleeping?" Vincent called out as he came into the room hours later.

I looked up and smiled. "Yeah. He groaned a few times, but that was it."

He pushed off the doorway and stepped over to me, resting his hand on my shoulder. "Celeste keeps calling. Dom got pissed and told her to stop. That Levin was busy."

I let out a soft, sad laugh. "Busy trying to stay alive."

"He's going to be OK. He's been shot before, you know."

"Really?" I gaped at Vincent.

"Yeah. Once in the shoulder last year." He pointed to a barely visible scar beneath one of Levin's dark tattoos.

I swallowed, hating this was their life.

"He saved me. A man came into the room and pointed his gun at me. Levin shoved me to the floor and took the bullet. I might be dead right now if it weren't for him."

"He cares about you," Vincent murmured.

"He has a girlfriend."

"He does." He gave my shoulder a squeeze. "You need to eat something. Dominic is making dinner. Let's let Levin rest."

I nodded and got up, gazing at Levin one more time before I pressed a kiss to his hand and let him go. Vincent led me out of the room and into the kitchen. Natalia was seated on a barstool, her gaze focused on a window where a squirrel was gathering for the upcoming winter. Fallon sat beside her on his phone, sending a text to who I assumed had to be Hail.

And Dominic was stirring sauce on the stove. Delicious smells permeated the place.

"He's making spaghetti," Vincent said as he ushered me to the table and pulled a chair out for me.

I sat, watching Dominic in his red apron, his black-framed glasses on his face, and his dark hair a mess. In that moment, he didn't look like a scary mob prince. He looked like a beautiful, sweet man, who was simply making dinner.

He glanced up at me and offered me the smallest of smiles before he went back to stirring.

"He cooks when he's stressed. Or he shoots stuff. Weird, huh?" Vincent said, settling beside me. "Never an in-between."

"I'll say," I said softly.

Natalia peeked over at me and winced. She looked how I felt.

Uncomfortable. Upset. Worried. I'd witnessed her do something I was pretty certain she'd never do without a gun pushed to her head. I didn't blame her at all and had zero animosity toward her. I just hoped she didn't resent me because of Dominic's decision to protect me and hurt her to do it.

When one considered it, it was probably the best option, despite it being so messed up. They would've killed her. I knew they would have.

I gave her a small, reassuring smile. Her lips twitched in my direction like she wanted to grin, but her eyes were glassy.

We weren't there yet. It was OK. Someday.

Dominic slid a plate of pasta at me before giving one to Vincent. I watched as he doled more out onto plates for Fallon and Natalia. When he handed Natalia hers, he gave her hand a squeeze. She stared up at him and gave him a slight nod.

I supposed it was his way of telling her everything that happened at his father's wasn't a reflection of who he was. He went to the counter and grabbed two large bowls of salad and two baskets of bread. He placed one of each in front of Fallon and Vincent before he finally filled the wine glasses and settled in beside me at the table.

"This smells delicious," I said to him. "I had no idea you could cook like this."

"I'm a man of many talents," he answered, reaching out and tucking a strand of hair behind my ear. "Eat, *mia regina*. You need your strength."

"Yeah, B. This shit is banging. Dom would've made a good chef if he didn't enjoy killing people," Vincent said around a mouthful of bread.

Dominic shook his head, and I smirked, almost feeling normal, even though everything in our lives suggested nothing was normal or good or safe. But we could pretend, even if only for a night.

I caught Fallon's eye, and he winked at me.

It was a playful wink, filled with his happiness. At least one good thing had come out of all of this. Fallon was one of us now.

FIFTY
BIANCA

"I think we should return to classes," Dominic said as I snuggled in bed beside him that night.

After claiming his cooking was the best I'd ever had and making him smile, I'd gone back to sit with Levin until I'd fallen asleep with my head on his mattress. Dominic had gone in and lifted me into his arms and carried me to our room.

"I thought we might be on your father's *Most Wanted* list," I said in a tired voice as he gathered me against his body.

"I think it would be easiest if we're there." He kissed the top of my head. "They aren't going to come shoot us there. Too many witnesses. It'll be the best place for us. Bolten has always been neutral ground. Then we can graduate on time and get the fuck out of there. We'll return tomorrow. Staying hidden like rats makes us look weak. We aren't weak."

"Like I care about any of that."

"*I* care about that. You're smart, *mia regina*. I want you to have a graduation. You deserve it. And I want people to know we're resilient."

I shrugged against him. Staying hidden didn't seem like a bad idea in my opinion.

"What about Levin? We can't just leave him here."

"Natalia is going to stay here and care for him," he said. He went quiet for a moment. "I didn't want to do that with her."

He didn't need to tell me what he was talking about. It was another ugly memory on repeat in my head.

"I know." I rubbed my palm over his heart.

"I don't regret it," he whispered. "I would've fucked her until she couldn't breathe if it meant saving you."

My chest tightened at his words.

"It was you. That's who I thought of while it was happening. I told myself you were sucking my cock. I told myself it was your pussy. I told myself I was doing it to save my queen."

"I-I don't want to talk about it, Dominic. I know you didn't want her."

The pain flared red hot in my heart as I struggled with the ugly memory of Natalia on her knees in tears with my husband's dick in her mouth. Of him pushing up behind her just before hell came crashing down on us.

We were quiet for a moment before he spoke again, "Vincent told me you had to shoot someone."

I cringed, my body tensing at the mention of it. Another ugly memory.

"Do you need to talk about it?" he asked softly.

"I don't know." I traced my fingers along his abdominal muscles, making him shiver against me. "I was scared. I just reacted when I saw him point his gun at Vincent. I didn't think. Then it was over, and he was dead."

Dominic took my hand and pressed his lips to my fingers. "In our world, no one cares who we kill within our circles. The police want us to finish one another off. We spend very little time dealing with them. They simply try to wrangle our little men. Those at the top never have problems."

"Are you saying I'm at the top and not to worry?" I looked at him hopefully. Not that I wanted to be at the top. I just didn't want to be in trouble.

"You're my killer queen. Heiress to my empire. You're fucking untouchable unless a bigger fish comes along and orders it," his voice tightened.

"Like your dad," I whispered.

"He could. I think he might be waiting to see what my next move will be." He was quiet for a moment. "I burned the house down."

"What?" I went up on my elbow and gawked down at him.

He gave me a sad smirk. "I hated that place anyway. Before we left, I turned the gas on in the kitchen. Then I shot the fucking stove as I ran out. *Boom.* Killed a lot of people, both sides. Father isn't happy with me.."

"But he's alive."

"Fucker is a cockroach, refusing to die," Dominic muttered, his gaze locking on mine. He reached out and cupped my face, drawing me to him. His lips met mine in a gentle kiss.

"I want you," he said against my lips. "Seeing you kiss Fallon last night upset me."

"You said—"

"I get upset whenever *anyone* kisses you. Vincent. Levin. Fallon. I'm jealous because it's not me, and you're mine."

"I'm here now," I said, kissing along his jaw.

"I want to put a baby inside you."

I paused my kissing to stare down at him. "I'm not ready for that, Dominic—"

"And I really don't think I give a fuck, Bianca. The only thing I can think about is burying my cock deep inside your tight, wet pussy and planting my seed in your womb. I want your belly swollen with *my* heir, a perfect combination of you and me. I want to feel my son's strong kick when I talk to him while he's growing in you. I want you to scream as you bring another powerful De Santis into this world. A piece of us that no one can erase or take from me. *I want it.*"

He flipped me onto my back in one fluid motion and settled between my legs as I stared up at him, my heartbeat roaring in my ears as he pushed my nightie up. My panties landed on the floor.

He dragged his finger up my center. "In here. This is where I want to hide." He shoved his pants down and pressed his cock to my damp heat. "I want to be a better man for you, but I'm not good. You know I'm not."

"We don't have to do this right now. We can wait a year or two—"

"No." He thrust into me, his hips meeting mine as I cried out against his sudden intrusion.

God, if he finds out I've been taking those damn pills, he'll probably completely lose his mind. Thank God I'd stashed them in my purse and had been able to sneak them while we've been here at the safe house. I'd be losing my own damn mind if I'd missed nearly a week's worth of birth control.

"Ah, Dom-Dominic—"

"Shh. Please, *mia regina*. I need this. I need my son because I need to keep you. I'll love you both so fucking hard you won't regret it. I swear it." He slammed into me again. Again. And again.

"That night with my father broke me. The thought of him touching you…of putting *his* baby in there. *Hell no.* Mine. *Fucking mine.* I need this. Fuck." He breathed out, thrusting in and out of me.

I reached for him, wanting to connect with him, but he pushed my hands over my head and held them there as he fucked me, his hips snapping forward in a delicious rhythm.

"Spread wider for me," he rasped. "I want you to give yourself to me. Take my cock, wasp."

I parted my legs farther for him. Something unhinged in my brain. His cock seemed to have that effect on me. He slammed into me, groaning, his breathing coming in soft gasps.

My impending release crept through me, the heat building with each precise piston of his cock inside me.

My body quivered.

"Yes, *mia regina*. Come for me. Give it to me, my good girl."

I cried out, clenching around his length as he nipped at my nipple. He released it as I shook beneath him. His hips moved faster until he came with a groan, filling me with his release.

He balanced over me, his body glistening with a sheen of sweat, trembling.

"I love you," he said thickly. "I'm not asking for your forgiveness.

I can't ask for it when I know this is who I am and it's what I want. Just know I fucking love you unlike anything else in this world. *Sei mia.* You are mine."

Denying him what he wanted wouldn't do a damn thing for me. Besides a part of me really fucking liked being his in all the ways he owned me. He wanted my submission. My compliance.

"You aren't going to save me by getting me pregnant, Dominic," I said softly, stroking his cheek with my fingers.

His green eyes searched mine. "But if they take you from me, then I'll at least still have a piece of you."

"They aren't going to take me from you."

He swallowed. "I'll kill them all and then fuck you in their blood. Our kingdom, wasp. *Mia regina.* No one will be brave enough to try once I'm done. And you'll have my baby. My *savage* little monster. Just like his daddy," his voice cracked. "But better because part of him will be you. The world needs him. I'll give him to the world. A gift after all my sins."

It was a beautiful sentiment. Children should make the world better.

He eased out of me, his fingers finding my pussy and pushing his release back into me. "I'll send the world a gift from us. For fucking with us. He'll be what our world needs. He will make my wrongs right."

The way he stared at me as he said the words made my breath catch. He was being serious.

"I don't get a choice in this?" I asked.

His gaze flitted over me. "No."

He didn't extend more explanation. He simply moved off me. I sat up quickly, but he pushed me gently to my back.

"I need to clean myself," I said.

He shook his head and leaned down to give me a tender kiss. "No. I want my come in you all night."

He got up and went into the bathroom for a few minutes before returning to me. Lifting the blankets, he crawled in beside me and dragged me into his arms.

"I know this doesn't make you happy," he said softly into the darkness. "But it's all I can think about. I *need* this. I'm not going to stop. You're going to have my baby."

"You'll force me?" I whispered.

"I don't want to have to, but if I must, I will. I will fuck you every moment of every day until it happens."

"What about Fallon and Vincent? A-and Levin if he comes back? What if one of them gets me pregnant?"

He bit my shoulder, making me cry out.

"I won't like it. But the baby will be mine just like it would be theirs. I protect mine. I just plan on getting there first. Don't underestimate me, wasp."

I swallowed and breathed out. There was no winning with this man. I'd just have to make sure to keep taking my pills and hope he didn't find out. I needed a little more time before I gave into him.

"I'm not ready to be a mom, Dominic. I haven't finished high school. And I'd like to go to college maybe," I whispered, caressing his cheek with my fingers. "Plus, I still don't know what happened to my dad. And let's not forget that people want me dead. What if someone hurt me while I was pregnant, and it made me lose the baby? I'd be devastated, and so would you."

He swallowed hard and frowned.

"I'm just not ready yet. Give me time."

"No," was all he said before he went silent.

We lay in the darkness until his breathing became deep and even, his hold tight on me.

I couldn't escape him even if I wanted to. And I didn't want to.

And he fucking knew it.

FIFTY-ONE
DOMINIC

Bianca smoothed her navy Bolten uniform down. I'd watched as she kissed Levin goodbye on his forehead as he drifted in and out of consciousness earlier this morning. Natalia had promised to keep him safe and comfortable. Alan was headed over to check on him. I hoped to hear good news by this afternoon.

The swelling in Bianca's face had gone down substantially. She covered the purple bruising with makeup and left her blonde waves tumbling around her so the stitches in her hairline weren't visible.

I'd fucked her last night and knew I'd upset her with my talk about a baby. But fuck, I wanted it. It was becoming a disease, eating at me, growing stronger with each passing day. She was my queen. I wanted us to have a baby. I also knew she really would be untouchable with a child in her. Her survival rate would be higher if she was impregnated by me, at least where my father was concerned. If he saw I was making an heir, he might be more inclined to pull back.

Or he might say fuck it then kill her and my baby to teach me a lesson.

But I was banking on him backing the fuck off because I really would put a bullet in his fucked up head. Pretty sure he got that memo when I blew his house up with him inside.

"You look beautiful," I said to Bianca.

Her blue eyes locked on me, and the worry eased away, making my heart pound hard.

My son could be in her belly right now...

"You can't tell my face is messed up?"

I ran my thumb along that bottom lip I fucking loved so much. "Wear your sunglasses if you're nervous about your eye still being a little swollen."

She pushed the Gucci shades I'd bought her up her nose. "How do I look? Like I survived a gun fight?"

"Like you survived the apocalypse and claimed the world as your own." I kissed her, bringing her body against mine and relishing in her heat.

When I bit her bottom lip, she let out a tiny whimper.

"*Sei mia.*" I nipped at her lip. "Tell me."

"Yours," she breathed out. "I'm yours."

"I want to fuck you again." I ran my hand beneath her skirt.

We were outside our dorm and definitely within the range of prying eyes, but I didn't give a fuck. I'd push her against the wall and take her from behind if the urge struck me hard enough.

And it definitely had.

"Easy," Vincent called out as he approached.

We'd been waiting for him to get changed.

"There are young eyes here," he teased.

I broke away from Bianca and winked as her cheeks darkened to crimson.

"And I want my turn with her," he added, moving to take her into his arms.

I held my arm out to stop him and shot him a warning look.

"Seriously?" he grumbled, halting in his tracks.

"She's my wife. That's all anyone here knows. I don't need rumors going around about her," I said. "We're dealing with enough as it is."

Vincent groaned. "Fine. But just so you know, people are already whispering about us. Didn't you hear I'm fucking her behind your back?"

"I heard," I grunted. "And in truth, I've walked in on your attempts."

"*Attempts?*" Vincent snorted. "It wasn't an attempt. I was balls out ready. I was going in."

I laughed at him and grabbed Bianca's hand. We walked through campus, my gaze darting around to make sure shit was OK. I noted Vincent doing the same.

Bianca's phone buzzed. She stopped to pull it out as we settled moments later at our table in the courtyard. Fallon was with the lords talking to Drake while Ivanov kissed on Stella.

"Hello?" Bianca said into the phone. She paused for a moment. "Don't touch my mother, you sick fuck—"

Immediately, I took her phone out of her hand and pressed it to my ear. "Who is this?"

"De Santis," a deep voice met my ears. "You little prick. You think marrying my daughter makes you both safe now? You of all people should know word travels fast in our circles. You're going to pay—"

I chuckled as Bianca stared at me with wide eyes. Vincent gave her hand a reassuring squeeze.

"Bianca isn't your daughter. And your empty threats don't do shit to me, D'Angelou. Make them. Hide behind them. But I'm coming for you. You're already dead and don't even realize it." I ended the call and handed Bianca her phone back. "Do not answer calls from him. They are to go straight to voicemail. Understand?"

"But my mom—"

"*Will be fine.* He needs her alive to keep talking to you. If he kills her, he has nothing."

She didn't look convinced but didn't press the subject as she pulled her bottom lip between her teeth, seemingly lost deep in thought.

I looked back to Ivanov. He noticed us and walked our way with his lords in tow.

"Vin," I said softly.

He straightened up and watched as they approached. Immediately, I rose and positioned myself in front of Bianca, who sat on the tabletop.

"Look what the fucking wind swept in," Vincent said as Ivanov and his crew stopped in front of us.

He was plus one today with some little piss ant named Trent Beyers. Five on two. Not good odds if they decided to throw down with us. But I'd been in worse situations.

"Trash," Vincent finished, smirking at the lords.

Fallon stood like a hard-ass beside them. Guy was a hell of an actor.

"Surprised you made it out alive. Heard your wedding reception was *a blast*," Ivanov said, giving me a shit-eating grin.

"Only because I blew it up at the end," I said in an even voice.

Drake scoffed.

"Heard poor Seeley caught a bullet. Is he dead? I don't see him here." Ivanov craned his neck around, pretending to look for him. "Ah, but looks like your whore made it out alive at least."

I shoved him hard in the chest, sending him back a few feet. His guys caught him. A second later, he stormed forward, going nose to nose with me.

"I don't have to finish you off. If your old man doesn't do it, the horsemen will. Heard you fucked with them too."

"I know what you did, you piece of shit," I snarled back. "Don't think you'll get away with it."

"I already have," he said back. "And once they kill you, I'll take my girl back. We'll all take turns on her. She'll wish she had died too."

I drew my arm back to punch him in the face, but Bianca grabbed my hand and tugged me back. I knew my wasp. She'd been counting numbers. Technically it would be three on two, but fucking Vasiliev had decked me last time, so really, he was a live wire.

"Aw, how cute. Your slut calls the shots." Ivanov smirked and backed away, his guys laughing at his side. All but Vasiliev, who was eyeing me with narrowed eyes. "Enjoy it, Bianca. When you're mine again, the only thing that pretty mouth of yours will be doing is sucking my cock."

He turned with his crew and began walking away.

"Hey, Ivanov," I called out, barely raising my voice.

He and his crew stopped to scowl at me.

"I'm giving you the chance to walk away and never look back. *To come clean.* I'm giving you a chance *to live*. This is that moment. Take it because I won't stop until I rule everything. Trust me when I say you don't want it to be you."

He glared before spinning and storming away, his guys flanking him.

It wasn't him I wanted to kill. I mean, yes, he was on my list. But Tate was the one I really wanted to end. The way he was staring past me at Bianca made my guts clench. Everyone knew how fucked up and twisted he was. And the fact he had his eyes on my wife only pissed me off more.

I'd kill him first. Then Ivanov.

FIFTY-TWO
VINCENT

Natalia was proving to be a very good nurse.

She called us multiple times a day when she first started staying with Levin. Then Levin started calling once he was up and moving about.

Nearly two weeks into his recovery, he was on the phone bitching to Dom while I kissed on Bianca in their room. I'd had to head off Celeste so many damn times that I'd switched up my walking route just to avoid her. I'd told her Levin was hurt and recovering, which had set the bitch off. All she wanted to do was visit him. Eventually, I told her to call his ass. If he answered, he could deal with her.

He still hadn't spoken to B. He'd asked me about her the first time we spoke, but after that, it was radio silence. B hadn't said anything about calling him. I suspected she was nervous, so I didn't push the subject with her.

I wasn't sure if them keeping their distance from one another was a good thing or not. I did know Levin was still talking to Celeste.

"He is?" Dom asked into the phone, his voice colored with surprise. "Really?"

I pushed B onto her back and slid my hand beneath her skirt.

"Vinny," she murmured, her fingers raking through my hair.

I hadn't fucked her since the night of the reception. Even Fallon had been left out in the cold with pussy. Dom insisted on hogging her, and it was starting to piss me off. He was becoming more obsessed with her getting pregnant, which was leaving the rest of us out in the damn cold. I didn't know how Fallon did it. His right hand had to have hella muscles at this point.

"Yes. Set it up.... I'll be there tonight." Dom hung up the phone. "Vin, enough," he barked at me.

I let out an exasperated groan and pulled away from B, who pouted.

"Man, for a guy who promised to share, you're sure a fucking cockblock. I haven't been laid in almost two weeks. If you aren't going let me fuck B, then you'd better put out for me."

Dom ignored me and grabbed his glasses. He slid them on and stared down at his phone for a minute before finally answering, his brow raised as he looked at me, "You couldn't handle me, Vin."

"What?" I sat up straighter and looked from B, whose eyes widened, back to Dom, who was scrolling through his phone, his dark brows knit.

"Isn't that what you wanted to hear?" He peeked over at me. "Or no?"

"I'll try anything once," I muttered, thinking back to me and Levin with B.

I noticed how B perked up. She wanted to see it, and I'd give her whatever she wanted. It was all about her anyway. I had no real interest in men, other than doing whatever she asked for. Maybe that counted though. I didn't give a fuck either way. I just liked making her feel good, which in turn made me feel good. I didn't care who was stroking my cock if it meant she was smiling. I wasn't so uptight about my sexuality that I wouldn't experiment. It all felt good to me.

Dom smirked at me before turning to face B. "I'm going to pick up Levin."

She sat up. "I-is he OK?"

"He's fine. He's ready to get back to work. He wanted to last week, but I wouldn't let him." Dom glanced to me. "Vander Veer is delivering. Tonight. We're going to meet with him to get the supply."

"You trust him?" B asked.

"Yes. He hates the Ivanovs, and he hates my old man more. Anything to fuck both is right up his alley. Plus, I have cash and an intent to fuck up their lives. He doesn't need much more motivation than that," Dom said.

"It's true," I assured B. "He was entertaining the deal with Ivanov because I suspect he just wanted to fuck them over somehow."

"What makes you think he won't fuck you guys over?" B demanded. "I'm sure he isn't going to come out and tell you he hates you."

"That's why I'm taking Celeste with me. I'll kill her if he tries to fuck with me."

B's eyes widened more. "You're taking her to see Levin."

"B," I warned.

"We're in a bit of a shit spot, wife." Dom put his phone away and adjusted his glasses. "I have a few loyal men. My father has the rest. I'm recruiting. I'm going to be fighting from every fucking side. I need whatever I can get, and that means doing things I wish I didn't have to do. If Levin needs to fuck his girlfriend to do it, I'll hold his dick for him so he can. This is war, and it isn't always fought the way you think it is. Sometimes we have to get dirty and do shit we don't want to do. You saw it firsthand when I had Natalia on her knees."

B glared at him but didn't bite back.

"When are we leaving?" I asked.

"You're not. I'm going to grab Celeste then meet up with Levin. Natalia has the Hummer, so she's taking Levin to the drop-off, and I'm picking him up then she's returning to the safe house. I need you and Vasiliev here with Bianca to make sure she's safe."

"So you're going with just Levin?" Bianca's voice held a note of alarm. "That's not nearly enough backup if you're ambushed and he's luring you out."

"I love the way you think." Dom stomped forward and leaned over B, pressing his lips to hers. "That's why you're my queen."

"Don't go," she whispered, twisting her fingers into his black button-down. "I don't want something to happen to you or Levin."

"I'll be fine. I'll bring a few of the court if it'll make you feel better."

She breathed out. "Promise?"

"Yes." He bit her bottom lip, making her whimper, before he sucked it into his mouth, hauling her closer.

She melted against him as he kissed her deeply before letting her go.

"I need to go," he murmured. "I have a lot to do." He backed away from her. "*Ti amo.*"

"I love you too," she said, releasing his hand.

He grabbed his leather jacket, having already changed out of his uniform, and stuffed a gun into his waistband.

"Keep her safe," he said to me as he strode to the door.

I followed him as he pulled it open and stepped through.

"You know what to do if shit goes south. Take her and run."

"I know," I said.

"Take her mind off things. I'm sure you and Vasiliev can come up with a few ideas if he can make it over," he continued softly.

"You want me to fuck your wife with Vasiliev?" I teased, eager to do his bidding.

"You know I do, Vin. I owe Vasiliev anyway. Let him fuck her. But remember the rules," he said, his voice so soft I had to lean in to hear him.

I studied his face, noting the discontent.

"She'll be here waiting for your big dick when you get back," I said, hoping to soothe him.

Deep down, I suspected he worried she loved Vasiliev more than him. Hell, even I considered it. She'd been willing to run away with him.

Dom reached out and cradled my face, pressing his forehead to mine. "Protect her, Vin. She's everything to me."

"Me too," I rasped, moving my hands atop his.

He breathed out, his breath feathering across my lips. "Promise me."

"Swear it."

He released me and left without another word. I watched him go, my heart hammering hard. I fucking hoped B's worries were nothing. As much as Dom pissed me off with his possessiveness over her, I didn't want to lose him. Or Levin. They were my brothers. My family. My best friends.

I tugged my phone out and closed Dom's door before turning to B.

"Want to take your mind off things?" I called out.

She nodded.

It was all the answer I needed.

"Pull your skirt up and spread your legs, baby. We're going to have a good time."

FIFTY-THREE
FALLON

"We lost the weapons deal with Vander Veer." Hail yanked his blond hair and let out a string of obscenities in Russian as I sat in the overstuffed leather chair in his room.

"That fucking bitch daughter of his," Hail continued. He glared at Drake. "I told you not to fuck that up. You saw Seeley move in. You didn't even fucking try."

"I did try. I tried to get her to fuck me at the bonfire, but she's all moon-eyed over Seeley," Drake snapped back, scowling at Hail. "She said she loves him. You know damn well he wormed his way beneath her skirt and settled there like a fucking disease."

"Which is why I told you to keep seeing her," Hail snapped back.

Drake grumbled and looked away.

"So what do we need to do now?" Tate asked. "It's De Santis who got the deal. You know he did."

"He's on the outs with his father. It's all over the street. Matteo hasn't issued a hit on him or Bianca, but I figure he's just seeing how shit plays out before he makes a move. If we're lucky, he'll take De Santis out before he becomes a bigger issue."

"Or the horsemen will," Tate said.

"Word on the street is the horsemen are out for blood," Trent added.

I glanced at him. Hail had started bringing him deeper into the fold lately. Trent was somewhere between Tate and Drake in personality. He was fairer but also a fucked up monster. He'd earned his place in the lords, that was for sure. Even though the shooting on the horsemen had been completely botched, Trent had still managed to pull it out of his ass and pin it on the kings. It was a good plan. An impressive one. Hail liked it. It had won him over completely, and now, Trent was one of us.

"They're going to strike soon. De Santis and his crew are as good as dead. I think we should probably figure out how to get Bianca away from him before it happens. Making him suffer her loss before he goes out would be fucking sweet," Tate continued. "We should film us fucking her and send it to him."

"Or we don't put that shit on video," I snarled at him. "You fucking idiot."

Drake snorted and shook his head at Tate. "You really are fucking stupid sometimes. I don't want to be on video raping some girl. In fact, I'm going to keep my dick away from her. You guys can have her."

"She's beautiful," Trent said, nodding.

I glared at him.

"Fallon gets her pussy first. It was decided already since he went through shit with the kings. When he's done, I'll pound her. She's already soiled, so I don't care if I'm first anymore. After that, I don't care what you guys do with the scraps," Hail said.

I inhaled deeply to calm myself. Drake pushed a baggie of powdered sugar at my chest.

"For you," he said as I took it.

"Why? Shit fucked me up last time," I muttered.

"Because snorting it should be fine," Drake said, doling some out from a bag into five lines. "My intel tells me the resident sugar daddy was having issues perfecting his injectables. Everything else is good." I watched as he tossed a bag to everyone else.

"I don't want to snort their product," Hail grumbled.

"You know it's good, man. Might want to consider getting the horsemen on our side. They might back down and run for us or something. Maybe De Luca won't like the dirtier side of things," Tate said, leaning down to snort his line.

"Or we take *his* girl and make him our bitch." Trent inhaled his line and wiped his nose. "He has a really fucking beautiful redhead. *Rosalie Bishop* is her name. Ass that doesn't quit. A set of tits on her you could fuck all night. Tight body. And she's quite a songbird." He opened the lock screen on his phone and pulled up a photo of a gorgeous redhead in a short, lavender dress to show us.

Yeah. De Luca had a beauty. She should probably run far away, or she'd end up like my princess.

"This guy," Trent continued, flipping through his phone and showing us another photo of a built guy, "is Fox Evans. He's the star quarterback for Mayfair. Full ride scholarship. They're already talking NFL." He flipped through his phone again and showed us another photo. "This is Cole Scott. De Luca's righthand man. He's fucking insane. Loses his shit and pretty much kills anything that gets too close to any of them, the redhead especially. It's not confirmed, but my intel says they all fuck her like some big, happy family."

I stared at the blond man in the picture. At first glance, the guy looked like an All-American, pretty boy, right down to his sparkling smile and blue eyes. But that was where it ended because when I looked into his eyes, like really looked, I could see the darkness floating in them. He was cracked for sure.

Trent scrolled again and produced a photo of another well-built guy with dark hair. He appeared more withdrawn than the other guys. He seemed haunted by more than past demons. It was like he was a ghost himself. I frowned as I took in his appearance. A good-looking guy, but damn, again with the eyes. Definitely haunted.

"Ethan Masters. This, gentlemen, is your sugar daddy. He's the guy who makes the product. He's the brains behind it. And again, rumor has it he's fucking the redhead too."

I exhaled as Trent pulled up a final photo. A handsome, young, Italian man. Dark hair. Dark eyes. He reminded me of Vincent.

"Lorenzo De Luca. Heir to the De Luca family. Largely connected. Deep ties in our world. His father runs a lot of shit in New York City, Detroit, Miami. Even Vegas. His reach is far and has extended into our territory. If Lorenzo keeps running the business the way he is, he could essentially take over our city within a few years. The good news is, Lorenzo doesn't really seem like he's too interested in taking over for his father. More like he goes through the motions because, with as well as he's doing, he could probably extend his reach and the city would fall under his control in less than a year. He's not pushing as hard as he could. Which confirms to me his heart isn't in it. He could be won over easily… I think." Trent darkened his phone and turned to Hail.

Hail nodded thoughtfully. "Well, I think we pissed him off enough. He's out for blood with the kings after we shot at his girl and his crew. Do we have a confirmed kill on any of them?"

Drake shook his head. "No. If one of them is dead, they're keeping it quiet."

Hail nodded again before leaning over the sugar and snorting his line. Sighing, I sat forward and snorted mine, not wanting to catch shit.

Please don't let me see fucking leopards and goats again.

My phone buzzed as Hail grabbed shot glasses and poured us all shots. I slammed mine back quickly and looked down at the text from Vincent.

V: You hungry?

I frowned down at the message and shot one back to him.

Me: I guess?

I let out a soft breath as the high took hold. *Fuck, that shit was good.*

V: Come eat.

A close-up photo of Bianca's pussy greeted me. I stared down at it in wonder. They were letting me be with her. The last two weeks had been torture. I may be a hybrid-king, but I still hadn't been able to touch my girl the way I wanted to. In fact, De Santis had made sure I'd kept my distance after we'd returned to Bolten. I knew his reasoning though. He didn't want any heat on me. He needed me with the lords.

"Who's texting you?" Tate asked.

I looked at him, my head a delicious mess. "Some chick. Says she wants to fuck."

"Which chick?" Drake asked, snorting another line before lying back on Hail's bed and letting out a breath.

"I don't want to say," I said. "I kind of like her. So I don't want to jinx it."

"She wants you to go fuck her?" Hail raised his brows at me. "And you're here, snorting sugar instead of getting your dick sucked? What the actual fuck is the matter with you, Vasiliev?"

"I'm just hanging with my boys," I said, my head taking a spin. *Fuck, the waves were intense.*

"You don't fuck enough. Go," Hail said, gaping at me like I was crazy.

"We haven't discussed what the plan is for Bianca," I said, sliding forward in my seat, eager to get to her.

"The plan is, we'll grab her when we get a chance. Hopefully, the horsemen will kill the kings, and she'll be free for the taking. That's it. For now, go get fucking laid." Hail poured another drink. "We're just going to celebrate the upcoming end of the kings tonight. That's it. You won't miss anything."

I jumped up. Fine by me.

"Thatta boy," Drake called out as Hail grinned.

Tate shot me a nasty look. He always was a jealous, little prick. He'd lose his mind completely if he knew who I was really going to see. That alone put a little extra skip in my step as I left the room, their loud laughter behind me.

FIFTY-FOUR
BIANCA

Vincent took a picture of me naked and sent it off to Dominic, I assumed.

"He'll enjoy that," he said as he moved in to kiss me.

I fell into the kiss easily. I was ready to beg him to move his hand from my breast to my aching pussy. He must have known it too because he laughed softly against my lips.

"What's wrong, B?" he asked. "Do you want something from me?"

"Yes," I whined.

A knock on the door made him ease away from me. He shot me a smirk before he got to his feet. I immediately covered myself with my blanket as Vincent answered the door.

"About time," he said, opening the door wider.

Fallon came into the room looking windswept.

"Sorry," he mumbled, turning to find me. The moment his gaze landed on me, he swooped forward and dragged me from beneath the covers, holding me to him. "Mm, princess."

"Hey," I said, squeezing him back.

He tilted my chin up and kissed me. "I missed you," he murmured, pecking at my lips.

"You've been drinking," I said back, my nose wrinkling.

"I'm not going to lie. I drank a little, and I'm high as fuck right now."

"Man, what the fuck?" Vincent said, coming to sit beside me. "You're always high."

"I hang out with fucking lords. Of course, I'm always high," Fallon shot back. "If you don't get high, you get fucked with. I don't need any reason to be fucked with right now."

"Whatever. I was going to spark up too, so I shouldn't bitch." Vincent reached into his pocket and pulled out a joint.

Fallon tossed a baggie of white powder at him. "Try this instead."

Vincent took it and stared down at it, a frown on his face. "What is it? I don't snort coke, man. Not anymore. I got so fucked on it one time that I lost my car and woke up in a dumpster with twelve rats fucking on me. I swore that shit off for good."

Fallon let out a huff of laughter. "It's not coke. It's powdered sugar from the horsemen. Drake gets it for us. It's *really* good shit. The high comes in these intense waves. And you can't overdose on it."

"Tell that to the fucking leopard and protein pants you were wearing," Vincent muttered.

"I shot up with it, OK? Shit was a bad batch. I've already tried this tonight. It's good. The great thing about sugar is there aren't any cravings for it after the high wears off. Like I'm totally fine."

"Have you been... addicted before?" I asked, cocking my head as I pulled the blanket up over my body again.

"Nah. Not really. I did heroin a few times, which can be a real bitch, but I stay away from that shit now. Drake knows it's a hard limit for me."

"But you've done coke?" I pressed as I examined him.

"Yes," he answered. "I've done a lot of fucking drugs, princess. Acid, heroin, coke, addy, Molly, sugar, weed. Anything you can think of, I've tried. Except meth. I don't touch that shit."

"Yeah, it's methed up," Vincent said with a snort. "It fucks your life in the ass. Ruins your skin too." He patted his cheek and winked at me.

I rolled my eyes at his joke and glanced back at Fallon. "I don't like you doing so many drugs."

"I do it because it's expected of me. Once I'm out of the lords for good, I'll be free to do whatever I want. I prefer weed, honestly. Mellows me out. Although, this sugar is pretty damn good." He looked at the baggie Vincent was holding. "You should try it. Know your enemy and all that. See what you're dealing with. You'll be surprised."

"Sure it's not poison?" Vincent asked, tossing the baggie up and down in his hand.

"I'll do it with you," Fallon said evenly. "Then we'll die together."

"Me too," I said, my heart in my throat.

They both gaped at me with raised brows.

"You're not dying on me and leaving me here with your bodies. If you go, I go," I said, nerves racking through my body.

The only thing I'd ever tried before was weed with Dominic.

"Fine. But if Dom finds out, we're blaming the new guy." Vincent held his pinky up to me.

I took it and smirked at him as he winked.

Fallon snatched the bag from Vincent then divvied out three lines. He snorted the first one with a rolled-up bill. I watched, fascinated as he let out a breath and closed his eyes.

"Yep. That's the shit right there," he said.

Vincent leaned down to the small bedside table and inhaled his line with the bill Fallon gave him.

He blinked for a moment. "Jesus fuck," he murmured, looking around. "That's intense."

"Good though, right?" Fallon laughed. "Who knew the air had a color?"

"Blue, like baby B's eyes," Vincent said, smiling as he stared glassy eyed at the empty air in front of him.

"You don't have to try it," Fallon said, taking my hand.

"I'm going to." Maybe it would take my mind off my worries. I leaned over and snorted the line, hoping it didn't kill me.

"Oh God," I breathed out a moment later as I reached for Fallon's hand.

He held my fingers.

"I-I feel like I'm floating. Like my head is moving fast, but everything is so slow and so… nice." I giggled.

"The rush will come and go for a while. It has a nice half-life," Fallon said, pulling my naked body onto his lap. His lips met mine in a deep, warm kiss that made my toes curl.

"I have to tell you something before we do this," he said.

"What?" I pulled away and frowned at him.

"I got really fucked up when Drake injected me, and I thought some other girl was you. I almost fucked her before Stella stopped me. I-I got her off in front of everyone at Hail's party." He stared down at the floor, his Adam's apple bobbing. "I swear I'd never do that shit sober. It's why I came to Seeley's room that night. I needed to tell someone. I felt so guilty. I still feel awful about it. I love you, Bianca," his voice cracked. "I just needed you to know it happened."

I cupped his face. "It's OK. I love you too."

His lips crashed against mine as he shifted me so I was straddling his lap.

"Easy, new guy. I've been waiting for like two weeks to sink inside her. You're not going to hog her. We do her together," Vincent demanded.

Fallon broke our kiss off and nodded. "OK. But I want to take it nice and slow."

"Deal." Vincent eased me off Fallon's lap and pressed his mouth to mine as I straddled him.

I melted against him, twisting my fingers in his hair as a wave of the drug's euphoria took me on a ride.

"God, fucking on this shit is going to be amazing," Vincent growled against my lips while I fumbled with the button on his pants.

I giggled as Fallon reached down to help me with Vincent's zipper.

"Teamwork," he said as I laughed again.

His lips were at the base of my neck while Vincent's moved along my collarbone.

"Who's going to help you out of your pants?" I teased Fallon as we finally got Vincent's pants off.

Fallon didn't get a chance to answer because Vincent reached behind me and undid Fallon's pants for him.

"We're even," Vincent panted, going back to kissing me as Fallon kicked out of his pants and boxers. He tugged his shirt over his head and tossed it to the floor behind him as Vincent did the same.

Then all of us were naked and in bed.

"Does Dominic know we're fucking his wife in their bed?" Fallon asked as he cradled my breasts from behind.

"It was his idea. Although, I'm pretty sure I'd have done it anyway. Suffered the consequences with a smile on my face." Vincent shifted and sucked one of my nipples into his mouth.

I let out a soft moan, which Fallon captured with his mouth as he turned my head so I could kiss him.

Vincent's fingers drifted between my legs. I went up on my knees, so he could maneuver however how he needed to.

A finger slid through my folds until he was knuckle deep in my heat. I rode his hand with wild abandon.

"Fuck yeah," Vincent growled, sliding another finger inside and pressing his thumb to my clit.

"Can I play too?" Fallon asked, his lips trailing along my neck.

I nodded. Fallon moved his hand to my core.

"I'm not pulling out. You'll just have to make your finger fit too," Vincent said as he plunged his fingers in and out.

Fallon eased his finger in alongside Vincent's. There were three thick fingers inside my heat. I moaned softly at the fullness.

"Can you take another?" Fallon asked huskily in my ear as Vincent sat up and sucked against the flesh of my neck.

I nodded, not sure if I could but willing to try. Fallon slipped another finger into me. I groaned against the burning pain as they worked in tandem to bring me to release.

"Come on, baby B. Come on our fingers," Vincent urged as the wet sounds of their fingers fucking my pussy echoed around us.

Fallon pressed his thumb to my back entrance, sending a jolt of electricity through my body. He breached my hole slightly as I panted.

Heat boiled in my core until it rushed out of me, my orgasm dripping onto their fingers as I moaned my way through it.

"Fucking beautiful," Fallon praised as I trembled against his naked body, my back to his front.

Both of them withdrew their fingers, leaving me to feel empty.

"No," I whimpered, desperate to have them back.

"Greedy girl," Vincent teased, rolling me onto my back. "Have some pussy, F word. The way you ate her that one night while we watched had her arching off the bed."

Fallon smirked and shifted between my legs as another wave from the drug hauled me higher.

"Fallon," I mumbled, completely blissed out as his tongue slid through my folds. I tangled my fingers in his hair as he licked and sucked, pushing my pussy up to meet his eager mouth.

"You like the way he eats your pussy, baby B?" Vincent asked as he dragged the tip of his dick along my lips.

"Yes. So good. Fallon," I called out as I pushed his face deeper into my heat.

His tongue lashed against my sensitive bud while he buried two fingers in my pussy.

"Open for me," Vincent said.

I obliged, and he slid his cock into my mouth. I came in Fallon's mouth seconds later. Vincent's dick choked my cries as he hit the back of my throat.

"Fuck, B. God, baby. Suck me." Vincent twisted his fingers in my hair and fucked my mouth.

Fallon got to his knees and lined up his cock with my pussy. He shoved inside me as Vincent continued his onslaught on my mouth, his dick hitting the back of my throat with each crisp thrust.

"I've missed your pussy," Fallon warbled, moving in and out of me with slow, precise thrusts, his cock bare. "It's the best pussy. Fuck. You're choking my dick so good."

"Try her ass if you think her pussy is tight," Vincent said.

"Can I fuck your ass, princess?" Fallon asked softly, pausing his fucking to slip a finger past my tight ring.

"Yes. Please," I panted when Vincent pulled his dick from my mouth.

Fallon thrust into my pussy a few more times before pulling out completely. He flipped me onto my hands and knees. I crawled over to Vincent, who was lying on his back, and straddled him.

"Come to fuck me now?" he asked, a knowing smirk on his lips.

I nodded and reached beneath me to stroke his dick. He jerked, moaning against my lips as we kissed.

Fallon tugged my face away from Vincent so he could kiss me. I tasted myself on his lips as his tongue wrestled with mine. I stroked Vinny fast, making him moan as I broke away from Fallon's lips. Fallon dropped down behind me. Fallon's mouth met my heat from behind, working me over as I went back to kissing Vincent.

Moments later, I came with a muffled cry against Vincent's lips. He swallowed it all down.

"That was hot," Fallon murmured, giving my ass a slap "Now let me see him fuck you."

Eagerly, I shifted, and Fallon guided Vincent's cock into me. Vincent shoved up in one fluid motion, spearing me with it. I cried out, falling forward onto his chest as he fucked up into me hard and fast, his lips on mine. I felt Fallon move behind me. Vincent slowed to a stop. Fallon gathered our juices and pressed them to my ass before the head of his dick kissed my tight hole.

"You're going to ride both our cocks, princess," Fallon said, gliding slowly into me.

I dragged in a short breath as he gripped my hips. Vincent sucked my breasts while Fallon slowly sank into my ass until he was buried to the hilt, both my kings filling me completely.

Then they moved. Thrusting. Shifting. Rough. Gentle. Hard. More. More. More.

I came again, tightening around Vincent's cock. He let out a shout as his release rushed out of him. Fallon followed a moment later, filling my ass. I lay on Vincent's chest with both guys still buried inside me.

Fallon slapped my ass and let out a soft laugh before he finally pulled out, his orgasm dripping down my crack.

"I'd fuck you with his come, baby, but I think I need a few minutes," Vincent said, placing a gentle kiss on the top of my head.

Fallon eased off the bed and went into the bathroom where he ran water.

"Did you enjoy that?" Vincent asked.

I nodded against him. "Did you?"

"Most definitely."

Fallon came back and pulled me off Vincent so he could settle me over his still hard dick.

"Guess what?" He kissed the corner of my lips.

"Mm, what?"

"I'm going to fuck you again." And with that, he thrust into me once more.

Vincent let out a laugh and moved to get behind me. Fallon slowed down to allow Vincent to push into my ass.

"Can't let him out-fuck me," Vincent grumbled, filling me.

I smiled against Fallon's lips, overjoyed at the situation and letting my worries float away.

At least for tonight.

Tonight I could have this with two of my kings.

FIFTY-FIVE
LEVIN

"I missed you, Levy," Celeste shrieked out as she threw herself into my arms.

I let out a grunt when pain shot through my guts and gave her a half-assed, one-armed hug.

Dom raised his brows but didn't say anything.

I knew what he was thinking. *Bianca*. She'd told me she loved me when she'd thought I was dying. I'd wanted to shout it back at her. I hadn't. I regretted it now because I had someone pressing her lips to mine who wasn't my bumblebee.

Dom looked away and stared out the window of his car as I pushed Celeste away.

"Levy," she whined with a pout.

"I was shot, Celeste," I said. "I'm feeling like shit still, OK?"

It wasn't entirely the truth. I felt loads better days ago, but Dom had made me stay behind, citing he needed me at a hundred percent in case shit went down soon. My rest and comfort were his top priority.

Honestly, it was nice having a break. I'd gotten to know Natalia and had heard about her love for my brother. At least, he left this world knowing what being in love felt like. And at least, she knew he loved her before the devil had stolen him away.

I'd heard about her sucking Dom's cock in order to save Bianca. It boiled my blood to know Matteo was such a sick fuck.

I prayed for Matteo De Santis's death as much as I prayed for my father's, which was a fuck of a lot.

"I'm sorry. Maybe I can make you feel better." Celeste's hand slid to my zipper.

This deal wasn't over yet. Tonight it would be. Then I'd have some sense of freedom.

I caught Dom's gaze in the rearview mirror. I couldn't read him though. Maybe he was telling me to stop her trek toward my cock or maybe he was telling me to go for it. I was still in this shit, so I let her pull my dick out.

I was still unsure about Bianca. She certainly hadn't tried to reach out. That had to mean something.

Celeste's warm mouth slurped along my dick. I swallowed a groan. She was doing a better job this time than she had the last dozen times she'd tried to suck my cock.

Fuck it.

I pushed up into her throat, making her gag. Dom smirked at me in the rearview mirror, his eyes still locked on mine. His wedding ring glinted in the moonlight. *Lucky fucker.*

I thrust up again while forcing Celeste's head down on my cock. She choked and gagged as I suffocated her with my dick down her throat.

When she came off my dick for air, her face was red, and she was breathing hard.

"You done?" I asked innocently.

She couldn't suck dick the way I wanted. It didn't matter how hard she tried. She'd never be Bianca.

"You're so rough. I don't like it," she complained, moving away from me.

Dom shook his head.

"What's so funny, Dominic?" she asked, leaning forward. "I'll suck yours if you want me to."

"Really?" He turned to look at her over his shoulder. "You'd suck my dick for me? Right now?"

She nodded. "You can both fuck me if you want. I don't care that you're married."

"You hear that, Levin? She wants us to fuck her, and she doesn't care if I have a wife."

"I hear it." I knew there was a catch. And I knew Dominic De Santis. Bianca was his whole world.

"Here's the thing though," Dom continued. "I don't want your chewed-up pussy when I have a perfectly good one waiting for me in my bed right now."

Celeste let out an indignant noise as she sat back in her seat, her arms folded over her chest.

"Seeley, control your whore," he grunted, turning forward.

"I am *not* a whore, Dominic De Santis. I just heard the rumors you and Vincent share Bianca. I thought I'd offer myself up, then all three of you could share me."

I scoffed and stared out the window. My dick was soft and back in my pants already.

"I speak for all of us when I say we really aren't interested." Dom opened the door as Vander Veer rolled up.

Our men got out of their cars behind him.

"That was fucked up," I muttered at Celeste.

"I'm just trying to make you happy. You're never happy. I figured if I offered myself to your friends, you'd want me."

"You shouldn't offer yourself to my friends. Especially Dom. He loves Bianca. She's his wife. He'd sooner die than fuck you."

"You're mad."

"I'm pissed," I said, not bothering to elaborate.

I got out of the car and adjusted my leather jacket. I followed Dom to where Vander Veer waited. Andrew, one of our court, pushed Celeste's door closed and shook his head at her. She was only allowed out if we needed her. Past that, she could keep her ass in the car.

"Ah, my future son-in-law," Vander Veer greeted me with a wink, his men armed to the teeth by his side.

"How's it going?" I grunted, reaching out and shaking his hand.

"I'm well. Heard you all had a little incident at the De Santis estate."

"My wedding reception didn't go as planned," Dom said in an even voice. "Ivanov's crew crashed it."

"Among other things, I hear," Vander Veer said conversationally.

"Among other things," Dom agreed.

"Well, no offense to you, Dominic, but your old man is a prick."

"I couldn't agree more."

Vander Veer smirked. "And that's why I gave the contract to you. I feel confident you'll fix both of our problems." He gestured for us to follow him.

When we reached the back of one of the SUVs, his men opened it and showed us the weapons cache in the back.

Dom nodded. It was a lot of guns. I picked up a nine and surveyed it. Vander Veer made quality products. It was perfection.

"Those are my favorite," Vander Veer said. "I'm including some ammo to get you going. The rest of what you need is on the way to the site you indicated."

"The balance of the payment will be in your account as soon as I get the delivery," Dom said.

"Fantastic. Well, it was a pleasure doing business with you," he said, holding his hand out for Dom to shake.

Dom took it and shook before they broke away.

"One last thing." Vander Veer reached into his jacket and pulled out a grenade. "A parting gift. I'm sure you'll find a good use for it. They're new. Extended detonation time. I've included a case, no charge, with the delivery."

Dom gazed down at the grenade for a moment before he stuffed it into his jacket.

"Until next time?" Vander Veer winked as Dom nodded and then backed away.

It was over. And we hadn't had to kill someone for once.

It was a first.

FIFTY-SIX
BIANCA

Fallon and Vincent fucked me until I couldn't stand on my own before I was bathed and put to bed between them.

Around two in the morning, Vincent got a text from Dom saying he was staying at a hotel with Levin, and they'd return in the morning. Knowing they were both safe and the deal went off without a hitch allowed the worry to ease from my body.

Fallon roused me just before sunrise to kiss me goodbye and promised to see me soon. I knew he had to go. It just really sucked. I didn't want to be separated from any of my guys.

I slid out of bed and went to the bathroom, where I got ready for the day, knowing Dominic would be there any minute since he was an early riser. I was just pulling my hair into a ponytail when Vincent wrapped his arms around me from behind and kissed along my neck.

"I missed you," he murmured, hugging me to his bare chest.

"Mm, you just saw me," I said with a smile.

"Did I?"

I spun in his arms and planted my lips on his. He fell into the kiss immediately, his tongue dancing against mine.

"You have a hickey on your neck, baby," he said, breaking away. "Dom might get upset about that."

"I don't care," I said just as I heard the doorknob in the dorm rattle.

Vincent rushed away from me and out to the main room. I heard Dominic's deep voice a moment later.

I quickly dressed in my uniform and came into the room expecting to see Levin, but he wasn't there.

"Where's Levin?" I asked, frowning.

"Probably in his room. He needed to drop Celeste off at her room. He said he was going to take a nap after that," Dominic said, his gaze raking over me. He shoved past Vincent and ran his fingers through my hair, angling my head back. "Why is she marked?"

"Dominic." I pushed away from him. "Stop. Why is Levin with her?"

"She stayed with him last night."

"What?" My throat tightened.

"It's probably nothing," Vincent broke in, shooting a look at Dominic, who was still frowning at the hickey on my neck. "Dom took her with them last night in case the deal went bad. She was basically a hostage."

Dom snorted. "She wasn't much of a hostage unless she gets off on shit like that. She offered to fuck me and Levin together after she sucked his dick in the backseat."

"What?" I snarled.

It wasn't just the fact Levin was still with her that got me. It was her thinking she could try to move in on Dominic, my husband. She'd already taken one of my guys. I wasn't going to let her take another.

"Does that upset you, wasp?" Dominic asked, giving the hickey on my neck a sour look.

I said nothing, simply striding past him and sliding my feet into my shoes.

"Baby B, where are you going?" Vincent called out as I opened the door and stepped into the hall. "B!"

I slammed the door shut and marched down the hall, going straight to Levin's room. I banged on the door until he cracked it open, his hair a mess.

"Bianca?" he mumbled, not opening the door further.

I kicked the door. It bounced off his chest, making him stumble back. It was enough space for me to slide through, so I took the opportunity and entered his room to find Celeste glaring at me from his bed as she sat on the edge.

"What the fuck is this?" I demanded, glaring back at her.

"*Excuse* me. Who the hell do you think you are barging into Levy's room?"

I reached out and fisted her hair, dragging her off Levin's bed. There was some commotion behind me. I peeked over my shoulder and caught Vincent and Dominic entering. Too fucking late. I was a woman on a mission.

Celeste fell to her knees on the floor, my fingers tangled in her hair. I yanked hard, making her cry out.

"Don't you ever proposition my *husband* again, you bitch," I snarled, giving her head a tug.

"Levy," she whimpered, clinging to my hands.

I jerked again. "He is *not* the one for you. Dominic De Santis is *mine*. Vincent Valentino is mine. Fucking Levin Seeley *is mine*. And you're fucking dead for touching what's mine." I released her hair.

But before she could get to her feet, I decked her in the face, sending her sprawling on the floor. She let out a cry and swiped at my feet, clawing at my legs as she screamed like a child.

She was fast though. One second she was on her back, and the next she was on her feet, shoving me. I stumbled back before I lost it. I launched myself at her, knocking her down again, pummeling any part of her my fists could get. She squealed and yanked my hair, a move that only pissed me off more. I hit her in the face, banging her head against the floor.

I saw red, and only red, as I swung on her.

Warm hands hauled me away. I fought against whoever held me, struggling to get to the crying bitch on the floor.

"Easy, B," Vincent soothed, tightening his hold on me. He brought my back flush to his front and kissed my cheek. "Easy."

My chest heaved in and out as I glared at Levin, who was dragging Celeste to her feet.

"Get her out of here," I snarled. "I swear to God, Levin. Get her the fuck out of here before I kill her."

Levin's blue eyes locked on mine. I thought he'd tell me to go to hell.

Instead, he stared at Celeste. "You need to leave. Go back to your room."

"You're taking her side?" Celeste wept. "After she attacked me, Levy?"

"Don't make me repeat myself," Levin said in a soft voice that sounded uncharacteristic for him. "Go. We'll talk later. I need to deal with this."

She shot me a glare and wiped at the blood dribbling from her nose before storming out, leaving me and three kings behind.

"That was hot as fuck, B," Vincent murmured in my ear, his cock hard against me. "God damn, girl. She didn't even leave a mark on you."

"Vin, let's give them some time," Dominic called out, backing away.

Vincent released me and went to the door with Dominic.

Dominic glanced at Levin, who was staring intently at me, his brows crinkled.

"Levin, call me if you need me," Dominic said, pulling open the door and stepping out.

"B, don't kill him," Vincent added before closing the door and leaving me alone with Levin.

We stared one another down for a long, silent moment before he spoke.

"Glad to see you're feeling better."

"Fuck you, Levin," I snapped.

"Fuck *me*?" He let out a soft laugh. "That's rich coming from someone who had *two* dicks inside her last night." He pointed to the hickey on my neck. "Nice, by the way. Vasiliev give that to you or Vin?"

"I don't recall since both their mouths were on me," I shot back.

He shook his head and went to his fridge to get a bottle of apple juice. I watched as he slowly drank it down, his stare locked on mine.

"Don't you just love apple juice?" he asked, licking his lips. "I'd offer you some, but it seems I'm out."

I ground my teeth at him. Apple juice was my favorite. "What's your problem?"

"I don't know what you're referring to. I was in my room minding my own business when you burst in here and started beating on people. So maybe you should tell me what *your* problem is." He raised his brows at me.

"You goddamn know what my problem is, Levin."

"Do I?" He shrugged. "Afraid I don't."

"You were almost dead two weeks ago. You took a bullet for me! I stayed by your side while we were at the safe house. Then I hear you're getting blow jobs in the backseat of Dominic's car, and *your girlfriend* is trying to get *my* husband to fuck her with you?"

He scoffed. "Dom didn't even entertain the idea for a moment, Bianca. He shut her down right away. No worries. Your husband is true to you."

"He's not the one I'm worried about."

Levin slid his empty juice bottle onto the counter and leveled his gaze on me. "Then who are you worried about? Last I heard, you hated my fucking guts, and I wasn't in the running to be your little bitch. Is that still true? You definitely didn't reach out to me once you came back to Bolten."

I swallowed and stared at him as he approached slowly, like a predator stalking prey. He stopped when his body was nearly touching mine.

He tilted my chin up to look at him. "I asked you a question. *Is that still true?*"

"They aren't my bitches," I answered softly. "They're who I love and who love me back."

"Am I one of them?" he murmured. "Do you love me, Bianca?"

His knuckles brushed along my jaw as he continued to stare down at me. "When I was drugged up on painkillers, I felt like I was in a dream, and you were beside me. I heard you whisper to me that you loved me. Was it just a dream?"

"No," I choked out.

"No what?"

"It wasn't just a dream."

A tear slid down my cheek, which he brushed away.

"Just say what you need to say to me."

"I'm sorry," I whispered, finally cracking. "For alienating you in my anger. I was wrong. I was furious. I was… so stupid. I regretted that shit the moment I said it. I wanted to take it back so many times. But then you got together with Celeste. I was so hurt. It made it so much worse. Then you saved me. I loved you and wanted you. I-I was just too scared to do anything about it."

"Why were you scared?" he asked in a gentle voice.

"I didn't want you to tell me you hated me," I said thickly. "I didn't want to hear that you loved someone else. I didn't want to let go if you did."

"But I don't love someone else."

"You don't?"

He shook his head. "I love *you*, bumblebee."

"You do?" I peeked up at him with wide eyes, my heart skipping.

His gaze darted to my lips. "Yeah. So much so I'd die for you. Or didn't you get that memo?"

I let out a blubbering laugh as he wiped the tears off my cheeks again.

"Make your move, bumblebee," he murmured. "I can't make it for you."

Screw it. I was going to take what was mine.

I crashed my lips against his, melting into his hold as his arms wound around me tightly. His lips parted, and his tongue slid along mine in a rough, fierce kiss. He lifted me into his arms, and I wrapped my legs around his waist as he pressed me against the wall, all lips and muscles and hands.

His kiss was demanding and brutal, just like I remembered. His palms held my ass as he ground his thick erection against my core. I moaned in his mouth as he hit a spot that made my eyes roll back.

His hands tightened on my ass until I hissed against his lips.

"You don't know what you fucking did to me," he growled, nipping at my bottom lip until I cried out. "I was in hell without you."

"I-I'm sorry." I wiggled in his hold until he lowered my legs, while still keeping a grip on my body. I undid his zipper and pushed his pants and boxers down.

He shimmied out of them quickly without moving away from me too much.

"How are you going to make it up to me?" He pressed, moving one of his hands off my ass and cradling my face. Slowly, he shifted his hand lower until he was at my throat. He rubbed a gentle circle on the sensitive flesh as I stared up at him.

"Anything. Anything you want," I said on a soft exhale.

"Be careful making a deal with the devil, bumblebee. I intend on collecting." He shuffled me off the wall so he could lay me in his bed, losing our shirts along the way.

He braced himself over me as my pulse roared in my ears.

"Are you OK?" I asked, noting the red, healing wound on his abdomen. I gently traced the area, now free of stitches, but still angry looking.

"Yes, I'm fine," he answered, cradling my breasts and burying his face in my neck. "I can handle you."

His declaration was good enough for me. I reached out and raked my fingers through his hair. He hauled my panties off and then my skirt, leaving everything in a pile on the floor. His mouth hardly left mine as he continued to kiss me, his hands roaming all over my body.

I let out a breath as he moved slowly down my neck, leaving a trail of hot kisses on my flesh. When he reached my breasts, he paid careful attention to each one, licking, sucking, and nibbling.

"Who left this mark?" he asked, nipping against the small hickey on my neck,

"I-I think Vinny," I managed to say.

His lips moved back to my breasts. He sucked hard against one, making me wince as he left his own mark on me.

With a heated gaze, he continued south, leaving more kisses behind. When he reached the apex of my thighs he breathed out.

"Spread your legs," he commanded softly.

I did so without protest. He swept his tongue up my heat, making me moan. He flicked his tongue against my clit before sucking it. A torrent of electricity and goosebumps raced across my skin as he tormented my aching center with his mouth. Nibbling. Licking. Flicking.

I writhed against his face as he brought me to a new high before pushing me over the edge. I tumbled freely, his name on my lips as he ate me to completion. When he was done, he crawled back up my body, his thick erection teasing my entrance.

"I love you," I whispered as he stared down at me.

He twined his fingers through mine and pushed them over my head, holding them there.

"I know, bumblebee. I know."

And then he pushed inside me, filling me completely, his low groan filling the room.

"Oh God," I choked out, wincing as he thrust into me again, his hips shifting in the most delicious way.

He hit the perfect spot inside me with each snap of his hips, making my toes curl and my back arch. I had no idea his hips could move like that. Fucking Levin Seeley was like doing an intimate dance where he took the lead. Each thrust made me cry out. Each breath he feathered over my face made me bow up against his body, desperate for him to inhale me and keep me inside him.

Levin Seeley knew how to fuck.

I was ready to come within seconds as he pounded into me at an even pace. Each time he thrust into me, each time he pressed his body against mine, each time he tightened his hold on my hands, made me want to scream his name until the devil heard me and crowned him king of the fucking world.

His gaze was on mine the whole time, his lips parted. He finally released my hands, resting more of his weight on me as he continued his assault on my pussy. I dug my nails into his back as his lips met mine. I pushed my hips up to meet his thrusts.

"Fuck," he groaned against my lips. "Just like that, baby. *Fuck.*"

His words sent me over the edge, and I came with a cry. He swallowed down my moans as he kissed me deeply, my body trembling beneath his. His rhythm picked up. The sounds of all the dirty things he was doing to my body were loud in the room.

He broke off our kiss as his breathing increased. I raked my fingers through his hair. He shuddered against my touch, goosebumps popping up along his flesh as his lips parted.

"Tell me you're sorry again," he rasped, slamming into me amidst my cries.

"I'm sorry, Levin. I'm so sorry," I moaned, clinging to him as he rocked in and out of my body.

He slammed deep again, nearly lifting me from the bed as he speared me hard and fast.

"Tell me you love me. Tell me I'm yours."

"I love you. I love you so much. You're mine, Levin. All mine. No one else's."

A low, sexy groan left his lips as he came hard inside me, his release filling me. He rocked in and out of me through it until his movements slowed and he pressed his forehead against mine.

"You're never going to get rid of me," he murmured. "You're mine now too, bumblebee."

"Promise?" I whispered, running my fingers through his blond hair.

"Swear it." He pulled away and stared down at me. "Be my girl?"

"Yes," I said, my heart dancing with joy. "I'm yours. You'll need to break up with your girlfriend first though."

He smirked at me. "What do you think I was doing when you burst into my room and started pulling hair?"

"You broke up with her?"

"No. I was in the middle of it until I was interrupted."

"Sorry," I muttered sheepishly.

He chuckled. "Don't be. I enjoyed it."

"Guess I'm a little crazy too."

He kissed me gently. "I like crazy. I love it. You're right where you belong." He grinned down at me.

The mask he'd been wearing for weeks was gone, giving way to who he really was—a sweet giant who gave a shit. There was no wall up. It was just Levin, a guy who loved a girl.

"We're OK now?" I asked, licking my lips nervously.

"Well, my dick is still hard inside you, and you haven't threatened to kill me in the last hour. I'd say we're the best we've ever been, baby."

I grinned. "Then we shouldn't waste it."

"I agree," he said, pressing his lips to mine before rolling me quickly so I was on top of him. "Show me more of what I've been missing."

So I did.

FIFTY-SEVEN
BIANCA

"My birthday is this weekend," Aubrey said as we strolled through campus together a week later.

Levin, Vincent, and Dominic trailed behind us somewhere.

We hadn't heard a word about Matteo wanting to kill either of us, but Vincent said it didn't mean he wasn't still considering it. According to Vincent's dad, Matteo was doing what Dominic had said, waiting, watching. Probably anticipating that the horsemen were going to kill us since they were still a very real threat.

Fallon reported the lords had been doing the same as Matteo, hoping and waiting. The ball was in the horsemen's court it seemed.

"Is it?" I asked. "We should celebrate!"

"I was thinking we could hit up Beats. It's this new club that opened. It could be a lot of fun." Aubrey stopped and looked at me. "Do you think they'd let you go with me?"

I knew she was talking about the kings. I was pretty sure she knew my situation with the three of them and Fallon without me saying a word. She'd caught Levin kissing me in the library two days ago, and Vincent didn't bother to hide his affection when she was with me. And she'd been the one who helped me see Fallon earlier in my relationship with him.

"Let her go where?" Dominic and his damn bionic hearing.

"It's Aubrey's birthday this weekend," I explained. "She wants to go to Beats and celebrate." I waited for him to say no.

He looked from me to Aubrey, who shrank away from his gaze.

"Beats?" Vincent stopped beside us. "I'm in."

"We really shouldn't leave campus," Levin said, joining us. "All things considering."

"Don't be such a stick in the mud, Seeley. We're kings. We don't cower and hide." Vincent looked at me and winked. "Right, B?"

I smirked. "I'd like to go, but it's Dominic's decision. Levin is right. It could be risky."

Dominic's gaze swept over me quickly. "I'll bring some of the court with us. We won't stay too long. Then we can come back to my room and party more."

"Really?" I asked, surprised he'd agreed.

"Yes. Vincent is right. We'll look like pussies if we just stay on campus. We'll have our guys with us. We should be fine for a few hours." Dominic took my hand and pulled me to him, placing a kiss on my wedding ring. "Are you agreeable to my terms, wasp?"

"Yes," I answered, biting my bottom lip as I peered back at him.

"Good." He hauled me closer and draped his arm around my waist.

Celeste seemed to pop out of nowhere.

"Levin." She stood behind us.

If I had to guess, she'd heard everything we'd been talking about. Levin had said their breakup hadn't gone well. She'd threatened to kill herself if he left, and he'd left her his knife to do it with.

Sounded like a total Levin thing to do. But even I could feel for her. Levin was a hell of a catch.

He groaned and closed his eyes before he turned to look at her. "Celeste, I told you to stop. We're done."

"I just want to talk," she said, taking a step closer. "I miss you, Levy. I-I'm sorry for whatever I did."

"You need to go. I'm not going to tell you again." Levin shot me a quick look.

I knew he cared about what I thought and felt, but I didn't want him to think I'd be mad over this. Sure, she was annoying, but this needed to be handled.

"You text and call me all hours of the night. I said we were over. I meant it. Understand that, Celeste," Levin continued.

"You said you met someone else," she whispered. "I want to know who. I think you're lying to me because you need time to think. All you have to do is be honest, Levy. I'll understand. I swear I will." She closed the space between them and rested her hands on his chest.

I started to step forward and tear her hands off him, but Dominic tightened his hold on me.

"Let this happen," he whispered in my ear.

I swallowed down my anger and waited for Levin's move.

"I did meet someone else. Now stop your shit, Celeste."

"I don't believe you," she said, her bottom lip trembling. Celeste looked like a disaster. Usually she was so put together. Today, her hair was a wild mess, and her mascara was smudged like she'd been crying before she accosted him.

"You're choosing them over us, Levy. I-I can let it go. I won't make you choose. I understand they're your friends. I think given some time though, you could find new friends. Ones who aren't so dangerous—"

"What do I have to do to prove to you we're over?" he snapped at her. "I'm sick of the late night phone calls and texts. I'm tired of you cornering me every chance you get. This is my crew. There was never a fucking choice, Celeste."

"But Levy... Just... please. I only want to know the truth. You keep telling me you met someone else, but if you did, she isn't here. That's why I think it's a lie—"

"You want fucking proof, Celeste? Is that what you need to get your shit sorted?" He stomped over to me and hauled me out of Dominic's hold.

Then Levin pressed his mouth to mine right in the center of the courtyard. The place was packed with students. When Dominic didn't punch him in the face and tear me away, I fell into the kiss, tangling my fingers in his hair as his tongue danced with mine while his hands gripped my ass.

When he broke away, I was breathless.

"Sorry, bumblebee," he murmured, thumbing my bottom lip. He spun away from me and glared at Celeste, who was staring at us with her mouth hanging open and tears in her eyes.

"You were right. I did have some weird crush on her. Apparently, she loves me too. So I'm here for it. And you need to not be." Levin twined his fingers through mine. "We're over, Celeste."

I knew we had an audience. I could see people gawking from the corner of my eye. Yet Dominic didn't intervene. He simply stood silently behind us.

"We are *not* over, Levy. I'll make sure you're back with me in no time," she snarled dangerously, her entire demeanor changing. "And I'll make sure she's dead."

This time Dominic did snap into action. He moved swiftly and was in her face in moments.

"Fucking try it," he growled. "If so much as a frown touches my wife's lips because of something you did, you'll regret your fucking existence." He reached out and gripped her face tightly. She peered up at him, fear evident in her eyes.

"I'll make sure your death is long and painful. Now go fuck off somewhere." Dominic released her.

She stumbled back. The hatred in her eyes sent a chill through me. Dominic stepped away from her and leaned in, kissing me while not pulling me from Levin.

"I love you, *mia regina*," he said against my lips before backing off.

"Well, shit. I love you too," Vincent said, sweeping me from Levin and dipping me before planting his lips on mine.

I kissed him back and let out a soft giggle when he righted me, a twinkle in his dark eyes.

"I didn't like feeling left out," he said when I shook my head at him.

"Guess the cat's out of the bag now," Levin said, glancing around at everyone gawking at us.

"It was going to happen eventually." Vincent pushed me into Dominic's arms, who immediately held me close.

"Yeah, I suppose," Dominic said with a sigh.

I followed his gaze to the lords, who were glaring daggers in our direction. Fallon offered us a quick smile before he schooled his face and put on a show with the rest of the lords.

"Come on. I'm hungry. All that animosity worked up my appetite." Vincent sauntered away from us, and Levin laughed.

"Fucking guy," Levin muttered.

"Aubrey, come on. We need to plan for this party of yours," Vincent called out.

Aubrey widened her eyes at me before scampering to catch up with Vincent, who was off and running with party plans.

"Are you mad?" I asked Dominic as I walked between him and Levin.

"No." He smiled over at Levin. "This is the happiest I've been in a long time."

Levin reached out and took my hand while Dominic kept his hand on my waist.

"Same, man. Same."

I couldn't argue, so I walked with my two kings, eager for the weekend.

FIFTY-EIGHT
VINCENT

I watched as Bianca sashayed toward me in her slinky, red dress, her blonde hair tumbling around her in soft waves.

"Look at you," I murmured as she did a little spin in front of me.

"Do you like it?" she asked, a nervous edge to her voice as she fidgeted with the crown necklace I'd given her.

"Like it? Baby B, I fucking love it." I placed a kiss on her lips, making her giggle.

"Come on," Dominic ordered. "Levin is waiting downstairs."

Bianca stepped away from me and moved into Dom's waiting embrace. He immediately wrapped his arm around her waist and led her out. I followed and took her hand. He shot me a smirk over her head. Now that the entirety of Bolten knew she was *our* girl, we didn't bother to hide it. I kissed her when I wanted. Levin touched her when he wanted. And Dom. . . well, he did what he'd always done—anything he damn well pleased.

We'd agreed tonight would be a quick outing then we'd come back to Dom and B's room and relax. We'd all get a fast break from campus and then be back before midnight. It should go off without a hitch.

When we made it outside, Levin was already waiting, having a heated argument with Celeste. I tightened my hold on B's hand because I knew she was getting tired of Celeste not giving up.

"What are you doing here?" Dom demanded as Aubrey came into view, looking nervously at the situation in front of her.

Her green halter dress looked good on her. I admired her for a moment, glad B had a decent friend in her. Aubrey made it a point to bring Bianca coffee every morning. Sometimes I'd sit outside Aubrey's dorm as they did girly shit together.

"I need to talk to Levy." Celeste gave Dom a defiant glare.

"Celeste, you need to let go. Levin has moved on—"

"With your wife," she cut in, pointing at B. "The fact that you're OK with it sickens me! She doesn't have half what I have or could give to him! He said he hated her. That she was trash—"

"I *never* said that," Levin snarled. "Get the fuck out of here. You're really pissing me off, Celeste. I told you we're over. I got some mediocre pussy and some shitty blow jobs. The best thing I got out of you was a weapons deal with your old man."

Her nostrils flared. "You'll be sorry. All of you."

She swept away, leaving us to stare after her.

Levin turned to B once Celeste was out of sight. "I never said that shit, Bianca. I fucking swear I didn't."

Bianca went to him and wrapped her arms around him. He hugged her back and blew out a breath.

"I know. And even if you did, you were entitled to your anger. I deserved it after the shit I put us through."

He tipped her head back and placed a kiss on her lips. "I didn't say it."

"I believe you."

He smiled down at her. "You look hot as fuck. I'm going to enjoy peeling this off you later."

"*We're* going to enjoy peeling it off her later," I corrected him.

Dom let out a soft laugh. Aubrey's face reddened, and she laughed, bumping shoulders with B.

And B? She grinned like she'd won the lottery. I liked to think she had. I was a helluva catch. These other fucks were bonuses.

"Come on," Dom said, nodding for us to follow.

Levin held B's hand, both seemingly happy just being next to each other. It was a nice change. For once, this shit was working out.

I strolled beside Dom and watched as he sent a text to Fallon about what we were doing. The poor bastard hadn't gotten any more of B since our night together. The lords and Dom kept him busy, but he never complained. Honestly, he was a good guy. I actually enjoyed the bit of time I'd been around him. The fact he loved my baby B to bits made it easier to like him.

"You going to tell B about her dad?" I asked as we continued toward the parking lot, Levin and B ahead of us with Aubrey.

"No. I'm still digging for more info. If he was a double agent, I want to make sure I know it before I go out and throw around accusations. Levin got the info from Celeste. We don't know much past what she and the F-Word collected."

I smiled at the nickname for Fallon. Guy could fuck. I'd see him bring B to the brink of explosion. No wonder she had a lady boner for him. Hell, even I couldn't deny he was pure sex.

Made me want to up my game even more.

We reached the gates and got into Dom's blacked-out SUV. B got into the very back with Levin. Aubrey sat in the middle row, and I got in the passenger seat. Before long, we were rolling down the highway, everything going smoothly and music playing. I turned to see Levin and B making out in the back. Aubrey gave me a frazzled smile, and I snickered. I was going to make it my mission tonight to get her laid. She deserved a good fucking.

As much as I wanted to crawl in the back and show B a good time with Levin, I knew I should let them be. To be fair, they were kissing and touching every moment they found. I knew it was irritating Dom, but he'd been keeping quiet about it just like I had. I figured he thought the same way I did when it came to them. If they were keeping the peace and shit was going well, there was no point in separating them.

Although, Dom did give us a stern talk about him wanting to be the one to get B pregnant. Making sure we understood where we were allowed to finish and where we weren't. So far she wasn't pregnant yet. While I didn't want my girl knocked-up so soon, I could appreciate Dom's reasoning. Levin had only grunted about it and promised he'd be careful and mind the damn calendar Dom had made tracking her lady-bits cycle. I suspected B didn't know about it because if she did, she'd have probably kicked him in the dick.

When we reached the club, Dom got us right in. We bypassed the line much to the dismay of the people, who'd probably been out there for eons.

"Wow," Aubrey said, taking in the club.

Reds, blues, pinks, purples, and greens decorated the place, the matching strobing lights adding to the effects. With a massive dance floor and dry ice pumping to the heavy club music, it looked like a fun place.

"I'll be right back," Dom said, shifting away from us.

He approached a bouncer. They spoke for a few minutes before the man spoke into the mic on his collar. A few moments later more men joined. Dom shook their hands. Then he looked over his shoulder at us and gestured for us to follow him.

"Think he bought the place?" Levin asked as we headed toward him at the bottom of a set of stairs.

"Probably," I said, checking to make sure Aubrey was still with us. I hadn't missed all the guys in the place scoping out her and B when we came in. I wasn't typically a jealous guy, but B did something to me. Took that part of me and twisted it into something even I didn't recognize.

We followed Dominic up to the VIP section. There was already a table waiting for us. He sat and snagged B, pulling her onto his lap and nuzzling her neck. She melted into him, his hands roaming up her thighs.

It got me hard just watching them. If we played our cards right, we'd end up with her beneath us in a few hours.

Levin poured some champagne that had been chilling at our table. I slammed it back, not bothering to be fancy about it.

"Gross. I hate champagne." I grimaced and stopped one of the shot girls and ordered us a bunch of shit.

We never got carded anywhere. *Who the fuck would be brave enough?* We were the kings and led by Dominic De Santis. A work perk for sure.

"It's good," Aubrey said, eying the flute. "It's, like, sweet."

B nodded. "I like it too."

"*Moët & Chandon Nectar Impérial Rosé.*" Dom took a sip. "Not terribly expensive, but decent enough to be sitting on the table for a few lushes."

I rolled my eyes. Of course, he didn't think it cost enough.

"We aren't lushes," B said, kissing his cheek.

His hand moved beneath her dress as her lips found his, and they kissed.

I caught sight of a guy sitting in a dark corner, his head cocked as he took us in.

I tapped the table and got Levin's attention as another dude joined the other. Both were young. Probably around our age. The blond one, who I'd seen first, spoke quickly to the one with dark hair, who'd joined him. The guy glanced in our direction, his facial expression not changing. He looked familiar. Like maybe I'd seen him on TV or something.

"Do you know them?" I asked Levin, trying not to be obvious as I kept a side-eye on them.

He shook his head and slammed back a drink. He may have seemed like he wasn't interested in them, but I knew he was tuned in, curious about why they were staring.

B and Dom finally broke apart, and Aubrey tugged her hand to get her to dance. Dom hesitated for all of a moment before he released her and let her leave.

"We're being watched," I murmured to him, sipping my drink.

"I know. There was a third with them when we arrived." Dom rose and slid his glass across the table. Casually, he walked to the balcony so he could watch B.

I moved to stand beside him as Levin left for the bathroom. I observed as B and Aubrey danced, both smiling.

"She looks happy," I said.

"Good," Dom replied, a small smile on his lips.

"I'm still jealous you got to marry her. Lucky fucker."

"I know." He stared over at me. "But she loves you, Vin. Never doubt how much."

I grinned, feeling light. Yeah, she did love me. I guessed I was a lucky fucker too.

"What are we going to do about our new fans?" I asked, feeling their gaze still on us.

"Keep an eye on them. It might be nothing."

"Or it might be something," I said.

"It always is." His face hardened as he stared out at the crowd like a king surveying his kingdom. "We'll stay for a bit longer. If things start getting more suspicious, we'll leave."

It seemed like a sound plan. *What was the worst that could happen?*

FIFTY-NINE
FALLON

"You need to slow the fuck down. I can't understand what you're saying when you're crying," Hail snapped as Celeste blubbered in front of us in his room that night.

I'd gotten the message from Dom that he was headed off campus with Bianca and the kings to celebrate Aubrey's birthday. He'd said they didn't plan on being gone long. *Beats*. That was where he was going.

I hated I was stuck behind with the lords, watching them get high while Tate got a blow job from some no-name, scholarship chick.

"Levin left campus with *her*. Bianca," Celeste said as Stella came in and took a seat beside me.

I cast her a cursory glance then turned my attention back to Celeste and Hail.

"Why do I give a fuck?" Hail asked. "You're not exactly welcome here, Celeste. Not after you fucked Drake over."

"I didn't," she exclaimed, wiping her nose. "Can you just listen? Please? Dominic De Santis is gone tonight. All the kings are. They have Bianca and Aubrey McIntire with them."

"They're off campus?" Hail perked up. "Where did they go?"

"I know about the horsemen and the shooting the kings did on them. Daddy told me it was really tragic. If I tell you, I want your protection if anything happens."

Hail nodded as I sat forward. Stella nudged my thigh.

"We'll make sure you're taken care of. I heard about Seeley leaving you high and dry for Bianca."

"He hurt me. He used me. I want him to pay. I thought maybe you could tip off those horsemen guys and tell them where to find the kings tonight."

Shit. Fuck. This bitch…

"I like the way you think. Tell me, and I'll see what I can do." Hail gave her a wicked smile.

"You promise you'll protect me?" She stared at him with wide eyes.

"Of course, I will." Hail held his hands out as Drake pulled his phone out.

Fuck… damnit…

"Tell me where the kings and their whore are."

"They went to this new club called Beats for Aubrey's birthday. They're there right now." Celeste let out a breath. "I want Bianca to die."

"Ah, come on now. I don't want that. Not yet," Hail said, glancing to Drake.

Tate grinned like the fucking lunatic he was. Trent smirked at me. I grinned, playing the part but dying inside to get to the kings and Bianca so I could let them know shit was going to go down.

"Well, I want them to suffer," she whined with a sniffle. "So however you can make that happen would be good."

"Sure. Trent. Make the call." Hail leaned back in his seat.

"We need to do something," Stella hissed.

The only way to get out of there was to fuck my way out. I grasped her hand and pressed my lips to hers. She went stiff beneath my mouth before she fell into it, her tongue gliding along mine.

"Oh, for fuck's sake. Get a room," Hail grumbled as Stella took the lead and straddled my lap, her fingers in my hair as she ground against me.

For fuck's sake. She was a hell of an actress.

"I know we have shit going on, man, but I'd like to leave," I said as Stella buried her face in my neck and sucked along my flesh. I wanted to flick her fucking nose and listen to her yelp just to get her lips off me, but I held it together.

"Is Stella the chick you're getting close to?" Hail's gaze raked over us. "You said you liked someone. Is it Stella? Because Stella is mine. I don't mind loaning her out, but she'll never belong to you guys."

"No," I said as she continued to kiss my neck. "I don't think that's going to work out, so I need to blow off this steam."

"Fine. Go. Trent is making the call. We'll just be sitting here waiting for an update anyway. No way we're getting involved in that fuck-fest. The horsemen are out for blood and will take the kings out for us. We'll swoop in and kill them once they're done with the kings. *Sovershenstvo.*"

"Thanks, man. Let me know how it goes. I'll, uh, try to answer if you call." I got to my feet, bringing Stella with me as she continued to paw at me.

I grabbed her ass, and she giggled. I led her from the room to the sound of catcalls.

The moment we were in the hall, I shoved away from her and ran with her on my heels.

"Where the hell are you going?" she asked as we made it outside.

"We gotta get to Beats. Call Dom. Try to warn him." I pulled my keys out and broke into a jog.

Stella stayed next to me. We reached my new car, and she slid into the passenger seat with her phone pressed to her ear.

"You should stay here."

"Fuck you, Fallon. I'm always excluded. I'm going this time," she said, ending her call to Dom and trying again.

Fuck.

"Fine. Try to not get killed," I said, tearing out of the parking lot on screeching tires, my heart in my throat.

"Text him. Call Vin or Seeley. B. Someone. Fuck."

Stella grabbed my phone and called from both our phones and sent messages, but no one answered.

Fuck. Bianca. Please be OK.

We tore through the streets as fast as I could go.

"Get my gun," I said tightly. "It's in the glove box."

"Jesus," she muttered, snagging the gun out.

I grabbed it from her and tucked it in my jacket.

"Are you really going to go killing people?"

"Won't be the first time," I muttered, making a hard right.

She cursed at me before going back to making phone calls.

My heart was in my throat. I needed a fucking vacation from all this shit. We all did. I'd suggest one at the next team meeting.

SIXTY
BIANCA

"Hey," a gorgeous blond guy said as I waited at the bar for my drink.

Dom had set up a running tab for us. I didn't plan on drinking a lot. I just wanted a little bit before we went home. It had been so long since I'd had any damn fun, so I was going to take full advantage as long as I could.

"Hey," I said, tapping my fingers on the bar.

Aubrey had gone off to the bathroom, and I'd promised to get drinks. I knew the guys were in the VIP area probably with eagle eyes on us, so I had no worries in my body as the guy leaned next to me, his rich cologne wafting out at me.

"What's your name?" he asked, his gaze skirting up my body.

I swallowed and gave him a nervous smile. "Bianca."

"Pretty." His blue eyes twinkled. "I'm Cole."

"Nice to meet you," I said, shaking the hand he offered.

"Are you here with anyone tonight? Pretty girls like you shouldn't be alone in places like this."

"Because of creeps?" I asked, cocking my head at him and narrowing my eyes.

He grinned. "Yes. Because of creeps. So are you alone?"

"I'm not. My friend is in the bathroom. My husband is upstairs. He's probably watching you right now."

"Husband? Aren't you a little young to be tied down?"

"We're unconventional," I said, glancing back to see where the bartender was with my drinks.

"I hear that." He ran his fingers through his hair.

A ring on his thumb caught my eye. It was pretty with a small gemstone embedded in it.

The guy was fit, I'd give him that. He probably had girls hanging off him left and right. He was about the size of my guys. Reminded me of them—muscles, height, looks. His clothes screamed money. His attitude said he was probably high maintenance. And maybe a little crazy, judging by the way his blue eyes kept darting around the crowd.

"Are you here alone?" I ventured as I continued to wait for my drinks. May as well make small talk.

"No, doll. I'm not alone. I'm here with my boys."

"Picking up chicks?"

"Hardly," he said with a laugh.

"Picking up guys?"

His grin widened. "You're funny. I like that. But no. Not guys either. Just out having a good time. So, what's your husband's name?"

"That's random," I muttered.

"Not really. What's his name so I know who to congratulate when I meet him for snagging such a beautiful girl?" He winked at me.

"Dominic," I said, crinkling my brows at him as I tried to figure him out.

He was a lot of pomp and smiles for someone with crazy written in his eyes.

"De Santis?"

I licked my lips. "You know him?"

"We haven't been formally introduced yet. But we will before the night is over." He slid a twenty onto the bar. "It's on me. Be safe out there, Bianca. Don't go anywhere alone. Plenty of creeps out there."

"Thanks," I said, watching as he turned and disappeared into the crowd.

What a strange guy.

"Here you go," the bartender called out, pushing two fruity drinks at me.

I nodded to the twenty, and he took it, thanking me.

"Girl, tell me one of those is mine," Aubrey said, coming up to me.

"Yeah, some guy bought them for us," I said, scanning the crowd for him.

Something didn't feel right. I took a sip of my drink and handed Aubrey her drink.

I caught sight of the guy talking to three more guys in a dimly-lit corner. The one with the dark hair and equally dark eyes stared back at me, making my breath catch in my chest. *Damn.* He was beautiful too. They all were. I peered up at the balcony to see Dominic wasn't there. He'd been there all night.

I frowned, my anxiety growing.

"Let's dance. I'm sure Dominic will want to leave soon," Aubrey said, finishing her drink.

I downed mine quickly and followed her to the dance floor, not wanting to get separated and not wanting to ruin her birthday. I told myself Dominic was probably comfortable and having a seat.

We danced to the music. One song after another. A shot girl approached and offered me a drink.

"From Dominic," she said in my ear.

I looked for him on the balcony but still didn't see him.

Whatever. If he was sending drinks, then everything must be fine.

I swallowed the shot and handed the server the empty glass. She moved away from us and deeper into the crowd. I went back to dancing with Aubrey and could have sworn I saw Fallon moving through the crowd to the stairs with Stella.

That couldn't be right.

My head spun. Heat rushed through my body.

"I need to use the bathroom again," Aubrey said, leaning in to shout in my ear over the pounding music. "You want to come?"

I nodded, wincing at the flashing strobe lights. I stumbled along behind her, the dizziness getting worse.

"Are you OK?" Aubrey asked as we stopped outside the bathroom.

"I-I don't feel well." My head gave a wicked spin.

"We can just go find Dominic," she said. "I can wait to use the bathroom."

"N-no. Go. Just hurry," I said weakly. "It's probably all the flashing lights and alcohol."

She hesitated for a moment. "OK. I'll be fast."

I propped against the wall in the hallway as she disappeared inside the bathroom. I hauled in a deep breath. My head was so light I thought I was going to pass out.

"You look unwell," a deep voice said from beside me.

I looked up to the voice's owner and saw he had two blurry heads. Dark hair. Dark eyes. He looked Italian. He was definitely the hot guy I'd seen earlier with Cole.

"I-I'm really dizzy. C-can you get my husband?"

"Of course. You want to sit down?"

I nodded, wincing. He held his hand out to me, and I took it. His hold was firm as he led me deeper down the hall. Lots of rings on his fingers. Holding his hand reminded me of holding Vinny's hand. I stumbled, and he caught me around the waist, helping me stay on my feet.

"Is there an office back here?" I slurred out.

There was no way I'd drunk enough for this to happen to me. Three drinks never did this to me.

"Yes," he answered gently, pushing open a door.

A rush of cool air hit my face. I stumbled again as he led me down the steps. A blacked-out SUV pulled up, and a door opened. My heart skipped as I realized I might be in a very bad situation. It felt like I'd blacked out during the walk and missed getting to the destination.

Cole, the blond guy from the bar, jumped out and grabbed me by the waist. I slapped at him, crying out as he hauled me into the dark confines of the vehicle. The door slammed shut, and the guy who'd brought me out got into the driver's seat.

"We going? Enzo?" Cole asked as I whimpered, continuing to kick at him. He let out a hiss as I caught him in the chest with my heel.

"One minute," the guy named Enzo grunted.

Enzo. Why did I know that name? My brain felt like a wall was being built inside it, and I couldn't get my thoughts to fall in line.

"For fuck's sake, where are they?" Cole growled, grabbing at me again.

I swung on him, making him grunt as I caught him in the face.

"They're here," Enzo said.

The door opened, and two more guys shoved a third in before getting in behind him.

"Fucking go. He was following us. Knocked his ass out," one of the guys said, slamming the door.

Enzo put the SUV into drive, and we squealed out of the parking lot.

I struggled against Cole as he worked to subdue me.

"*Jesus fuck*, help me. She's wild," Cole called out as I kicked him in the chest again.

One of the guys grabbed my wrists. We struggled as I tried to fight him. He was bigger and stronger than me, his hard body pressed to mine as we wrestled in the backseat.

"Don't. Stop. Please," I cried out, thrashing against him.

"You're making it worse on yourself, doll," Cole said through gritted teeth as he secured my ankles.

The guy on me finally got my wrists bound, and I breathed hard as I stared up at him.

"Please," I choked out. "Don't—"

"Sorry," he said, really sounding like it as he duct-taped my mouth.

I sobbed as I glanced at the figure slumped on the floor.

Vinny.

The guy who'd duct-taped me made fast work of securing Vincent's hands and feet. I cried out as he jammed a needle into Vincent's neck.

"You aren't going to kill him yet, right, E?" Cole grunted as E sank back in his seat.

"No. It'll just keep him knocked out so he's easier to handle. He punched Fox in the face right before we knocked him out. Nearly put him on his ass."

The guy named Fox glanced at me. He had the prettiest blue eyes.

His gaze raked over me quickly. "She's De Santis's wife?"

"That's what she said. Judging by the rock on her finger I'd say it's the truth," Cole answered. "Plus, one of his henchmen came looking for her. Pretty sure she is married to Dominic."

"Knock her out," Enzo called out, making a hard left.

I watched in horror as E slid forward with another needle in his hand.

"I really am sorry, peach. This might hurt a little."

I cried out behind my duct tape, the sound muffled and barely audible as E poked the needle into my neck.

Son of a bitch. Not again.

I sank into the darkness, not sure if I'd ever be able to claw my way out this time. The way things were looking, it was a no.

SIXTY-ONE
DOMINIC

"D-Dominic! Dom!" Aubrey clutched her chest as she dragged in deep breaths.

Immediately, I went on high alert as I got to my feet.

"What's wrong? Where's Bianca?"

"G-gone. I-I can't find her. She wasn't feeling good. We went to the bathroom, and she was waiting in the hall for me. When I came back, she was gone. D-did you send her a drink?"

"What?" I frowned. "No."

"She drank something, and now she's gone. The shot girl said it was from you."

Levin moved to the balcony and peered out at the crowd as Vincent turned away from us. I followed his gaze to see Fallon and Stella rushing to us.

This isn't fucking good. My chest clenched. All thoughts on the possibility of her going back to dancing left me. We'd just dealt with some asshole shoving me and shouting about me stealing his drinks.

Diversion. It was a fucking diversion!

"Where's Bianca?" Fallon demanded, breathless.

"Missing," Vincent said, his voice shaking.

"The horsemen. Celeste is pissed. She told Hail where you were tonight. Trent made the call to his contact, so the horsemen know you're here. We need to get the fuck out of here. We have to find Bianca," Fallon rattled off, his eyes filled with panic.

"Aubrey, where was she last?" I demanded.

"In the hallway by the bathrooms. I'm sorry, Dominic. I-I-"

I turned away from her tears and focused on my men. "She couldn't have gotten far. Find her. Check everywhere."

Everyone scattered like roaches in the light as I drew in a deep breath, my mind racing a mile a minute.

"Where is she?" I snarled, staring out at the dance floor from the balcony, hoping to catch a glimpse of her below.

Fallon stood beside me, staring out at the writhing bodies.

"Fucking Celeste," I snarled. "She's dead."

"Hail offered her his protection," Fallon said tightly. "I can't be seen with you. I don't see her up here. I'm going down to the floor to look for her."

I didn't stop him. Instead, I took the backstairs down and called her phone from the quiet. It rang several times before her voicemail picked up. I called again. And again. Nothing. My guts twisted as my heart thudded hard, my pulse roaring in my ears.

I can't lose her. Fuck. I need to find her.

I ran to the dance floor and forced my way through the thrashing bodies, looking for Bianca.

"She's not here. Vin went to check the bathrooms," Levin said tightly.

I swallowed. "Check out front. I'll look in the back. The court is searching too."

"Dom, if what Fallon said is true, the horsemen—"

"Just find her," I said thickly. "We have to find her."

Levin nodded and rushed off, leaving me standing in the center of the dance floor. When I didn't see her, I moved to the back hallway and asked a bouncer if he'd seen her.

"Red dress? Hot blonde? She left with De Luca. Not ten minutes ago."

I swallowed, my blood running cold.

"Lorenzo De Luca?"

"Yeah. Out the back. You didn't hear that from me."

I pushed past him and rushed to the back doors, flinging them open. Nothing.

"Fuck," I snarled, raking my hands down my face as my blood roared through my veins.

Something dark on the ground caught my eye. I picked it up. *Vincent's wallet.*

FUCK.

I pulled my phone out and called Levin. "They have Vin and Bianca. I'm in the back lot. "

I didn't wait for his answer. I hung up and stared up at the stars.

"Give me strength," I whispered, breathing out. "And don't fucking let those assholes take them from me."

Levin pulled up with my SUV moments later. I hauled open the passenger door and climbed in wordlessly. Fallon was in the back on his phone, typing out a text.

"Stella and Aubrey are going back to Bolten in my car," he said tightly, darkening his screen as we sat.

"Where do we go?" Levin asked softly, his hands trembling.

"I honestly don't have an answer," I said, my head spinning.

How the fuck had I let this happen? Both Vin and Bianca. They could already be dead. My guts churned with the nausea of what it could mean. I'd fucking die with them. I'd kill myself because I didn't want to go through this world without them. The drunk fuck had been a distraction. Probably someone they'd sent up to us.

My phone rang. I stared down at a number I didn't recognize. Levin and I locked eyes as I answered it and lifted it to my ear.

"Hello?"

"Dominic De Santis," a rich, deep voice greeted me. "I wish I could say it was a pleasure to finally speak to you, but I'd be lying."

"De Luca," I snarled back, trying to quell the rage boiling in my veins. "Where's my wife? Where's Vincent?"

"Both out cold at the moment."

"I'm not the fucking guy who shot your shit up."

"Sounds like something someone who shot my shit up would say when I have his hot as fuck wife and best friend, doesn't it? I mean, you see my predicament, right?"

"What do you want? I can prove I'm not the guy."

"I want you to die, De Santis. It's not like I'm asking a lot. Give yourself up to me and *fucking die*. It's simple, really. Your life for your wife's. I won't be able to release the other one. Unless, of course, you'd rather die for him instead of her. *A soul for a soul.*"

"The lords did the shooting. They lied and left our calling card. I was at my fucking wedding reception when it happened." My hand shook as I pressed the phone to my ear. "We're at war with them over a bunch of shit. It wasn't me who did that to you."

"Your life for hers, De Santis. Or his. Your choice. I must say it would be a shame to lose her though. She really is beautiful. And this dress. Her tits are real, huh? *Fucking nice.*"

"Don't you dare fucking touch her. I'll come to you. Where are you?"

"The warehouse on Ninth and Broadway. I'll make it nice and easy for you. First floor. No weapons. No cops. You show up with any of those things, and I'll kill them both on sight. *Capisci?*"

"*Capisco,*" I said tightly.

"Within the hour. My finger is getting itchy. Tick tock, De Santis."

The line went dead.

"Ninth and Broadway. The old warehouse on the corner," I rasped, my chest tight.

Levin peeled out of the parking lot. I pulled a gun out of my glove box. Then I grabbed one from under my seat and handed it to Levin along with a magazine for each of us.

"Hope you have a weapon," I said to Fallon.

"I do. Several," he said, his voice a soft grunt.

"We don't know what we're up against, Dom—" Levin started.

"Does it matter?" I snapped. "It's our girl, and it's Vin. De Luca wants my death in exchange for one of them. It's either her or him. One of them has to die according to De Luca."

Levin tightened his hands on the steering wheel. "Son of a bitch."

Fallon adjusted his jacket and scrubbed his hand down his face. "I'll die in place of Vincent."

"You're not getting the fucking glory, you fucking Russian dicklick," Levin snapped.

"If Bianca loses Vin, she'll fucking die of heartbreak. I'll die so she won't feel his loss, you fucking German taterdick."

"And then she'd mourn you," I shouted. "It's a no-win situation. Whatever happens, whoever survives, just fucking take care of her. Keep her happy. Take her far the fuck away from this shit and never let anyone harm her again."

We fell silent as we continued our trek. I breathed out, an idea taking shape. I opened the glove box and pulled out the grenade Vander Veer had given me.

"Is that a fucking grenade?" Fallon asked as I glanced back at him and then to Levin, who gave me a slow nod, seemingly on the same page.

"I fucking hope they can catch," I said softly, gripping the grenade tightly before I put it into my jacket pocket.

I hadn't started the night out thinking I was going to die, but my life never went to plan. I expected to die at some point like this. If I got to take out a few cocksuckers on my way out, then I was ready to pull the pin.

If dying for someone I loved was how I was going out, I'd gladly take my last breath with her name on my lips. For wasp, I'd do anything.

Always.

SIXTY-TWO
BIANCA

I stared at my captors as they talked in a room near where I was tied to a chair. Vincent was slumped over across from me in his seat, his hands and feet bound to the metal bars of his chair.

With the tape over my mouth, I couldn't call out to him. I struggled against my bonds, hoping to break free. What I'd do once I got free was another story. I couldn't carry Vinny out on my back. The only thing I could do was run and hope I made it out to get help. My head was still fuzzy from whatever drug they'd given me.

"Easy, Bianca."

I snapped my gaze to the owner of the voice. *Cole.* The beautiful blond. He stood in front of me. I'd been so focused on breaking free I hadn't noticed his arrival.

I stared up at him, trembling. The other three guys joined him, all large and menacing. And totally captivating. I bet they broke plenty of hearts with the women they encountered.

"We're going to take the tape off, if you promise to not scream," the one with the messy, dark hair and blue eyes said. "OK? Nod for me."

I nodded, my heart in my throat.

He stepped forward and peeled the tape off my mouth. I gasped at the pain before letting out an ear-shattering scream.

"For fuck's sake," Enzo snarled as the blue-eyed guy taped my mouth again.

I bucked as hard as I could against my bonds, glaring at them while silently vowing I'd seriously kick some ass if I managed to get free.

"Bianca. Come on now," Cole said "Doll, this isn't going to get us anywhere. We only want to talk, OK? Talk to us, and things might go better than you expect. So we're going to take the tape off again, and you're going to be good. Right?"

I glared at him.

He nodded. "Go on. Take it off."

The blue-eyed guy came back and pulled the tape off again.

"I'm sorry about that," he said, looking like he might mean it as his dark brows crinkled.

"Fucking assholes. Do you even realize how *fucked* you are once my husband gets here?" I seethed, glaring at all of them.

"I think it's him who's going to be fucked," Cole said with a smirk.

"W-who are you?" I asked, my voice shaking as I tried to calm myself with a deep breath.

"My name is Fox," the blue-eyed guy spoke up. "This is Enzo, Cole, and Ethan," he continued, nodding to each in turn.

"The horsemen," I whispered, saying aloud what I'd been fearing. "You're the leader." I looked to the dark-haired guy, who'd taken me in the hall. *Enzo.*

"We all lead in one way or another," he said, kneeling in front of me and pushing a blonde wave away from my face. "But yes, I suppose I am."

"Are you going to kill me?"

My heart jumped in my chest as I waited for his judgement.

He cocked his head as he studied me. "You're really beautiful. I'd honestly hate to hurt you, but yeah, I'm going to kill you if De Santis doesn't show."

My chest constricted more. "What about Vinny? Please don't hurt him."

"Vincent Valentino. A king." Enzo clicked his tongue. "Well, my dear, he's part of the problem, and the deal I struck with your husband dictates he dies."

"What? No. *Please.* Dominic wouldn't want that. H-he wouldn't make that deal! *I* don't want that. I'll do anything you want. Just let him go."

"Anything?" Cole asked, perking up.

Ethan let out a sigh, and Fox shot him an irritated look.

"Anything. With or-or for any of you," I said, nausea roiling in my guts at the implications.

"I don't know how the kings do their negotiations, but I don't fuck my hostages," Enzo said, his dark gaze gliding over me. "Although, in another life, I may have taken you up on your offer. You really are so damn beautiful."

"You're married too." It wasn't a question. He also had a ring similar to Cole's on his thumb.

He gave me a smile. "Something like that."

"Then you know what it would feel like to have her taken from you. That's what you're doing to me."

He reached out and swiped a tear off my cheek. "I know exactly what it's like. I've lived that particular horror a few times already. I don't much care for it."

"The kings didn't do what you think they did. Dominic didn't order the shooting. It was Hail. *Mikhail Ivanov.* He's the son of S-Sergio Ivanov, head of the Bratva. He pinned it on the kings so you'd take them out and clear the way for the Ivanovs. Hail is a monster. *He* did this!" I pleaded.

"The thing is, we're all monsters," Enzo said gently. "Unfortunately, when one monster attacks another, we fight to the death. Everyone is a liar. We don't know who's telling us the truth. Even if you're being honest, De Santis is still a threat. Best to cut the head off the snake than risk it biting me when I'm not looking. We put our trust in family, and you, Bianca De Santis, are not our family. I hope you understand."

"I'm not lying. I swear I'm not. What do you want me to do?

Please. I'll do it." I let out a cry of anguish. "You don't have to do this!"

Enzo stood and strode away from me.

"What we want you to do is watch and learn," Cole said as Fox stepped forward and pressed the tape back over my mouth.

Tears streamed down my cheeks as my body shook from sobbing so hard.

Ethan said nothing, simply watching in silence, his body tense as his gaze raked over me with a haunted look.

"I sincerely hope you learn from this and take the second chance De Santis is going to give you to pick better men to fuck," Cole continued.

Cole followed Fox back to the small room with Enzo.

Ethan approached me, a sad look on his face.

"Do you love him?" He nodded to Vincent. "We only plead and bargain for those we love."

I nodded miserably, my face soaked with tears.

"That's how it is with us. Our girl loves us four. We've been where you are. I would've died for her too. Take what Cole says and run. De Santis is going to die for you tonight. Don't let his sacrifice be in vain."

Bile burned my throat as more tears fell.

"For what it's worth, I truly am sorry. If there was another way, we'd do it. This is hell, peach, and here there are no angels. Just us demons spurred on by revenge."

He backed away from me with a sad look on his face. The rest of his crew came back out.

Vincent groaned in his chair, his eyelids cracking open. Cole reached out and yanked the tape from Vincent's mouth, making him curse softly. I sobbed harder as Enzo reached out and fisted his hair, pulling his head back and putting a knife to his throat.

Vincent looked at me as he swallowed.

"One of you is going to die tonight. Pretty sure it's going to be you," Enzo said, pressing the blade harder into Vincent's neck.

A bead of blood blossomed out. I rocked in my chair, hardly able to draw in a breath as I cried.

"Is that a fact?" Vincent rasped, wincing.

Enzo slid the knife across Vincent's throat, marking him with a thin, red line that trickled blood but didn't cut deep enough to cause much harm. Although, I was sure he'd sport a nasty scar from the attack.

Vincent's head fell forward as Enzo released him.

I shook violently in my seat.

"We don't need to make her watch," Ethan said softly.

"How will she remember if she doesn't get to see?" Cole asked with the air of someone simply discussing the weather.

I knew he was crazy.

"I agree with E. She shouldn't see this," Fox said tightly, shooting Cole an irritated look. "It's bad enough you sent her the drink and drugged her."

Guess that explains where the drink came from. Cole must have bought it and told the shot girl he was Dominic. What a dick.

Cole scoffed and gave me an apologetic look. "Sorry. I thought we figured this mess out. You don't want to listen to us argue over killing him, do you?" He tore the tape off my lips as Vincent shouted for him to get away from me.

"Tell your lover boy goodbye before he passes out from the pain."

"Vinny," I choked out. "Vinny."

"I'm not going to die, B."

Enzo twirled the knife in his hands. In a blur of movement, he shoved the knife into Vincent's thigh and left it there.

"Fuck!" Vincent groaned, panting as blood dripped onto the dirty concrete floor.

I screamed hysterically.

"Here's what we're going to do," Enzo said easily, twirling another knife and circling Vincent's chair. "I'm going to ask you questions, and you're going to answer me. If I think you're telling the truth, I won't stab you. If I think you're lying, it's going to hurt."

"Don't. Please." I struggled against my bonds again.

Panic took over my senses. Breathing burned my chest. My vision was still foggy from the drug they'd given me.

"Shh, doll. Just watch. I don't want to have to hurt you too." Cole pulled his gun out and dragged it down my chin and over my breasts. "You be a good girl and just listen like I told you, OK?"

"Did Dominic De Santis order the hit on me and my crew?" Enzo demanded, the blade flashing quickly in his hand.

"N-no. Fuck," Vincent groaned, panting. "Ivanov did."

Enzo swung down and jammed his knife into Vincent's other thigh, making both Vincent and me howl.

Enzo nodded and clicked his tongue as he brought out a third blade from his leather jacket. "Why did we find a kings' calling card at the scene?"

"Ivanov was pissed that Dom took Bianca from him. Hail was out for re-revenge. Bianca had an arranged marriage to Ivanov. He abused her. She came to us for help. Dom fell in love with her. We all did. Dom m-married her to keep her safe."

I cried out as Enzo swooped in and pressed the blade to Vincent's cheek.

"I'm not fucking lying, you goddamn psychopath. If you're going to keep fucking stabbing me whenever I tell the truth then fucking kill me," Vincent said breathlessly. "I'm not a fucking human pincushion. Prick."

Enzo backed away, chuckling softly.

"So you're swearing the lords are behind the attack?" Fox asked, his arms crossed over his chest.

"That's what I fucking said. This is Ivanov's way of getting you fucks to clear the board for him. You're playing into his hand. Fucking goddamn newbie asshats."

Cole's fist collided with Vincent's face, making Vincent's head snap to the side. My throat was so hoarse from screaming for them to stop that my pleas came out broken and soft.

"Be *nice*, Valentino," Cole admonished. "There's no need for name-calling."

Vincent spat blood onto the concrete and glared at Cole.

"Fuck you, pussy. Kill me if you don't believe me, but you'd best bet it won't be the last time you hear my fucking name. The kings are more than just me and De Santis."

"Oh, we heard," Enzo said. "That fucked up old man of De Santis's, Matteo. We know all about him. Which brings me to my next question. Actually, it's Ethan's question."

Ethan stepped forward. "Do you know a girl named Macy?"

Vincent breathed out, a look of confusion flitting across his face. "M-Macy? I don't know, man. I know lots of girls. You'll have to be more specific. Did she have big tits and an ass that didn't quit? Was she into being fucked in public? Red hair? Blonde? Fucking purple? Details matter, cunt."

Cole punched him in the face again. Vincent's eye swelled as he smirked at Cole.

"You hit like a bitch."

Cole struck him twice more before Enzo stepped in to stop him. I whimpered softly and squeezed my eyes closed, praying hard for a miracle.

"Do you know Macy or not?" Ethan asked again.

"I *don't know*." Vincent was silent for a moment before he let out a snort.

"What?" Fox demanded.

"I only know of one Macy. Matteo De Santis grabbed her near the Mayfair campus. He put her in the palace. He forced her to suck Dom's cock. When Dom tried to help her, Matteo had her brains blown out to teach Dom a lesson about weakness. Dom knows her better than I do. It was him who had to wash her brains off his face."

My stomach rolled with Vincent's words. *Matteo was a fucking monster.* I made a silent vow to make sure he was taken from this world before he could hurt anyone else.

Ethan let out a shaky breath and licked his lips. "Macy is dead?"

"If that was your Macy, she is, unless she can survive a bullet to the skull," Vincent said.

"That's too bad," Enzo murmured, his eyes downcast.

Ethan turned away and ran his hands over his face, a muscle thrumming along his jaw.

"Dom tried to stop it. He tried to help her. He's not his father," Vincent said fiercely. "If you stupid fucks would listen, you'd realize you're being set up. The kings want to take Matteo De Santis down as much as you do. He's the biggest fucking monster there is."

Enzo swung forward and drove his blade into Vincent's shoulder. Vincent let out a loud groan as steel met muscle, his face contorting in agony.

"We're all fucking monsters," Enzo breathed out before stepping away, leaving the three knives embedded in Vincent's body.

Vincent was losing too much blood. His shirt was drenched in it. Blood pooled at his feet. His face was pale, and sweat dotted his forehead.

Enzo turned to Cole. "Kill him."

"No. No. No!" I cried out. I bucked against my chair, screaming Vincent's name. I didn't even see Ethan approach me, but I felt the bite of his needle in my neck and his lips at my ear.

"I don't want you to see this, peach," he murmured. "Sleep. It'll be over when you wake."

My vision grew cloudy, and my head lolled to the side as I stared at the pain in Vincent's eyes.

"I love you. Forever my B," he choked out before my world spun black a final time and all I was left with was the fading roar in my ears.

EPILOGUE
ETHAN MASTERS

Her chest heaved as she struggled against her bonds. I could already see the ugly red welts encircling her wrists.

With each desperate tug, my heart cracked a little bit more. It took all I had to keep my cool because all I saw in that chair was my sweetheart, Rosalie, twisting and desperate. It wasn't the kings' girl in agony; it was mine.

The reason why I was now part of some sick, fucked up torture session which was all too reminiscent of what I'd watch Rosalie suffer through not long ago was beyond me. She'd been terrified too.

I hated this.

I wasn't this guy.

This. . . *monster*.

But I knew what was at stake. I knew to protect who I loved it meant someone else's love had to go.

The world was wicked like that.

It still didn't sit well with me.

It was killing me inside.

Macy was dead. Vincent Valentino had confirmed it. She'd been so special to me. To us. She was the one who. . .

Fuck. I couldn't think straight.

To know she was gone...

Macy. Was. Dead. She's dead.

How long until it was one of us? Until it was Rosalie, my sweetheart?

The syringe in my pocket pressed against my thigh.

It didn't matter if this poor girl was the wife of our enemy. She was innocent and didn't deserve to watch someone she loved die.

And he was going to die if something didn't give. The three knives sticking from his body dictated that.

The blood pooling at his feet dictated that.

The fucking horsemen dictated that.

All in the name of love.

"Kill him," Enzo ordered, his face filled with a ruthlessness which made my blood run cold.

"No. No. NO!" Bianca, the blonde beauty screamed, her sobs creating an earthquake in her body as she shook. "Vin. Vinny! VINNY!"

My guys told me to let her watch. But I wasn't that guy. I'd been in the same position as her. It still fucking haunted me.

"I don't want you to see this, peach," I murmured in her ear, pulling the syringe from my pocket and jamming it into her delicate neck. "Sleep. It'll be over when you wake."

Vincent's name continued to fall softly from her lips until her lashes fluttered and her head slumped to the side.

"I love you. Forever my B," Vincent choked out as she went still.

My heart shattered in my chest over his vow to her.

Cole raised a brow at me. "Really, E?"

"You wouldn't understand," I muttered.

Fox shot me a sad, knowing look.

"If B is hurt, I swear I'll come back and haunt you fucking pricks," Vincent snarled. *"Cazzi del cazzo. Ti maledico in questa vita e nella prossima. Lo giuro."*

I had no idea what he'd said. I glanced at Enzo, who narrowed his eyes and kneeled in front of him.

"You curse me in this life and in the next?" Enzo murmured. "I'm already fucking cursed, *re morto*. We all are, my *dead* friend."

"Dom won't let this go unpunished," Vincent rasped, his face pale, sweat dotting his forehead.

"I'm truly hoping he's everything I've heard he is." Enzo shoved the knife in Vincent's thigh a little deeper, making Vincent cry out. "But just in case, we best give him something to fight for."

My gaze shot to Bianca passed out in her chair.

"It's OK, man," Fox said softly to me. "It sucks. It hurts. Stay focused though, OK?"

"I already regret this," I answered.

Fox nodded. "I get it, but we're *in*. For life. You know what that means."

"I know," I whispered. I fucking did know, and I hated it with my entire being.

This scene would become just another nightmare which kept me awake at night. I didn't know Bianca, but I knew her pain. I didn't want that for her, but like I'd been told countless times, this was war. This was what *being in* looked like. We'd done far worse already. And we'd continue to do worse until the devil claimed our fucking souls.

Enzo stood and looked to us. "It's time to see what the kings are made of. We've already seen what the lords can do. In this new world, we aren't heroes, E. Remember that."

I nodded tightly.

In this new world, we were the monsters.

In this world, I would become one of the biggest monsters of all.

All in the name of love, power. . . and sugar.

Pre-Order Deadly Little Promises, book three in the Kings of Bolten now.
Deadly Little Promises: Kings of Bolten

Thank you for reading Pretty Little Sins! Please consider leaving your review. The release date is just a placeholder date. Deadly Little Promises releases Fall 2022.

**Want to know about the horsemen? You can read their story in the completed Black Falls High series before you read about them in college this fall with the kings. Also an audio series.
Get it here: In Ruins: A Black Falls High Novel**

Need more dark bully reverse harem goodness? Flip ahead for a preview of Church: The Boys of Chapel Crest, a dark bully ASYLUM reverse harem or get it here:
Church: The Boys of Chapel Crest

ACKNOWLEDGMENTS

Big thanks to my alpha readers. Mahida, Crystal, Erika, Rebecca, The Jess's, and Valarie. Thank you to my editor. She's the sparkle in these words.

Thanks to my readers and fans, my ARC readers, and my little family.

Finally, I have to acknowledge all the voices in my head. You guys. . . *shakes head*. Thank you for driving me crazy.

Good grief. I even talk to myself here.

ABOUT THE AUTHOR

Affectionately dubbed Queen of Cliffy, Suspense, Heartbreak, and Torture by her readers, USA Today bestselling author K.G. Reuss is known mostly for making readers ugly cry with her writing. A cemetery creeper and ghost enthusiast, K.G. spends most of her time toeing the line between imagination and forced adulthood.

After a stint in college in Iowa, K.G. moved back to her home in Michigan to work in emergency medicine. She's currently raising three small ghouls and is married to a vampire overlord (not really but maybe he could be someday).

K.G. is the author of The Everlasting Chronicles series, Emissary of the Devil series, The Chronicles of Winterset series, The Middle Road (with co-author CM Lally) Black Falls High series and Seven Minutes in Heaven with a ridiculous amount of other series set to be released.

Follow K.G. at the links below and on TikTok!

https://vm.tiktok.com/ZMexyRPcE

Sign up for her newsletter here:

https://tinyletter.com/authorkgreuss

Join her Facebook reader group for excerpts, teasers, and all sorts of goodies.

https://www.facebook.com/groups/streetteamkgreuss

CHURCH

THE BOYS OF CHAPEL CREST

Sirena

Eight Years Ago

"Wanna know a secret?" Seth's blue eyes raked over me.

"I don't know. Do I?" I looked from the small, white mouse in his hands to his face, shivers rushing through my body.

Seth Cain was my neighbor and best friend. We played together every day after school and often spent the nights together on the weekends, underneath our blanket fort, giggling over ghost stories and talking about the latest video games.

I loved to sing and dance, and he'd even made up a song to hum for me that I added words to. He hummed it all the time, even when I wasn't singing. We called the song "Roses and Whiskers". Or actually, I did. He rolled his eyes at the name I picked out, but it fit the words I saw in my head for his tune. A curious kitten nosing through the roses and getting scared when a thorn caught her paw.

He'd gotten in trouble at school a few days ago for humming the song during a test and had been sent to the principal. It had made him angry. So angry that he'd thrown his book at Mrs. Baker. He'd been getting weird since his dad moved out a year ago.

Hateful. Cruel. Terrifying. Sometimes he talked to people who weren't even there. It scared me.

But he'd been my best friend since we were in diapers. If anyone could help him, it was me. Whenever Seth got into a fight at school or got mean, I was there for him. I swore to him I always would be. I always tried to draw his attention away from the invisible people he spoke to. I didn't want anyone to think he was strange because he was perfect to me.

I let out a shaky breath.

"C-can I hold Oscar?" I asked, cupping my hands to accept the mouse his mother had purchased for him for fifty cents down at the pet shop.

Seth said it was her way of keeping his mind occupied and teaching him responsibility. Plus, it gave him someone real to talk to when he was alone. Seth was already responsible as far as I was concerned. He practically raised himself since his parents were always working. And now with his dad gone, his mom worked two jobs.

Seth cocked his head and narrowed his blue eyes at me, his dark hair falling across his forehead before handing me the tiny creature.

He glanced to his right and frowned, talking to someone who wasn't there just like he'd done at lunch today. "She won't hurt him. She loves him."

I took the mouse, breathing a sigh of relief and ignoring his words.

"Hey, little fella," I cooed into my cupped hand, hoping whatever gloomy thoughts going through Seth's head would go away.

Seth turned his attention back to me and watched wordlessly. I could see the wheels spinning in his ten-year-old mind.

"We're moving," he said after a beat. "That's my secret. Mom doesn't want me to tell anyone. *No one does.* She met someone new. His name is Philip. *I hate Philip.* We're leaving in the morning."

I looked up at him in surprise. "Where are you going?"

Seth hadn't mentioned a Philip before. But I had noticed a strange man coming into their home over the last few months though. Seth also hadn't let me inside his house for the past two weeks either, claiming his mom was busy cleaning. I guessed that meant packing. It was unlike Seth to keep secrets, especially big ones like this, from me. My tummy ached when I realized I might be losing my best friend.

He shrugged. "I don't know. Somewhere. It won't be anywhere good. Philip is a bad man. *We all know it.*" His expression darkened with his words. "I don't think I'll be able to see you anymore."

"Maybe you'll go with your dad?" I asked hopefully, ignoring how he said *we,* like it was more than just him.

He frowned and shook his head as he addressed someone who wasn't there. My heart raced as I thought about what him leaving meant. His dad still lived on the other side of town. If Seth stayed with him, we'd still be able to see one another.

Seth scowled and focused on me again. "No. Screw him. Mom said he left us for someone half her age. I guess I'm getting a brother or sister and a new mom and dad because of the people they left each other for. It's messed up."

I winced. My dad had left my mom when I was seven. I remembered wondering where he went and why he never came back. Mom told me he was dead to us and to never think of him again.

As if reading my mind, Seth spoke, "It's different for me, Rinny. Your dad just disappeared. Mine found someone better and decided I wasn't good enough, so he's having a whole new baby. Then my mom started seeing Philip. He touches. . ." his voice trailed off as he schooled the pain from his face. "I'm going to get revenge. *We are.*"

A storm cloud passed over his face as he gestured to whatever invisible things he saw.

"Revenge? How?" I frowned, wondering what Seth was cooking up in what had become a gloomy mind. All I knew was if someone was hurting my friend, I needed to get him help.

"I'll kill the baby." He shrugged like it was nothing. "Then they'll take me away, and I won't have to see Philip. Killing someone is a good plan. *They* said so. It's not like anyone cares about me anyway."

I wet my lips, worry creeping through me. This wasn't my best friend.

"*I* care about you. You can't kill a baby, Seth. It'll be your new baby sister or brother. You're supposed to love it and teach it things. Like with me and Cady. I taught her how to braid her hair yesterday."

He was quiet as his breathing rate increased, his serious gaze fixed on me. He jerked and glanced to his right, a frown marring his lips again. His hands shook as he swallowed. He stood silently for a moment before he spoke, "A-are you sure?" he asked in a soft, worried voice. He seemed to be listening for a moment before he said, "O-ok."

I took a tentative step back as his focus snapped back on me. Seth had never turned his violence on me. He'd always been kind and sweet, taking care of me as much as I took care of him.

Something seemed to break within him in that moment. It was like a lightbulb had gone off over his head.

"I don't want to love the baby." He glared at me before closing the distance between us and shoving me.

I cried out as I tumbled to my backside. I hit my head on the concrete floor, making my vision swim and my tummy churn. Oscar fell out of my hands and scurried off, squeaking as I struggled to sit up.

"Don't you get it, Sirena? I hate it. *I hate everything.*" He kneeled beside me for a moment.

I reached out to him, thinking he was going to apologize and help me up, but he surprised me again and fisted my hair. I let a wail out as he tugged so hard, I thought he'd pull all the dark strands from my head.

I fought back, slapping at him. He drew back and punched me in the face, dazing me. Seth was stronger by a lot and twice my size. Even at ten, he looked a few years older than other kids our age.

If the hair pulling wasn't enough, the hot trickle of blood flowing from my nose let me know this wasn't one of Seth's wrestling games. He'd never been mean or cruel to me before.

"Stop. Stop!" I cried out, struggling beneath him as he shifted to straddle me.

He released my hair, but his fists kept flying at my face.

"Seth! Seth!" I tried to cover my head as my best friend in the whole world went crazy and beat me on the dirty, cracked cement of the old shed on the back of his parents' property.

I was no match for Seth Cain though. Black spots dotted my vision as my arms fell limply to my side.

Seth's sobs and his soft words tickled my ears as I lay beneath him, my body hurting. "You'd be better off dead, Rinny, than to spend another moment in this stupid world. *They told me that. They said I'm saving you.* It's what friends do, right? Sirena?" He stopped hitting me. His warm breath washed over my face as I stared up at him through bleary eyes. "I love you, Rinny. You're my best friend in the whole world. *I'm saving you.* I promise I am. Wait for me to get there, OK? In heaven? Things will be better then. We'll be best friends always. I swear it. No more hurting here. I don't want anyone to ever hurt you. I'm so sorry. You'll be safe forever. Mom says angels always go to heaven. I promise I'll find you."

Relief flooded my body as he moved off me. The sounds of shuffling and scraping made me wince before I managed to crack my eyelids open to find Seth looming over me with a shovel.

"Roses and whiskers
Don't stop the purrs, mister.
This world is too big
To go it alone
So follow me through the thicket
And just try to fit through the thorns.
I'll be right behind you.
No need to be alarmed."

He sang the song in a shaky voice before the words faded away and became a hum. A soft song I used to adore so much.

As much as I wanted to stop what I knew was coming, my body felt like lead. I had to make the effort though. I rolled onto my stomach and made a feeble attempt to crawl away. It was useless. The shovel swished through the air, the humming louder. With a crack the shovel came down on the back of the head, sending me to my tummy hard.

The last thing I saw before the darkness claimed me was Seth's white shoes, my blood splattered on them.

As my vision faded, so did his words.
I'll be right behind you
No need to be alarmed.

Read Church now
Church: The Boys of Chapel Crest

ALSO BY K.G. REUSS

Black Falls High: In Ruins

Black Falls High: In Silence

Black Falls High: In Chaos

Black Falls High: In Pieces

May We Rise: A Mayfair University Novel

When We Fall: A Mayfair University Novel

Double Dare You

Barely Breathing

Barely Alive

Church: The Boys of Chapel Crest

Ashes: The Boys of Chapel Crest

Emissary of the Devil: Testimony of the Damned

Emissary of the Devil: Testimony of the Blessed

The Everlasting Chronicles: Dead Silence

The Everlasting Chronicles: Shadow Song

The Everlasting Chronicles: Grave Secrets

The Everlasting Chronicles: Soul Bound

The Chronicles of Winterset: Oracle

The Chronicles of Winterset: Tempest

Hard Pass

Kings of Bolten: Dirty Little Secrets

Kings of Bolten: Pretty Little Sins

Kings of Bolten: Deadly Little Promises

The Middle Road

Seven Minutes in Heaven

Printed in Great Britain
by Amazon